# Joscelyn

# The Revolutionary War Novels
# of
# William Gilmore Simms

1. *Joscelyn*
2. *The Partisan*
3. *Mellichampe*
4. *Katharine Walton*
5. *The Scout*
6. *The Forayers*
7. *Eutaw*
8. *Woodcraft*

Revolutionary War Novels

1

# Joscelyn

by

## William Gilmore Simms

*With Introduction and Explanatory Notes*

Published for the Southern Studies Program
University of South Carolina

THE REPRINT COMPANY, PUBLISHERS
SPARTANBURG, SOUTH CAROLINA
1976

This volume was reproduced from a 1975 edition by arrangement with the University of South Carolina Press



Reprinted: 1976
The Reprint Company, Publishers
Spartanburg, South Carolina

ISBN 0-87152-235-7
Library of Congress Catalog Card Number: 76-10257
Manufactured in the United States of America on long-life paper

**Library of Congress Cataloging in Publication Data**

Simms, William Gilmore, 1806-1870.
Joscelyn.

(Simms Revolutionary War novels ; v. 1)
Originally published in the Old guard, Jan.-Dec. 1867.
Reprint of the ed. published by the Univ. of South Carolina Press, with new introd and explanatory notes.
1. South Carolina—History—Revolution, 1775-1783—Fiction. 2. Georgia—History—Revolution, 1775-1783—Fiction. I. Title.
PZ3.S592Si vol. 1 [PS2848] 813'.3 76-10257
ISBN 0-87152-235-7

# Contents

# Acknowledgments

The cooperative efforts of a number of organizations and individuals made possible this publication of Simms' eight novels of the Revolution in South Carolina. It had been originally planned to include them in the Centennial Edition of the Writings of William Gilmore Simms, published by the University of South Carolina Press. However, a textual study of the novels indicated that a new edition, newly set in type, would be desirable for only one of them, *Joscelyn*. Accordingly, the Editorial Board of the Centennial Edition, consisting of James B. Meriwether, General Editor; Keen Butterworth, Textual Editor; and Mary C. Simms Oliphant, John C. Guilds, and Stephen Meats, decided to omit the remaining seven novels from the edition and to seek another publisher to bring them out with new introductory and explanatory matter, but with their texts reproduced by photo-offset from the Redfield edition of Simms' works, originally published in the 1850's.

*Joscelyn*, with an introduction and notes by Professor Meats and its text established by Professor Butterworth, was published in October 1975 by the University of South Carolina Press as volume XVI of the Centennial Edition, with the Seal, as an Approved Text, of the Center for Editions of American Authors. When Thomas E. Smith of The Reprint Company agreed to undertake the publication of the Revolutionary novels as a set, the University of South Carolina Press agreed to license the reissue of *Joscelyn* (without its textual apparatus) so that all eight novels might, for the first time, be brought out together.

The Southern Studies Program of the University of South Carolina, of which Professor Meriwether is Director, agreed to provide appropriate historical notes and introductory matter for the set. The preparation of the notes was carried out as a collaborative project by graduate students in the Southern Studies Program, under the direction of Professor Meriwether and Professor Meats. A grant to the Southern Studies Program by the South Carolina Committee for the Humanities, in support of a series of public seminars on Simms and the Revolution, directed by Professor Meats, aided greatly in the work upon the notes for the set.

When planning for publication had been completed, the South Carolina American Revolution Bicentennial Commission gave the project its endorsement and agreed to purchase 150 sets to be used for educational purposes within the State of South Carolina. Special thanks are due to John Hills, Director, and to Bradley Morrah and Sam P. Manning, Chairman and Vice Chairman, respectively, of the Commission, for their interest in and assistance with this project.

In the preparation of the historical notes for these volumes, the assistance of E. L. Inabinett, Director of the South Caroliniana Library, and of his staff was invaluable. Thanks are also due to Charles Lee, State Archivist of South Carolina, and to his staff; and to Professors George C. Rogers, Robert Weir and David Chesnutt, of the History Department of the University of South Carolina. Editorial assistance on the notes was provided by Elisabeth Muhlenfeld and Dianne Anderson of the Southern Studies Program, and by Margaret C. Thomas of The Reprint Company. Special thanks are due to Mrs. Oliphant for making available her great store of knowledge concerning her grandfather's life and work.

James B. Meriwether
Stephen Meats

# Introduction

William Gilmore Simms was South Carolina's and the South's leading man of letters in the 19th century. He was born in Charleston on 17 April 1806 and died there on 11 June 1870. During his long literary career, which began in 1825 with the publication of his first separate work, *Monody on the Death of Gen. Charles Cotesworth Pinckney*, Simms wrote and published twenty-seven novels or romances, five collections of short fiction, eighteen volumes of poetry, two of drama, four volumes of history and geography, four of biography, and five volumes of reviews and miscellaneous prose, a total of sixty-five volumes. Probably an equal or greater amount of material was furnished to various periodicals and annuals during his career, including four novels that appeared serially in magazines between 1863 and 1869. As an editor, he brought out three volumes of the works of other authors and four miscellaneous anthologies, and was associated editorially with a substantial number of significant periodicals, among which were such South Carolina newspapers as the Charleston *Courier* and the Charleston *Mercury*, and such journals as *The Magnolia*, the *Southern Literary Gazette*, the *Southern and Western Magazine and Review* and *The Southern Quarterly Review*. As his many published addresses attest, he was also a popular lecturer on a variety of subjects, and he left a number of works, including one of his finest short stories, in manuscript at his death.

As a student of history, Simms' interests ranged over nearly every stage of the development of western civilization, beginning with ancient Greece and Rome and carrying through to European history of the age of Napoleon and after, but he was most interested in the history of the western hemisphere, particularly in the way the early Spanish, French and English settlements evolved into the nations of his own time. Evidence in his correspondence and in his published reviews and notices indicates his extensive knowledge of contemporary and older accounts of these eras and events. In his historical writings about most places and periods, he shows himself to be only a student of history rather than a historian—that is, he depended for his knowledge entirely on the previous researches and writings of the real historians in these fields. But his study of the American Revolution, particularly in South Carolina and the South, was quite a different matter. In these areas he possessed the historian's knowledge of primary sources—personal and official correspondence, legal documents, diaries, eye-witness accounts, and other records—as well as being thoroughly familiar with all the published histories, biographies, memoirs, records, and volumes of correspondence available. He owned a large archive of Revolutionary War manuscripts himself and had access to other extensive private collections. Although his own manuscripts were predominantly of Southern and South Carolina interest, they did not concentrate exclusively on these areas. His collection also contained considerable numbers of the letters and other papers of prominent civilian and military figures of the Revolution from nearly every one of the original thirteen states, including, among others, large collections of the correspondence of General Washington, General Greene, Henry Laurens while President of the Continental Congress, John Laurens while Washington's aide-de-camp, and the Baron DeKalb, as well as smaller numbers of letters by Patrick Henry, John Adams, John Jay, General Horatio Gates, Governor Jonathan Trumbull, and Samuel A. Otis. Simms was also intensely interested in the local legends and traditions of the Revolution in South Carolina and spent nearly a lifetime collecting such materials in his travels around his native state and in his correspondence with local historians and antiquarians.

Simms put his extensive knowledge of the Revolution to use in a wide variety of article- and book-length works over a period of nearly forty-five years. Among his most notable non-fictional publications on the Revolution are *The History of South Carolina* (1840), which devotes nearly two-thirds of its length to the Revolution; full-length biographies of General Francis Marion (1844) and General Nathanael Greene (1849); *South-Carolina in the Revolutionary War* (1853), a book defending the importance of the state's contributions to the conflict; a volume of the war correspondence of Colonel John Laurens for which Simms wrote a biographical memoir of Laurens; extensive articles on such prominent Revolutionary figures as Governor John Rutledge and the Baron DeKalb; biographical sketches of nearly a dozen Revolutionary soldiers and civilians for various biographical and historical works; a substantial number of lectures on topics ranging from particular battles to individual men; and many book reviews in which he uses his own primary knowledge of the Revolution to support, expand upon, or to refute the work he is evaluating. Simms was also instrumental in encouraging other amateur historians to write down the results of their researches by publishing their works in some of the journals he edited, particularly in *The Magnolia* and *The Southern Quarterly Review*.

But Simms made the most extensive use of his knowledge of the history, legends and traditions of the Revolution in the series of eight Revolutionary War novels which constitute the most ambitious treatment of the conflict by an American author of the 19th century. Concentrating on the progress of the war in South Carolina, these novels were written and published in the following order:

1835 *The Partisan: A Tale of the Revolution.* 2 volumes. New York: Harper & Brothers. Revised edition, entitled *The Partisan: A Romance of the Revolution*, New York: Redfield, 1854.

1836 *Mellichampe A Legend of the Santee.* 2 volumes. New York: Harper & Brothers. Revised edition, New York: Redfield, 1854.

1841 *The Kinsmen: or the Black Riders of Congaree. A Tale.* 2 volumes. Philadelphia: Lea and Blanchard. Revised edition, entitled *The Scout or The Black Riders of Congaree*, New York: Redfield, 1854.

1850 *Katharine Walton: or, the Rebel of Dorchester. An Historical Romance of the Revolution in Carolina.* Philadelphia: A. Hart, 1851. Revised edition, entitled *Katharine Walton or The Rebel of Dorchester*, New York: Redfield, 1854. A shorter version was first published serially in *Godey's Lady's Book* (February-December, 1850) with the title "Katharine Walton: or, the Rebel's Daughter. A Tale of the Revolution."

1852 *The Sword and the Distaff; or, "Fair, Fat and Forty," A Story of the South, at the Close of the Revolution.* Charleston: Walker, Richards & Co. Revised edition, entitled *Woodcraft or Hawks about the Dovecote A Story of the South at the Close of the Revolution*, New York: Redfield, 1854. First published serially in semi-monthly supplements to the *Southern Literary Gazette* (February-November, 1852).

1855 *The Forayers or The Raid of the Dog-Days.* New York: Redfield.

1856 *Eutaw A Sequel to The Forayers, or the Raid of the Dog-Days A Tale of the Revolution.* New York: Redfield.

1867 *Joscelyn A Tale of the Revolution.* Columbia, S.C.: University of South Carolina Press, 1975. Volume 16 of *The Centennial Edition of the Writings of William Gilmore Simms.* First published serially in *The Old Guard* (January-December, 1867).

Because the order in which the eight novels were published does not follow the chronology of the Revolution itself, they should be read in this sequence in order to follow Simms' narrative of the conflict: *Joscelyn; The Partisan; Mellichampe; Katharine Walton; The Scout; The Forayers; Eutaw;* and *Woodcraft.*

*Joscelyn* portrays the civil war in the back country in the late summer and fall of 1775. This was the first open warfare of the Revolution in the South, involving the citizens of South Carolina and Georgia who took either the whig (American) or loyalist (British) side. The next three volumes of the series are closely linked and can be considered a trilogy. With the first of them, *The Partisan*, the action of the series skips to June 1780, immediately after the fall of Charleston in May. Simms uses several representative though fictionalized characters to show the development of partisan resistance to British occupation. The main historical event of this novel is the Battle of Camden (August 1780) in which the crushing defeat of the Southern Continental Army threw the entire responsibility of resistance on the irregular volunteer forces under Francis Marion and other partisan commanders. *Mellichampe*, the second volume of the trilogy, centers its narrative around a different set of fictional characters in following the activities of Marion's band in its struggle with loyalist and British forces in the Santee River area in the fall of 1780. The third novel in the trilogy, *Katharine Walton*, picks up the narrative involving the fictional characters of *The Partisan* in September 1780 and describes the impact of the war on their family fortunes over a period of several months. Much of the novel portrays the social life of the British garrison in Charleston and the participation of various civilians in the American war effort. *The Scout* opens in May 1781 not long after the Battle of Hobkirk's Hill and ends in June after the British abandonment of the star-fort at Ninety Six. This novel concentrates on the struggle between partisan forces and the outlaw bands that operated under British authority in plundering the central portion of the state around the Congaree and Wateree River areas. The retreat of British forces toward Orangeburg and from there to

Charleston due to their inability to maintain their outpost at Ninety Six is the subject of *The Forayers* and its sequel, *Eutaw*. The central historical event of these two novels is the Battle of Eutaw Springs (September 1781) which virtually ended British domination in South Carolina. The final novel, *Woodcraft*, begins just as the British are evacuating Charleston in December 1782, and portrays the difficulties experienced by soldiers and civilians of South Carolina in making the transition from the lawless disorder of the late stages of the war to a condition of relative peace and civil order. Most of the action of the novel occurs on a ruined low country plantation on the Ashepoo River.

## *JOSCELYN*

Although Simms apparently conceived the idea and did some of the research for *Joscelyn* as early as 1858, the actual writing of his eighth and last novel of the Revolution did not take place until after the Civil War, in 1866 and 1867. Its serial publication in the New York monthly magazine *The Old Guard* was suspended after the issue of December 1867 with several chapters still needed to finish the stories of the central characters. Even though *Joscelyn* as a separate fictional narrative is in some ways incomplete, in it Simms nevertheless accomplished his purpose of giving "the *opening* scene in the grand drama of the seven years' war of the Revolution in the South."

*Joscelyn* was not brought out in book form until its publication in 1975 by the University of South Carolina Press, with an introduction and notes by Stephen E. Meats and the text established by Keen Butterworth. The text of the present volume was reproduced by offset from the first impression of this first book edition.

# JOSCELYN;

## A TALE OF THE REVOLUTION.

"I thank my memory, I yet remember some of these articles, and out they shall."

—[ *King Henry VIII.*

# CHAPTER I.

## INTRODUCTORY—THE WHERE AND WHEN.

It was a pleasant day in summer, a few years ago, which I spent, in company with my friend, the late eminent Senator in Congress from South Carolina, General Hammond, (so well known as among the most philosophic of our statesmen,) at the Sand Hill, or summer residence of the venerable Mr. John Bones, a gentleman who, for so long a time, has done the honors of the city of Augusta, Georgia, in giving hospitable welcome to the stranger. The season was gratefully mild, the atmosphere fine, the site conspicuous, and the scene such as fully satisfied the eye, in commending a pleasant landscape to the fancy. We sate, after dinner, in the shadow of trees, and with some delicate Rhenish wine in our beakers, and a box of choice Cubanas at hand, we gazed out and down upon the contiguous city, which spread away beautifully below us, with its tall towers and spires, and stately dwellings blending gratefully with the green foliage of trees, stretching away, along the winding course of the Savannah, until lost in the heights and thickets of the primitive realms of wood. The scene around us was hushed in the deep mellow stillness of a midsummer afternoon; the leaves overhead were slightly stirred by a pleasant breeze which swelled, gathering vigor in its wing, as it struggled up from below, to reach the height. At moments a twittering bird darted overhead, speeding, without a song, from covert to covert. No hum from the city reached our ears, and we naturally fell into a mood of contemplative chat, which was almost reverie, as, recurring to the past, we retraced, from infancy to a vigorous maturity, the growth of the goodly and wealthy province of trade and commerce, which spread away beneath our eyes.

By little and little we wandered back to that remoter period when this whole realm was first laid bare to European eyes, and when the first bold adventurers from the Old World penetrated the mighty thickets which once overspread these plains. Memory, calling imagination to her aid, portrayed for us the aspects of the scene, at that inspiring moment when the brilliant cavalcade of Hernando De Soto wound its way beneath these hills, and moved down upon the plain, passing in gorgeous procession beneath the gigantic avenues of oak and pine, and cypress, on his way to the waters of the Mechachebi, (Mississippi,) pursuing that magnificent, but melancholy march, to the grandest of all his discoveries, in the great river which was to yield him nothing but a grave!

There it was—there in the very heart of yonder city, in a blended empire of forest and morass, that he encamped, for a space, with his gay and gallant cavaliers—a thousand knights in armour, shining in the sun—all well mounted, on coursers, mailed like their riders, and brilliantly caparisoned, as well for pageantry as war.

Never, down to that period, had Spanish adelantado set foot in the New World with such a glorious cavalcade, surpassing far the petty bands which followed to wondrous triumph the lead of Cortez and Pizarro. They had caught the inspiration of war in all its grandeur from the long-protracted conflicts of their people with the no less chivalrous Saracens of Granada; and, wild with miraculous deeds and chimerical hopes, they had rushed to join the train of De Soto, on the saddest expedition that ever baffled the hopes and fortunes of the most sanguine of all self-deluded adventure! But we are not to pursue their history.*

Enough that it was all vividly recalled to us, as we sate upon the slope of the sand-hills, and gazed down upon the spacious city of Augusta.

There had De Soto made his encampment. Thence had he sent forth his pioneers. Hither had the prince of the land sought him either in hate or amity; and it was just across the river that he had been guilty of that greatest crime in his career—the seizure and imprisonment of the gentle and loving princess of the Indian Prov-

---

* Let the reader look for it in the new and beautiful edition, published by the "Bradford Club," of New York, of the Portuguese narrative of De Soto's expedition, as found in the supplement to Hakleigh, but here given to us in a new and excellent translation from the pen of Mr. J. Buckingham Smith, of Florida.

ince of Cutachifiqui—a province of which the Uchees are supposed to have constituted the largest element.

Musing or conversing upon these old dramas in our New World, the transition was at once natural and easy to times less remote, and, indeed, in some instances, within the memories of living men, and to events of more recent experience, occurring in the same neighborhood.

We lingered naturally over the revolutionary period, and over the facts in several cases, of persons, still well remembered as actors, on one side or the other, during the period which is said to have tried men's souls, as if all periods did not try the souls of men, when these are fit for any trial.

The absolute in history and the old local tradition gave us food for reflection and discussion, and little snatches of anecdote, dimly remembered details of domestic strife and excitement, brought up the names of the Hammonds, the Cummings, McCoys, Joscelyns, the Conynghams, the Alexanders, the Hamiltons, the Coopers, Brownes, Griersons, and many others, who had conspicuously figured on this scene of action some ninety years ago, and of whose habits, characteristics and performances much was still remembered by my two friends, and subsequently by others whom I sought for information.

Yes, on these very sand-hills, nearly on the same spot where we sate together, on that pleasant summer afternoon, smoking our cigars and quaffing our Rhenish, there opened certain tragedies of passionate local interest, blending, here and there, with the grand drama of the American Revolution, then at the beginning of its action.

Here, nearly on the very spot occupied by the fine mansion of our host, stood a modest cottage, some ninety years ago, which occupied one of the few in the precinct—the very centre of a pretty little farmstead, under good cultivation; and, from the shelter of this cottage, and under the shadow of these great trees, a group had gathered, ninety years ago, to discuss the prospects and probabilities of war—to open all the fiery seals of civil feud and persecution, and plan those enterprises of peril which were destined to cover the land with fire, and drain thousands of its bravest hearts of the life-blood which makes States famous.

The city, then but a hamlet, lay below, as now. But the little group, there and then assembled, looked not forth upon the scene with those emotions which possessed our party. We were in the full enjoyment of repose. We had leisure for the contemplative, and for the play of such fancies as would have been a mere mockery in that former day of those earnest and vindictive passions which were rising in their souls. They were absorbed in the opening of a grand action—a gigantic tragedy over the proscenium of which hung an overshadowing fate, with great black wings, and breathing forth mephitic vapor from its nostrils, which was to overspread the land with the direst pestilences of war.

Of all these things our little party spoke, for all their results had been realized. Persons and parties and events were recalled, and made to pass before us, like the shadowy spectres that rose before the vision of Macbeth in the cavern of the witches. It is for us now, if possible, to recall the events in which these shadowy forms were to be the actors—to clothe them with flesh and blood, and find for the action its local habitation and its name. I have, since that pleasant day in midsummer, gone over the fields, and possessed myself of the events; have sought from history whatever details she could afford, and, seeking the aid of other friends among the old inhabitants, have invoked from the old Druids of tradition, the domestic record, the personal event, the secret motive, the local feud, the thousand small details, by which we blend the national history with little groups, here and there, who played their parts in its progress, under the goading influences of those various hidden impulses, passions or vanities which sometimes make men conspicuous in history against their will. The fruits of these studies and researches must be sought for in the chapters which follow.

Of the friends who sate with me that midsummer day, but one survives. The noble intellect of Hammond can no longer teach or inspire in the circles which honored his mind and manhood. He has escaped those evils to his country which, in some degree, he had anticipated; for his was the prophet mind, which, in studies of the past, shapes the passages of the future; and in the solution, by a bold induction, of the mysterious problem of humanity, not unfrequently delivers itself in prophecy.

## CHAPTER II.

### MALCONTENTS IN COUNCIL.

In the lane leading to the cottage—a lane of original forest trees such as grow chiefly along the sandy slopes of the South, and where the lands swell into little hills, having long central ridges—a young man, some twenty-three years of age, was slowly making his way. He was a goodly-looking youth, tall, well set, of graceful and easy carriage, who seemed rather disposed to lounge than to walk, as if disturbed with uncertain thoughts not yet resolved into a purpose.

He wore a dress which was decidedly Scotch—a tartan plaid suit of that fashion, so well known of the time, "when George the Third was king." It was close-fitting, and fully displayed the symmetry of his figure. A good pair of Scottish legs, well formed, were conspicuous in the plaided stockings, and his small-clothes were of plaid also, but of a different pattern. He wore no shawl or cloak; only a doublet, not dissimilar to that of the blouse, but longer in skirt, and more graceful; briefly, something of the well-known hunting shirt, borrowed from our red men and mountaineers, in part, and which was commonly known among our people as the "split-shirt," because of the opening in front—a mere split, which partially exhibited below a vest not unlike that of the present day, but of enormous length, reaching, as was the fashion of the time, almost to the hips. The costume was a modification of the European, so as to suit the condition of the half-forest country in which the wearer found his abode.

The stuff worn—the tartan—showed the youth to be of Scottish origin. But his place of birth was Georgia. He carried a long rifle on his shoulder, known and famous among the mountaineers of that day in the South as the "Deckard" rifle. A brace of squirrels and some birds swelled out the pouch at his girdle, and showed how he had recently been employing himself, and with what success.

As he emerged from the lane, and was making his way slowly across the little court-yard in front of the cottage, he was encountered by a young damsel, of seventeen, or thereabouts, who suddenly darted out from the cover of the shrubbery, and met him as he came. And she, too, judging by her costume, was also of Scottish origin. Her kirtle was of plaid, and she bore the Scottish type, very decidedly marked in all her features. She was a tall damsel, graceful of movement, very fair to look upon, with the merriest laughing eyes of blue, a fair, white, lofty forehead, surmounted by masses of the richest golden hair that ever hid away in its folds the sunshine of an oriental day. These masses, partially bound up, terminated, however, in the brightest ringlets, curling naturally, that ever flowed freely over the white shoulders of a village beauty.

These were brother and sister, very like in features, and very loving, as became their close relationship.

The girl had shown some impatience to meet her brother—had evidently watched from afar, and waited his approach. Her movement was hurried, and she exclaimed, as she drew nigh:

"How you have stayed, Wattie. You are waited for impatiently. They have been out asking for you a dozen times, and father seems almost vexed that you are absent."

"Why, who's here, Annie? Who are 'they,' for whom you have no names?"

"That Cameron!"

"Aye! *That* Cameron!" he exclaimed, repeating her words, and his brow darkening as he spoke, while his lips grew rigidly compressed together. "Well, he is here again?"

"He is not the only one. Tom Browne is with him, and you may be sure, Wattie—"

"That they come for no good! Would to God that my father could shake himself free of these men! Have you any notion of their business now?"

"Only that it is something which has warmed them all into a passion. They've been a good two hours in the hall, and they all seem to talk at once sometimes. I hear papa's voice very high, as if under great provocation; and, every now and then, I hear the sharp, shrill, harsh tones of Tom Browne. Cameron is louder, too, than usual in his speaking; and all of them, as I tell you, are greatly excited about you, as I think."

"About *me?* Hardly, my sweet little sister. What have I to do with Browne or Cameron, and what should they have to do with me? I loathe them both."

"I don't know; but they've been calling for you. Browne went to your office, which he found locked up. Papa then came to me to know where you were, and when I told him that you had taken out your rifle, he cried out:

"'Ay, it will come to that! The rifle has its eloquence when the time comes, and we shall all need to know how to use it—we cannot guess how soon.' This was as nearly as I can remember what he said."

"You see from that, Annie, that the affair does not concern me. It is this wretched matter again of the Crown and the Colonies. It makes me sick to think of it. Browne and Cameron are kites that scent the carnage. I would to God that they were both of them in ———."

"Oh! fie, Wattie."

"In heaven, my child, and with better right to possess that kingdom than either of them can now assert. Surely, Annie, there is no blasphemy in such a wish."

"Ah! Wattie, but that was not what you meant."

"No, indeed, puss, and I might well wish them in any other place, when I reflect upon the mischief into which their cunning may involve my father; but they shall not succeed, if I can help it."

"How can you, brother? You know that you cannot hold out against papa, when he flies into his passions."

"It is not easy; but I must now."

"Ah! if you could."

"I tell you I must; for I see the troubles that threaten him through these men; but, look you, Annie, when did you see Martin Joscelyn last?"

The damsel blushed to the very ears, and, looking down, answered hesitatingly:

"Not since Tuesday evening last. But why do you ask?"

"Look you, Annie, that tell-tale blood of yours will some day betray to Martin himself what it too clearly tells to me."

"Oh! Wattie, how can you think so? I should die rather"—

"Hush, and do not be foolish! Only beware and do not let your heart leap so quickly into your throat. Our father, I fear, has no love for Martin, and shows him a cold shoulder when he comes hither, though he knows that he comes to me, and that he is my most intimate friend. Let him not see that my sister thinks even more favorably of him than her brother."

"You are unkind, Wattie."

"I meant to be kind only, my sweet little foolish sister; and my warning was to spare you some suffering. Keep down the heart; for a season at least. This is no time for love and walks in the groves together, without a word between you, which word you should probably tremble yourself to hear. Enough now"—

At this moment a harsh voice at the window cried out:

"Why there's Walter now! Why does he not come in? Why do you not send him in, Annie? Dogs and devils! can I get nothing done that I desire? Am I never to be master in my own house? Come in, Walter. We have waited for you half the day."

At the first accents of his voice the girl disappeared in the shrubbery, making her way to the dairy. The young man replied very quietly, and as if unmoved by his father's impatience:

"I will be with you directly, sir. I will but wash my hands."

There was an impatient ejaculation in reply, something very like an oath, followed by—

"Never matter about your hands. There are some things that cannot wait upon soap and water. If you stop to wash your hands, you will think it necessary to find a towel to wipe them."

"Very likely I shall."

"Well, in with you quickly," was the response, and the old man left the window.

The youth did not hurry himself, however. He coolly proceeded to perform his ablutions in the porch of the dwelling; used the soap freely, and deliberately employed the towel, the old man watching his proceedings through the window, and bestriding the floor at intervals, under a self-chafing process, which made his cheeks glow as with the heat from a furnace.

Having satisfied himself that his hands would now bear the inspection of his guests, the young man took up his rifle and bird-pouch, quietly entered the hall where he was awaited, carefully hung up his rifle upon the rack of deer antlers over the door, cast down his bird-bag on a table, his cap beside it, and ran his fingers through the massy shock of light brown hair which overspread his forehead.

All these things were done as quietly and coolly as if no other parties were present, having claims on his attention; and without any recognition given to the three several persons who were silently in waiting, watching all his movements.

The group consisted of the father, an elderly person of some fifty-five years, a hale, florid, fiery Scotchman, of bluff manners, and grizzly hair and beard. He was over the middle size, stout of limb and muscle, and was still capable of great endurance and of much activity.

His companions, Cameron and Browne, were both much younger men. They, too, were also of Scottish type and natives of the old country. The one was the sub-agent of the crown among the Indians of the colonies of Georgia and the Carolinas. Browne had been a trader among the red men. This traffic, for a long period, had been carried on mostly by Scotchmen. They penetrated into all the obscure regions of the South, and by their general industry, shrewdness, intelligence and courage, laid the foundations of great families as well as great fortunes. We owe to these sources, chiefly of the Scotch-Irish, some of the most eminent men that the country has produced. But this aside.

We turn once more to the group now assembled in the parlor of Malcolm Dunbar.

A keen, quick glance of the eye showed to the young man, Walter Dunbar, their several aspects in a single moment. His first glance was upon the face of the man named Cameron. There he beheld, in features comparatively smooth, that sinister sort of smile which looks so very like a sneer, that one feels tempted to floor the wearer, at a glance, with a single blow of the fist. Such was the feeling of Walter, just as if he himself had received a blow.

But the young man subdued himself, and, with a slight inclination of the head, turned away his eyes till they met with the coarser and more savage countenance of Browne. To him, also, he bowed slightly, and now, looking at his father, he slowly drew nigh to the table where the parties had been sitting, and where, from the quantity of papers and memoranda which lay scattered before them, they had evidently been greatly busied.

As the eyes of the young man settled down upon these papers, Cameron rather hastily drew nigh, swept them together with his hands, and, without arranging, proceeded to bundle and tie them together in a single package.

Walter turned away with something like loathing in his look, and stood patiently confronting his father.

"By my faith, Mr. Walter Dunbar," said the old man sharply, "you are something deliberate in your movements this morning."

"Not more so than usual, I think, sir."

"Ah! but I think differently, sir."

"It may be so, sir. There are periods when we require to be unusually deliberate. It is, at all times, due to my profession that I should be deliberate. Unlike medicine, which requires that the physician should be prompt, and should lose no time either for or with the patient, the lawyer has need to save all the time he can—"

"And his breath, too, sir, we should trust, if only the better to cool his porritch. But have you no civil courtesy for our friends here?"

"I have acknowledged their presence here, sir, with the usual courtesy."

"What! you mean with a little nod, a sort of twist of neck or bob of head, sir. That seems but scant courtesy, I'm thinking, to such old friends of the family, sir."

"Scant as the courtesy may be, sir, it is one which neither of them has had the courtesy to acknowledge or return."

Cameron exclaimed, with a polite smile:

"Oh! surely Mr. Walter is mistaken. I did return his bow; I did indeed; but just at that moment he turned away his head—and—and—"

Browne surlily said:

"I gave as good as I got. I am not much given to ducking my head, particularly to young fellows, and—"

Whatever else he might have said was stifled in a low guttural muttering, which might have been designed for a chuckle.

"Well, well, this is a foolish sort of business, and no more words need be wasted upon it. Son of mine need not mount the high horse when he meets with the friends of his father—"

"Friends!" was the single ejaculation of the son.

"Yes, sir, I say 'friends,' and what have you to say against it? But let us stop this badgering. We've no time to waste; and what you've said, Master Walter, about your profession, only reminds me that it is in the way of your profession that we would have a talk with you. My *friends* here think so well of your professional skill and ability, that they wish to engage your services in a great case which is shortly to be tried in this country."

"Ah, sir, I shall be pleased with any opportunity to try my hand professionally, though the devil himself be the client."

"Your want of scruple is delightfully professional. It is clear you must succeed. Well, sir, what say you to the great case at next popular assizes of 'The King *versus* the Colonies'?"

"Perhaps, Mr. Dunbar," said Cameron, "the parties will be better described as the 'Crown *versus* Rebellion and High Treason,' for such, it seems to me, are the real contestants in the case."

"Right, sir; the Colonies, if let alone, the people, sir, would go in their proper tracks, in becoming harness, but for these pestilent traitors, these nabobs of the country, whose ambition and vanity are perpetually goading all parties into strife, under all sorts of popular delusions, the rights of man, and heaven knows what not; the very sort of talk, sir, which, as the good book tells us, converted one-third of the angels into rebels and devils, and outcasts and patriots! Well, sir, what say you to this grand cause before the

Commons of Georgia, speaking for yourself as a lawyer and a good citizen?"

"And when is this great trial to take place?"

"What! you have not heard of this gathering which is announced for Augusta next Friday? Is it possible that you should not have heard, when it is in the mouth of everybody?"

"I have heard," answered the young man, gravely, "but had no idea that this gathering was to decide a case of so much importance either to Crown or Colony."

"Well, if you have heard of the issue that is to be made up—of the decision time only can speak—my question may well be repeated. How are you prepared to become a party to the argument?"

"I do not see how I need to become a party at all. But there is another question, if I am to engage in the case. The point of inquiry, then, must be, which of these two great parties am I to advocate?"

"Ha! can it be, my son, that you doubt? Can a son of mine deliberate, or hesitate, between loyalty and rebellion—the Crown, or the traitors who would pull down the Crown? I'll not believe it! No, no, Walter, you are jesting with me. Do not, I pray you, my son, trifle with me on a subject so sacred! This is not a time, nor this a subject for jest. No, nor for coldness and indifference. You cannot doubt between our sovereign and his subjects. Speak, sir, speak out, my son, and say what I am to hope—what to fear? Great God! that I should, on such a question, be troubled with a doubt!"

The son was moved. He paced the room for awhile in silence, and then answered, with evident uneasiness:

"Perhaps," he said, still in very deliberate accents, as if measuring the import of every word, "perhaps, sir, I should have phrased it more professionally if I had asked which of these clients is best prepared to respond in fees?"

"If that be the only, or the real question, my young friend," interposed Cameron, "I have the sufficient answer in readiness. There can be no doubt of the ability of his Majesty the King of Great Britain to compensate amply all who serve him loyally and well, and even *my* report alone, if I may be permitted to say so, made to his Excellency Lord William Campbell, will suffice in your behalf—"

He was here interrupted.

"Thanks, sir, for your courtesy," said the young man, coldly, "but I must not be understood literally when I speak of compensation, as to a mere lawyer, in a case that affects the life and welfare of a nation."

"Well spoken, my son! You are right, Walter, to discriminate between your duties to yourself as a lawyer, and to your king as a loyal subject. It were base now, and in such a case, to speak in the one for the other character. But you will have your rewards for loyal service, though you lose the ordinary fee of the lawyer. Your sovereign's gratitude—a nation's peace—your own conscience, and all the best sentiments of the human heart, among honorable people—will reward the loyal service which shall stand forth to check rebellion, and to answer and refute the specious arguments of treason! It is a grand cause—a great occasion, which lies open before you; and the credit which will follow your successful advocacy of our cause will be a perpetual source of reward, of never-failing profit! You must have seen the rapid progress of this treason. It has spread through Carolina, from the seaboard to the mountains. It is spreading here. It must be checked! A brave speaker now, full of the cause, and earnest in his plea, will do wonders with our people. They are just now at a turning point of opinion, as it were, when everything will depend upon a fearless and capable speaker. We look to you. We have few others to whom we can look. Many old favorites have gone over to the new opinions, and the common people know not whom to trust, or what to believe. Now is your time to win a name for yourself in the colonies, and acquire the lasting favor of your king. Prepare for the argument with all despatch, and with all your best determination. Saturday next the traitorous, insidious orator of Carolina, Drayton, will be here. He has, through his Georgia emissaries and allies, summoned our people. He will address them. He will endeavor to inoculate them with his pernicious, infidel doctrines of the rights of man; as if God had no rights, and appointed men no rights under God. Grapple him, my son, and, under God, boy as you are, he will be overthrown, even as the giant of the Philistines was cast down by the pebble of the shepherd boy of Israel."

The old man paused, rather through exhaustion than will. He was too much in earnest not to have much more to say.

The young man was troubled. He remembered the words of his sister, hinting at his weakness. He resolved to be firm, and, at least, not to commit himself in the matter, but he knew not the degree of his own weakness.

Browne muttered, but loudly enough to be heard—

"He is more of a stone than a man, if he can hold out after that!"

He meant himself to be heard.

Cameron replied to Browne in tones which were audible also.

"Wait! He is right not to be hurried. It is too great a cause to be treated rashly. A wise man must be allowed the privilege to think and decide for himself. In the case of a tiger like yourself, Browne, you have only to be hungry to decide where you shall dine."

"And I thank God that it is so. No long graces for me before meat!"

The father meanwhile resumed his plea.

"You are silent, Walter. Do not answer me at all, if you lack in faith and loyalty! If you are touched by this treason, leave me! But if not, think of these people—about to be led blindfold, like sheep to the slaughter. They tell me that but too many of them are already won over by the cunning eloquence of this arch-traitor, Drayton. Who, but yourself, is here to answer him before the people? It belongs to your race and blood to do so; it belongs to your profession that you should not be a laggard or a skulk at a time when the rights of your sovereign are threatened! Our friends here can give you proof, argument, and show that your duty."

"Why do not our friends here undertake this duty themselves?" demanded the youth, more quickly than usual. "Here is Colonel Browne, who has never shown himself slow of speech when he has anything on his mind; nay, he somewhat prides himself, as I hear, on his capacity as a preacher to the people, and his severe inflexibility of purpose. He alone can do so effectually who has full faith in his own argument."

The father rose impatiently.

"And what if it be their duty, and what if they should shrink from their duty? You do not mean to tell me that you would shrink from yours? Can it be, my son, that you doubt of the duty to your king—that your loyalty fails at a moment when treason is rampant and spreading over the land? Great God, shall it be that son of mine has drank of the deadly poison?"

The tremor of the old man was so great that he grasped the table with one hand for his support, while with the other he smote it heavily at each spoken sentence! His eyes glared savagely upon his son, whose face began to lose all its former immobility, and to exhibit unwonted signs of that emotion which had been hitherto kept under close suppression within. In the meantime, and while thus struggling with himself, the grim old ruffian, Browne, interposed, and in a cool, phlegmatic manner, replied to Walter's previous question to himself and Cameron.

"You have rightly asked, Mr. Walter, of myself and Mr. Cameron. He can, no doubt, answer for himself. On my part, as to my full faith in my own argument, that is for myself to feel and know; and when I feel and know, I am not the man to suffer any speech of mine to belie and make fool of my faith. I act up to it, with tooth and nail, if necessary, and leave the consequences to take care of themselves. That I do, and ever shall express my convictions, freely and fearlessly, everybody who knows me will readily believe; and, whatever comes of this business, you may be sure that I shall take my proper cue at the proper time, and find my proper place in the ranks for the fight. But I am no orator, and have not that gift for public speaking, which you are said to possess, quite as well as this man, Drayton. You may not have had so much practice, but you are said to move people's feelings when you speak, and that, I take it, is the first business of speaker or preacher. Whether your father and friends are mistaken in your opinions, in respect to this matter, I don't know, and hardly care; but it does seem to me to be very strange if, considering who your father is, and how you have been taught, you should now prove to be any other than a loyal and dutiful subject of the king of Great Britain. But that is all for you to consider. I know where *I* am, and how I set down my foot; and when I do so plant myself, then everybody knows where I am to be found!"

There was a good deal in this speech, and in the manner of its utterance, calculated to gall the spirit of the young man, who answered promptly, and with some asperity.

"My faith, sir, is my own, and I will suffer no man to question it, whether by direct charge or by insinuation. I trust that when the time comes for its trial, I shall not be found to shrink from my duty. But I am not prepared to recognize as duty the things that are prescribed to me, arbitrarily, by other men. Matters have been thrust upon me to-day for which I have not been prepared, and I must weigh well this matter of duty, on a subject so entirely new and complicated, as closely, with the mind of the lawyer, as with that of the man."

"You can't, sir!—you can't! Impossible! As regards the king, sir—his majesty—your duty, sir, as a loyal subject demands—"

"The duty of a subject, sir, not that of a slave! If kings violate law, they forfeit authority. The law is superior to any sovereign!"

"And who shall pronounce upon them, upon the law, upon the sovereign?"

"All men who are themselves just, and who suffer from a king's misdoings. Have you forgotten your own history, sir, and that of England? But, sir, pardon me if I say that neither yourself nor your friends are fair judges between me and my people. You have a king here, but I have a people also. You are all of that foreign kingdom. I am a son of the soil—a native of the country—kindred with its people—trained in a long course of exercise to share in their sympathies—to feel when they are hurt, and to relieve them if I can; and, though I freely say to you that I see no good reason for open resistance to the crown, yet justice bids me equally to declare that the people of these colonies have serious and good cause for complaint, which king and parliament have shown but too little disposition to remedy."

"Heavens give me patience!—This boy! This miserable boy. Why he is already speaking the language of that arch-traitor, Drayton, and his aristocratic crew along the seaboard!"

"No, sir, not exactly."

"Well, yes, there may be a hair's breadth of difference between you. He'll split the hair with you, and be reconciled!"

"Do not drive him from us," was the whispered sentence of Cameron, as he drew the old man to the window, where he endeavored to soothe his anger. The youth continued as if there had been no interruption.

"It is true that the people threaten, and I disapprove of that; but, sir, is it not true that they too have been, and still are, threatened with the rod of power?—and to you, sir," addressing Cameron, "I beg to put a single question."

"Well, Mr. Walter."

"Are you not even now stirring up the red men of the mountains to descend upon this people? Have you not been addressing them with speeches meant to goad them into fury, and ally them in arms against the people of this colony? You have supplied them but lately with arms and ammunition—"

"And why not, sir?" cried the impatient father. "All manner of warfare is legitimate against rebellion! Rebellion, sir, is the crime against God himself, and every agent, and every instrument we can bring to bear against it, is properly employed in maintaining the divine right!"

Again Cameron led the old man away to the window, where Browne seized upon him, while Cameron answered the charges of the young man.

"My dear Mr. Walter, you are entirely misinformed. You must not listen to such idle stories, which have been gotten up in Charleston to drive that honorable gentleman, Colonel Stuart, out of the country. They would drive me out also; and these stories are the Raw-Head-and-Bloody-Bones fictions, meant to awaken the terrors of the people, and force them into the embraces of the rebels. There is no truth in them. My official position compels me to constant intercourse with the red men, and I urge them all the while to be pacific. As for arms and ammunition, they have no more than the annual allowance which has been given them for the last seven years and more. Are you satisfied?"

The youth answered vaguely. Indeed for some moments he had not seemed to listen to him, being apparently wrapt, if not lost, in his own troubled thoughts.

While Cameron was yet speaking, Browne had released the old man, and both had returned to the table, at which the former quietly reseated himself, and began drumming on it with his fingers. The father meanwhile followed with his eyes every movement of his son, who had now begun rapidly to pace the chamber to and fro, evidently under the pressure of emotions which he found it difficult to subdue. He had mistaken his own strength. His sister knew it, or rather knew his weakness, better than himself, when, at the porch, she exhorted him to firmness during the coming interview.

The father at length rising from his seat, and staggering rather than walking, approached his son, arrested his rapid pace, and suddenly threw his arms about his neck, exclaiming, in husky and almost choking accents:

"Oh! my son!—my son! You will not break your poor old father's heart. How I have loved you—what hopes I have set on you—your honor, your talents, your loyalty to king and country—you do not know. Do not disappoint all my hopes. Do not shame the old man's loyalty by your own failure. You will speak to our people. You will seek to keep them from this mad rebellion. You will answer this man, Drayton; you will confound his insidious arguments, his cunning arts, his glozing eloquence. You have it in you to do so. You, too, can be eloquent on such a theme. I know what you can do if you will but try. Tell me that you will speak to him and to the people—that you will try—that you will do your best for king and country. You may not think altogether as I do; but you do not, cannot go with these wild fanatics, who, in the name of liberty, are training the minds of men to anarchy, and precipitating a general ruin on the country. Even if their argument be right, we are not prepared for the independence they court, nor for the struggle which is essential to secure it. These surely are your opinions no less than mine. Tell me, my son, that you will speak. Say it, O! say it, if you would not have me madden—if you would not have me fling you from my bosom, with the old man's curse upon your head."

His sobs at length silenced this passionate appeal. He clung about the neck of the youth, while the tears flowed freely from his eyes. The youth swayed to and fro under his own emotions; and at length, with the most mournful tones, and with the saddest emphasis, he replied:

"Oh! my father, you have prevailed. I will speak as you desire; but you know not what you have done. I foresee all the mischief which must follow. I will combat every suggestion which may seem to lead to disaffection and war; but I will enter into no argument upon the abstract principles now asserted in this issue. The policy is one thing, but the principle another. I may combat the one, but you must leave me to be silent on the other. I cannot speak what I know not to be the truth. The time will come when it will assert itself, and when no man will dare to question. Plead as you will, with blind loyalty, which sees a divine right in the crown which I see only in the people—assert as you may, and believe, if you will, in the right of a foreign power to rule, according to its pleasure, over other States three thousand miles away, but the claim involves a falsehood and must, if permitted, result only in a despotism. I have no such loyalty as you. I do not pretend to it, and cannot, even though your agonies force me to be silent where my conscience might compel me to cry aloud. But I will argue for the patient waiting of our people, for their continued endurance; for their avoidance of all occasions of strife and commotion; in the one hope that temperance and moderation may quiet passion, smooth the way to wisdom, and so procure them justice in the end. This is all that I can promise. And even this will work mischief to my own hopes. It will place me in apparent antagonism with my people, in whom are all my hopes, and who possess all my sympathies. It will, besides, be of little use. It will do no good; arrest no passion; above all, offer no check to that popular movement which lies in the very nature of things, and which must grow finally into an impetus which will prove irresistible, no matter what the odds. Remember my words, gentlemen. The very course which some of you are now taking, asserting everything for the crown, denying everything to the people, and preparing even for their destruction, rather than abandon a solitary prejudice or opinion, will precipitate the struggle which can have but one termination in the end. I will speak as I have said!—no more!"

The father would have answered with new arguments, and a fresh appeal, but Cameron arrested him, and while these two conversed together at the window, the son hurriedly left the apartment. The father was about to call him back, and would have followed him, but his companions restrained him. He groaned bitterly, wringing his hands, as he exclaimed:

"Cold! cold! He will never do. He is all ice at heart. He does not *feel* with us, my friends. He cannot make himself felt by others! And what does he mean by that rigmarole about the truth prevailing at last?"

"Patience! patience! old man!" said Browne, laying his hands on his shoulder, and literally pressing him back into his seat.

"Enough has been gained for one day. Enough, that your son has promised you to speak. Do not doubt, when he once begins, that he will speak to the purpose. He will be hurried forward, after he has once begun, much faster than he designs. A young man, having the gift of the gab, and proud of it, does not well know, when he once begins, where he will stop. As he warms up, the very opposition which he will meet will carry him off his legs, and what he lacks in loyalty will be supplied by self-esteem and the love of approbation. The passion of the orator will trip the heels of the lawyer; and in the heat of conflict with a rival, he will rather look to victory before the people than to the maintenance of those cold philosophies which now chill his loyalty. Let him alone; enough that he is pledged to speak. I will wager a crown that before the day is out he will begin to meditate his speech, and how he shall say it."

"It is well! It is perhaps as you say. But Wattie has not much vanity. And what does he mean when he speaks of mischief to himself?"

"Oh, that is as to his prospects as a lawyer. A *crown* lawyer, and a favorite with the king, he need not care a button for mere popularity."

The old man sighed. He began to see, or to suspect, that there were other problems involved in the great popular issue, which were beyond his ken. But the policy of his associates was not to suffer him to brood in this direction, and Browne interposed:

"The one matter settled, and, as I think, just as we wish it, let us now see to other things. These dispatches from Lord Wm. Campbell?"

"We must keep dark on that subject," answered Cameron. "We dare not use them yet. They will do hereafter, and will then produce the better effect, especially when the rebels shall more fully show their hands."

"Nevertheless," said Browne, "there is reason that *we* should see them, and I must have copies of them for other eyes."

"Here they are, but for our own perusal only. Here are the dispatches of the Governor, under cover to Colonel Stuart. Here are Stuart's own private advices to me. He has had to fly to Florida. We shall have the arms and ammunition, nevertheless, just as we desire. Here are the Governor's own assurances."

"But how get them up from the seaboard? We want them in the mountains. We need them for the backwoods' people as well as for the Indians. There is Fletchall's Regiment, which alone will need a thousand stand of arms, and the whole country along the Saluda and the Broad, the Tiger and Little Rivers, and especially in the 'Dutch Fork.' The Scotch and Dutch settlements are all with us; or can be worked by the Cunninghams, by Fletchall, Kirkland, Pearis, and others. Five thousand muskets will not be one too many, and a few swivels will be needed also. The question is how to get them away from the seaboard. The rebel patriots are very vigilant, and the Committees of Safety are busy in every precinct."

"That has been cared for. The plan of the Governor will be to forward our supplies, by night, in boats, to the heads of Ashley and Cooper Rivers. Say near Dorchester on the one, and Monk's Corner on the other river. Thither we shall dispatch trusty parties, who will muster there secretly, and move upward only by night. We have also another plan by which the rebels themselves shall help us to supplies. They are about to dispatch a baggage train, with arms and ammunition, for the supply of their friends in the interior. I have a plan of organization by which these shall all be captured."

"Ah!" cried Browne, rubbing his hands, "that is something like it. By the way, friend Dunbar, where could Mr. Walter have got his information about these supplies for the Indians?"

"I really do not know."

"They have no real information on the subject. It is only a reasonable conjecture. They propose to do the same thing themselves, and naturally give us credit for a like policy."

"It is clear to me, Cameron," said Browne, "that Master Walter was not wholly satisfied with your explanation and denial on that subject."

"Very like! But that will not matter much in the end. He has some active associates, who are not only not with us, but whom we believe to be working bitterly against us. There are the two Joscelyns."

"Ha! the Joscelyns!" cried the old man. "Which of them?"

"Both; and they are both visitors here."

"One of them, Martin, the younger brother only. The other, Stephen, rarely comes hither. He keeps a school somewhere over on Beach Island, and is said to be a smart fellow, though I could never see it. But he is a cripple, you know, miserably deformed, and goes little about the country. As for Martin, he seems a good boy enough; I thought well of him, but if you suspect him—"

"Suspect! I *know* him to be active among the rebels. We have him and his brother both upon our list as traitors."

"He shall never darken my doors again," cried the old man.

"Don't be foolish," said Cameron. "Let him come if he will. He will be on his good behavior while here, and you can have him under your eye. To let him know that you suspect him, is to put him on his guard. It will be time enough to denounce when we are prepared to destroy."

"I must probe Walter about him."

"Better not. The surgeon will only probe when he is prepared to operate; and your son is in no mood to submit to any operation now. Once more, my old friend, let well enough alone. As for the elder brother of these Joscelyns—"

"Oh! he's a poor cripple; he can do nothing."

"There you miss it mightily—a poor cripple, indeed, and possibly not the one to take up arms, but we have him down as a most viperous malignant, who has been writing the most audacious letters to the people about the king."

"Who would have thought it? And I thought him little better than a simpleton."

"One of the best heads in the country! I tried him once, a year ago; and before I knew where I was, he had wormed his way into my memory and brain, in such a manner that he came very near plucking out from its hiding place one of my most valuable secrets. Simpleton, indeed! I, too, was simpleton enough to think him one, and came near paying the penalty. Were he not a cripple, and so deformed, you would find him one of the most dangerous malignants on Savannah river."

Here the conference may end for us, not that it stopped here. It was continued throughout the day at intervals, and late into the night, when Cameron, who was laying *perdu,* and did not dare to show himself in the neighborhood, was conveyed by Browne, under the cover of the darkness, across the Savannah river, whence he made his way up to his princely domain of "Lochaber," on Little Run, preparatory to an excursion among the Cherokees, where he was even then busy in subsidizing for the cause of his Majesty.

Young Walter Dunbar did not reappear to his father that day or night. He had left the place, in fact, after a brief conference with his sister. The old man was especially uneasy, as for two days more he could see nothing of the son. Meanwhile, we may do the youth the justice to say, that whatever might be his employments, he was not surely engaged upon the matter or manner of his speech.

# CHAPTER III.

## STEPHEN JOSCELYN.

While this scene was in progress, at the cottage of old Dunbar, upon the Sand Hills, there was one person, a few miles distant, even then, who brooded earnestly over the same subject, but in quite another temper, and with arguments, for himself, in his own faith, which led him in the opposite political direction.

We have heard something already, from the preceding conversation, of one Stephen Joscelyn, a cripple and a schoolmaster. He has been described as a malignant, hostile to the royal cause, and of great capacity to do it harm. Let us visit him at the "old field" school, some eight miles from Augusta, and but a short distance from the Savannah river. But we are now on the east, and not on the west side of that stream.

Beach Island, in South Carolina, has long been famous for the fertility of its soil. It had the same reputation in revolutionary times. There were many planters of considerable wealth, for those days, who occupied its rich bottoms and prolific plains. Its seasons were mild and genial, and the means of life were abundant. Beach Island had, besides, a considerable population of the class of small farmers, all of whom lived prosperously. It possessed, also, we are free to admit, some wild tribes, restless, and of irregular habits, who were *nomades* rather than residents. The population was mixed and of various kinds. There were wild men who lived wholly by hunting and fishing—their labors, though not themselves, being wholly tributary to the wants of the thriving town of Augusta. These persons were always eager after excitement, and readily yielded themselves to any party or influence which promised them exercise in fields where the restless blood would find impulse and employment. They gathered to the muster ground, to the horse race, the barbacue. They were always present at the

Court-House, at sale days, and during the sessions; and their convivialities were rarely limited within the rules of prudence and propriety. Generally well mounted, on fast horses, which they well knew how to manage, they rode through the forests without needing a well-beaten pathway. They were thus the very sort of people to constitute an irregular cavalry; to scout, skirmish, purvey, and explore. They belonged, in brief, to that class of pioneers who were the first in our country to penetrate the domain of the red man and the wild beast, and to prepare the wilderness, the swamp and forest, for the advent of civilization. They had their uses.

Here, then, in all this precinct especially, as in a large part of the contiguous country, were associated, but not assimilated, the antagonist forces of a wild nature and a refined society. On one hand rose the beautiful domain of the wealthy planter, who had brought the highest culture from the schools of Europe; on the other hand was the low hovel of the wild man, where no flower grew, where all was coarse and savage, the chief possessions of which were bear and deer meat in abundance, hanging from the rafters, and a rude hospitality which freely shared with the stranger the small physical comforts of the humble cabin.

Gradually these people were in training for the advent of a superior civilization. Their wives and daughters had just begun, following the example of wealthier neighbors, to plant the rose and the shrub-tree at the porch, and to appreciate that education for their young the benefits of which they had not themselves enjoyed. And so rose in this, as must be the case in every sparsely settled agricultural region, what was long known, in our interior, as the "Old Field School."

An old field, denuded of its soil by long cultivation, was abandoned to the waste. Possibly an ancient log-cabin still remained upon it. This was repaired, or a new one built, and this always in some spot sufficiently contiguous to the more populous settlements. The children, girls and boys, were frequently taught together, in the same low edifice, and might be seen daily trudging to their tasks, bearing in their satchels bread and meat rather than books. Books were scarce. A few will always suffice where the schoolmaster himself is competent, and has the judgment to perceive how superior to every other was the ancient system of *oral* instruction.

Books, in recent times, are provided rather for the benefit of the teacher than the pupil. But we must not digress.

The "Old Field School," on Beach Island, with its few books, had its fair proportion of pupils, girls and boys, in very equal numbers. Their ages ranged between eight and sixteen. Some of the males, indeed, seeking, at a late period, to supply their early deficiencies of education, were to be found of eighteen or nineteen, and in a few cases even of twenty-one or more years, painfully struggling through their arithmetic and grammar. These were mostly the children of poor people, or persons of very moderate means. Occasionally, however, a farmer or planter of sufficient wealth, would send his son to the "Old Field School," preferring contiguity to the supposed advantages of more expensive institutions, and, perhaps, as was the case here, preferring the one particular teacher for his son. Stephen Joscelyn had a reputation with many, not unlike that which we have heard delivered from the mouth of Alexander Cameron.

His school-house, which was of well-squared logs, of good size and shapely to the eye, occupied a corner of an old field, long thrown out of culture, and now thinly sprinkled with a secondary growth of scrubby and water oaks, field pines, persimmon, and the frequent China tree. The building itself was completely surrounded by these latter beautiful shade trees, growing in clumps, and affording, in summer, a finely sheltered play-ground for the children. Of these, a goodly number attended the school of Stephen Joscelyn, and they generally throve under his rule. He was a favorite among them; gentle and patient, adapting his lesson to the capacity of the pupil, and seeking, in every possible way, to discover, in the case of every individual, in what that capacity lay.

But we need not dwell upon his processes. It is enough to report that he was held to be generally successful. He had won the confidence of the parents, in winning the affections of the children, and, by his calm, grave, sedate, gentle and unobtrusive manners, he secured a welcome in all the households within his province. His fine talents, prompt judiciary thoughts, and graceful and forcible expression, compelled additional acknowledgment from the best classes, by which, in process of time, he was lifted gradually into a sort of local authority, which was amply shown by the frequent references made to him as an arbitrator for the adjustment of difficulties among his neighbors. His judgments, founded at once upon great good sense and an innate love of justice, were rendered logical, and in a measure legal, by his knowledge of English law, which was considerable. His leisure hours were usually surrendered to this study.

But it is time that we should make his acquaintance. Let us, without ceremony, penetrate his school-room, and see him in his seat of authority.

As you behold him now, seated at his desk, you are impressed with the remarkable strength and beauty of his personal aspect. A noble and powerful bust, great massive shoulders, supporting a head of magnificent dimensions, covered with a thick shock of fine brown hair, great blue eyes, with heavily-arched eye-brows; a mouth, firm but sweet, and a full, Grecian nose, gave you the impression of a mind not only of large development, but of equitable poise and balance. The breadth and fullness of the chin, the *pose* of the head, upon an ample column of neck, the general symmetry and mutual dependence of the several features united to assure you that you were in the presence of no ordinary, certainly no vulgar mind. Air, carriage, manner and tone, all indicated the perfect gentleman; and the general gravity of expression in the face, while it denoted a spirit that might rise into passionate determination, was yet softened into sweetness by a uniform expression of sadness. The eyes, though soft, clear, and very full, were yet singularly sad, save when the countenance brightened up in the warmth of conversation, when they at once partook of the general animation of all the features.

See him where he sits, and you would conceive him to be, physically, a perfect man as well as gentleman; a Diomed, or Antinono; powerful of frame, large of limb, of great muscle and activity, and wonderful symmetry as well as endurance; and, in many of these respects, you would not be disappointed.

But when you see him rise and attempt to move, you would then readily conceive why it is that such a person should subside into the master of an "old field" school. You then perceive the cripple, whose motions pain you to behold, which are made doubly painful to your eyes because so completely in antagonism with the otherwise perfect symmetry and grand development of the physical man.

From his earliest childhood he had been a cripple. Born of vigorous parents, he gave, for a time, every promise of a healthy infancy; but, during this tender period, an insidious disease—considered by the physicians to be scrofulous—the result of some hereditary taint, had shown itself; and when he was about two years of age, his mother despaired of her child's ever being able to stand alone. The left leg was drawn up, shrivelled, and shortened, the knees and toes inverted; whilst its fellow kept pace uniformly with the general development of the body, which, as we have shown, was unusually vigorous and athletic. At seven, when his companions were gambolling afield, trapping partridges, smoking rabbits out of their hollows, hunting birds, and robbing nests, his only exercise was taken in a little go-cart, rolling about the level inclosure, the subject of pity to all who saw him, and of perpetual pain and anxiety to his parents.

But the boy had a soul and spirit which loathed the inaction to which his misfortune seemed to doom him. While his earlier durance continued, and when but six or seven years of age, he became a great reader, especially of the Bible; the Old Testament, with its wild mysteries, its strange rites, its ghostly prophets and savage warriors, appealing to his imagination, so as to constitute a something compensative for the physical privations which he was perforce compelled to endure. He was also fortunate in a Plutarch. He gained, in some degree, through these and other books, at the expense of his comrades, for what he may have lost in play. For awhile he literally devoured books, and a wonderful memory tenaciously retained what he thus acquired. But books did not satisfy his *temperament*, though they gave grateful employment to his *mind*. He very soon began to evince—strange contradiction—a passion for *horses;* a preference which his father judiciously fostered; and before the boy was quite twelve years of age, he could ride with the boldest of his associates, vaulting, or rather scrambling into the saddle, without any assistance. Once seated, he looked the Centaur, defying the most vicious colt to cast him from his seat.

In that attitude, no one would suspect his infirmity. As a horseman, he gave no evidence of weakness, want of limb, or deficiency of muscle. The upper part of his frame was unusually massive; his chest broad, as we have described; head and throat of corresponding size; his arms long and sinewy; and long before he grew to manhood, he was noted, throughout the country, not only as a great fox-hunter, but by his singular strength of wrist and hand. He had practiced with quarter staff and broadsword, and his only exercise was taken on horseback.

Such, in brief, was Stephen Joscelyn. Though a cripple, his affections were still divided between the exercises of field and forest, and the study of books. Latterly, in consequence, perhaps, of his occupation, the influence of the books prevailed. But we shall see! There is, yet, perhaps, an undecided conflict between them, which this story must develop.

The business of the school is well begun. The mingled hum of voices is heard from the children conning their several lessons. There is the wonted buzz at once of study and unrest. Stephen Joscelyn only interposes when the murmur shall become impertinence. He is indulgent, and knows too well the value to the *string* of the relaxation of the *bow*. He allows for the tenderness of gristle and sinew in the child, as he knows what is due to the early breaking in of the wild colt. It is only the stupid, or the brutal, that makes the mouth callous, by too frequently straining upon the bit.

He has borrowed some of his notions of education from the schools of the Greek masters. He is not for restraining the physical movements, fettering the boy or girl for five mortal hours on a stiff bench, to the harm of the yet unhardened sinews, and the enfeebling and curvature of the spinal shaft, which evils are, in our day, the too frequent consequence of the cruel habit of concentrating the entire tasks of the day into the morning hours only. He will, in fine weather, take his pupils into the open air, under the shady trees, and hear them recite, and teach them as they walk to and fro together. And, at a signal, he, the cripple, will play with them like any other child; will bend their bows for them, and use his own; will shape the feathers and sharpen the arrow; will teach them the sleight of hand which helps the strength, to hurl the *pilum;* will train them to such precision in the use of the *discus,* that each shall become prouder in his growing progress to perfection, day by day. And when they behold his strength and agility, and skill, and feel his care and sympathy, they see not that he is a cripple; they know him not as the pedagogue, but the father and the friend.

But the labors of the school are interrupted. The sudden tramp of horse's feet is heard without; and soon the door is darkened by a shadow; and a figure enters; a hale, rough backwoodsman, of hardy, honest face, smiling good humoredly around upon the children, and marching boldly up to the teacher as to an old acquaintance, he offers his hand, which is taken promptly with a hearty gripe, while the stranger exclaims, with a voice well trained for forest use in whoop, hallow, and high occasions:

"Well, Stephen, how is it with you to-day? Got any larning to spare to me? I'm mighty in need of it, I tell you."

"Nonsense, Dick Marvin; you have quite as much learning as you need, and as much good sense. But what brings you here to-day?"

"To get a favor out of you. I want to take young Dick away from you."

"What! take him from school?"

"Yes, jist that, Stephen."

"I hope not, Dick! Your boy is doing well, and I hope to make a man of him. I trust, Dick, that you do not mean to deprive the boy of all chance of becoming a man, by turning him into a mere horse boy, as is too much the habit with base and slavish people."

"No, no, Stephen! No fear of that! I was only funning with you. I know too well what you're adoing for Dick; and all that *riles* me, and hurts a proud stomach, is that the chap's a gitting quite too smart for his fayther. Ha! ha! He bothers me a'most every night, with his big dictionary words, and his great diskiveries in 'rithmatic and gography."

"Well, I have not taught him *that* lesson, Dick. He should have more respect for his father than to shame him before folks."

"Oh! I don't quarrel with the young rascal for that. As Malley Seibels said to Jacob Simpson, when he 'pologized for kissing her all on a suddent, 'Don't 'pologize, Mr. Simpson, I rayther likes it.' So I rayther likes to see my chap show himself smart to the comp'ny, though he does so at his fayther's expense. I am quite willing he should grow to be wiser than his fayther."

"And what do you mean by taking him away?"

"Only for a day! I wants you to give him a holiday-chance to-morrow, as I wants him to go with me to Augusta town, to the great meeting."

"What great meeting?"

"What! you hevn't hearn?"

"Not a syllable."

"Wal, I swow! And you didn't know that all the country's agathering to go thar, and hear the famous speechifier, Drayton, from the *Salts*, who's to talk to us, and tell us how stands the whole case atwixt the King and the Colony."

"Is it really so, Dick?"

"It's a born truth, Stephen."

"I'm very glad you've told me. I should like to hear Wm. Drayton myself, and on this question, especially; and I'll not only give Dick holiday, but the whole school shall have holiday also."

"Hech! boys, do you hear that?" said Dick Marvin.

"Hoorah! hoorah! hoorah!" went up with united voices from the whole school.

"No more work to-day, Dick! You've spoiled this morning for us; so the dogs get two days instead of one. I'm something of a boy myself, and shall be glad of the holiday."

"No harm that, Stephen. *They* won't be any the worse for it; and they'll come back, every gentleman's son of 'em, ready to do double work, and so make up for lost time. Play is a great part of edication, Stephen, I'm a thinking; and holiday, to a boy, is jest something better than a Sunday—it has a brighter sort of sunshine."

"You are *speaking* more wisdom than you *know*, Dick Marvin; and your philosophy, if put properly into practice, would save thousands from drunkenness, and make thousands of wiser men. But sit down, Dick, while I speak to the children."

Dick Marvin flung his fox-skin cap upon a bench, and threw his great length of legs after it, occupying a portion of two seats, which enabled his feet to arrive at an elevation something greater than his head. Here he shut his eyes, while Stephen Joscelyn, after a short talk, dismissed the boys to play. When they had all tumbled out headlong, with a rare sense of mirth and freedom, Dick Marvin, taking out his pipe and filling it, produced flint and steel and tinder box, and made for himself a light. A few puffs of smoke, to settle his ideas into something like shape, and he spoke as follows:

"What I wants, Stephen, is to larn and know. When I've larned a thing and know it, I can then set down my feet fairly on the square, and snap my fingers at the devil. Now this quarrel betwixt the Congress and the King troubles me; for you see, I kaint altogether get the right hang of it. I don't see how the cat's gwine to jump, and I don't like to git down from the fence till I can clairly see upon which side of it the mad bull is gwine to run. Hyer's one man telling you one thing, and another man another, and they mixes it all up with so many words, that the devil of an idee kin I pick out from the whole. I wants to do what's right, and take the right side, and then, ef the thing concarns me at all, I'm ready to pitch in, though the cry is 'no quarter!' They tell me thar's gwine to be fightin', and I don't like the idee; for though I've *fit* the Ingins, and pretty hard, too, with several narrow escapes of having the feel of a red devil's fingers in my hair, yet the time's gone by when I could say, without oneasiness, 'I'm ready for any brush!' I was a younker then, and didn't much care for any thing; but wife and children makes a pusson old mighty soon, and when you've got them, and sich a boy as my Dick, and sich a gal as my Sally—you know Sall—and she's now mighty nigh gwine on to fifteen; and when thar's a snug farm to 'tend to, and allis smooth and looking well, and doing well, it's hard to think upon the breaking up and the hard chainces that comes along close a'ter the heels of war. Now, Stephen, every body knows you to be a mighty smart man, with a head chock full of books, and a tongue that's jest as smart as wisdom can make it; and I want you to tell me something to set me right, and set my mind at ease, and put me in the reason and the right of every thing in this quarrel; for I don't like this leaping in the dark 'till that time comes, when a man's bound to take it. Now, Stephen, jest you give that big head of your'n a scraitch or two, and blaze away with all your wisdom."

"Not so easy, Dick. I may have wisdom enough for one—myself—but not for two. I have satisfied myself on the subject of this quarrel, and you will always know what course I shall adopt. It is not always easy to explain to another the reason that moves oneself; and there's never a good reason, my friend, where there is not some feeling in it; and this feeling is a more difficult matter still to explain. But I do not wish to enter upon the subject at all. You propose to hear Judge Drayton to-morrow. He can, no doubt, and probably will, explain everything satisfactorily. I do not know that I can anticipate him; nor is it proper that I should. He comes from the seat of government, as well as information. He will know, a thousand times more than I do, of the condition of things. I am going, myself, to hear him, and be enlightened by him. You will do the same thing. Come by here to-morrow at an early hour, and take me in your way. We will ride to Augusta together. On the route, I may tell you what *I* think and feel, and Judge Drayton will tell you more. He is one of the great men from the Low Country, who is perfectly familiar with all the 'inns' and 'outs' of politics. Let me remind you that I go to hear him as a *teacher*. I do not doubt that he will teach well. You will bring your son with you?"

"Won't I? He's a smart boy—You says it yourself. I want him to hear and larn as well as myself."

"Very good." After a pause—"Dick, you can ride?"

"Kaint I, then?"

"Dick, in all the quarrels of the world, the great body of men have shown themselves always as mere animals. They may have brains; but, under the influence of great excitement, these brains become animal brains. Then it is that men show themselves in their true colors. One is the hare-brain, which jumps and gets out of breath without any good reason; one is the fox-brain, which knows how to double and dodge, and will a thousand times rather pursue a crooked course than a straight one; one is a wolf-brain, which is only brave when desperately hungry; one is a tiger-brain, which has a passion for drinking blood, but never that of any other beast that can show him tooth for tooth! The lion-brain is more brave and more magnanimous, and it has power. But the best brain of all is that of *manhood*, which seeks always to be just; can always afford to be generous, and when exercised without fear, and with a good conscience, is lord over all the beasts. The conflict before us is one which will bring all these beasts into exercise. It is for you and me, if we can, to find and put in active service the brain of our best manhood. Study for that, and you must be wise."

With these words, a certain time having elapsed, Joscelyn put the bugle to his mouth, and winded a noble blast. Presently the children came bounding into school, and were instantly subdued to quiet by a word. They had fed as well as played. The teacher then spoke to them as follows:

"There are some tall boys among you," he said, "who may well persuade their fathers to take them to the gathering to-morrow. You will hear one of the great statesmen of your country speak on matters well worthy to be known, and which must vitally affect your interests hereafter. It is proper that you should hear him. He will probably teach you much better than I can. Hearken to his words and understand them, if you can. It will not be difficult, if you pay proper attention, for the good speaker can always make himself understood, no matter what his subject, by the humblest of his audience. Go, now, my children, and behave yourselves as you should. I shall hope to meet some of you at the gathering to-morrow, for I too shall go thither, with the hope to acquire information, and I trust knowledge. We will try and learn together."

And so he dismissed them. Dick Marvin soon took his departure also, with his boy, promising to join Joscelyn at a certain hour in the morning.

Left alone, Stephen Joscelyn sate in moody meditation, brooding in silence, and in a sort of reverie which made no exhibitions calculated to inform us of the subject of his thoughts. In some respects, he was a lonely man. His infirmity probably tended much to confirm him in a habit of solitude. There were books about him, but now he did not read. His temperament, implied in his powerful physique, was one designed for action. Nursed in solitude, he was keenly sensitive, and possibly but for his temperament, which was ardent in a high degree, he would have shrunk wholly from society. It is not easy to conceive how much one suffers, who, from natural or other disabilities, is forced to feel a disparity between himself and fellows, in whose ears a bitter voice perpetually murmurs, "you are unlike other men. You cannot feel their confidence in society, in man or woman. Lo! all eyes behold your deformity. All fingers point to that miserable member which you are forever striving to conceal."

Such a voice speaks forever in the ears of the cripple, when he possesses innate sensibilities of great keenness, which have been trained by superior tastes. They quicken these sensibilities. They keep them perpetually sore. It may be they harden the heart in time against man and woman. Happy he who shall escape this danger; who shall learn to bear his sufferings with an humble spirit which sorrows over, but does not quarrel with his destiny.

At length, whatever the meditations of Stephen Joscelyn, a deep groan broke from his bosom, followed by vague ejaculations, from which, however, we may gather some clue to the subject of his brooding moments.

"Unloved! and all alone! Shall it be so always? Will the one fond, earnest craving to be loved, never be satisfied? Must I, alone, of all, be denied the communion of some sympathizing nature, to see me and know me as *I am*, through all my deformity? And yet to love, not only vainly, but weakly! To yearn towards one who can satisfy no craving of thought or mind; who appeals only to the sensuous and dependant fancy! This is the curse over all! To be decreed to feel a passion for the object from which the thought perpetually revolts, but from which it vainly struggles to be free. This is the misery! I must escape from thought to action. Better the headlong race, the struggle, the catastrophe—sudden bolt of doom in the desperate and wild issue where one obeys only the fiery impulse of his blood, than this brooding day by day in humiliating reveries and fancies which must end only in atrophy or despair! It must be so!—and yet! But no! I can deceive myself no longer! *She* loathes the cripple! I see it in all her looks! I read it in all her motions! Nay, more, so little is she *human*, or *woman*, that she does not seek to conceal her dislike—and shall I still—"

The rest of the speech was lost. He stopped himself suddenly, as if there had been a listener at the entrance. Then he rose from his chair, went to the door and threw it wide, looked forth, returned to the desk, and proceeded to put his papers in order. This done, he closed up doors and windows, and mounted his horse, a powerful black charger which stood fastened to a neighboring tree; and, once seated, he presented as noble an aspect of knighthood as ever shone in ancient tournament.

He rode fast, and it was not long before, having traversed something like a mile and a half, he stopt in front of a neat cottage, the entrance of which was gracefully festooned with flowers.

This was his lodging place. He had board here, with an excellent old lady, Mrs. Kirkland, a widow, well known and respected in all the neighborhood. He looked up as he drew nigh to the gate. A beautiful girl sat at one of its windows, as he gazed and caught her eye. She immediately ran and passed out of sight. The cloud suddenly overshadowed his brows, his lips were sternly compressed on the instant, and he murmured bitterly as he rode slowly to the stable:

"Ay, it is even so! I am not one whom she can abide to behold. She can see but through the eye of sense, and the cripple offends her sight! Oh, God! why, with all this strength on which I pride myself, must I be still so weak? To waste a precious love on so frail a thing! I must assert my mind—my manhood! Bitter though the medicine, I must cure me of this heart-fever, lest I grow to scorn myself."

## CHAPTER IV.

### GRACE AND ANGELICA.

"It was Stephen Joscelyn's horse?" said the old lady, with her knitting in her lap, and the needles plying fast between her fingers while the stocking grew.

"Yes," answered her daughter, Angelica, as she crossed the chamber, and took her seat in an opposite corner.

"And why did you start so, my dear, and leave the window? Did you expect any other person?"

"No, mother; but he looked up at me."

"Well, what harm in that? A cat may look at a king, they say."

"Yes, but they don't say that the king must look back at the cat."

"You're sharp, Angey. But where's the harm of Stephen Joscelyn looking at you?"

"He stares at me so, mother."

"Well, that's only a proof of his liking, Angey."

"And who cares for his liking?"

"Fi, Angey, my child. Stephen Joscelyn's liking can do you no harm, and better his liking than his dislike, my child. It seems to me, Angey, that you do not treat Stephen as you should. He's been a good friend of ours, and has taken a great deal of pains in teaching you and Grace. The truth is, Angey, I'm thinking that it's more than liking that he has for you, in particular. He loves you, Angey."

"I know it, mother, and that's what I don't like! What right has he?"

"Oh! he has a right to love whom he pleases, my child. You can't forbid that, Angey, and, more than that, he has a right, if anybody has, to be loved in return—"

"Not by me, I can tell him. I can't forgive him that following me with his eyes, and looking so into mine, with such a stare, as if he wanted to eat me up—the poor, miserable 'dot-and-go-one' that he is!"

"Angey, my child," cried the old lady, indignantly, laying down her knitting in her lap, and looking at her artful daughter with eyes of equal displeasure and surprise—"what possesses you to speak in such language of so good and noble a gentleman as Stephen Joscelyn, and one to whom we owe so much? Do you know what he has done for us, Angey?"

"Yes, I know, mother; but that gives him no right to think of me."

"I don't know that, Angey; but I do know that it makes it a duty with all of us to think kindly and gratefully, and even lovingly of him. He has been the best of teachers for you and Grace, Angey."

"Well, but you have paid him, mother."

"Money cannot pay for all sorts of obligations, nor have I ever been called upon to pay Stephen, even in money, what I should have had to pay other persons for the same services. You must not forget that when your poor father died, it was Stephen Joscelyn who settled up the affairs of the estate, collected the debt, put the farm in order, and for more than two years superintended everything, and never once asked or received a copper for all these services. Had I got any other lawyer, he'd have sweated the property down, I tell you, one-half."

"But he's lived with us all that time—has had board and lodging free."

"You silly child; you perverse! When will you come to your senses, and see things as you ought to see them?"

"I'll never see Stephen Joscelyn with your eyes or Grace's."

"I wish you could!"

"Let Grace marry him if she pleases, and she looks at him now as if she were not unwilling—"

"Hush, Angelica! You have no right to speak thus of your sister. I wish you were more like her. If you would look more into her eyes, and less in the looking glass, you'd be a more sensible child. But remember one thing: whatever you may think and feel with regard to Stephen Joscelyn, I shall expect that you will always be careful to treat him as one whom your poor father loved and honored; to whom he confided everything before he died, and who put our little property into his hands for management, knowing it would be safe, and husbanded with care. How would he be shocked to hear the manner in which you speak of him who has been for so many years the best friend and the sole guardian of his family. I tell you, Angey, that if you do not love Stephen Joscelyn, I do, and so does Grace Kirkland."

"Yes, indeed!" with a meaning laugh, "that's plain enough."

"Once more I warn you, Angelica; you are no more to trifle with your sister's name than with my feelings or those of Stephen Joscelyn. Well, if you ever get so good a man for a husband. You will go farther, but may fare worse. You are a vain and foolish girl, flattered by your own face, and do not know that if the fine face sometimes wins the husband, it is the fine soul which must keep him."

The young beauty left the room, humming the fragment of a song. The mother sighed, and trembled. She had reason to be anxious. Such dialogues as these had been somewhat frequent of late, but Angelica had not gone quite so far before in the expression of her antipathies.

It was her misfortune to be a beauty, and to be conscious of her charms. She was a gay, graceful creature, of sunny eyes and hair, features at once symmetrical and piquant, full of animation, with full, pouting lips, always armed with a lively play of feature, and intellectually endowed with a certain gift of fancy, which was apt to show itself in repartee. But she had her caprices, her humors —was variable as the weather, and, from having been a spoiled child, because of her juvenile graces, had grown to be a spoiled woman, the effect of which was sometimes to mar all her graces.

Reaching her own chamber, she paused before the mirror, let down her hair, and as she smoothed out the wavy masses, which terminated in ringlets nearly reaching to her knees, she murmured audibly—

"And such as he to think of me with love! Oh! how I hate him for his impudence!"

This was strong language, especially after the lecture of her mother. But when was the too conscious beauty ever wise?

And he of whom she spoke?

He was just then entering the house, below stairs, having been delayed at the stable in a conference with his groom. Slowly, and sadly musing as he came, he drew nigh the porch without seeing that he was waited for, until at the very entrance, when he found himself suddenly confronted by a young woman.

This was Grace Kirkland, the elder sister of Angelica, but without any portion of her beauty.

Grace was homely. The face was fair and sweet, but the features, blended or separate, were without any special attractions. Her hair was long, like that of her sister, but of coarser fibre, and far less etherial hue. It was brown, and so was her complexion. But the dark and shaded eyes were dewy, and not wanting in brightness, and the general expression of her features was pleasant.

If the consciousness of beauty was strong in her sister's mind, her's was not less possessed of the consciousness of her own homeliness. She was modest, accordingly, to humility, amiable and solicitous to please; yet, so unobtrusively, that her solicitude seemed always the most natural conduct, proper to herself especially, and so grateful to those whom she approached.

"Ah! Grace, what have you there?"

"Some buttermilk, Stephen, fresh from the churn. I have brought this bowl of it for you."

"But, where's your share?"

"Oh! we have all drank already."

"You are very good, Grace."

"Thank you; but tell me that you find the buttermilk good, and I shall be satisfied. I churned it myself."

"It is excellent—so cool, so sweet. You do everything well, Grace." And, handing back the bowl, he laid his hand on her shoulder, and looked gratefully into her face, nor did he—blind and insensible that he was—perceive that her eyes drooped beneath his glance, and the swarthy nut-brown of her cheeks was suffused with a glow, like sunset, that almost made her handsome.

Grace hastily retreated with the bowl to the pantry, and there sate, with the door closed, her cheeks still burning and her heart palpitating, and she knew not then the secret of her own emotions, and it more than once occurred to her that she might be suffering from some secret infirmity of constitution—a heart-disease, perhaps, of which she had sometime heard as having once before been the case in her mother's family!

Verily, she was right! It was a heart-disease of which she suffered, and we are not sufficiently the physician to say where she will find her remedy.

Meanwhile, Stephen Joscelyn has hobbled to his little chamber, in a shed-room, on the ground floor. It was an humble lodging-place; the walls unplastered; the floor uncarpeted; the room poorly furnished, with its truckle bedstead, its homely set of drawers, or bureau, its pine table, and washstand of the same material, and its few oaken chairs, of country make, with seats of oaken splits, rudely intertwisted. And there was a little book-case in the room, containing some hundred volumes, among which were a few treasures from the masters—a Homer, of Pope; an Æschylus, a Shakspeare and a Milton. There were also certain of the essayists, of recent reputation. It was not a very valuable collection in the eyes of a book-worm, but it had been made to yield all its values—and they were great enough for any student—to its possessor. The books had been all well thumbed, and their contents were nearly all well stored away in memory.

Over the chimney hung a broadsword which the father of Stephen had used in the Indian wars of the colony. The ambitious son had trained himself to its use also, while on horseback. A long rifle was suspended above it on supports made of the antlers of the buck, firmly fixed to the naked studs of the wall.

And these were all the objects of interest that met the eye in the chamber of Stephen Joscelyn. He seemed at this moment to regard none of them; but, throwing himself into a chair, he appeared to surrender himself to a moody humor, chewing the cud rather of sad and bitter than of grateful thought. His eye watched the distorted limb which was crossed upon the knee of its more noble fellow. He laid his hand upon it, and the cloud grew darkly over his brow. At moments he spoke in murmurs, and the subject of his meditations was to be gathered from his occasional ejaculations, which seemed to be extorted from him by a sense of pain more than usually acute.

"It is well, at least, that I can ride! Would that I could *live* on horseback! Well that I can use rifle and sabre; that the sinews and the limbs are stronger than the soul! Yes, would that I could *live* on horseback! This world of ours needs savage muscles, and reckless hearts, and audacious courage, and daring enterprise. It does not yet need books. It will not need them for a hundred years. There is a manhood of the time, which demands no studies such as mine—which shares none of my cravings. I must exercise that sort of manhood, and the field seems opening to me as to others. I will make myself feared, if I can, and make myself loved! I will prove that deformity is not necessarily feebleness. They shall know that I am strong—strong of limb as of will—and the Time is calling upon me to go forth into those fields in which the athlete mocks the bookworm! I see what awaits us. The old struggle is to be renewed. The ancient despotism is still at work, and Power will again take Justice by the beard, as it has ever done before, and tear away the barriers of Right and Law, and License shall break the head of Authority. Everything shows it to me, a foregone conclusion! I will hear Drayton to-morrow. He ought to know. He will probably deliver all that is necessary for our people to know; and, if he be, indeed, the statesman which he is said to be, it can scarce be possible that he shall escape those conclusions which crowd upon me as inevitable. We shall be all at once involved in the struggle of a dreadful war—shall be engaged in the deadly wrestle, and without a warning.

"And how, with such a prospect before my soul's vision, how should I dream of home delights, and Peace beside the hearth, and Love watching, and smiling welcome at the door!

"Love, indeed! Love! And I to dream of love! Ha! ha!—and with this!"

He smote the crippled limb as he spoke.

"No, no! give up such dreams, Stephen Joscelyn! It is no time, nor are you the person, to be dreaming of 'Amaryllis in the shade,' and twining fetters for the soul, from the 'tangles of Naera's hair.' No, no!"

"This is no world
To play with moments and to tilt with lips;
We must have bloody noses and crack'd crowns,
And pass them current, too."

"Ah! my beloved Shakspeare—thou universal voice! I must leave thee; but thou shalt be with me still! Thou wilt cling to me forever. I shall hear thee at all hours, and thou wilt speak to every feeling of my heart; to every need of my mind; to all passions; all emotions, all hopes and fears, and every necessity. Thou shalt also speak to me—sweetest, yet sharpest of all satirists of the sex—of woman; what she is *not,* and what she should be. I have thee by heart as I have little else, and thy lessons give fervor to my resolve. I will shake off this miserable insanity of weakness, and assert my proper manhood. It is an oath in Heaven! So help me, Heaven!"

He was summoned to dinner.

Here, once seated, it seemed that he *had* shaken off all the turbid humors which had so recently darkened his mind. His manner was light, graceful, and even gay. Not a forced gaiety, but that reckless sort of abandon, in which the spirit seems to shake off all its fetters, in very desperation, and mock its own previous weakness with a levity, the bitterness in which is perhaps hardly perceptible to itself.

"My dear Mrs. Kirkland," said Stephen, "I am about to give myself a holiday, and I feel already the sense of freedom. I have given the school holiday for the rest of the week, and shall visit Augusta to-morrow. Can I do anything while in town for yourself or the young ladies?"

"Why, Stephen, that is something now for you, taking holiday! And what carries you to Augusta?—what are you going to do there?"

The question was thoughtless, and something unfortunate.

"Show myself, my dear Madam—show my admirable proportions; the symmetry of my figure, the graces of my movement. I have *my* vanities as well as other people, and expect to become the observed of all observers. Don't you think that I shall make a great sensation? I shall be judged by my outside, Mrs. Kirkland, for that is the common method; and, judging thus, the good citizens will give me credit for great moral loveliness! How fortunate it is that we do judge by the outside. How terrible it would be were the spectator to be able to pierce the rind to the core—penetrate to the soul or heart—and see what a foul and leprous thing may be harbored in a beautiful form and figure—the venom of the serpent under the polished and diamond-mottled skin!"

This terrible speech was delivered in the gayest and liveliest manner, the eyes of the speaker embracing, as it were, the whole table; bright and blazing with sarcastic fires, while the pleasantest smile played about the mouth.

It paralyzed the circle. The thought at once occurred to both Angelica and her mother, that the conversation between them had been overheard, and yet, upon a moment's reflection, they felt that to be impossible; for they knew the moment when he rode to the stable, and the period when, after some delay, he had reached the house, where Grace had met him at the porch.

But the speech was received in dead silence. The cheeks of Angelica paled, and then instantly flushed, while the mother looked about her with a troubled and bewildered countenance.

"What!" said he, in merry tones, "have you nothing to say which shall encourage my hopes? Do you not see that I am as much excited by the idea of holiday as the boy first let loose from school, with a month's freedom for his Christmas in the country? Do you not perceive how grand are my anticipations of pleasure?—and how should I find this pleasure unless by display, provoking vulgar admiration, and compelling people as they pass, to turn about and ask, 'who is that? what a noble figure, what a fine carriage, and especially what a stately walk!' I have been wasting time, my dear Madame, too long upon these acquisitions which do not tell outwardly and upon society. I have been cultivating the Muses to the neglect of the graces. I am going to put myself to school. I hear of a grand ball to-morrow night. You will hear of me there in a lavolta. I will show to the fair women of Augusta that I, too, possess those personal charms and accomplishments which the world deems so necessary to success!"

Stephen Joscelyn seemed disposed to talk against time. He was playing a part, of course. Mrs. Kirkland was confounded. The eyes of Grace filled with tears, and she left the table and the room. He did not seem to notice her departure. His eyes fastened upon the face of Angelica; keen, quick, sharp, piercing, as if he would look her through, and she, abashed at a certain humiliating self-consciousness, dared not encounter his gaze, which her instincts told her was yet fixed upon her, and her only.

Mrs. Kirkland at length seemed to arouse herself. The only awkward consciousness which she entertained was felt on behalf of her daughter. She felt that the style and manner of Joscelyn was eminently appropriate, supposing him to have heard the conversation between herself and daughter. But this she did not suppose; yet she wondered at the instinct which had divined it.

"Really, Stephen," she said, "I never heard you talk in this way before. I confess, Stephen, I wonder at you, and—"

"Verily, my dear Mrs. Kirkland, you may well wonder at me. I sometimes wonder at myself. But you see that I begin to persuade myself that I am a wonder-provoking person, and so I go to-morrow to Augusta, proposing a great sensation upon the streets. My time will be greatly employed in dancing, the graces, and other agile exercises; but I shall still have time to attend to any little commissions for yourself or the young ladies; so please—I would become the courtier as soon as possible—allow me the pleasure of executing your commissions, whether of friendship or trade; in other words, in the parlor or the market-place."

The air of the speaker was still that of good-humored banter. But the old lady was still bewildered. At length, however, she made out to reply:

"Well, Stephen, I shall thank you to buy me a couple of sacks of salt, and some other articles, and I will make you out a list. I deal, you know, with Moore and Robson. There's a netted head-dress, too, that I'd like you to take up to Annie Dunbar—"

"Happy to do these things, and more—a fine young girl, Annie—a fine woman, I should say."

"She's all that—and very pretty, I think, Stephen. Don't you think so, Stephen?"

"More than pretty, Mrs. Kirkland. Her beauty is nobly intellectual. It is not idiotic—not a simpering Venus, but a sylph who had been touched at her birth, by the wand of Minerva. She is, in truth, a very lovely woman."

"Just my opinion, Stephen. Happy the man that gets her for a wife."

"Happy Annie, if she can get the proper sort of man for a husband. I shall be glad to be the bearer of the head-dress. She is a favorite of mine, and, now that I have resolved on making a figure in society,

I don't know but I may fall in love with her myself. By the way, a good phrase that; *fall* in love—oh, love! oh, love! what a headlong falling business it is!"

"Really, Stephen, you surprise me to-day. I never—"

"Haven't I told you, my dear Mrs. Kirkland, that I am a very surprising person! I have first discovered the fact myself, but intend to lose no time in acting upon it; I shall surprise everybody as I have surprised you, and now that you give me the opportunity, I shall endeavor to surprise the fair Annie Dunbar. She is, in truth, a delightful creature, and I shall employ a goodly hour in persuading her that I am an Adonis. What a pity that she has such an old tiger of a Pasha for a papa!"

And in this fashion Stephen Joscelyn beguiled the dinner hour away. Grace only, of all the family, perceived that he had eaten nothing.

The old lady, when she had reached the apartment with her girls, exclaimed:

"Well, if I didn't know that Stephen never drank a drop of liquor, I should say to-day that he was much the worse for it! What can be the matter with him? Can it be that he has heard something which you girls have said?"

"Oh! mother, impossible," said Grace.

"It's only his insolence!" exclaimed Angelica.

"Angey, my child, you must stop this. You show a very bad spirit towards Stephen, and somehow he sees it."

"Well, if he does?" answered the wilful girl.

"It will be a sorrowful day to me if he should part from this house in anger. If anybody, you, Angelica, have brought about this mischief, and for what? Because you think he loves you! It's perfectly monstrous! I trust you may never get a worse husband."

Angelica derisively began humming an air, and sauntered out of the room to her own chamber. A pleasant smile flushed her countenance! Her ideal was a something better, and it was with the thought of one lover that she chafed at any allusion to the other.

That night there were no readings and explanations from the poets, as usual. Stephen did not come forth to supper. He kept his room.

"One of you girls carry Stephen a cup of tea," said the old lady. Tea was still a luxury in sundry parts of the country, though under the ban of patriotism in society.

"He will wait long enough before I carry him one," said Angelica.

"Grace, my child, will you carry him a cup of tea?"

"Mother!" said the young woman, pleadingly. What did she mean? The old lady rose impatiently.

"I will carry it myself. He must be sick. Such a change as has come over him to-day makes me fear that something's wrong with him. He must be sick, and seriously."

Grace started from her seat, took the cup from the hands of her mother, saying, meekly:

"I will take it to him, mother."

And she took it to Stephen's room, and rapped gently at the door, and murmured, hesitatingly:

"Stephen, mother sends you a cup of tea. Will you take it?"

He came to the door, and received it in the calm, grave, sweet, quiet manner, as of old, and he said:

"Thank you, Grace. You are very kind."

"Are you unwell, Stephen?" she asked quietly enough, but with some effort.

"Yes, Grace, as all men are unwell who know not *well* to do. Troubled, Grace, and sad and thoughtful, but not sick, if that is what you mean. Thank you, now. There—good night."

And he gave her his hand, and slightly pressed her fingers between his own, and said again, very gently, if not tenderly,

"You are a good girl, Grace. God be with you in mercy."

And Grace, somehow, slept very sweetly that night, and had pleasant dreams; but Stephen was wakeful, and Mrs. Kirkland said at breakfast the next morning that she had heard him pacing the floor till after midnight. Poor Stephen; he was struggling with his demon, and the struggle is not likely to be soon ended.

## CHAPTER V.

### GATHERING OF THE CLANS.

Dick Marvin and his son came along bright and early next morning, and found Stephen Joscelyn already in the saddle. There was quite a cavalcade, proposing the same progress. Dick had mustered some half dozen of his neighbors, who, with their sons, all mounted, and some of the boys riding double, were all as eager as Dick himself to acquire political wisdom. There was Hal Watson, and Sam Perkins, and Sam Cochran, and others, hard-riding fellows, farmers and graziers, a very fair representation of the yeomanry of the precinct. They took their way by the Galphin and Redclyffe settlements, beautifully planted along the heights looking over the Savannah River to Augusta; and it required no long time, on fleet horses, to reach the river and cross at the "Sand Bar Ferry."

The party discoursed together as they proceeded, and Dick Marvin was especially anxious, riding close beside Stephen Joscelyn, to beguile or provoke him into speech upon the topics of the day. The rest of the company were quite as solicitous to hear, Stephen Joscelyn being an oracle among them all. But he was not in the vein, and probably thought it better that they should first be prepared by the arguments and evidence which Drayton was expected to deliver. He waived the subject, accordingly, but skillfully, and contented himself simply with throwing out certain leading ideas and passing suggestions, meant rather to promote than to satisfy curiosity. As they drew nigh to Augusta, the party rapidly increased in numbers. Men joined them, riding in from all quarters, and all on horseback—all good riders and well mounted. Stephen Joscelyn beheld them with flashing eyes. He said to Marvin:

"Dick, I asked you yesterday if you could ride?"

"And I told you, Stephen, I couldn't do much of anything else. But you know'd that before; and what made you ask?"

"I thought of the time coming, Dick, when I should have you at my elbow, and a hundred more, just such persons as you, all born, as it were, on horseback, and each going at speed, with a broad-sword flashing in the sun."

"And you think it will come to that, Stephen?" demanded the other, somewhat anxiously.

"As sure as yonder sun shines in heaven."

"Well, if it must be so, so be it! And you may be sure, Stephen, that I'll be close to your elbow, whenever you take the saddle for the drive. I believe in *you*, Stephen, and when a man don't know anything himself, he kin only look for the virtue of the article to the person he most believes in. That, I think, is the most sensible respect of wisdom."

"It is what the great body of mankind has been compelled to do in all ages, and what they will still need to do for a thousand years yet to come," replied Stephen, fully comprehending his companion, in spite of his high-flown phraseology. Dick had always, as he said himself, a few dictionary words at his command, and was rather pleased, as we have seen, that young Dick, his son, so well resembled him as to beat him at his own weapons. Stephen concluded the subject by bidding him keep his ears open, and hearken attentively to what might be said by the orator of the day.

The town was already crowded with people, when just as the party of Joscelyn reached Main street, they encountered Captain Sam Hammond, from Snow Hill, who rode in at the head of his troop of Carolina Horse, escorting the expected speaker, who had spent the preceding night at Snow Hill. Another troop, under Captain Hamilton, of Georgia, next rode in at a fast trot, waving caps and shouting bravely, as wild a set of boys as ever started on a scout, or foray, or fox-chace.

The face of Stephen Joscelyn was all in a glow, and he could scarcely restrain himself from rising in his stirrups, and sending forth the *cri de guerre*, the trumpet peal for the charge! But, at this moment, he found his brother, Martin Joscelyn, beside him.

"You here, Steve?"

"You see! But no thanks to you! Why didn't you send me word of what was going on? Had it not been for our friend, Dick Marvin, here, I should have never known a syllable of the gathering, or of the political and oratorical treat which we are promised."

"Ah! Dick, how are you, old fellow?"

"Bright, Martin, as a bee in an apple blossom. How's you?"

"All of a sparkle."

"That's sensible, and answers to the sunshine. We're gwine to have tall talking to-day, Martin. Has he come?"

"Who?"

"Who else but the Judge, Drayton?"

"Here he comes now, in Captain Hammond's carriage."

"Let me have a peep at him. There!"

The whole party pressed forward. The troop of Hammond was surrounded, and suddenly, the signal given by Captain Hamilton, his sturdy Georgians sent up a wild halloo, lengthening into huzzas that filled the welkin for five minutes, and provoked a thousand echoes from more distant throats, which joined in the music, from the mere love of it, without knowing what was the particular occasion for it.

Drayton rose gracefully, and bowed, hat off, on each side of the beleaguered carriage. The party of Stephen Joscelyn now commanded a full view of him.

"He's a mighty good-looking chap," said Marvin, "and seems as if he could do mighty handsome talking; but he looks a leetle too young, I'm a thinking. He kaint be over thirty, ef that."

"He's about thirty-five."

"And he's been a Jedge in our Israel, a'ready!"

"And a good one, too, Dick. He's got the old head on the young shoulders."

"It's a pretty big head, too, Stephen, much like your own, though yours is much the biggest; but he wears his hairs in curls, like a woman, and how I hate them cussed twists and ties at the back of the head, and that white flour in the hair."

"It's the fashion, Dick."

"Dem sich a fashion, I say! How much better now, would he look ef he'd jest let his hair alone, as you do, or crop it short like mine, and only stick his fingers through it of a morning. I don't see the use of combs, when a fellow's got his own ten fingers."

The face of Drayton was a fine one. There was a sufficient height and breadth of head for command. The eyes were full and clear, with a mild, genial expression. The mouth was firm, with the lips slightly inclined to compression; the nose was large, long, and inclining to the Roman. A white neck-cloth of clerical aspect, protruding ruffles of fine cambric at the shirt bosom, and a full suit of black —such was his costume, his small clothes being of silk, as were his stockings, and he wore silver buckles in his shoes.

The hour had arrived. The crowd had ceased to be tumultuous. There was something like order in consequence of the general expectation. This was shared by all parties, though as yet the lines between parties had not been very clearly drawn or defined. This day's events were looked to for bringing about this result. There were parties present, however, about whom there could be no mistake. Some men are inevitably fixed by public opinion itself. Some are as inevitably fixed by the habitual formation of opinion for themselves. Circumstance does its work with the greater number—circumstance and their supposed selfish interests.

Among those who were present on the ground, in all their strength, were the loyalists—men who, no matter what the circumstances, were committed to the Crown. A large proportion of these were foreigners, and of these the Scotch was the more conspicuous element. The Dunbar family, or rather the old man, the father, the Camerons, Browne and others, who were always to be found at roll-call; these were the types of the rest. They were all present, Dunbar, Browne, and many more; but not Cameron. He feared to show himself, and as we have seen, had taken his departure under cover of the night.

These men had taken position in near neighborhood to Drayton. Young Dunbar was present, occupying a position between his father and Browne. These two were but imperfectly assured of their own orator. It was sufficiently evident to them that the duty imposed upon Walter Dunbar, under the name of loyalty, was ungrateful to the young man, and they sought, by such arts as they knew, to bolster up his resolution, or rather to keep him to his enforced pledges. On one hand, the father renewed his entreaties, always passionately made, and warmed into anger in degree as his son showed himself cool. Browne alternated between sneer and suggestion, and furnished sometimes the goad, where the father furnished the persuasion.

Between the two, the young lawyer was ill at ease. His countenance was very pale, but his lips were compressed, and he seemed resolved, at all events, to go through with his task with all the strength that he could command.

It was little thought by any of the other parties present that there could be found anybody who would be bold enough to reply to Drayton. His reputation as an orator would naturally discourage disputation, while the friends and the supporters of the *movement* party were quite too numerous to suffer any reply to be of much avail in arresting it.

And so stood the parties when Drayton rose to speak.

Drayton was an accomplished speaker—not a Cicero, nor yet a Demosthenes, but copious like the former, with less of the poet and more of the statistician and politician. His manner was easy and graceful, quite natural, and singularly sweet and persuasive. There was a gentle soliciting in his voice, which, soft and musical, was yet strong and clear. His eye possessed the same sort of soliciting expression, which won that of the listener, without his consciousness. Voice and eye consorting, the matter of deep interest, and logically presented, the orator won completely the attention of his auditory.

He proceeded to show what were the true relations between the Crown and the Colonies; what were the rights of the people under the British Constitution; in what manner these rights had been invaded, and what would be the dangers to American and even British liberty, if the aggressions of Parliament and the Crown were permitted to continue and to grow.

To this period, none of the politicians, taking up this argument, had gone beyond the expression of a purpose to have the popular grievances redressed. There was no suggestion of independence. That was a bird to be hatched from the gradual growth of the egg of strife and revolution. The American statesmen were to move cautiously, and rather let events *grow*, naturally, than suggest the form, character, or extent to which the progress was to conduct. Results were not to be named or predicted, lest men should recoil from those preliminary steps which yet, as is the case in all revolutions, could only reach one terminus.

Drayton was thus cautious in his speech, and studiously disclaimed anything beyond the purpose to obtain redress of grievances, and security for the Colonies under the Crown, the Constitution, and their several charters, against the invasion of all these by an usurping Parliament, or faction.

The orator led his audience with him to this extent. There were no dissenting voices. The applause was frequent, especially where some strong epigrammatic phrase was employed to round happily a paragraph with the assertion of the people's rights. Even the party headed by old Dunbar and Browne listened with patience, and to this period felt that there had been nothing said to which legitimate objection could be taken.

There was a brief pause, in which the speaker seemed to be gathering himself up for more impressive matters. He resumed:

"Thus have I shown you, my countrymen, the relations which, at present, exist between the Government of Great Britain and the people of these Colonies. You have seen what are the wrongs under which we live, and the rights for which a brave people ought to be willing to die. Let me now say to you that we can repel these wrongs, and can maintain these rights, if we are only true to ourselves and to one another. A people is never so sure of their liberties as when deeply impressed with an earnest love of their country. And *this is our country*—not to be yielded to the spoiler; not to be robbed of its profits or possessions by any *foreign* government; to be ruled by, and among ourselves, and for the benefit of our own children. If it be not so—if a foreign and remote government is to interpose, and with insolent strength to stretch its gigantic arms over three thousand miles of sea, to tear away our harvests when the fields are golden with the grain, the produce of our own labor, of what avail is our labor? of what hopes or securities are we possessed for our children? What country can we call our own, and what the use to labor, or indeed to live? Better, far better, that we should fold our hands, abandon our fields to naked fallow, and depart from a region which is not only unblessed by security, but in which our only inheritance is shame."

"Better fight!" cried a sturdy voice from the crowd, and there was a clash and clattering of sabres.

"Aye, better fight!" was the echo from a hundred voices.

There had been murmurs among the loyalists at several of the utterances of Drayton in this portion of his speech; and old Dunbar and Browne had been eagerly thrusting some things into the ears of Walter Dunbar. The young man heard them in moody silence, and simply nodded his head. Martin Joscelyn eagerly watched his countenance. They were close friends, and the latter knew enough of the young lawyer to begin to suspect the sort of use which the two loyalist leaders had prepared to make of him. He whispered his doubts to Stephen Joscelyn. But the latter replied:

"Impossible! He cannot be such a fool! It would ruin the poor fellow forever!"

"You will see! He has his weakness, and the old man is a terrible despot. If I could only get to whisper a moment in his ears."

"If what you suspect be true, you are too late! Keep where you are, and leave him to work out his own deliverance if he can! Hush!"

This little dialogue, with the popular interruption, had occupied but a few moments of time. Drayton had resumed, seizing, with the promptness of a practised debater, upon the ejaculation of the crowd as furnishing the key-note for a new beginning.

"Yes, my friends; you are right! Better fight for our possessions than yield them to the spoiler! Better die a thousand deaths in the harness for our liberties than tamely surrender them into the hands of the tyrant! But I trust that no such necessity awaits us. Indeed I could promise you that you would escape from all the dangers of war—would emerge from this contest with all your rights intact and compact—with all your securities of property and right and law, if, as one man, you will unite in the common cause! Let the Parliament of Great Britain but understand that the people of America have but one voice, and that they unite in one great determination to assert their rights, and the usurpation will quickly cease! But, unhappily, there is not that degree of union among us, in sentiment, policy and opinion, which is essential for producing this effect. The people and Parliament of Great Britain are encouraged in their aggressions by the traitorous counsels which they receive from America. There are among us, I regret to say, but too many pensioned and malignant wretches who feed their own venomous natures, while they stimulate to daily usurpations that government to which they look for pay. These are our worst enemies! These are they, the very canker in the heart of the country, who keep us from our rights, and invite daily wrongs and trespasses upon our people! And unhappily, they exercise but too much influence here at home in abusing the minds of the ignorant, and in working upon the fears of the people. Not content with these injuries, they are now busily engaged in the worst work to which men could put their hands, under the instigation of the devil! We have the proofs in our possession of most treacherous conspiracies set on foot for our undoing, and for the massacre of our innocent people! Secret plans are in progress for supplying arms to the disaffected and the ignorant among us. We are well aware of the plans of the traitors! And a still worse work has engaged their venomous and barbarous imaginations, inasmuch as they have already begun to poison the minds of the heathen savages upon our borders; to unite them into bands of war, and encourage them, at a given signal, to descend at night time for the massacre of our women and children along the frontier. Driven by his fears, and the consciousness of his deep and dreadful guilt in this respect, John Stuart, the Crown agent among the red men, hath fled incontinently from Charleston, and taken refuge in Florida. His assistant, his agent—the facile instrument of his hands—Alexander Cameron, who dare not show his face among our people, is now busied among the Cherokees sending the 'red stick' throughout their towns, and prompting a chorus of war songs from the Saluda mountains to the Tennessee!"

"That's a d—d lie!" cried a loud voice, hoarsely, from the crowd. The voice was that of Browne, who could no longer restrain himself, and whose mutterings for some time before had become audible to the circle just about him. There were other parties about this circle who had been attracted thither by these mutterings. Scarcely had he spoken the offensive sentence when he was felled to the ground by a terrible blow from the fist of Captain Hamilton.

All was confusion, and a general rush took place in the direction of the fallen man. Drayton was silenced during the commotion.

Browne struggled to his feet, and bravely enough rushed on his assailant, who stood ready, confronting him with a display of those formidable knuckles which had already laid his cheek open to the bone.

Hamilton wore his sword, but he made no show of using it. Browne was entirely unarmed, but he was a powerful man also, of heavier build, but less agility than Hamilton, and, perhaps, less muscle, as he had less youth. Blows were exchanged between them, and again Browne went down under the fist of Hamilton.

He was then rescued. By this time certain parties, among whom Martin Joscelyn and Walter Dunbar were conspicuous, succeeded in parting the combatants, and lifting Browne to his feet. His eyes were bunged and blackened, and his face literally dyed in blood. They made a way through the crowd, and hustled him out, though with some difficulty, followed still by a crowd momently growing more and more excited. Martin Joscelyn and two or three others, however, supported Browne to a neighboring tavern, where his wounds were washed and dressed.

He submitted, in sullen silence, to their services. He called for spirits, and a bottle of Jamaica rum was brought to him, of which he drank freely. Joscelyn then left him, with the counsel not to suffer himself again to be seen in town, but to get away at nightfall. He grinned ghastly at them in reply, but spoke nothing; yet, long afterwards did Martin Joscelyn remember the terrible ferocity, the vindictive and terrible meaning which spoke, audibly enough, in that ghastly grin of demoniac malice and suppressed rage!

He returned to the assembly just in time to hear the voice of Walter Dunbar, and his heart sank within him. He loved Dunbar; passionately loved his sister, Annie, and knew so much of the brother—of his somewhat anomalous moral and mental constitution—that he almost shuddered as he heard his voice! He knew that the young lawyer had fine talents, but it vexed him that they should be exercised in a cause to which he himself was hostile—to which he believed that Walter himself was cold, if not hostile, and to which he had only lent himself under the imperious influence of a father, whose will, if not capacity, was far superior to that of his son. But Martin could do nothing now. He could only listen, with all his misgivings, and, unable to reach the side of Walter Dunbar, he made his way to that of Stephen Joscelyn, who was sternly gazing upon the young speaker, with a mingled expression upon his face of pity and resentment.

# CHAPTER VI.

## WALTER DUNBAR.

"He has bungled from the beginning," said Stephen Joscelyn, in a whisper, to his brother; "has begun with an essay, dealing in generalizations which begin too far off for his subject. In truth, he is afraid of his subject, and falters already. He lacks directness, and seemingly all aim and purpose."

"His heart is not in it," said Martin.

"No, indeed, nor his head either! and the headstrong old man at his elbow is his evil genius. He is doing the very thing which will make the young man break down—prompting him at every sentence."

Sure enough! old Dunbar could be seen to nudge the speaker with his elbow, to jirk his coat-skirts, and to mutter at his shoulders. The youth was restive under this annoyance, and it told on what he had to say. But this was a petty annoyance compared with his main difficulty. As Martin Joscelyn had remarked, "his heart was not in his subject," and his head was too honest for his heart, and would not second its enforced utterances. Besides, he had to overcome a prodigious lee-way, in the wake of the accomplished speaker who had preceded him, to say nothing of the consciousness by which he was oppressed, that the sympathies of his audience were not with him. But he struggled on nevertheless, with all the effort of a lawyer, to make if possible the worse appear the better cause. There was in his speech a strange admixture of polished didactic sentences, with rude and abrupt turns of language as of thought, which moved Stephen Joscelyn to say, in a whisper to Martin:

"He has been writing and memorizing his speech, and has forgotten parts of it. His case is like that of Hamlet, who had prepared his apostrophe for the meeting with the ghost, and forgot the best parts of it in his fright when the ghost did appear."

This was most probably the case. Walter Dunbar, unwilling to speak on the occasion, was yet, when forced to do so, ambitious to appear to advantage. He mistook the process. Instead of letting his mind alone, and looking for its proper provocation to the speaker whom he was to answer, he undertook to elaborate beforehand a reply to the arguments which he had not yet heard, and could only conjecture. Had his heart been with his subject, he probably would not have made the mistake. But, conscious of his utter lack of sympathy with his subject, he threw all the responsibilities upon his head, was cold, accordingly, and, when most elaborate, was most tedious. He made repeated efforts at new beginnings, endeavoring, by a fresh start at intervals, to break away from the monotonous meshes of his first entanglement, but only sank deeper into the "slough of despond" at every labored impulse.

It is the common error of speakers who are conscious of failure, that they will still speak on in the hope to retrieve themselves. It is not easy. The audience began to grow indifferent and heedless, if not impatient; some loud yawns were heard; Drayton looked on and listened good-humoredly, but carelessly, and sometimes with a smile; old Dunbar, chafed in his vexation, broke away from his son's side, dashed back to him again, and exhibited all the signs of the keenest anger, as well as mortification. The scene was becoming absolutely painful to many of the spectators, even those who were fully of the movement party. Martin Joscelyn grew fevered, and almost as restless as old Dunbar. Stephen Joscelyn now regarded the young man with eyes of pity. Walter Dunbar was, in some degree, a favorite of the people; he was amiable, and much had been expected from his known abilities. A feeling of regret and disappointment pervaded the crowd, and this was very soon apparent to the eyes of the orator himself. Again and again he strove, in fresh efforts, to recover position—to rise above the merely essayical, the dead level of vague generalization, in which he had pitched the key-note of his speech from the beginning—to simulate passion—to call in the aid of fancy, and, by rhetoric, to make up the deficiencies of argument and power. But all in vain! He was still, at best, only coldly correct and elaborately dull. The genius would not answer to the call, and at length he broke down utterly at a point, in which, from the greater emphasis of his voice and manner, he appeared to think that he moved upon sure ground.

One of the points which Drayton had urged in his speech, and which had made a great impression upon the crowd, was that in which he had charged upon Stuart and Cameron a design to bring down the red men of the interior upon the frontier colonists; providing them with arms and ammunition, and organizing them, on the side of the Crown, in anticipation of a war which was thus seemingly premeditated.

This was just one of those charges to arouse all the apprehensions of the people, and to provoke them to a wild excitement, acting upon their opinions through their fears, and exciting their passions in behalf of those abstract principles which the great body of a people scarcely ever grasp except through the medium of their passions. The charge was dreaded by Cameron, and we have seen how brutally it had been denied by Browne when advanced by Drayton, and what had been the result to himself of that denial. It was essential that young Dunbar should combat this charge also; and, on the strength of the solemn denials made him by Cameron himself, he boldly challenged Drayton to produce the proofs which he had alleged to be in the possession of the Committee of Safety, in relation to the accusation.

"Such a charge," he said, "so discreditable to an officer of the Crown, so shocking to humanity, so justly calculated to arouse to passionate fury the whole of the people, should not be made in wantonness, and without the most conclusive evidence. It cannot be true, and I appeal to the honorable Commissioner from Charleston to produce his proofs on the spot, or at once atone, by a frank confession of error, for this most cruel assault upon the fair fame of men who bear his Majesty's commission. I pause for a reply."

"And you shall have it," answered Drayton promptly, rising in the carriage, and drawing a packet of papers from his pocket. He added:

"And when *you*, sir, shall know *me* better—nay, sir, when you shall the better know what the honorable statesman, or the orator, owes to *himself*, you will see that it cannot be possible that he shall wantonly, and without proper authority of proof, assail the character of any person, whether he be the official or the humble citizen!"

Deeply did the face of the young man redden under this keen rebuke. He unhappily, in appearing on this occasion, did not well know what the orator owed to himself. The humiliating consciousness of this truth made the shaft strike home. Drayton proceeded:

"Does any gentleman present know the handwriting of the Hon. John Stuart and that of his assistant, Alexander Cameron, Commissioners for the Crown of Great Britain, among the red men of Carolina, Georgia and Florida? I have here, luckily, the original letters of both these persons, intercepted by our Committee of Safety, which will fully confirm to you what I have said of the atrocious and damnable scheme of these two men, under the instigations of Lord Wm. Campbell and the devil, to bring down the murderous savages of the mountains upon the women and children of our frontiers. Here, in their own hands, shall you read the proofs, so boldly challenged, of their infamous designs of midnight fire and slaughter among our innocent people. Let any of you who are curious, any who know the signatures of these men, examine these documents for yourselves. There must be many among you who will be able to say whether these papers be or be not genuine. Let me hope that the gentleman who has challenged the proofs be among those who will examine them. If I mistake not, he himself will be quite competent, of his own knowledge, to decide upon their authenticity."

He held the papers up as he spoke. He read aloud their contents, which were in full confirmation of the charge which he had made, and a dozen or more persons, among them Captain Sam. Hammond, a leading man in the neighborhood, drew nigh, and examined the papers. So did Walter Dunbar, who turned away in silence, and made his way back to the spot whence he had spoken. All the other parties pronounced loudly in behalf of the genuineness of the documents.

"Is the gentleman satisfied?" demanded Drayton.

"We have been deceived, sir," was the reply of Walter, looking not to Drayton, but to his father. The old man glared at him with a face in which rage and scorn were equally conspicuous. Then, in his insanity:

"Oh! fool and blockhead!" he exclaimed, loud enough for everybody to hear. "That such a cause should be lost in such worthless hands!"

He wheeled about as he spoke, and pushed his way through the crowd. Walter followed him, under a sudden impulse, and called to him the single word, "Father!"

The other looked round for a moment with a scowl of direst bitterness, waved him back with both his hands, as he cried:

"Come not near me! Hence! Find your way into some rat-hole, and die!"

This was very terrible, shown to the entire crowd through which he was making his way. The young man fell back, as if he had received a mortal blow. He staggered about blindly for a moment, and Martin Joscelyn was in the same instant at his side.

"Who is it?" asked the young man, with a bewildered stare.

"Martin—Martin Joscelyn."

"Ah! my friend! let me take your arm! Somebody has struck me on the head, I think! I am very weak, and—Martin!"

The next moment he had fainted in the arms of his friend.

# CHAPTER VII.

## THE BARBACUE.

Drayton offered his carriage, and the insensible form of Walter Dunbar was carefully lifted into it. Martin Joscelyn, with a friend, entered with him, and had him carried to his own lodgings, where, for the present, we propose to leave him.

The effect of this scene upon the multitude was one of unmingled horror, which soon gave way to an unqualified indignation at the brutal ferocity of the father. Had he remained on the ground he would have hardly escaped the fury of the mob, and there were those present who needed only a few words to impel them to pursue and lynch him—that wild sort of justice which is so often the resort of an ignorant population in sparsely-settled regions.

It was some time before the business of the day was resumed. Drayton was again called upon, and his discourse was addressed to the exciting exhibition which had just been made.

"You see before you, my friends, in the melancholy scene of wild and ferocious temper which you have beheld, the sort of passions which are at work among too many of our people. Where the father strikes down the son with stabbing words, can you wonder if the same temper shall whet the tomahawk and sharpen the scalping-knife of the savage? You heard the words of the young man to his father, when the proofs of this murderous conspiracy against our people could no longer be denied. 'We have been deceived!' said he. No doubt the young man had been deceived! But the father was *not* deceived. He, the son, had been used for a purpose; and, as a blind instrument, not seeing the way he went for himself, has baffled the expectations of those who employed him. I have other proofs. Alexander Cameron, of Lochaber, who plays the part of a feudal baron in that quarter, as he does among the Indians, was harbored here, in these very precincts, but a few nights ago. He did not dare to show himself. He knew his danger from his own consciousness of guilt. It was natural enough that a son should be deceived where one of the instruments of deception was his own father! But be not ye deceived! Look to yourselves! Look to the traitors that harbor among you, speaking smoothly to your faces, in open day light, while at midnight they conjure the murderous savage to your firesides! You will find deceivers enough, even where you least expect to find them. Be vigilant, watchful, and always prepared. It is half the battle—a battle already more than half won—where your enemy is made to understand that the victim he would destroy has his armor on, his weapon ready, and his beacon lights in full blaze to warn his neighbor. Organize, arm, be watchful, and beware of the deceiver! He will come to you in all guises; and that of the sleek official will prove one of the most dangerous, especially where you have been accustomed to his exercise of authority. Prescription and usage are amongst the greatest foes to popular freedom, since *habit* is among the greatest tyrannies of mankind."

Much more was said; but we do not propose to reproduce the oration of the past. Enough that we exhibit its action, and show so much of the orator as provides the impulse to the actor.

There were other speakers, most of them speaking briefly, however, and merely in compliance with the calls of their friends and neighbors. It was to the surprise of no one more than himself, when, while eagerly looking and listening to others, Stephen Joscelyn suddenly heard his own name cried aloud. It was caught up by scores of eager and willing echoes. He would have wheeled his steed out of the circle, but friendly hands grappled the animal by the bridle, and held him fast to his place.

"You don't git off, Stephen," cried the familiar voice of Dick Marvin. "We've got you to the very ring of the sarcumstance, and you've got to pour forth in all the peculiars of a fervorous inclination. You've got to give tongue on a hot trail, and follow close on the haunches of the biggest buck that ever carried ten fingers on his horns. Blaze away, Stephen, and give the boys a genywine taste of the music of a lean beagle on a long chase."

"Dick Marvin, you're the devil."

"No, no, Steve. I'm only the devil's man! And I'm your man, you know; and so you see where *you* air, and what's the sort of consideration that's upon you to show the tongue you carry in your head. Blaze away now with a *rip* that shall make these fellows snort agin, with the feeling of a righteous combination."

"Devil take you, Dick! Let go, and let me out! Haven't you had speech-making enough for to-day?"

But Dick was tenacious of his hold upon horse and rider, and the crowd grew vociferous. Stephen found that his own school urchins, several of whom had accompanied their fathers, contributed, in no small degree, to his arrest, and their juvenile pipes kept up the clamor of his name, much longer, perhaps, than those of larger people.

He was evidently not to escape. Nor was he a man of affectation. That fiery nature had been more than once overboiling, at fever heat, during the proceedings of the day; and the full mind, the ardent temperament, and the copious fancy, were usually too cogent with him to suffer him to hesitate where circumstance itself seemed to interpose against it.

He obeyed. He burst into speech with an epigrammatic sentence. He seized upon the salient points of his subject. He made them dramatic. He depicted the British monarch as a Dutchman, who, with short arms and a bulky body, was striving to overreach a world! He showed the enormity of the attempt to rule the people of a vast and foreign hemisphere by the monarch of a few island parishes. He made a mock of this, and of all the proceedings of Kings, Lords and Commons, with their big wigs meant to bolster up their empty heads. He took the details of Drayton's speech, and made a vivid dramatic sketch from each. Taxation without representation was lauded as a judicious process of paying one's debts out of other men's pockets; subscribing to the purse of St. Peter, by picking the pockets of all the other saints, then swindling the Church of Christ out of the whole deposit, and dividing it equally among the heathen gods, of whom Bacchus, Mammon and Venus were the most potent still, though passing, each of them, under the name of a virtue or a saint! But the satire ceased when he came to exhibit Stuart and Cameron among the Indians, presenting the weapons of war with the torch, the tomahawk, and the scalping-knife. Of these agents, he made a terrific picture.

But to describe the speech were impossible.

"I said I was the devil's man, Stephen," said Dick Marvin, "and, by Jingos, wasn't I right? Dod dern you, man, you've kept my blood running, hot and cold, cold and hot, for a full hafe an hour! and I could listen to you for an hour longer! And look you how the jedge is staring at you! He's a'most frightened, I'm thinking. It's a new sort of talk for him, I reckon."

"A very remarkable man!" said Drayton to Sam Hammond. "Will you bring him to me, and let me know him?"

"We shall meet him at dinner, judge. It will be difficult just now to make his way through the crowd. You are probably not aware that he is lame. He is, as you say, a very remarkable man; and but for his lameness, it would be difficult to say what he might not attempt, and what not perform. He has great versatility, and great boldness of character, and is true as steel."

"What does he do?"

"He teaches school on Beach Island, but has studied law, and, I believe, practises it on a small scale among his neighbors."

"Bring me to know him as soon as convenient, Captain. Such a man must not dwell in obscurity. He is a man to be greatly useful now. His is the very sort of talent for popular use."

We are not so sure that Drayton's tastes were quite satisfied with Stephen Joscelyn's speech, for he was of the old classical school, and symmetry and finish were essential among his standards; but his mind and judgment had been taken by surprise by the reckless audacity with which Stephen had sported with his topics, and he had a lurking notion, especially when he witnessed the effects of his speech, that Stephen, though a less practised orator than himself, might yet possess a somewhat better knowledge of what was best suited for his audience; and this, by-the-way, is the first great secret in all popular oratory. Repeating his request to bring Stephen Joscelyn to him while at dinner, Drayton rode from the ground, followed by the cheers of the multitude, and escorted by the troopers of Hammond and Hamilton.

But he was disappointed. At the dinner, or barbacue, Stephen Joscelyn did not make his appearance. As soon as he could extricate himself from the crowd, which he did only after shaking hands with hundreds, and narrowly escaping the embraces of scores besides, he had taken his way quietly out of town, having first made the desired purchases for his good landlady, Mrs. Kirkland. He had made his escape alone, none of his neighbors being prepared to forego the barbacue, and the exciting scenes and sensations by which it was usually accompanied. Stephen reached home long before nightfall.

Home! Stephen Joscelyn's home!

We will say nothing more of that at present; but, reporting him safely to have reached the cottage of the Widow Kirkland, we will ourselves return to Augusta, where the business of one day is not to end with nightfall even.

When men of our forest country leave their homes for a visit to the distant town or city, they try to recompense themselves for the previous solitude of agricultural life. Of the thousands of persons gathered at this meeting, few will, like Stephen, return to their homes on the same day. The barbacue and its beverages, its songs, sentiments and speeches, will consume the rest of the day; and there will be scores of groups and congregations at scores of other places, who will trench fearfully before sleep on the small hours of the night. In this period events shall occur which need to be reported fully in this sober chronicle.

Of course, every one knows what is meant by a barbacue. In a neighboring grove, an ox, entire, undergoes the roast over a pit. He is *barbacued*. There are smaller barbacues in progress, also, of sheep and goats. Hoe-cakes are browning at numerous fires; wagons and other vehicles surround the charmed circle, and barrels of "apple-jack" (apple brandy), and kegs of Jamaica rum, and molasses beer and cakes, and other junkets, are to be found in certain other wagons, over the ends of which a gay, green bush gives sufficient sign of the creature comforts which they contain, and are prepared to furnish.

At a little distance a party is engaged at rifle practice, shooting at a mark for a prize, probably a bullock, possibly the rifle itself, at so many dollars or shillings a shot. A wrestling match hard by has gathered together its crowd. Whoops and halloos declare for the successful shot, or ring out in honor of the triumphant athlete. Some older parties are grouped more deeply in the thickets, at play with a *deck* of well-thumbed and greasy cards. In these sports the interval between the speech-making of the morning and the preparation of the barbacue for dinner is fully consumed.

Time passes. The horn suddenly sounds for dinner. The tables are quickly filled, and anon the orator of the day re-appears, is received with cheers, and seats himself on the right of the chairman.

The feast proceeds. After a while, the toast-drinking begins; Drayton is toasted, and, while speaking, the company is startled by the sudden presence of Tom Browne, who appeared, ghastly of aspect, bruised, if not bleeding, and grinning savagely upon the circle.

He forced his way to the table, and by dint of deliberate and determined pressure between those already seated, secured a seat for himself, into which he struggled with some difficulty. It was apparent that he had been drinking. Between his partial inebriation, his mortified self-esteem, his naturally unruly and savage temper and the sentiment—call it loyalty or what you will—which he held to be at stake in the presence of Drayton and the proceedings of the day, he was just in the mood for mischief, and, with the natural restlessness of a diseased spirit, vexed with himself and everybody else, he threw himself in the way of provocation, evidently resolved to seek, if not to give it. But he was prepared equally for both, and impatiently waited for the occasion.

Seizing upon a bottle of rum which stood near him on the table, he poured out half a goblet, and swallowed the terrible potation, without water, at a single gulph; then, with a scowling smile, of mixed scorn and defiance, he glared around upon the company with the air of one who would have said: "I am ready for any one among you!"

There was a strong feeling of indignation aroused by his presence and his bearing; but our forest population is habitually good-humored and indulgent. They are irritable, but not malignant, easily goaded to passion, but soon quieted; and, after a first gush or outburst of feeling, easily persuaded to forget and forgive, and, remembering the severe handling which the trespasser had already that day been compelled to endure, allowance was made for his conduct, and the larger portion of the company were reluctant that the circle should be thrown into disorder, especially in the presence of their distinguished guest. There were some few, however, who needed but a look or word from some superior to thrust out the offender, neck and heels—aye, and to subject him to worse punishment, but their indignation, lacking the needed suggestion, expended itself in numerous and savage looks, which Browne answered in a similar manner.

The feast continued. Browne ate nothing, but he was not equally abstinent in drink. At length, the chairman gave as a sentiment:

"The Continental Congress," and moved that the toast be "drank standing."

All rose except Browne. Some of those beside him endeavored to persuade, and urged him to rise; but he planted his elbows firmly upon the table, with his chin between his hands, and the chairman said aloud:

"Let him alone, my friends. He is too drunk to know what he is about, and certainly too drunk to stand."

Browne answered only with a ghastly grin, which was made more hideous to the spectator by the great gash upon his cheek.

"The Continental Congress!" repeated the chairman. The toast was drank with three times three. When the shouts had subsided, the intruder staggered to his feet, raised himself into the most erect attitude, lifted his cap, and, with savage glare of eye, ranging around the table, and, finally, fixing itself on Drayton, he roared out:

"Here's damnation to the Continental Congress and all its friends!"

This was too much to be borne. Instantly, every person present was on his feet, and, in a few seconds, the offender was hustled out of the circle—torn out of it, in fact—and, but for Drayton, Hammond, Martin Joscelyn and a few others, would have been summarily subjected to some one of those brutal punishments which, in that day, were applied equally to all who wilfully came in conflict with the ascendant party, whether Whig or Tory.

It required very great effort to rescue the madman—for madman at the time he was—from the rough grasp of those who had him in their clutches. Meanwhile, he strove manfully, but in vain. He was found to be heavily armed with *couteau de chasse* and a pair of pistols, and sought to use them. But they were plucked from his grasp, or bosom, and he was thrust from the ground, Martin Joscelyn and two or three others undertaking to send him out of town.

They took him out of sight, at least, and he seemed suddenly to become resigned to their guidance. With a strong effort of will, not inconsistent with his inebriate condition, he mastered himself sufficiently to put on upon the instant every appearance of a quiet and reconciled submission; and, having disposed of him at a quiet lodging place, at the lower end of the town, and exacted from him a promise to depart across the river as soon as night should set in, the party left him. They previously gave him to understand that there were those in town who could not again be restrained, in the event of a renewal of his provocations. And he tacitly admitted his danger from these rude hands, and by a nod—for he did not speak—he seemed to assent to all that was required of him.

The party returned to the barbacue, late in the evening, and found the company breaking up. Drayton was just driving off with Captain Hammond, whose guest he continued to be, and, while at Snow Hill, he continued to enjoy the escort of Hammond's Light Horse. Other parties, the more staid and aged, were departing also for their several abodes. But there was a goodly number of the Peep-o'-Day Boys, who, almost as a matter of course, would make a night of it. Augusta that night was to have the echoes awakened long after the chimes of midnight. Others again, more soberly inclined, who remained in town for business the next day, found quarters at the houses of sundry of their city friends. Dick Marvin and his son were of this number, persuaded to it by the invitation of Martin Joscelyn, who said to him:

"Dick, you will lodge with me to-night; I've much to talk with you about, and wish to ask you some questions especially touching my brother, Stephen."

"I reckon, Martin, that nobody can tell you about Stephen Joscelyn with more expeditious partiality than Dick Marvin."

"Well, I know that. You will stay with me? I have two rooms, besides my office. I've got this poor fellow, Walter Dunbar, in one of them, and he's in such a state that I would not have him disturbed, and I'm thinking he needs to be watched throughout the night. You can assist me in doing so; and when your boy, Dick, is asleep, we can pore together over certain matters, about which, touching Stephen, I am somewhat concerned. You will stop with me—will you not?"

"Ask me if I won't be considerate of particulars, and satisfy you and myself and young Dick together? Fact is, Martin, I looked to you to ax me, and, if you hadn't done so, I should have constituted myself for lodgings with Martin Joscelyn for the rest of the night without axing leave or favor."

These three were all seated snugly in the private room of the latter, which adjoined his law office on one hand, and Dunbar's office on the other. They were quietly conversing on the business of the day, when the door was hurriedly thrown open, and a fourth party entered, in great haste—one Gideon Walker—one of those men who, with Martin Joscelyn, had succeeded, as they fancied, in leaving Browne in a state of equal quiet and serenity.

"How now, Gid., what's the matter? Whose horse has broken halter?" was the demand of Martin.

"Would you believe it, that d—d madman, Tom Browne, never minding what we told him, and what he promised, has gone out, and pushed his way to Andrew Griffith's, the very last place in the world to go to, for a dozen or more of Hamilton's troopers have gathered there for sleep and supper, and he's a gone coon if he trees them, or they him! Old Weatherby's just told me about it, and he says that Browne's got weapons again, and he's just as drunk as ever, with a sober sort of devil in him, so that he walks as steady as a bear at a stake, though the fever is burning in his brain, like a furnace, all the while. He's just in the humor for a fight with all the world, and Hamilton's men in particular; and, unless we make another trial to get him off, there will be mince meat made to-night out of human collops."

"What's the use?" said Dick Marvin. "Let him get what he goes for. Ef so be he's bent on his own salvation by a short cut, in the devil's name, let him take his own course on the broad road to satisfaction."

"Very good doctrine in the devil's name," replied Martin; "but, in God's name, no matter what he is, we must try once more and save him from the devil."

"But, look you, Martin, how if he stands upon the matter of his own salvation, and won't be saved in God's name? How then?"

"Shut up your oven, you parrot, and come along with us. What we seek to do must be done quickly."

And the three sallied forth together, followed by the boy, Dick, who was not to be left behind.

# CHAPTER VIII.

## THE LYNCHING PROCESS.

Browne, though left under watch, had escaped from the lodging-house unobserved. He had made his way to the shop of a cutler, and bought a large, sharp knife, and a single pistol. These he carefully secreted about his person.

His proceedings, for a man still half drunken, were singularly cool and deliberate. There is a sort of temperament tenacious as the grave of its purpose, which still works to the proposed end, in spite of any loss of physical equilibrium; in which passion is still subordinate to will, and works, however irregularly or confusedly, under a fixed mental purpose. Hot-headed at once and cool, Browne was of bull-dog peculiarities, and the liquors which fired his blood seemed to have but little effect upon any determined action suggested by his brain.

This, perhaps, is a characteristic of the Gael, generally. It was especially so of this man. Though persevering in an unwise and imprudent object, he was yet as religiously circumspect in all the details necessary for its prosecution as if his whole intellectual nature was in hand, and as if no unbalanced faculty remained to contest, in his mind, with the perfect ascendancy of aim and purpose.

With like directness he made his way to the "Full Moon" public house of Andrew Griffith, who kept in one of the side streets near the present market-place, and but a few doors out of the main, or Broad street. It was a second or third-rate house, designed for those who wished to lodge economically, and yet enjoy those social freedoms which, among this class, are very apt to degenerate into licentiousness. Good suppers were provided here; and there were tempting beverages; and private rooms, or crypts rather, were at hand; snug, not easily found; where stakes were set on games which lacked in every attraction, save to those who desired the shortest possible processes in the acquisition of money. It was to this place that Browne, either with foreknowledge of the place, or led by an infallible instinct, now made his way.

He was met on the threshold by the keeper of the house, Andrew Griffith. Without speaking to Griffith, he was about to push his way in; but the latter civilly resisted him.

"Better not come in now, Mr. Browne—better not."

"And why not?"

"There are persons in here now, who wish you no good. *I* wish you no harm, and it is for your own safety that I beg that you will go away."

"Harm! and why should I fear harm? What do you see in me that you should suppose that I fear any man's ill-will?"

"It is not whether you fear, Mr. Browne. I don't mean that. I don't suppose you are afraid of any man. But that's not the thing. A brave man may be as brave as Julius Cæsar, yet he may be 'sassinated for all that. And I don't know that any man's chances are the better for having half-a-dozen upon him at the same time, just as Julius Cæsar had."

"Pooh, pooh, Griffith! You are talking strange things—strange and foolish! Julius Cæsar, indeed! Who cares about Julius Cæsar? I did not ask for Julius Cæsar. I never said a word about *him*. Do you mean to say that you have such a person in your house at this very moment?"

"No, sir; but I have some customers here now who are no better than Julius Cæsar, I'll venture to say, and whom you would just as little like to see as Julius Cæsar."

"I must see them all, Griffith—Julius Cæsar and the rest. They're all my friends, I've no doubt; and we must drink together! I must see my friends, I tell you."

"And I tell you they're just now your worst enemies."

"And we're commanded to love our enemies, you know! Ha, ha, ha; beautiful doctrine that, Julius, very beautiful doctrine! I must go in, Julius, and love my enemies."

"Hark'ee, Mr. Browne," said the landlord, in subdued tones, but in manner the most emphatic, "hark'ee, sir, the house is full of Captain Hamilton's troopers. Now you know what I mean, and what you've got to expect."

Griffith was quite mistaken in regard to the effect he thought to produce.

"Captain Hamilton's troopers, eh? The very friends I desire to see! All of them my friends, Griffith; beautiful boys, all of them; very brave and beautiful fellows. I am impatient to see them, Griffith; so stand aside, old chap, and let me embrace my friends."

Griffith protested, and still would have occupied the doorway, but Browne suddenly seized him by the shoulder, and with a single whirl transferred him from the porch to the pavement without. No sign of drunkenness or feebleness in that demonstration of the physical man. The dogged and tenacious *will* had corded up the muscles to the utmost exercise of their power, and perhaps Tom Browne never showed himself more powerful than when he was thus, as it were, in the white heat of drunkenness.

He gave no look to the man whom he had laid prostrate, but without more ado passed at once into the house, and into the hall, a great apartment, where some six or eight of the rough-riders of Captain Hamilton were grouped at ease, in all attitudes, and in every situation, with each his tankard beside him, and with pipe in mouth. The room reeked with tobacco smoke, and through the cloud it was not easy to discern the face of the new comer, or those of any of the party in possession of the hall. A small table stood in the centre of the group. The heels of one of the party rested upon it, amidst two or three pewter flagons, and as many more of delph.

Having nearly reached the centre of the hall, Browne paused a moment, the better to take in, through the cloud of smoke which spread throughout the hall, the aspects of the party. Having satisfied himself, he advanced.

"Who is it?" demanded one of the party, "Brighton?"

"Brighton, to be sure," was the reply; "all the bright ones."

"Where's Moore and Jackson? Where did you leave them?"

"Just entering the gates of hell, as an escort to the Continental Congress."

The whole party started to their feet at this reply, and one of them exclaimed:

"It's Tom Browne, by all the pipers."

Another cried out fiercely:

"What do you want here?"

"To see your Julius Cæsar, your great Captain; he's a friend of mine. You're all friends of mine and the devil."

"Drunk as ever," cried one.

"Crazy drunk," said a second. A third, somewhat cooler, and more ferocious, cried out: "Pitch the scoundrel out."

"Clear out, you bloody scoundrel, before you lose your scalp," was the exhortation of another.

Browne, seeing this speaker, approached the table upon which his heels rested, and seized one of the mugs of liquor.

"What, rascal, would you steal my drink before my face? Put it down, I say, before I brain you."

"Ah, Julius, is it you? Here's to our better acquaintance."

He lifted the vessel as he spoke, as if he would have drunk, but suddenly, by an adroit turn of his wrist, flung the contents of the cup into the trooper's face, and then hurled the empty vessel after it.

With a savage yell, the fellow sprang towards his assailant, but was encountered with a blow of his fist which laid him prostrate on the floor.

All was uproar in an instant. The troopers made a rush in a body together upon the intruder, but were confronted suddenly with the huge knife, nearly the model of the modern Bowie, which Browne flourished fearfully in their faces as they came on. His left hand, at the same moment, displayed the huge horseman's pistol which he carried; and, both of these weapons, conspicuously presented to their eyes, made them pause in the onslaught. Where the bullet or the stroke seems meant for general distribution, no individual desires especially to appropriate its dangers exclusively to himself, and, on such occasions, prefers modestly to yield precedence to any of his associates. True valiancy always carries with it a certain prudent circumspection.

It was so with our troopers; not that they were dastardly. They were simply taken by surprise; and, after the fatigues of the day, stuffed with food, and perhaps a little overcharged with their beverages, they did not exhibit that audacity, in such cases, which is, perhaps, the only real secret of success. The very fact that Browne had drunken but not eaten, was favorable to his own recklessness; and, standing upright, and beholding their incertitude, he spoke to them in language of the most cold, yet savage intensity, of mingled hate and scorn, and insolence.

"And ye are the salt of the earth, ye scum! Ye are to purge the Commonwealth, and to put your beggarly bodies on the seats of Kings, Lords and Commons! Where are your Julius Cæsars, your Draytons, and your Dauphins, and your Hamiltons and Hammonds? ye vile curs that sit in judgment upon better men! Do I not know ye? Ye would assert the rights of man, and ye are not men! I can buy every soul of ye for a button! Your souls are at the bottom of your flagons, and a gallon of rum will buy every dog of ye to sell his grandmother! Here, take your flagons, and look after your souls. There's for you, skunk! for you, hound! for you, mongrel! for you, whelp!"

And, as he uttered these epithets, he hurled the several mugs of liquor, with their contents, at the heads of the troopers, and yelled with delight to see them dodging the missiles which, drunk as he might be, he aimed at them with no inconsiderable dexterity and skill.

Trooper nature could not long endure this treatment; furious now, they rushed upon him in a body, reckless of the danger, and, with a howl rather than a shout, he welcomed the assault. With steady hand and aim he fired his pistol, then hurled the empty weapon at their heads, and slashed desperately with his knife.

His bullet scarred the shoulder of one of the troopers; his knife gashed the cheek, and had nearly severed the carotid of another, when they bore him to the floor, and the struggle became pell-mell, while the table went over in the melee.

Browne fought like a tiger, with tooth and nail. A roar from one of the troopers, as he withdrew a lacerated thumb from between the jaws of the madman, showed that he was reduced to his natural weapons. The knife had been wrenched from his grasp, and Ben. Clymer, a huge Georgia trooper, now sate astride his breast, and, with a tremendous flourish of his *couteau de chasse*, prepared to pass the keen edge of the weapon over the throat of the prostrate man, when his arm was arrested by the powerful grasp of one from behind.

Martin Joscelyn and his friends had not arrived a moment too soon. A group had followed him in. Andrew Griffith had brought up some of the *posse comitatus*, and had been fortunate in finding

Captain Hamilton himself. But for his timely arrival, it is doubtful whether Martin Joscelyn and his companions could have saved Browne from the fury of the thoroughly enraged troopers. One of their comrades had been shot, another slashed with a knife; and though luckily neither wound had proved serious, yet they breathed nothing but revenge. They were not easily pacified, and but for the fact that their Captain was well supported by other and strong men, it is doubtful if he could have succeeded in saving the victim.

This, however, was done at last. The men, sternly rebuked by their Captain, and overawed by his threats, suffered their assailant to rise to his feet. But no sooner had he done so, than with a tiger spring he rushed upon Hamilton, with arms stretched out, and his fingers curved and half contracted, clutching at his throat, as with the claws of the vulture.

But Hamilton was on the alert, and he encountered the assailant with a blow of his fist, which sent him once more as incontinently down as he had been prostrated in the morning.

"The fellow's mad," said Hamilton, seeing that his men were about to fall once more upon the prostrate wretch.

"Mad with the hate of hell in his breast," growled one of the troopers, while murmurs from the rest clearly echoed the opinion, and resented the interposition of their Captain.

"Silence, men; I tell you that he is mad. We must rope him."

All parties were agreed to this stern measure. Griffith found the rope. In securing him, it was discovered that he had not escaped scot-free. He had received a knife gash on his shoulder, and another cut on the fleshy part of the thigh. Neither was serious, and after bandaging his hurts, a brief conversation privately followed, and it was agreed that he must be borne across the river that very night. His own safety required it. His escape already had been sufficiently narrow; and, from the temper of the troopers, it was feared that, in another collision, they would scarcely stop at taking his life. Besides, his presence was odious in the eyes of the community.

A cart was promptly procured, and under an escort of three, led by Captain Hamilton himself, Browne was carried across the river and lodged with a person named Floyd, who was not unfriendly, an old man who promised to take care of him.

At parting, Hamilton spoke to him kindly; expressed his regrets at the harsh and compulsory measure which he had been compelled to employ, and warned him, as soon as he was able, to quit the neighborhood.

"If you remain here long," said he, "I would not give a shilling for your life."

To all this he gave no answer. But his eyes, with intense stare, were fastened upon the speaker all the while, and the physiological student might have seen that the madness, the vindictive rage of the demon, had not gone out of them or out of him.

When the party was gone, the savage man rose up—he had been released from his bonds—and shook his doubled fist in the direction of their retreating forms.

But he spoke never a word. He received the rude but kind expressions of old Floyd with sullen silence; said nothing; asked for nothing; answered nothing, until some hours after, when he silently rose from the spot where he had been seated all the while, and in the same silence walked out of the cottage.

"Where would you go, Mr. Browne?" asked the old man. "You are not well enough to travel. Your hurts—"

"These!" said he, with a laugh of scorn. "These scratches!"

"Pretty sharp scratches, I should say."

"The bites of a cur. I do not feel them. The bite is here," touching his head.

"But why not stay here? Where would you go?"

"I go to my work. From this day my work begins. You will hear of it, old man. Ay, you will hear! The country will hear—hear and feel. I thank you, old man. Your name is Floyd—Floyd! I must remember the name, for your good. You are feeble—you cannot fight; but you have meant me kindly. May God, my poor fellow, forgive you your many sins."

And so he went—went out on foot, pursuing a wilderness track, making his way in the direction of the little village of New Windsor, in South Carolina.

"Guess he's crazy," said old Floyd. "Only to think of his praying God to forgive *my* many sins, and not having a single prayer about his own. He's gone crazy from his hurts and bruises. And what's the work he's to do? and who's going to hire a creature like that for any sort of work; but he's powerful strong: I'm glad he's gone, for that face of his'n has kept me in a sort of narvousness ever since he came. He's wrong in the upper story, I'm athinking."

Perhaps old Floyd was right. We shall see.

Martin Joscelyn congratulated himself on having done a good thing in assisting to rescue Browne from his enemies. Captain Hamilton also reviewed his own course with complacency. But Browne felt but little gratitude to either of these persons, and certainly none to the latter. Martin had very soon reason to suffer some misgivings himself as to the extent of the service done for the loyalist. While he and his friend Dick Marvin were returning home from the "Full-Moon," they encountered a group of Hamilton's troopers at the corner of the street. Some of them were of the party engaged in the fray. They had been joined by others of their comrades. To these were added a half score of the "Peep o' Day Boys," who had been setting the streets to rights, and were ripe for any mischief. One of the troopers addressed Martin after this fashion:

"Well, you've got that scoundrel off, *this time*, Joscelyn, but it won't be so always. You think you were doing a merciful thing by him, but mark my words, if he lives long enough, he'll make you repent that you ever passed between his weasand and my knife. He'd just as lieve murder you as he would any of us. I tell you he's got all hell in his heart. Better for all of us that you and the Captain had jest let us alone, when we had him down, with a keen edged weapon fairly making a straight line across his throat."

"Oh, pooh! Burnett; you are too bloody-minded. What can he do? Besides, he's really mad for the present. He'll be sober by to-morrow."

"No more mad than you. He knows what he's about. The liquor only feeds his natural passions. He's drunk, no doubt, and has been drunk all day, and can keep drunk for a week and never lose his senses. But he's not safe yet. Let him—"

Here he was interrupted by one of his comrades, who nudged him with his elbow, and in a whisper said:

"Don't you be giving tongue, like a cur after a rabbit! Hush up!"

This was enough. A few words more, and the parties separated, Martin Joscelyn and Marvin making their way home to the lodging of the former. It was now near midnight.

Meanwhile, the troopers, with sundry of the "Peep o' Day Boys," had a long secret consultation, and agreed upon a plan of meeting next morning by daylight.

"We've to find out where they left him. You, Fink, will see the Captain. He'll be apt to talk out. We must try and be at the ferry by sunrise."

And they went their several ways. They did not meet so early next morning as they had arranged to do. They overslept themselves. Food, fatigue, and liquor had done their work, and with full heads and moist eyes, they found themselves, near midday, on the banks of the river, and waiting for the ferryman.

It was twelve before they got over. They soon obtained clues on the track of Browne. They traced him to the cottage of Floyd; but the bird had flown. Unsuspicious of evil, Floyd gave what information he could touching the route taken by the fugitive; but his information was of little value, and was, indeed, but little needed, by a race of men versed in all forest experiences, who could take the trail, with equal facility, of bear, deer and turkey.

"He's crazy," said Floyd, when they were leaving him; "crazy as a loon. Why what do you think he said to me when he was going? Why, he axed God to forgive *me* my many sins, but never a word did he say about his own! Only think, *my many* sins, as ef he had studied them all out in the arithmatic, and as ef he had no need to ax for any marcy for himself. He's ondoubtedly as crazy as any man that ever worked himself into a straight jacket."

The report of Floyd did not change in any respect the purposes of the party in their pursuit of the fugitive. They were of that class of persons who delight in the exercise of any unwonted power, and the license of a time, which supersedes one authority, without establishing another, was grateful to the self-esteem which, at periods of regular order, is necessarily under that restraint and rebuke in which vanity finds nothing but humiliation. To such people the mere exercise of power is a singular pleasure in itself, and this exercise is never more gratefully felt than when it is engaged in inflicting pain. The two most favorable pretexts for this exercise, in its most cruel forms, in all ages, have been those of patriotism, or liberty and religion.

If Browne, at any moment, fancied himself safe, after being delivered by Hamilton and Joscelyn, and abandoned to himself at Floyd's, he was grievously disabused of his error, when he found himself overtaken by the hunters, about sunset, and when within a mile of the smokes of New Windsor.

They found him lying beneath a tree, and engaged in bandaging his wounds anew, as well as he could, with green moss and strips torn from his own shirt. He stopt in this performance the moment he beheld them. He at once fully conceived their mission. He was utterly disarmed, he was feeble from exhaustion, he was helpless. He submitted to his fate, and without murmur or entreaty.

The scene is not one to be dwelt upon. Enough, that the miserable fugitive, now incapable of resistance, was subjected to the torture, as it was known and practised among this forest population in their wild ideas of justice. In the name of liberty, they subjected the fainting wretch to the scourge, and smeared over with tar and feathers, torn by the lash, he was left fainting to the care of one good Samaritan, a woman, who found him senseless on the wayside.

He had borne the punishment without a plea for mercy, or groan of suffering, till he sank senseless beneath their strokes. He was unconscious of the further infliction of the tar. When he awoke to consciousness, sore and suffering, he found himself on a mattress in a homely hovel by the wayside.

"Were it not better that I should die?" he asked himself.

Days elapsed before he could answer this question.

"No! if I have survived all this, it is clear that God means that I shall still live. If He means that I shall still live, He means that I shall live to work! And how work? What is to be done? Need I ask when such men as these still live? When others beside myself must still endure the torture? I must work. I feel what is required at my hands! The torturer must be made to feel the torture. I must drink blood! 'Vengeance is mine,' saith the Lord; but shall not the Lord employ, for His vengeance, the creature of His own hands? I *will* live! They shall feel me yet! Woman, I thank thee. Peace be with thee."

And, heeding not her prayers that he would not depart till his wounds and bruises were entirely healed, he went forth once more into the dim paths of the forest, never heeding the darkness now rapidly coming on, nor the frightful exhibition which he made in his garments of tar and feathers, which matted beard and hair, covered hands and feet, and made of him a monster to the sight, even as he felt himself growing a monster in his own imagination, decreed to rage and rend, when the opportunity should arrive, as the appointed agent of the God of vengeance.

## CHAPTER IX.

### OUTBREAK.

Stephen Joscelyn reached his home, or rather the cottage of the widow Kirkland, at an early hour of the afternoon. He had but a few passing words with Grace, the elder of the two daughters, who met him at the porch with smiling eyes of welcome, which pleasantly lighted up her otherwise homely features. The beauty, her sister, was no where visible. She, as we have already seen, had never welcome for the cripple; and while he smiled amiably back to her sister, her smiles in no wise compensated his heart for the absence of the other.

To Grace he delivered the packages which he had brought, together with a note from Annie Dunbar. The young ladies were intimate, were cousins, indeed; and the intercourse between them was quite as frequent as their separate abodes would admit.

Stephen Joscelyn retired to his own chamber to brood. His unemployed hours, out of the school-room, were now chiefly employed in meditation. His mind and heart were at conflict; and, between the distractions of the country and the misdirected and hopeless nature of his affections, in the false direction which they had taken, he found it difficult to arrive at such a degree of composure as is requisite for thought and study. He could only indulge in unprofitable reveries which saddened without strengthening.

He reviewed the events of the day, recalled the comprehensive and classical speech of Mr. Drayton, recalled his own, as far as this was possible, but he had spoken too entirely under a gushing impulse to remember exactly what he had said. He only recalled its effect upon the crowd, and his cheeks glowed with a grateful consciousness that he had not spoken in vain; nay, that he had spoken successfully, and in full sympathy with the emotions of his audience. The reflection forced him upon a new track of thought.

"And why should I not pursue this track, and see whither it shall lead? Why waste time with those emotions, earning simply the bread which feeds and the clothes which cover me? Am I not endowed for better things? Do I not dream of grand debates by night? Do I not meditate deep issues of argument by day, and do I not involuntarily speak those things which men call eloquence when they hear? Does not the strong instinct thus speak perpetually within me, as with irresistible overflow, and would not this seem to prove the natural endowment? Where the instinct is so strong and coercive, would it not seem to argue in behalf of the gift? Is it not that mysterious something which in earlier days men called inspiration—that sacred madness which drove poets into prophecy, and established the oracles of the true God, even in the temples of the heathen!

"But the age no longer suffers the prophet, and scorns the poet! What then? Shall I be dumb because there be oracles no longer? Is this man, Drayton, silent because he is recognized only as lawyer or orator, and not as a prophetic teacher of the future? He can prophesy! All *great* men are prophets! The future is read in the past, and in that volume of humanity which always lies open to him who has the observing eye, the thinking mind, and the will to shape his thoughts to action. And his province is also open to me. Why not pursue my profession? Why not make the law an oracle for my people?—the law, that perfection of man's wisdom, in which he seeks, though at immeasurable intervals of distance, to emulate the Perfect Law, which is the true God!

"I must do it!

"And yet, what is the prospect in the present condition of the country? More stirring necessities are at hand—trials for thought and courage which shall utterly obscure the feebler decrees of courts and juries, and task the souls of men to the crisis of a mighty revolution. I behold it looming up in the distance, a shadow which grows larger every day, and which is destined, I doubt not, to envelope all our sky! Great Britain will never forego the exercise of that power, which, knowing the provincialism of the colonies, will not see that they too possess a power, in their own certain growth, which, after a long struggle, they shall themselves comprehend, and which shall be able to breast her own! In this impending conflict the laws will be silent!

"But shall this prospect discourage me? What shall I lose of the certain now by the adoption of my true profession? Is it *not* my true profession? I believe it. I feel it in me, the power to persuade, to convince, to inspire my people. I shall not for a long season realize its profits. But what do I need for life? Are the means of life—such a life as mine—not as easily attainable by law as by these daily drudgeries of the pedagogue? What are my needs—what should be my wants beyond the simplest necessities of life? Coarse brown bread, a few ounces of meat daily, and such clothes as keep from cold and cover nakedness—no more! What should I do with fine garments, silks and satins and broadcloth, but expose to vulgar ridicule the deformities of the cripple!"

And, with a bitter smile, he gazed upon the crippled limb, and sate for a while in silence. His musings soon again took the form of soliloquy.

"At all events, I must quit this dwelling. Here I feel that I am weak—weak to very feebleness of heart, and doubly miserable, as I not only love in vain, but love unwisely! Alas! for the melancholy conflict between heart and brain! That one should despise the poverty of aim in his own affections!

"And yet, she is very beautiful!—very beautiful! But, lacking heart, how loathsome to the thought her very beauty! I must fly from its fascinations; I must go hence! I can endure this misery no longer!"

He rose and took down his books. But he strove in vain to read. He could not fix the letters in his eye. Thought wandered, and, with a deep groan, he replaced the books upon his shelves, and paced the room with awkward movement, but with the stride of one in whom the most powerful passions were busily at work, and not to be kept down by will.

Night came on; and still he strode to and fro, though no sunlight now stole into his window with its golden reassuring smiles. A tap at his door, and the kindly voice of Mrs. Kirkland summoned him to supper.

He had not dined. He felt in no humor to sup. The full head, the sad heart were fatal to appetite. But he went forth, and the good widow met him at the door with her wonted smiling.

"You must have been in a brown study, Stephen, for I called you three times before I got an answer."

"Rather a black than a brown study, my dear Mrs. Kirkland," was the reply. "I needed no supper, being busily engaged in chewing the cud of bitter and vexing thought."

"I'm sorry to hear you say so, Stephen. But I don't wonder at it. You read too much—you study quite too hard for your health."

"Alas! my misfortune is that I read too little. Could I yield myself to books, and study them more and men less, it would be the better for my peace and happiness. Books never offend or pain me."

Thus speaking, and while he seated himself at the table, he murmured to himself the melancholy speech of Hamlet: "Man delights not me, nor woman neither!"

The eyes of the elder sister watched him with a tender interest, looking askant, as she poured out the tea. The younger looked elsewhere.

"And where did you dine to-day, Stephen? You must have come off too soon for the barbacue," inquired the old lady.

"I do not think I dined at all," was the somewhat vacant reply. "If I did so, I have forgotten where."

"Not dined to-day! Why, my dear son, what could you have been thinking of?"

"I know not that I thought at all, Mrs. Kirkland. I have felt no appetite either for food or thought."

"You are certainly the strangest person, Stephen—"

"And, naturally enough," he replied, looking downwards. His glance, the expression of his countenance, told all parties what was uppermost in his mind. They had but too frequently before beheld him in this mood, and fully comprehended what he meant. The deep-toned utterance, full of feeling—the one sudden glance of the eye, full of significance—sufficiently betrayed that feminine weakness of his thought of which he was himself ashamed. A thousand times had he said to himself:

"What a coward's thought it is! How unworthy of manhood! Why a surgeon, in twenty minutes, with knife and saw, would remove the monstrosity! A bullet, in a single second, would relieve me forever of its presence! Why should a man live on his legs as if there were no brain to support him in his own and the eyes of other men?"

"Yes, I am strange!" he said aloud—"strange to myself no less than to others. It is not wonderful, Mrs. Kirkland, that it should be so. In degree, we are *all* strange in some sense of the word, as depraved in thought or feeling as in figure or movement!"

A long pause followed this speech, and the party silently sipped their tea. Even Stephen made some show of sipping his. But at length the elder sister broke the awkward silence.

"You have not told us, Stephen, of the gathering to-day."

"What should I tell you, Grace, save that there was a great gathering; quite a crowd, indeed, for Augusta? The people flocked in from all quarters—from all the surrounding country—for a circuit probably of ten or fifteen miles; in gig and chaise, and on horseback, making a great show, without much variety. Suppose a crowd of our people, all eager, noisy, and excitable, and you can readily conceive the sight. The aspects are sufficiently monotonous."

"But the speaking, Stephen? Was there much of that? Was Judge Drayton there? Did he really come?"

"He was there, and spoke according to engagement."

"And how did you like him?"

"Very much, indeed. He speaks well, and thinks well, and was quite familiar with his subject."

"But," said the younger sister, now for the first time speaking, and with something of a sneer on her lips, "but I suppose he said nothing which *you* did not know before?"

He gave her a single look, and with deliberate effort answered calmly:

"Much, Miss Angelica, and fully came up to all my expectations, satisfying all my doubts. He was full of facts which our people knew not, and of which I was quite as ignorant as any of his audience."

"But, did he speak well, Stephen? Was he what is called eloquent?" was the query of the elder sister.

"Hardly, in any very elevated sense of the word. He spoke well, however—lucidly; with great good sense, much frankness, and seeming candor, with a nice classical polish, but, perhaps, with a suavity and sweetness, a delicacy and finish which, lacking in passion, or much warmth or enthusiasm, could not exactly be ranked as eloquent speaking. He spoke to the purpose, and with grace. He satisfied the desires of the people; gave them the information which they needed, and argued, from his premises, clearly to most logical conclusions. I do not know, indeed, that any one present was better satisfied than myself; and, from what I could see and hear, I am inclined to think that the greater number of persons present, were all well satisfied. They were certainly well informed."

There was a slight hesitancy of manner, in the look and language of the elder sister, as she continued:

"And was there nobody to answer him? Were there no other speakers? None on the other side? for I suppose there must be two sides to every question."

"Some other speeches were made, but after Mr. Drayton's, they need hardly to be considered, and will hardly be remembered. Perhaps it would be well for the parties if they could have been forgotten as soon as spoken."

"Indeed! and why so? Were they so bad, Stephen?"

"They were not calculated to do much credit to the speakers. Indeed, it is a somewhat perilous thing to follow in the wake of an accomplished orator, like Mr. Drayton. We have not the men for that here."

"But who *did* speak, Stephen?" demanded the elder sister, pressing her question. He answered, somewhat reluctantly:

"Young Dunbar—Walter—spoke."

"Ah!"

"Well, how did he do?"

"He was unfortunate, I think. His heart did not seem to be with his head, and his speech was all uphill work. The sympathies of the audience were not with him, nor do I think did his own inclinations serve to do justice to his mind. Poor fellow! I was truly sorry for him! His exhibition was most pitiable."

While Stephen was thus speaking, the younger sister had risen from the table and moved in the direction of the door. There were some symptoms of agitation and excitement in her manner while he was speaking, which were apparent to all but Stephen himself. He was, in fact, addressing himself to the elder sister chiefly, in reply to her questions; and, though he looked round to the movement of the other, as she rose from table, his eyes were quickly averted from her. But, when he paused from speaking, standing just within the door, she spoke, and with such an outburst of passion as to confound all present, and especially the party to whom her speech was a reply.

"Ha! ha! ha! You to speak of Walter Dunbar in terms of pity! You! You! He is as much above you in mind as in body! *You* to speak of him as a pitiful fellow! You! He shall know what you have dared to say! Pitiful fellow!"

Her face was inflamed with passion. She had lost all power of self-control, and, stamping with her foot, as she spoke, she continued to launch at him language pregnant with all the bitterness in her vocabulary.

"My child! my child!" cried the mother, starting to her feet, and rushing towards her, "my poor child, you are crazy!"

"Neither crazy, nor crooked!" was the reply, at which her sister clasped her hands together and exclaimed:

"Oh! sister! Oh! Angelica! what have you said?"

"What you cannot gainsay—what is true!—neither crooked nor crazy! and for such as *he*—ha! ha! ha!"

With a look of scorn and loathing, she flung wide the door, and darted through it in the direction of her chamber.

The mother followed her.

It was in utter dismay and consternation, rather than anger, that Stephen said to the elder sister:

"What does all this mean, Grace? What have I said?"

She came to him, caught his arm in her grasp, and in a flood of tears exclaimed:

"Oh! forgive her, Stephen. You did not know—you did not know!"

"Know what? I know nothing."

"She is engaged to Walter Dunbar. She was engaged more than a week ago."

His arms suddenly dropped beside him. His head sank forward—but only for a moment. He stood erect in the second instant after.

"I forgive her!" he said, solemnly. "I forgive her! May God help her and preserve her—and—forgive her even as I do!"

And pressing his lips upon the brow of Grace, with all a father's tenderness, he quietly left the apartment, wearing a wonderful look of calm and quietness.

He left the dwelling itself in a little while after, and very soon the tread of his horse's feet was heard at full gallop, as he rode away from the cottage.

In another moment, the mother re-entered the room and found the elder girl bitterly sobbing.

"Oh! mother! He is gone," she cried. "He has left us, and I fear he will never more come back. That cruel, bitter speech, has driven him away forever!"

# CHAPTER X.

## THE OLD TIGER IN HIS DEN.

It is a great misfortune where the sensibilities work too actively at the cost of the mind. They are essential to its proper working, but they must be kept subordinate. They should be tributary always, and never allowed to obtain the mastery. The sensibilities may be trained to a diseased activity. This is one of the dangers of a purely domestic education. The world has peculiar uses in roughing the sensibilities, and subduing them to proper service. Strike the true medium between making them acute or obtuse and they become graceful and beautiful servitors to will and reason. Stimulate them to abnormal activity, or render them callous by brutal suppression, and you render both will and reason traitors to the endowment of the mind, whatever that may be. In the one case you enfeeble, in the other case you brutalize the soul.

We need not inquire by what course of training Walter Dunbar became enfeebled through the diseased activity of his sensibilities, to the injury of his mental, and perhaps moral nature. Something of his defect may have been constitutional—something was undoubtedly due to a pernicious training. Injudicious praise, which stimulates vanity, is at the bottom of much of the mischief which is done by family training. In the pride of a parent's heart, indulging in fond, and, perhaps, mistaken anticipations of a son's performances, he stimulates the vanity without increasing the powers of his boy. A rough disregard, a seeming indifference to the juvenile performances of the young, would be far more judicious treatment.

How far old Dunbar's expectations—how far Walter's own ambition or vanity, may have led to the failure of the latter, in his late effort, need not task our inquiry. It was certainly due, not to a deficiency of endowment, or of acquisition, but to the false relations in which he stood, because of his previous opinions, when he undertook to be the simple mouthpiece of his father and the other loyalists who had succeeded in substituting their united *will* for his own. His heart, as some one said justly, was not in sympathy with his mind. His heart was honest, and his head weak, if not dishonest—the natural disease of professed politicians, and too much the case with persons engaged in the legal profession, unless, indeed, they succeed in subduing and making callous the sensibilities, when the pure intellect fully triumphs over the moral, and the advocate shows himself equally able and unscrupulous.

The struggle of these sensibilities, the want of sympathy with his subject-argument, the sense of mortification following upon defeat, and the savage anger of his father, all united to destroy Walter Dunbar's equilibrium. We have seen, from its effects upon him on the ground, how acutely he suffered, and what nice sensibilities, morbidly acute and aroused, were at work to baffle his powers, and, in some degree, to discredit his manhood. We shall see that those effects were not ended with the simple fainting fit which left him temporarily senseless. From this he recovered after awhile, in the chamber of Martin Joscelyn, and beneath the ministry of the physician. But in recovering from this fit, it was not to recover his senses. His evidence of consciousness was delirium. He raves! His fever rages, and his brain is threatened by the keen and tense strain which has been made upon it. Joscelyn and his friend Marvin watch him all the rest of that night, when they had helped to save Browne from the ferocity of Hamilton's troopers. They had returned just in season to assist the physician in getting the young man back into the bed from which he had leaped in his delirium. By morning he had grown worse, and in his anxiety Joscelyn had called in another physician. The two shake their heads doubtfully, and when two physicians unite in shaking their heads over a patient, his friends may, naturally enough, apprehend the worst of results. By sunrise Martin Joscelyn has mounted his horse, and is on his way to old Dunbar's house upon the Sand Hills.

We have heard already that, hitherto, Martin Joscelyn has been a frequent visitor at Dunbar's; nay more, it has been hinted to us that he is something of a favorite with one member of the family especially. We have been told that he was an intimate of Walter, and from Walter himself, in conversation with his sister, we gather that he found the welcome of the gentle Annie particularly grateful always. He was no less a favorite with that ancient maiden, Miss Janet Porter, the aunt of Annie, who presides, as chief matron, over the establishment of Dunbar, being the unmarried sister of his late wife. Miss Janet is quite a demure, domestic lady, not over warm in her deportment, rather stately, in fact; but very fond of her niece, and very cordial in her treatment of Martin.

The Pasha, in his dressing-gown and slippers, was still the occupant of his chamber, when Martin Joscelyn rode into the court-yard.

He encountered the fair Annie in the piazza. She had heard the horse's tread, and like an innocent damsel, instead of peeping through the blinds, like a knowing one, had fairly gone out to see who was the new comer. He alighted, hitched his steed to the swinging limb of an oak, and entered the piazza.

Here was opportunity. Even Miss Janet Porter had as yet failed to make her toilet. The eyes of the girl were bright. Her heart was light; for though her father had shown himself quite the savage on his return home, yet he had revealed nothing of her brother's hapless failure of the day before. She knew not the particular occasion of the father's anger; but this mood was so frequent a thing with him, his passions were so easily roused, and so unruly, no matter how small the opposition that angered him, that no surprise was now felt at his ill-temper; the girl and her aunt usually taking care, when he was in his rages, to keep out of his way as much as possible till the storm had blown over.

The opportunity was present; but the heart of Martin felt in no mood to take advantage of it. As he silently pressed her hand, she beheld the sadness of his aspect.

"Why, what's the matter, Mr. Joscelyn?"

"Mr. Joscelyn, Annie!" he said, reproachfully.

"Why, what would you have me say, Martin? Are you not Mr. Joscelyn—Mr. Martin Joscelyn, and the good friend of Walter Dunbar?"

"And yours, Annie."

"Well, yes; I suppose so. You say it, and I must believe you," she answered, coquettishly.

"And something more than friend, Annie—is't not so?"

The color grew more richly red on her cheeks as she replied:

"Oh, hush! there—and tell me what makes your face so cloudy, when you come to see me, as I take for granted you do."

"I do come to see you, Annie; but I also come to see your father."

"Oh!" she replied, hurriedly, looking around her, "you must not speak to him now. He's in one of his most awful passions—has hardly spoken to Aunt Janet or myself since he got home yesterday. He seems terribly out of sorts at something, and we dare not ask him."

"I know all. I can tell you."

And the two make their way into the parlor, and they seat themselves together on the sofa; and Martin takes her hand in the tenderest grasp of his; and he speaks to her in those low, sweet tones that lovers use, though nothing of love did he speak—that was, perhaps, sufficiently understood between them; but he told her of the scene of the day before—of Walter's failure—of the father's brutal speech, and of the subsequent serious illness of her brother, and the tears fell fast and thick from the eyes of the maiden as she listened, and in frequent broken murmurs she said:

"Poor, poor brother—he has a hard time of it—has always had—but what is to be done, Martin? Have you done nothing?"

"All that I could do, Annie. I have been watching him all night. I have Doctors Ford and Chauncey with him now, and my good friend, Dick Marvin. You must do the rest, Annie—you and Miss Janet. I have come to let your father know, and to get you and your aunt to go and nurse him. He needs your attendance."

"But how can I? Oh! Martin, how can you think it?"

"Think what?"

"How can I go to your lodgings, Martin? The thing is impossible."

"And why impossible, Annie?" asked the simple-hearted fellow.

"Why, don't you see I can't? Go to your lodgings, Martin! No! How can you think of such a thing?"

"Really, I don't see why not. I came to ask your father to let you do so; you and Miss Janet. I see no reason why not. Your brother's condition needs female attendance. He must have it. Men do not understand these things. At least I don't. Women make the best nurses. I'm sure, Annie, if I were in your brother's place, you could do more for me than a thousand doctors."

"Thank you, Martin, for your good opinion; but don't you see that it's impossible for *me* to go to *your* lodgings?"

"My lodgings! You dwell upon *my* lodgings. They are very good lodgings, as comfortable as any in town. I hope, dear Annie, that they will be your lodgings too, some time or other, though when the time comes, I shall try to give you a great deal better."

"Oh, thank you! but you must wait till the time comes. For the present, I cannot go. You must bring Walter home, Martin."

"Impossible to move him now. He's raving with a hot fever on him, and the doctors say it will be his death to move him. We must not excite him in any way. If one speaks above his breath, if a chair moves, or a door creaks, he's for jumping headlong out of bed. They've had to shave his head already, and cover it with blisters."

"My poor brother! I must go and see Aunt Janet, Martin, and see what she says. Meanwhile, I'll send a message to father."

"Send your aunt to him, Annie."

She hurried from the room to Miss Janet's chamber, and Martin, while waiting for her return, very coolly stretched himself at length along the sofa, and, from the fatigues and sleeplessness of the last night, was rapidly lapsing into drowse, when he was suddenly startled into an unpleasant consciousness by beholding the person of old Dunbar standing before him, and by the tones of his voice sounding most harshly in his ears. The stern old Baron, in dressing-gown and slippers, unconscious of any visitors, had silently descended the stairs, and was quite as much confounded as Martin himself to find the latter so free-and-easy, comfortably stretched out on his parlor sofa, and half asleep.

"Well, sir, who are you?"

Martin started up, and replied:

"It's me, sir—Mr. Dunbar."

"Me!—oh! you are, I believe, Mr. Martin Joscelyn! And what are you doing here, sir?"

"I came to see you, sir."

"Ah! you came to see *me!* Well, sir, be pleased to understand that I have no wish to see *you,* nor any of your brood. I shall be better pleased, sir, to see you out of sight! Do you understand that, sir?"

"But, sir, the important matter upon which I came will—"

"There can be no important matters, Mr. Martin Joscelyn, between us, now or hereafter. I owe you no money, sir. I have no claims upon you. There need be no time wasted between us."

"But really, Mr. Dunbar, you must hear me."

"Must, sir! must! I never suffer any man to use such language to me, and particularly a young one. Shall I humbly request to be relieved of your presence? I will entreat, sir. I am perfectly calm and mild, sir, as you perceive, entreating where I might command. You will do well, sir, not to provoke me to forget myself, and to enforce what I now request."

All this was said with an assumption of the meekest manner, and with ironical tones, very deliberately, with great slowness, if not sweetness. The wrath, like a pent-up volcano, ready to burst forth, was concealed in a cloudy vapor through which no mocking sunlight made its way—a sort of Indian Summer atmosphere—the storm to follow after!

"Was there ever such a man?" was the almost spoken exclamation of Martin, which he, however, kept to himself. He became feverishly anxious, as he exclaimed:

"Your son, Mr. Dunbar. Your son."

He was interrupted as before.

"Ay, ay, sir; my son! Well, sir, in regard to him, it will be well that I should tell you that if I have any interest remaining in him, sir, it only prompts me to beg of you as a particular favor, that you will drop his acquaintance, as I now propose to drop yours. The less intercourse you have with him, or he with you, the better for both parties. And I shall be the better satisfied with both of you."

Desperately, Martin exclaimed:

"He's sick, sir; very sick, sir; dangerously sick, sir; wretched—"

"He has need to be so, sir. Let him get well if he can, sir; and show himself more of a man—"

"He's deathly sick, sir, with two doctors—"

"Enough to kill any man! Were he a reasonable person, one would suffice."

"But, Mr. Dunbar, for God's sake, sir, and Walter's sake, listen to me, listen to reason—"

"You and reason!—ideas improperly associated, sir. May I hope that you will now depart?"

"Will you not hear, sir? Your son is now at my lodgings, sick."

"The sooner you turn him out the better. His practice will never pay for his lodgings. Speech-making that turns the stomachs of all other men, will be sure to make him sick."

"My God! what can I say?" This was spoken aloud.

"Nothing, if you please. Nothing that you can say will please me."

"You *shall* hear me, sir, though you strike me," replied the young man, now resolutely confronting the irascible old Scotchman.

"Ah!" was the single exclamation of the latter, as he compressed his lips and ground his teeth together.

"Yes, sir, you *shall* hear me, though you strike!"

"It may come to that," was the muttered reply.

"Be it so, sir! But hear you *shall*, before I depart. I came to serve you, and not to offend—to tell you that your son is dangerously ill, with brain fever, and that Doctors Ford and Chauncey, the best in town, are attending him, and are greatly anxious for his life."

"Well, sir, have you anything more to say? Have you finished?"

"The substantial fact, sir, yes! I would suggest—"

"Suggest nothing, if you please; and now, if you please, you may take your leave. I have listened to you patiently, young man, and you have shown yourself obtrusive. You have presumed upon my indulgence. But I will not be angry, sir, and I wish you a good morning."

"But, sir, you will come—you will send—"

"Good morning, sir."

"He needs nursing, sir"—and the now desperate Martin shrieked out the words.

"Good morning, sir; good morning."

"Great God! what a man!"

"Cudjo," cried the old man at the top of his voice, while bowing Joscelyn towards the entrance. The negro, in another moment, appeared at the door.

"Mr. Dunbar, sir, this is terrible. Your son, sir, Walter Dunbar—in another day, sir, you may have no son."

"Cudjo, see this gentleman out. Get his horse. Wait upon him, sirrah, to the gate; close the gate when he goes, and see that he never enters these doors again."

"Sir, Mr. Dunbar, I have not deserved this treatment."

"Good morning, sir."

At that moment Miss Janet Porter entered the apartment, a tall, thin, stately lady, simple of manner and costume, and of features rather calm than rigid, more grave than sad, evidently a person of well-balanced character, influential without being demonstrative, and impressive if not solicitous.

"Mr. Joscelyn—Martin"—said she kindly, "good morning."

"That's what I've been telling him for the last twenty minutes, but the party seems quite too demented properly to understand the King's English."

The old maid seemed at once to understand the situation. She had possibly overheard something of the dialogue between the parties. At all events, the temper of her brother-in-law was no enigma to her. She smiled good-humoredly to Martin, but only to be seen by himself, as she said:

"Go, now, Mr. Joscelyn. Your business is understood. Your mission is properly at an end. What is proper for us to do will be done; make yourself sure of that."

"And what the deuse do you know about the matter, madam?"

Martin Joscelyn did not wait to hear her answer to this apostrophe. As she had said, his mission was fulfilled, and no further speeches or language would avail, he well knew, to make the old man a more patient listener, or render him more accessible to reason.

He left the room with a sense of relief, Cudjo following close behind him, but gazed in vain about him for a last look at, or word with, Annie Dunbar. Cudjo held the horse as Martin mounted, and, as the latter witnessed the broad grin upon the negro's countenance, he said, throwing him a shilling:

"There, Cudjo, old fellow. You are to remember to shut the gate in my face, should I come again."

"Ki! Mass Martin, what ob dat? Enty you kin hitch de horse 'mong de scrubby oak, and slip round to de back ob de garden? You knows de way by dis time, I reckon."

Cudjo had evidently some experience of the ways and means of the young people, and just as evidently had no such hostile feeling to Martin Joscelyn as his old master entertained. He picked up the shilling, carefully wiped it of the sand, contemplated the face of his Majesty upon it, and deposited it in a secret pocket of his coat; then, watching the departing horseman, he muttered gratefully to himself:

"Martin Joscelyn always be's a gentleman. 'Taint de fus' ob his shillings I hab in dis pocket."

# CHAPTER XI.

## THE CRISIS.

There is an old Greek epigram which tells us that every man, no matter what his prowess, in due season, meets with his master. It is one of the modes by which fate rebukes vanity and teaches her best lessons of humility.

Our Baron, Dunbar, savage as he was, and truculent in his dealings with his children, and with most others, was yet not an exception to the rule. He found his master, if not his match, in his maiden sister-in-law.

Miss Janet Porter was a calm, quiet gentlewoman, of few words, and very amiable manners and disposition. She knew her man, and, without any demonstrative processes, asserted, when she pleased, a counter authority to his, which usually served to check his excesses of passion whenever these seemed to promise any mischievous consequences. She never *appeared* to run counter to his will or wishes; on the contrary, she very rarely permitted herself directly to oppose him; and, perhaps, one secret of her authority lay in the infrequent assertion of it. She had a happy art of assuming things on *his* behalf, and, studiously avoiding discussion and even inquiry, she seldom gave offence to his self-esteem. He submitted quietly to an authority which he did not *fear*.

Possessed, as we may assume, not only of the tidings brought by Martin Joscelyn, but of the particulars of his most unpleasant conference with her brother-in-law, her tact was beautifully displayed, when, after Martin's departure, she quietly said to old Dunbar—

"Do not trouble yourself about this business, my good brother. I'll see to it. Women are better nurses than men, and I have sufficient experience at a sick bed. Of course, it will be better—nay, absolutely necessary—that some one of the family shall see to Walter. It must not be devolved upon strangers."

"Why, what do you know about this business, Janet? What's the matter with Walter? Where is he?"

"I know all, my brother. The case is a most important one, and I fear the worst from what I hear. But I trust——"

"From what you hear? The worst? Why, what did you hear that I have not also heard? My son is somewhat sick, they tell me, but I suppose there's nothing much the matter with him. Some feeling of mortification, pride, disappointment, and——"

With well-acted surprise, Miss Janet replied:

"Why, did not this young man, Martin Joscelyn, tell you everything?"

"He told me nothing, I believe! He only wanted some pretext for coming here, and indeed I have no doubt that my son sent him to see how the land lies, and what is the prospect of his being restored to favor. He really told me nothing."

"Is it possible? And Walter lies absolutely at the point of death—raving in delirium—threatened with brain fever, with two physicians, Ford and Chauncey, constantly in close attendance—his head shaven, and covered with blisters!"

"Janet! You surely don't mean that my son is in any real danger?" demanded the old man, somewhat hoarsely, and with staring eyes.

"Danger! It is astonishing that these young men cannot say what they have to say, and make themselves understood. But there is no time to be lost. I shall take Annie with me to her brother. We will nurse him together."

She was leaving the room, but suddenly returned, and, with grave looks, and in subdued tones, she said to him:

"It will be well, perhaps, brother, if you will devote this morning to seeing about the family burial place. It has been neglected for several months, and is now full of weeds. Have it cleaned up this morning, and put to rights as soon as possible."

"Janet, my dear sister," said the old man, approaching her with a shudder, "can it be; have you really any apprehension in regard to—to—my son?"

"There is hope while there is life, my dear brother! Walter is young, and of vigorous constitution, and he is in good hands. Ford and Chauncey are the best physicians we have—"

"Oh! d—n the physicians! I will go myself. I will see—"

"No! You shall not! I will not suffer it, nor would the physicians admit you. Do you stay where you are."

"What!—not see to my own son, and he——"

"Dying, perhaps! But for that very reason, you must not see him, nor he you. Were he to hear your voice now, in his delirium, the effect would probably be fatal!"

"Great God! His father's voice!"

"Brother Dunbar—my poor, headlong and headstrong brother!—I have heard what has probably not reached your ears! It was *your* voice—your harsh and cruel language—that felled him on the ground at the barbacue, and which now fills his brain with delirium! Yes!—his father's voice; he was felled by it as with a shot! He must not hear it again, my brother, until he shall no longer fear it as a mortal terror. But let *me* go now, and do you take *your* warning. Go to your knees, and pray God that the wounds with which you have stricken that poor boy, may not prove mortal!"

The manner in which this was spoken was admirably adapted to the terms employed. It was sad, very sad, indeed, and conveyed its full lesson of rebuke; but it was not reproachful. She could pity the old man as well as his victim, and, while teaching him a needful truth, in respect to himself, could do so without any gratuitous cruelty. There are two ways at least of probing a deep wound, and the differences between the two processes are shown daily in the manipulation of the different surgeons. Miss Janet disappeared, while the old man covered his face with his hands, and staggered back into the parlor. With a groan, close followed by an oath, he exclaimed:

"What a miserable fool and brute I have been! My son, my son, forgive me! I know not what I said. But, no! I said nothing, nothing to do harm! I was vexed, goaded, stung, mortified, maddened, and tore myself away, but surely I said nothing! Did not that fellow, Joscelyn, tell me something of this? He spoke about brain fever. Yes! and blisters! and—O! what a passionate old fool I am!—my son! my son! Come back to me, Walter—my son!—my son!"

And, groaning in the bitterness of his self-reproach and apprehension, he threw himself prostrate on the floor, covering his face with his hands, and uttering deep moans at intervals, mixed with the frequent ejaculation:

"My son! my son!"

But, in a little while, he started up with a cry.

"The family burial-place! Ah! to be cleaned!—to be put in order, and for whom? My God! my God! have mercy upon me! Spare him!—spare him, O! Father of mercy, for his own sake, if not for mine!"

Miss Janet Porter, at parting, had found it necessary to inflict a keen and piercing wound. She had done enough, and paused just at the right moment. She knew the old man better than he knew himself—comprehended fully the fact that, in his arrogance and self-esteem, he had really not allowed himself to hear, or to take in, the import of anything that Martin Joscelyn had sought to communicate. In the confidence of his strength—the strength of his will, the intensity of his prejudices, and the gigantic force of his passions, his reason was not to be reached by one whom he already beheld with a sinister aspect. He regarded Martin Joscelyn as one who was engaged in beguiling his son from his loyalty, and he was too much bent on goading the young man, and driving him from his presence, with sharp sarcasm, to be, in any degree, conscious of the full force of that revelation, which, made to him by another party, went directly home to his feelings. It was necessary that Miss Janet, in order to reach his reason, should penetrate through the crust of arrogance and self-esteem, and strike keenly at his heart itself. It was done, in her peculiar way, firmly and fearlessly, but tenderly still. She touched him to the quick without irritating his self-esteem.

We leave him to the restlessness of those tortures which a conscience suddenly awakened knows but too well how to inflict.

Accompanied by Annie Dunbar, Miss Janet drove down to the lodgings of Martin Joscelyn. He met them at the entrance.

"How's Walter now?"

"Just the same!"

"And now, Martin, you must give up your room to me and Annie," said Miss Janet. "You can find other lodgings for yourself."

"Yes, certainly, but I must see Walter, you know—must stay with him."

"To be sure, you shall see him—that is, when it is altogether proper, or when you shall be needed. You can be within call. But, if he be out of his head, the fewer who see him the better. You can understand that. You are also to understand that these are *our* lodgings now, not your's. Let us go to him."

When the ladies entered the chamber, they heard the voice of Walter in rapid utterance. He raved incessantly, while all his limbs were kept in almost equally rapid and spasmodic motion with his tongue. His arms were thrown out wildly, his eyes rolled with a hazy sort of glare, the pupils greatly distended, and always in motion.

Miss Janet approached the bed, grasped the wrist of the patient with all the strength and pressure of her fingers, fixed a steady and keen penetrative glance upon his eyes, and, in really very stern accents, such as we should have scarcely looked to hear from her lips, she said:

"Walter, my son, do you know me?"

For a moment his eyes rolled wildly, then seemed uncertainly to flicker, as it were, like the flame of a dying candle sinking in the socket, and at length steadily encountered the intense gaze in her's. A moment after, he murmured:

"Yes, aunty, I know you!" and he returned the pressure of her hand.

Something had been gained! It was the first show of consciousness which he had given since the preceding midnight. A strong will had coerced the wandering reason back to its proper place. But for a moment only! In another instant he was again raving, with eyes rolling wildly as ever, and every limb in spasmodic activity, tossing to and fro.

But something had been gained, and Miss Janet persuaded herself that she might at intervals thus continue to coerce into consciousness the wandering intellect—not that she held it desirable to do so. She had a theory that the aberrations of the mind, during these fits of delirium, and under the stimulating effects of fever, were among the *remedial* processes of nature, and necessary for the relief of that strain and tension of the brain which otherwise, following one fixed idea, would be found insupportable. To recall the mind occasionally back to consciousness, she deemed an equal necessity, but she could not well explain why. Psychology may be found to do so. It is enough that such was her theory, and that she acted upon it, and successfully; that is to say, she found, on several occasions, that by word, look and sudden grip of the patient's wrist, she could compel his attention, and momentary recognition of herself or other parties.

But only for a moment. She ventured upon nothing more, and prohibited all attempts at conversation.

And so, day and night, these two women, aunt and niece, watched by the bedside of the dreaming and distracted sufferer!

They employed the two rooms of Martin Joscelyn, who found accommodations, however, in a low chamber in the attic. He was not to be separated from his friend; he, too, was devoted; always watchful, yet never obtrusive, the ladies had no reason to reproach him, though he sometimes sought his compensation in a silent squeeze of Annie's hand whenever they happened to meet under good opportunity. But this was only a rare delight, and to be valued accordingly.

Every good physician who is honest acknowledges the value of the nurse as his most essential agency of cure; and when she happens to be a Florence Nightingale, he can then repose with confidence in the promises of art and science.

Walter Dunbar was fortunate in his nurses. Never was solicitude more gentle, more watchful, and less obtrusive than the ministries of those two women, his aunt and his sister. Miss Janet had the experience; and the eager love, the desire to serve, soon enabled the observant and watchful Annie to acquire in a short time that perfect intimacy with the duties of the sick chamber and its necessities which are among the essential qualities and uses of the nurse. Day and night they watched the sufferer, separate or together, with a judicious ministry. And how beautiful this watch! In the deep, still hours of the midnight, when the heart of the great city sleeps, when greed and avarice and appetite find rest, there are bright, clear eyes, that glisten in the faint lamplight—glisten with their own tears, as they hang over the feeble and suffering form, and listen to every faint murmur from his fevered lips! That murmur may be a word of hope—it may be a premonition of the last sad struggle with the mighty wrestler, Death! To watch and weep without a moan; to moisten the feverish lips; to adjust the disordered pillow without disturbing the sleeper; to stoop and catch every murmur from his lips in dream, and sigh where you cannot speak—suffer agonies, yet watch on; this is woman's work!—and O! how beautiful does she appear when engaged in this sad but holy service! Would you see woman when she is most beautiful—when she is most worthy to be seen—look in upon her, as Martin Joscelyn does now, at midnight, and behold her as he sees Annie Dunbar, unconscious of his presence, and ministering, as we have shown, to the suffering brother, by whom she patiently sits, and over whom she sadly weeps, but without daring once to sigh.

It is the fifth night of her watch, and it is felt that the crisis approaches of her brother's fate. The physicians have so pronounced. For four days and nights he has slept never a wink. He has been all that time a raver, in the wildest delirium, with every limb in spasmodic motion, as we have already described. His few brief fleeting intervals of consciousness have been those which were *compelled*, at moments, by the stern eye and voice, and the tenacious grasp upon the wrist, of Miss Janet. He must sleep to-night, or he must die!

Gradually, hour by hour, the relaxation of the nervous energies seemed to increase. The limbs at length subsided along the couch. The eyes became closed. Only slight murmurs continued to escape from his lips. He was at length silent. It might be the gentle repose which promises recovery, or that exhaustion of all the powers which can only terminate in death.

Did he now sleep, the enemy baffled, or did this repose imply that exhaustion which must be fatal?

This was the fearful question that Annie Dunbar put to herself. She was at this moment the sole watcher. Exhausted by her own watch, Miss Janet had sunk to sleep in the easy chair. Trembling with her doubts, yet unwilling to trouble her aunt, Annie suddenly caught a glimpse of Martin Joscelyn at the entrance. He had entered noiselessly, only in his stocking feet. She motioned to him, with finger on her lips, to be silent; and, silently rising herself, she stole to meet him at the door. In a whisper, she said:

"I know not, Martin, if he sleeps or not—but it looks so like death, Martin!"

He entered, noiselessly as before, stooped his ear down to the lips of the sick man, and, after a brief pause, moved away himself, and motioned her to follow. She did so, and he whispered her:

"He sleeps! Let him sleep as long as he can. Everything will depend on his sleeping. Do not wake him by any means. No noise. Dr. Ford will be here by daylight, and it is now quite two o'clock."

He left her, but returned again at dawn. The patient still slept. Martin took his seat beside him, while Annie and her aunt retired to the adjoining room to make their toilet. Soon after daylight, Dr. Ford arrived, and was ushered into the chamber. He did not venture to feel the pulse of his patient. He stooped and listened to his breathings, which had become slow and regular, broken only occasionally by a sighing sound—seemingly of a deeper-drawn respiration, rather than any expression of pain or suffering. While the two thus sate together, Walter opened his eyes, and murmured:

"Is it you, Martin?"

Consciousness had voluntarily returned from sleep. The crisis had passed.

At this moment, the wheels of a carriage rolled up to the door and stopped. Old Dunbar had arrived. He could no longer resist his anxieties. The evening before Miss Janet had apprised him that the crisis had arrived—that a favorable change must take place that night, or they might abandon hope. He had come accordingly; he had not slept that night. The Nemesis had been at his pillow, with her scorpion wand, and his remorse of conscience aggravated every injustice of which he had been guilty to his son—every harsh utterance, into the blow that had proved him mortal! For once the Baron was unmanned; his fears had got the better of his pride and arrogance; he was no longer ambitious of making himself felt by others, in the keen feeling of his own apprehensions.

The doctor went below to meet him. He anticipated the question which the father found himself unable to articulate.

"We have hopes of him now," he said. "He has had a good sleep; he has awakened in his senses; the fever has entirely left him; he raves no longer, and the circulation has become regular."

"Oh! thank you, thank you, doctor. Let me go to him now."

"That you cannot do."

"What!—not my own son!"

"Were he twenty sons, you must not see him, nor he you."

"But, doctor, I will only look at him, and speak to him gently and lovingly, as a father should."

"He must neither see nor hear you, Mr. Dunbar, at present. Indeed, such is his condition, that it will be a week before he can be permitted to see or speak with any person, those alone excepted who are engaged in watching him. His life hangs upon a hair, and the very tones of your voice, Mr. Dunbar, or the glance of your eye, may bring back his worst symptoms, under which he will certainly sink from exhaustion."

"But, you say he has his senses?"

"Yes, but not his strength, and even reason, and the proper use of one's senses, require, for exercise, a certain amount of physical strength which he does not now possess. You must be patient, Mr. Dunbar."

Relieved suddenly from his worst fears, the ancient devil of resistance, opposition and obstinacy was beginning to reassert himself in the old man's bosom, and, unconsciously, he raised his voice to a louder pitch than before. Immediately, with looks of alarm, Miss Janet made her appearance from the sick room, took the old man's arm, led him aside, and said:

"Go home now, brother, unless you would do mischief. Your voice has reached us in the sick chamber, and *he* has heard it. His excitement has again begun, and you must go."

"Go?" said he—"Go, and leave him *now!*"

"Yes, go, satisfied, as you must be, that, while I am here, Walter will need no other presence."

"But," with a groan, "Janet, give the poor boy this. He has no watch, and I have bought him one. It is a fine one—all gold, capped and jeweled. I bought it on my way down."

The maiden lady took the watch with a sad smile, and a quiet tear trickled down her thin cheeks, as she gently pushed the old man from the entrance, and into the street.

"Poor old man!" she murmured to herself—"To think of such a toy at such a moment!"

She was turning away, having seen him fairly out of the house, and on the sidewalk, and was preparing to follow the doctor up to the sick chamber, when a chaise appeared in sight, approaching the entrance, which, she saw, contained Mrs. Kirkland and the fair Angelica.

Miss Janet caught a full glimpse of the invading party before she had re-entered the house. She readily conceived their mission.

"Here comes another trouble!" said she to herself—"I must send them off too."

Old Dunbar was just preparing to drive off as the new comers approached. She arrested him quickly, and promptly gave him employment.

"Brother!" said she, "here come Mrs. Kirkland and Angelica. They will be wanting to see Walter. They must not be allowed to do so. If his own father cannot see him, of course they cannot."

"Of course not!" said the Baron, decisively.

"Make this clear to them, if you please, and keep them out. For my part, I shall just give them the time of day, then go into the house, and lock the door."

This was said very positively.

"I will watch the door all day, Janet, if you say so, and keep *everybody* out!" was the reply of the Baron.

"It is just as well," quoth the other, as the Kirklands, mother and daughter, drove up to the sidewalk. Miss Janet was as good as her word. She simply shook hands with the new comers, then told them she must leave them, as she could no longer be spared from Walter.

"We will go in with you, Janet," said Mrs. Kirkland.

"That you can't do yet," was the reply. "Walter can see nobody."

"Not a soul!" said the Baron. "Even I, his father, am not permitted to enter his room."

"But we have come to nurse him, papa," said Miss Angelica.

"Yes," said Mrs. Kirkland, "we have come to help Janet to nurse him. We are women; and women, you know, are the only proper nurses. Janet and Annie must be quite worn out with their long siege of it."

Miss Janet had stolen away, while old Dunbar engaged the visitors.

"He has nurses enough," said he, "and more than enough; and, what's more, we can't change 'em now! He's better—doing well, if let alone. Let that content you. But he's just out of sleep, and the least excitement now—a mouse running across the floor—the mere dropping of a pin—might bring on his delirium again. He's still in a very ticklish condition."

"Oh! we shall be more still than any mouse, papa, and we won't drop a single pin!" said Miss Angelica, as she caught his hand in both of her's.

"It don't matter, my child. It's forbidden. The doctors know best! Janet knows best! It's the doctors' orders—two doctors—Ford and Chauncey—the very best physicians in all Georgia, and Janet has given strict orders to the same effect; and there's no better nurse in Georgia than Janet—none half so good in Carolina, and hardly her equal in all Christendom and Cochin-China to boot. So important is this caution now, in the case of my son, that I am set here to watch and keep off all intruders! and I'll do it! I am a sentinel here! I march to and fro all day, between that barber's pole and yonder sycamore, and no one enters here without special permission from Janet or the doctors."

And, flourishing his coach-whip, the Baron enforced his expressed determination, by such a smack of it, as made him apprehensive, a moment after, lest the report of it should be heard in his son's chamber.

"But where's Janet gone?" asked Mrs. Kirkland, looking about her, and missing her for the first time. The door of the house was closed—securely closed. Angelica was already trying at the lock, from which the Baron sternly drew her away.

"It's no use, Angey, my child! We have our orders! We are on duty here to see that they are obeyed! You must submit. I am very sorry, my child—very sorry, Mrs. Kirkland—law is law!"

Mrs. Kirkland looked displeased. Her vocation as a nurse, upon which she prided herself quite as much as did Miss Janet, was set at naught—was under disparagement.

"This is very strange treatment, cousin," she said. "I, surely, have a claim to be here; and this poor child, considering her relation with Walter, has a right to be at his bed side. It is her right, cousin!—her right!"

"Pooh! pooh! my dear madam, don't talk of rights! Everybody seems to be asserting some sort of rights in these latter days. As his father, one might suppose that I, too, have some rights to be at my son's bedside! Yet, you see, I am denied; and I submit, and acknowledge the propriety of my own exclusion! They somehow think within—the doctors and all—that the *right to live, on the part of my son,* is paramount, just now, to your rights as well as mine, and that neither you nor I have any right to kill him with mistaken kindness. I remember, my dear cousin, to have seen a very fine woman killed once—yes, madam, absolutely murdered—by the prayings and psalm-singings of a goodly Christian congregation! The physician forbade, and told them that his patient was in such a state, that he would not answer for the consequences. But their Christian fervor was not to be resisted. They pushed in, set up a terrible howling over the sick bed, and the poor woman, in two hours and twenty-five minutes after, was in Abraham's bosom! She went out of the world raving. They had murdered her body, the better to save her soul!"

The Baron grew eloquent in the satisfied self-esteem, which was never so well pleased as when in the assertion of authority. Mrs. Kirkland grew peevish, and Angelica pouted, and finally wept.

"It is so hard, so cruel, papa, to keep me from dear Walter!"

"Some natural tears she shed, but dried them soon!" as being found to be wholly shed in vain. The Baron was inexorable; and, with an exulting sense of his triumph, he rejoiced to see them drive off, having gallantly offered his hand to assist them into the chaise.

This the pique of the old lady moved her to decline, while the young lady, moving briskly to the opposite side of the vehicle, was enabled to help herself into it before he could make his way round to assist her.

Relieved from these parties, the old man now persuaded himself that other dangers of the same sort might again occur—that these women might come back—and that duty required him to continue his watch, as a sentinel at the post, during the rest of the day, and he did so. The disappointed ladies, unwilling to return to Beach Island without realizing some of the uses of a visit to the town, consumed the rest of the morning in shopping—Miss Angelica being greatly exercised in her fancy in deciding between two loves of bonnets just brought into market by the famous milliner of Augusta, Madame Pequillon.

## CHAPTER XII.

### THE FUGITIVE.

The convalescence of Walter Dunbar, under the judicious watch and ministry of his aunt and sister, continued without interruption, though some weeks elapsed before it was deemed safe to remove him to his father's house upon the Sand Hills. Some weeks more were required to put him fairly upon his legs, and restore him, in some degree, to his former strength. His youth and a good constitution finally prevailed for his full recuperation, though, in the case of a mind so sensitive and delicately constituted, they did not suffice to make him forgetful of the mortification of his defeat at the barbacue. There was an element of self-esteem—we should, perhaps, more properly call it vanity—which kept him sore on this subject, and it was found among his friends that he had lost some portion of his former good temper—was irascible in conversation, and any reference to the speech at the barbacue threw him into an irritable mood, in which he did not seem to care to distinguish between his friends and indifferent parties.

But the course pursued towards him had been, and continued to be, soothing. Much indulgence was accorded to him, even by his father, though the terms between them continued to be cold, and very unlike their former relations. In the moment of the old man's apprehensions, and, when he feared the young man's death, the claims of nature were permitted to prevail, and find recognition in his bosom; but, with the passing of the crisis, the habitual arrogance, self-sufficiency, and dictatorial will of the father reasserted themselves, and it was perceived by all the family, that, though forbearing all offensive speech, when the two had any intercourse together, the opportunities for intercourse were not welcomed by the father, and a seeming distrust—of his public opinions doubtless—rendered the latter averse to much or frequent communion with his son.

It was while young Dunbar was still an invalid, too feeble to leave the lodgings of Martin Joscelyn, that old Dunbar received a visitor at the Sand Hills, who came secretly, by night, and lay there *perdu* at intervals for several weeks. This person was named Alison, though it appeared subsequently that he passed under several names. He brought despatches from Cameron, Kirkland, McLaurin, Fletchall and Pearis, the loyalist leaders among the highland population, to Dunbar, who, holding the same faith with these men, though of superior moral to most of them, occupied a position in the precincts of Augusta, and along the Savannah river, not dissimilar to that which they sought to maintain along the Saluda, the Congaree, Broad, and other rivers in the hilly or mountain country. In this way, from district to district, from the Blue Ridge to the seaboard, the loyalists, through the agency of Cameron and others, had established a series of relays, posts of rests, points of rendezvous, and agents for a rapid telegraphic communication between the extremes of the country, with lateral agencies, which, from Augusta, south, so far as St. Augustine, were all in working order.

Dunbar, at Augusta, a stern old influential Scotchman, was expected to play the same game in this precinct which the leaders in the highlands were engaged in, and with much greater prospect of success.

We have seen already with what timidity Cameron, Browne and Dunbar, not to mention several other names, were required to proceed at Augusta. That town was of sufficient size and importance, even in that day, to exercise a large influence upon the contiguous forest population. It was, in brief, as towns and villages must be in all agricultural countries, one of the chief fountains and well-heads of intelligence. The professions here will be more exigent and self-improving, and a stationary and growing population in daily attention, will not only possess more knowledge, but be much more active in employing it, along with energies which are always thrice as pressing in the use of it, among a trading than a farming population. It very soon became evident to Dunbar and the rest that their policy in this precinct must be to lie low, keep dark, wait events, and keep well in hand whatever resources they possessed, till the time when they could profitably use them.

At first, the leaders of the loyalists in and about Augusta fondly fancied that they might boldly oppose the current, and by open demonstrations, take the field against the party which had already secured a large foothold of popularity in the adoption of the title of "Liberty Boys." This title rallied the young under the revolutionary banner. We have seen how fruitless was the effort to withstand the progress of the revolutionists, when, in an evil hour to himself, young Dunbar was put forth and goaded on to take up the gauntlet of Drayton, and meet that practised speaker in debate. Could we only realize fully to ourselves the large hopes which old Dunbar had rested on this effort, and the large calculations which he had made on the acknowledged abilities of his son, we shall be at no loss to account for, if not to excuse, the savage ferocity with which he had treated the boy upon his short-comings as an orator, and his utter break-down on the occasion. The cause of loyalty seemed to him to be wholly lost in the failure of his son to meet, with adequate argument, and more glowing eloquence, which was needed to restore the balance between the parties, the speech of this arch-traitor who was aiming to tear down the throne. No allowance was made for the youth of the speaker; and no account was taken of those possible sympathies with the cause of the revolutionists, which certainly took from his ability to speak on the other side. It was not possible, with the despotic will of old Dunbar, to conceive of the possibility of a difference of opinion between his son and himself. Nor was he yet disabused in this latter respect. He ascribed the failure of Walter to the overawing influence of Drayton's reputation; to the sinister friendship of Martin Joscelyn; and, which was quite as mortifying, to the inferiority of those endowments which he had hitherto assumed to be absolute and large possessions of the young man.

It was the night of that day when, relieved from all immediate apprehensions of his son's fate, he had kept watch upon the house to keep off all intruders. Having received, at evening, the assurance from Miss Janet that the patient continued to improve, he drove home; and after supper, was summoned to receive Mr. Alison, who made his appearance just when the old man was making preparations to retire. He brought with him such credentials as were instantly acknowledged, and which compelled the old man, willingly enough, to sit till a late hour, read his dispatches, and listen to the verbal reports made by Alison.

These were full of interest. Briefly, the highland population were everywhere in commotion, and, in some precincts, in arms. The ancient feuds between the Regulators and Scovilites, of a previous day, if not generation, were all revived, though under new names. One of these parties had shown itself as revolutionists, the other as loyalists. One proclaimed "Liberty," the other the "Crown." The Scotch and Irish colonies, the Dutch settlements, the French, all separate, and with little communion between them, were led severally by parties and chiefs, approximating the feudal baron in character, each governed by national sympathies, by the love of power; moved by local jealousies, or by passions and vanities which it is not now necessary to define. We must refer to the histories of the times for the details, if these be desirable.

The curse of the colony lay in the absence of homogeneousness. It was enough for Irish and French merely to hear the cry of "Liberty" on one hand, and that of loyalty on the other; something more, as respects the Irish, to know that the Scotch were generally loyal. With the Dutch settlements, which were numerous, their ignorance of the English language was unfavorable to the eloquence of Drayton, especially while they remembered that George III. was a Prince of the House of Hanover, and that his good, old-fashioned German visage was stamped upon every piece of money which they garnered up. Besides, as a people poor in circumstances, and generally ignorant, it was a sufficient argument by which to decide thousands adversely to the *movement* party, that the people of the low country, with whom it originated, claimed to be *a gentry*, almost a nobility, whom it was their peculiar sneer to speak of as *gentlemen*, and to describe opprobriously as "*nabobs*." Most of the people of these interior settlements were new comers, and had inhabited the country for a brief period of only eight or ten years.

The mission of Drayton, who had gone among them soon after leaving Augusta, had been productive of various excitements. He was accompanied by an eloquent preacher of the Gospel, Mr. Tennent, and by others of German origin, who might be supposed likely to exercise some influence over people of their own stock. They had full commissions from the Council of Safety, and could confer commissions. Companies of infantry and cavalry were organized, and one body of "Rangers," under Major Mayson, captured Fort Charlotte, on the Savannah river, expelled the British regulars in charge of it, and possessed themselves of its guns and ammunition. These were transmitted to the keeping of Captain Kirkland, who was posted at Ninety Six. This man, a Scotchman, and the brother-in-law of our widow at Beach Island, betrayed his trust, and went over, with most of his men, who were mostly foreigners, also, to the loyalist party of his section. He thus became associated with a sturdy and dogged race of men, who finally raised the King's standard openly, and began to organize troops in his Majesty's name, and, under commission from the Royal Governor, Lord Campbell, at Charleston, Col. Fletchall, the leader of the loyalists, soon collected a force of fifteen hundred men about him—a force, properly led, capable of overawing the whole country between the Broad and the Savannah rivers. Had the energies of Lord Campbell been such as to have allowed him to venture his own person into the interior, and taken command of these people, the highland region would probably have been lost wholly to the revolutionary cause.

Fletchall, who was, substantially, a feudal baron in his precinct, had no military talents to support his social popularity. He was a mere instrument in the hands of shrewder, abler and more courageous parties; and these, in a country so sparsely settled with communities at once remote from each other, and wanting in homogeneity, having so large a force in arms, already well concentrated for action, might well entertain the strongest anticipations of the full success of the royalist cause. At this time, be it remembered, the militia of the whole province comprised but thirteen regiments, twelve of foot and one of horse; in other words, as the regiments consisted, in that day, of but five hundred men, the whole disposable force of the colony was about seven thousand fighting men. Fifteen hundred in one section alone, and that so remote from the capital and the larger settlements, might well become bold enough to attempt any enterprise. Moses Kirkland, in immediate command of this force, under Fletchall, was now meditating the capture of Augusta.

Such, in brief, was the tenor of the despatches brought to old Dunbar by Major Alison. Of course, there was a great deal more. Alison, who had been a militia captain in Georgia, had hopes to subsidize a force in the immediate neighborhood of Augusta. He was well provided with British commissions, in blank, his own already having been filled out with the rank of Major. Arms and ammunition were to be supplied by Lord Campbell, through various media, and Alison had already in possession a goodly handful of British gold for the better persuasion of reluctant understandings. Already had he tried the efficacy of this latter influence, and it was not long ere he had nightly visitors at the Sand Hills, of that rank and *vile,* who are quite willing that Mammon should for them represent the cause of the better Deities.

But while the loyalists were thus active, showing energy and determination, if not good conduct, it must not be supposed that the revolutionists were idle. Drayton and his associates had done what they could, by argument and persuasion, at various places of importance in the highland region. They had met their opponents in argument, at numerous gatherings of the people and the militia—had, perhaps, worsted them in the discussion, as at Augusta, but without obtaining any substantial conquests in their change of feeling or opinion. The argument, to have been successful with these people, should have been addressed to their feelings and sympathies, and a due regard to the proper conciliation of these, was the great necessity when dealing with a people jealous of the social superiority of the low countrymen, and with their self-esteem perpetually irritated by the very efforts of the Commissioners to persuade and teach. This argued for the assumption of superiority, on the part of the revolutionary leaders from below; and, when the proof of this intellectual and social superiority became sufficiently evident, in the numerous discussions which took place at their assemblages, the soreness which vexed self-esteem spread and grew into a sort of moral gangrene, which penetrated to the core. Perhaps, too, some mistakes of Drayton and the other Commissioners contributed to the partial failure of their mission of persuasion. They discriminated unwisely between the local factions and their leaders, among several of whom there had been long and bitter feuds, engendered by the old conflicts between the Regulators and the Scovilites, and unwisely, in some instances, they gave their preferences prematurely to inferior men, when the same preferences would have secured the abler. In the business of conferring commissions, also, certain injurious mistakes were made, by which militia officers of inferior rank, and, perhaps, ability, were promoted, in the new organizations, above their former superiors. These things had a great and very mischievous effect upon a people, already jealous and suspicious of the parties who came among them to conciliate and counsel.

Still, the work of Drayton went on. He made speeches, and treaties and compromises, and played the politician as well as he was able, in a country and among a people with which and whom he was unfamiliar. He was misled, and frequently deceived, and encountered much treachery. But he did not wholly rely upon negotiations. He organized troops wherever he could. He issued commissions superseding those of the crown by those of the State; and, possessed of secret powers from the Council of Safety, he prepared to use them with efficiency, employing force, whenever events should so ripen as to make it politic to remove all masks. His sagacity enabled him to conceive that this period was rapidly approaching.

So much for the tidings brought by Alison to Dunbar, most of which were wholly unknown to him before. And while Alison remained, the occasional guest of the old man, making his house a sort of headquarters for the loyalists in the precinct, and working secretly through them, upon the surrounding country, he continued, from time to time, not only to receive, but to transmit intelligence, as well below as above, corresponding with the highland leaders on the one hand, and the Governor, Lord William Campbell, in the harbor of Charleston. His lordship by this time had taken refuge on board of one of the King's ships of war, then lying in Rebellion Roads, from which he threatened the city. The summary of events, thus given, will enable us sufficiently to comprehend the relations of the two parties now doubtfully struggling for ascendancy in the highland country, and neither yet prepared, or, perhaps, willing, to come to blows. They were soon to receive a decisive impulse from a fiery messenger already on his way, bearing the torch which should convert discord into war, and fix for a while the attitude of the rival contestants for power.

Browne is on his way upward!—We have seen in what manner, and with what abruptness, and in what mood, he left the dwelling of the [Words missing. See textual note.] him solace. But his solace was of a very different sort from any which she could offer. A stern, grim spirit had taken possession of his soul, and the demon of Revenge, working in his bosom, had clothed himself, in his eyes, with the character of a religion! Solemnly dark were the images that filled his mind, and vexed all the impatient energies of his thought and fancy, with the direst images of hate. He was attended ever by a cloud that seemed to him a wing of Fate, and he heard forever a goading voice in his ears that bade him go forward, whetting the knife as he went, and preparing for a bloody feast, in which only could he satisfy the thirst which consumed him, and the hunger which almost rejected all ordinary food with loathing; and with this cloud hovering above him, and with this voice of the vulture singing to all his senses, he pursued his way through the wilderness afoot, finding common food unfrequently, shelter rarely in human homes, yet never once suffering from privation, and never to himself acknowledging the exhaustion from which he not unfrequently dropped by the wayside, or reposed from, on the roots of trees beside some running water, where he quenched his thirst.

There is an insanity which never loses its wits. It is embodied in the intensity of a single purpose, good or bad, supported by an ever-watchful and tenacious self-esteem, in which no vanity mingles. The madness which comes from vanity, or entertains it in large degree, is usually witless—without purpose—a thing of ever-varying caprice, to be easily diverted from its object. Its objects are those of the child chasing the butterfly, plucking flowers only to pull to pieces, and led off by that will-o'-the-wisp, a bodiless Fancy, in the chase of every fire-fly that flickers about the woods.

The madness of Browne—for such it was—belonged to the first of these two classes. The madness lay in the entire concentration of his whole mind upon the single purpose, and that purpose was in conflict with law!

But, however erring in direction, all the human faculties were held well in hand for its support. Browne did not fail, or neglect, to use all necessary precautions in the prosecution of his object. Whatever he knew, from thought or experience, his wits, of whatever nature, were duly exercised, even as required, in the persevering aim which he had in his mind. Though he slept beneath the tree, he economised his strength in frequent appeals to sleep, seasonably, taking care never to travel so far without rest, as to lessen his ability to accomplish his whole journey. So, too, without any sense of hunger, he yet, at regular times, and whenever the opportunity offered, secured food, and from the dwelling where he might have slept to-night, he procured the necessary supply of provisions for the morrow. This he carried in a little wallet of woolen, thrown over his shoulder, and pendant from a stick. He knew many persons who dwelt along the route, who were understood to be of his own ways of thinking. There were Scotch graziers as well as shop-keepers on his way, with whom he was always sure to find succor. Nor were the Dutch settlers less accessible to the wants of the wayfarer. In approaching parties who were of doubtful politics, he made use of one of those little arts, which all parties find it convenient to employ at times, which were used as signs among loyalists by which to assure them of the true quality and character of the stranger, whatever his costume or disguise. Thus, for example, a *crown* piece, always kept conveniently in the pocket, was dropped on the highway, or at the entrance of the cottage, in the presence of the other party. Should he say:

"Would you lose your *crown?*" you knew yourself secure. Browne had money, which he had contrived to conceal about him—for those who flogged and tortured did not rob him—and with this he paid for his entertainment, when he failed to find it tendered to him by the hospitable. In this way, with all subordinate faculties in hand, tributary to the concentrated purpose of his mind—which was yet an insanity—he contrived to make his way successfully, an object of wonder and even terror to many, grateful to few, from New Windsor, until, late one sultry day in August, 1775, he reached "Ford's Station," on the Enoree river.

Here he paused, going into cover on his arrival, his presence known only to the host at the station, who was also a Scotchman, who knew him well, but failed, as well he might, to recognize him.

His aspect was scarcely human. He bore about him all the proofs of the late cruel treatment which he had received from the troopers of Hamilton. At least, he ascribed to them—which they denied—the coat of tar and feathers which he then still partially wore, and of which he refused to be cleansed. Huge gouts of tar, mingled with feathery fragments, hung from his matted hair and beard. His hands were still similarly coated with the tar. His clothes, smeared in like manner, and torn in many places, were those of the most miserable

Gipsy that ever starved at the trade of beggary and theft; and yet withal he carried himself as proudly as a conqueror. He did not beg. He did not whine. He scarcely answered a question; he rarely put one, save to the parties whom he well knew to be with him, and then his question was about "the cause;" and when he spoke, it was with the solemnity of one who delivers judgment. He could, however, be passionate and imperious of speech, under provocation, without losing, for a moment, any portion of that stimulating and tenacious purpose which had become, to his mind, its all-pervading law!

No wonder that he had wakened wonder, and sometimes terror, wherever he came upon his route. His present host, when he discovered who he was, would have found him better clothing—would have removed from his person all the wretched proofs of the brutality from which he had suffered. But this, for the time, he resolutely refused.

"It is not the hour!" he replied. "That hour will come, but not yet! Much must first be done. Something, too, will need to be washed out in the blood of sacrifice! Soap will not answer! And the blood must not be of goats and lambs, and the innocent herds of the fields. Felon blood must flow to wash out the stains of the felon. Heed me not in these regimentals, friend; they do not make the man. Learn to know the man *through* his garments, and in spite of his seeming shame! Give me to drink!"

He swallowed the stoup of apple brandy which was handed him, at a single gulp, and without water.

"I must sleep now! Show me where to lie down, where none shall see me till to-morrow! And—then!"

## CHAPTER XIII.

### HOW THE STRIFE BEGAN.

To-morrow, and what then?

The manner and matter of Browne's speech were equally significant. His wild aspect, savage solemnity of air, deep tones, and authoritative manner, equally impressed the humble host, who conducted him to a lowly shed-room, in the rear of the building where he kept his shop. He showed him the rude framework of pine plank, slightly raised above the floor, upon which a mattrass was spread, but without covering of any kind. But the season of the year made all covering unnecessary. Before laying himself down, Browne called for another stoup of the brandy—not in any soliciting manner, but in tones of command. The host was submissive, and Browne having drank, bade the former remove his lantern and leave him to his sleep, which he was quite willing to do. Though well knowing his man, and being of the same faction, he felt uneasy and troubled as he reflected upon the strange conduct of his guest, and the remarkable change which had come over him. He beheld his condition, and could readily conceive, from what he knew of the brutalities which had characterized parties in their savage feuds with their neighbors, to what Browne had been subjected. He could also fully understand that the violent passions of the man had given such provocation as, in public opinion, seemed to justify this usage. But he dared ask him no questions, and Browne volunteered no explanations. He kept these in reserve for other occasions.

During the night, the landlord, who slept in an adjoining room, was frequently disturbed by the voice of the fugitive, as if engaged in earnest conversation with other parties. So deeply was he impressed with this opinion, that he finally arose, and, taking his lamp, re-entered the shedroom where he had left him; but, to his surprise, found him in his bed, his limbs all composed, and buried in deep sleep, but speaking at intervals, in passionate bursts, which seemed quite sufficient to awaken any sleeper. But they had no such effect on him. He slept on, not quietly, it is true, but no doubt with unbroken slumbers, till broad daylight.

The morrow had come!

Somehow, Browne had obtained information, somewhere on his upward route, that this day was destined to be an eventful one among parties in this region. It was one of the strongholds of the disaffected men of the highlands. Here, Col. Fletchall had command, and his regiment of militia was one of imposing character; at once formidable in numbers, and, from the general ignorance of the foreign population, easily accessible to the arts of designing leaders, and, in some considerable degree, the loyalist leaders of this precinct were men of ability and character. Fletchall had popularity, but was feeble; but the Cunninghams, the Kirklands, the Pearises, the Robinsons, were all shrewd, hardy and energetic men, of strong fiery passions, a stubborn will, with some intelligence, and adroit managers of men. These, stimulated and supported by such persons as Stuart and Cameron, who were royal officials, and their subordinates, McLaurin, McLean and Mins, all of whom were Scotchmen, felt themselves confident of strength and in full command of the situation. Fletchall they used as a tool, and they shaped his purposes and governed all his proceedings. This day was assigned for bringing together all the leaders, with the militia of the precinct, for a meeting with Drayton and his brother Commissioners, who were to argue for them the existing relations between the crown and the colony, exhibit and enforce the alleged aggressions of the former, show and urge the rights of the latter, and persuade the people generally, if so they might, to subscribe to certain articles of "association," by which, in the end, to coerce the government of Great Britain into a recognition of the popular rights, and the surrender of all those claims of the crown which were denounced by the Congress as usurpations.

Fletchall could not well deny to the Commissioners the assemblage of the militia; he was temporizing with them, and, accordingly, he issued his orders for the gathering to the several captains of his regiment. But as the argument had been already prejudged by the loyalist leaders, and as they were quite unwilling that their people should be exposed to the persuasions of Drayton, or the effects of his oratory in any way—for this they were quite unable to answer—they resorted to subterfuge in order to defeat the chance of success on the part of the Commissioners. The captains in several instances forbore to summon their men to appear, or told them that they might or might not appear at their own pleasure; that the order was not imperative, and that their conduct in the matter was wholly optional with themselves. The result was that, instead of an audience of fifteen or eighteen hundred persons, there was but a scant three hundred on the ground.

The leaders, however, having thus kept their men from the hearing, contrived to be present in force themselves. It was, perhaps, fortunate for Drayton and his associates that, of the three hundred persons present, a large proportion were those who were not only favorable to the revolutionary movement, but had already signed the articles of association.

It was evident to Drayton and his party, as soon as they arrived on the ground, that a very bad spirit was at work, not only to defeat their objects, but, if possible, to precipitate some violent proceedings. The loyalists appeared well armed, with sword and pistol; but the Commissioners wore private arms themselves, and some of the friends who accompanied them, suspicious of danger, were armed also in like manner.

Drayton, in terms that might be construed into reproaches, drew Fletchall's attention to the fact that his regiment was by no means represented on the ground; that not a fifth of them was present, and he somewhat imperatively demanded to know if they had been properly summoned. Cunningham replied for Fletchall, and said, very coolly, that, for his part, he saw no good reason for the assemblage.

"As for ordering my company to assemble," said he, "that I could not and would not do. I told them that the assemblage would be purely voluntary; they might come or not, as they thought proper. But, if they were satisfied with their present opinions, on public subjects, there was no need that they should come to listen to the addresses."

Several captains present said the same thing, adding: "The Colonel, (Fletchall) left it to themselves to come or not as they pleased, and told us it would not matter if the men staid away. They might be sure that he would not be angry with them for doing so."

Drayton turned to Fletchall, and he too answered cavalierly.

"The truth is, Mr. Drayton," said he, "this is no lawful muster, and it was only to comply with your request that I issued any summons at all. It is optional with the men whether they want to hear political discourses."

"But the orders of the Council of Safety, Colonel Fletchall, these are imperative. Your commission, sir."

Cunningham and Kirkland both answered, in very nearly the same language, saying:—

"Our commissions are from the King. We recognize no Committee of Safety here."

But we need not dwell upon these preliminaries, which Drayton judiciously shortened as much as possible, proceeding to the main business of addressing the audience, however small, which had assembled. He spread before them the "articles of association," which they were solicited to sign. He proceeded to expatiate upon the uses and absolute necessity of such articles, and this necessarily conducted him to the principal subjects of difficulty and discussion: the false relations existing between the crown and the colonies. In this discussion he arrayed before the assembly the leading tenets of republican liberty, which have been subsequently relied on in the assertion of the independence of the colonies. He showed that the colonies were able to go alone; that their numbers were quite sufficient to support the fabric of the State; that their people possessed the necessary qualifications of morality, knowledge and intellect for self-government; that, whenever this condition should be reached by any people, there was neither right nor reason in the claim of any foreign or remote nation to govern them from abroad; that any people submitting to such usurpation were only fit to be enslaved; were slaves already, in spirit, and must sink into a condition of slavery; that the rule of right and reason required that all governments, to be safe and beneficial, must exist only by the consent of the people to be governed; that, to be taxed without representation, was the perfection of tyranny, constituting the very worst feature of that oriental despotism which placed a province at the mercy of a foreign satrap, with the wholesale privilege of plunder for himself and master, &c.

We need not pursue these details, or indicate the several points made by the speaker. Ninety years of experience as independent

States have confirmed the propriety of these assumptions to the people of the United States, until they have grown to be the recognized standard of all good government, avowed and recognized as law in the minds of the whole of the States of North America.

Drayton spoke at length, and spoke eloquently, and, for a time, the loyalist leaders seemed disposed to give him a patient hearing. This was induced, perhaps, by the temper of the people present, who listened with interested attention and in the utmost good order. But, in the midst of the speech, forcing his way through the crowd, Browne suddenly made his appearance, without any warning, and, perhaps, without the knowledge of his presence, among his own associates. He spoke to none, but simply pressed on through the multitude, until he confronted the speaker, at the distance of a few paces.

His appearance produced a sentiment of surprise, amounting almost to terror. The persons whom he jostled to make his way into the circle readily yielded him a pathway, as soon as they beheld his condition. They shrank from contact with the foul and ragged garments, besmeared with tar and feathers. The matted hair—for he came in hatless—still hung heavy with tarry gouts, as did the beard, which was literally massed together beneath and about his chin with the resinous ooze, which, in the hot season of the year, continued to drip at moments upon his breast and hands. His eyes, almost starting from their sockets, glared out like those of an owl forced to face the sun at noon day. But it will be easier to conceive than to describe his condition and appearance. It produced a strong and painful sensation. At first, his most intimate friends and associates failed to recognize him.

"What!" he cried to Kirkland. "You do not know me! Ha! ha! ha! It is, indeed, a wonderful transformation. I owe it to Liberty, my friends—the cause of Liberty! Liberty is a great cause! It makes, as you see, a bird of Paradise out of a common crow! Look at me, and behold the blessings and the benefits in store for you, at the hands of these new apostles of Liberty, with their fine speeches and virtuous declamations! Look at me, and admire the charities which the gentlemen of the seaboard have in store for us poor plebeians of the backwoods!"

"Great God! It is Browne!" cried Kirkland.

"Ay, Browne! You hardly thought it possible that the Browne could be made so suddenly so fair! This is the magic power of Liberty. Go below—seek out the 'Liberty Boys' of the heroic Captain Hamilton, and get yourselves a liberty cap such as mine, and the clothing of charity which Liberty is to confer, in such a beautiful and close-fitting uniform as mine! Ay, they will make you a fit-out for freedom which shall last something longer than any British uniform!"

"This is a shocking spectacle!" exclaimed Drayton, with disgust and horror.

"A shocking spectacle! Ha! ha! ha! That you should say it! What! You do not find it beautiful, even though put on in the name of Liberty? I say it is a beautiful sight, to charm all lovers of the fine fresh doctrine of the rights of men and the blessings of free government. It is the form which charity takes, my brethren, when it preaches philanthropy, and confers liberty as a blessing and a right by the hands of violence!"

And the madman—deliberate as death—schooled his mind to its purpose, and with a savage concentration of his will, sported with his own loathsome appearance—held up his tarred hands to the audience—threw open the ragged vestments from his bosom—exhibited the clotted masses of tar and feathers upon neck and breast, and, baring his shoulders, displayed the swollen and bloated marks which had been left upon them by the scourge, still raw in many places, with the clotted gore caked along the edges of the wounds.

"Who could have done this?" exclaimed Drayton, with a feeling of mixed loathing and pity, which he did not struggle to conceal.

"Who!" shouted the victim. "Do you dare to ask? Your creatures!—the commissioned creatures of your Council of Safety—the 'Liberty Boys' of your great hero, Captain Hamilton, of Augusta, having special license in the name of the rights of man—of the new Goddess of Freedom, whom you would raise to silence all freedom of speech, where it happens to conflict with your purposes."

"False, sir—false as hell!"

"What! dare you deny these wounds—these beautiful scars in the flesh, written by the scourge in blood! Do you mean to say that I have put them there with my own hands? Do you dare deny this beautiful handiwork of these troopers of Hamilton?"

"I deny that for this proceeding they had any sanction from the Council of Safety."

"Ah! God keep us! You are a lawyer! You are a lawyer! able to make your own spider webs that only enmesh fools, while you have secret avenues of escape for yourselves. No! perhaps your Council of Safety did not say to the 'Liberty Boys' do this, in this particular instance, Tom Browne being the victim; but they chuckled over the deed. Can you deny that they *have* sanctioned—nay, *ordered*, this performance, in Charleston, in many cases, where, asserting the privilege of speech and opinion, which you would deny to all those who differ from you, men have been borne through the city on carts, clad as you see me now, amidst the blows and whips and revilings of the mob; and you looked on, and smiled, and cried out 'Well done, brethren! Liberty demands that Terror shall sit beside her as she goes in state, and Brutality shall prepare the way for her march even over crushed bodies and bleeding hearts'?"

Drayton was silent. His conscience smote him with the truth of the charge. He knew, too well, what Browne could not confidently assert, that *he himself*, as chairman of the Council of Safety, had, in some instances, himself written the orders prescribing this brutal punishment as the proper agency for suppressing opposition in the city. The reflection was no way grateful to him, and he felt, for the first time, the cruel doubt, whether, in the name of Liberty, he had not consented to the grossest outrage upon Humanity. It was a subject not to be dwelt upon with complacency in his present or in any situation. Nor could the art of the lawyer, nor could the natural endowments of the man, provide him with a ready answer to the fierce, natural eloquence of the outraged victim, thus exhibiting the horrid proof, in his own person, of the truth of his charge, and illustrating its terrible cruelties by his own loathsome condition. The madman had become endowed with a speech of fire, which sped like a lightning shaft through the assemblage. He had employed the same mode of argument with Mark Antony, when he showed the bloody robes of Cæsar in the sight of the Roman populace.

The effect was indescribable, and yet all the parties present had been familiar with this mode of punishment. It had been adopted from the British themselves. It had been freely employed by the leaders among the Regulators and Scovilites, many of whom were present. It was reserved for the insanely aroused victim, in the present instance, to present it, for the first time, to their minds in all its horrid naked enormities.

The silence of Drayton, itself—he, usually so prompt of speech, so ready to answer, so capable of all the glozing arts of the orator—seemed to give confirmation to all the extremes and charges of his assailant. For the moment he was dumb.

"And this is what we are to expect," shouted Kirkland, "if we dare to differ from these nabobs, who would tear down the throne of Great Britain! Here they come amongst us with smooth speeches—all lies—about the rights and liberties for which we are to shake off our allegiance to the King, and crown them with the power which shall make dogs of our people. We owe this to your fine speeches!"

He shook his fist at Drayton, as he spoke. Drayton replied:

"He owes it to his own!"

"Liar!" cried Browne, pressing forward. "It was you who set the hounds upon me. You have been the instigator of all the mischief that now threatens the lives and safety of all good men in this country—you, with your accursed smooth speeches, about your scoundrelly congresses, and councils and committees, that sit in Charleston, and hatch conspiracies against the laws, that you may ride into power, and rule as the tyrants of the land. What prevents that we seize upon you now in the very act of your treasons, and sacrifice you to the peace and safety of the country—that we give you a taste of that punishment which has been bestowed on me?"

"You will try it at your peril," was the answer. "Hear me, my friends," continued Drayton, addressing the assemblage. "I deeply regret the outrage which has been perpetrated on this man. I now bitterly regret that any such outrages should ever be committed, since the claims of humanity should be always paramount, and no cause should require her sacrifice. We have all, perhaps, grievously sinned in this particular. This cruel punishment, for mere differences of opinion, has been but too frequently resorted to. You, too, well know how commonly it has prevailed in this very region; and unhappily, the better taught among our people have but too frequently, in their own passions, let loose the wolf-dogs of society against those whom they held to be deserving of any punishment, where the laws did not readily reach the offender. We are all but too apt, in the moment of passion, to lose sight of the consequences of passion, and the evils which may arise from a too ready compliance with its demands. I confess that the spectacle before me, for the first time, impresses me with the feeling of horror which it should excite in every heart not dead to humanity."

"Ha! ha! Very good!—very comical! The lawyer is at his work again! The argument changes with the climate. It is now your bull that gores my ox! You are now on *our* ground, and you can now see how wicked you have been when you felt strong upon your own. But the cunning is not quite deep enough out of sight. It will not help you here! We have you here, where we are strong, and, by the eternal devil, you shall pay the penalty."

"Aye!—by ——!—and why not? We've a long reckoning to settle with these fellows, and the sooner we begin to square accounts the better!"

Such was the speech of Kirkland, seconding that of Browne.

It was now seen that the latter was armed with a butcher-knife which he had snatched from the stall of his host of the preceding night. He had concealed it in his garments until the present moment, and now flourished it aloft while making a forward movement in the direction of the Commissioners. Kirkland's sword was drawn even while he spoke, and he, too, made a forward movement.

Drayton, Tennent and the rest of their party stood apparently unmoved, but evidently watchful. They were armed.

Cunningham, Robinson, and one or two others advanced at the same time; and, as Drayton beheld them, mistaking their purpose, and assuming that there was a combined movement to set upon them, half drew his small sword, but the Rev. Mr. Tennent interposed, and stayed his hand:

"Not yet!" said he—"not yet! Let us forbear till the very last moment. They will hardly attempt more than intimidation. Let us not precipitate the matter, and force them to extremities."

In a moment more it was seen that the object of Cunningham and Robinson was not assault, but the arrest of any demonstration of this sort on the part of the two most infuriate and inveterate among them. Browne was forcibly held back by Cunningham, and Kirkland by Robinson. They struggled violently for release.

"Hold me not back, friend!" quoth Browne to Cunningham. "Hath not the time come? Is not the victim delivered into our hands, and may we not execute judgment upon him? It is the judgment of the Lord!"

"Aye!" cried Kirkland. "He is the proper victim! He is the man—the orator, the great leader, and arch-traitor among the rebels. He is the proper victim for the sacrifice. It is not the hounds that run down the game, but the cunning hunter who sets them on. It were something gained if we only cut the tongue of treason! I ask for nothing but his tongue!"

He freed himself from Robinson, and resolutely advanced towards the Commissioners. Browne, at the same moment, shook himself free from the grasp of Cunningham. These, with several others, now grappled with the two once more. Browne apostrophised the crowd, in that half biblical phraseology which he had imbibed, no doubt, from his old Covenanter origin. He had evidently come to regard himself, in his insanity, as one chosen to minister at the altar of sacrifice.

"Yes! now is the time, my people!—now is the accepted time! The Lord hath delivered the enemy into our hands. He hath come to judgment of his own free will. Here is the proper altar of sacrifice, and the victim stands before us. Let us hew him down, even where he stands. Now is the time to wash out our own sins in the blood of the traitor. I have a two-fold commission for the sacrifice. The Lord commands that we put away the evil doer from among us—the Belial, who, with smooth and serpent tongue, would persuade us anew to pluck and eat of the forbidden fruit; and I have the warranty, besides, from our sovereign lord, the King of Britain. Look and read, my brethren!—and see that you no longer vainly oppose yourselves to the judgment of your heavenly and your earthly sovereign."

He drew from his tattered garments, as he spoke, a sheet of parchment, with heavy seal, which the nearer bystanders soon perceived to be a formal commission, creating and constituting Thomas Browne as a colonel of colonial infantry, in the service of his Britannic Majesty, signed by Lord William Campbell, Governor of South Carolina.

"Behold, I say!" he continued; "and read your warranty for what you do in mine. Let there be no surprise, for the Great Jehovah—

aye, and, following Him, the sovereigns of the earth—choose the agents of their power, even as they please, and lift up the lowliest instruments of earth for the overthrow and abasement of the most lofty. Though you behold me clad in this loathly garb, bestowed by the 'Liberty Boys,' of whom yonder smooth-tongued orator is the leader—though I be wretched and mean and miserable, as you behold me—yet have I been chosen by the mightiest of all powers, to do the work of justice upon the offender. With this commission of the crown, I call upon you to gather around me—to follow where I lead—and, when I bid you, to seize upon this insolent rebel, and bind him, so that I may make of him a bloody sacrifice, even now, and here, in the name of the Lord Jehovah, and of our lawful sovereign, George the Third, King of Great Britain. I command you, my people—follow me! Follow my commission! It bears his stamp and seal, and carries the signature of Lord Wm. Campbell, Governor of the Province of South Carolina."

And, shaking aloft the commission with one hand, he brandished his knife with the other, and made a desperate bound at the little circle, which had now formed a ring about the orator.

For a moment, all was confusion and uproar. The scene had reached its crisis.

Drayton stood calmly erect, with his hand upon his small sword, which still remained undrawn. But the pistols of his friends were in each several grasp, and the followers, who were trustworthy, now pressed forward, with compressed lips and dilating nostrils, preparing for the *mêlée* which now seemed scarcely possible to avert.

Fletchall sate upon a fallen tree, seemingly unconcerned. Kirkland followed, as if to second all the movements of Browne. Their murderous intentions glared out in the eyes of both these savage men, different in expression and degree, but both indicating the fellest purpose; and the sword of Kirkland, in an instant, was actually threatening the breast of Drayton over the shoulders of one of his friends, who stood, unconscious of it, pistol in hand, with his eye fixed only on Browne.

A single stroke at that moment—the shot of a pistol, or the thrust of a sword, must have precipitated the murderous struggle which now seemed inevitable, in spite of all the efforts of Cunningham and

Robinson to keep back Browne, while others were engaged in like efforts to restrain the rage of Kirkland.

Just then all parties were brought to a sudden pause in the action, by a sudden cry—a sort of stifled shriek—from Fletchall, the chief of the loyalist party, who had been hitherto sitting quietly, if not indifferently, in the back-ground, a willing witness to the progress of that mischief which he did not seem willing to oppose. He did not care to participate in the proceedings, which he yet did not choose to arrest. For this he was too cowardly. But he was not unwilling that other parties should incur the hazards of opening the game, the cards of which he was yet in hopes to play. He had looked on, apparently with the greatest indifference, as the strife increased in warmth. Picking his teeth with his knife, he sometimes grinned, scowled or chuckled, during the progress of the wild discussion, especially while the infuriate assailants were badgering the orator by whom his vanity had been offended.

But, as the strife warmed into violence, he silently rose, and was making his way out of the crowd, when he felt himself suddenly seized by the throat, and found himself in the grasp of a powerful Irishman, one Orrin O'Brien, who had followed Drayton's party to the ground. O'Brien, thrusting his fingers between the throat of Fletchall and his neckcloth, gave it a single twist, which forced from him the choking cry which had brought upon the parties the attention of the crowd. All eyes were quickly turned in this direction, to behold Fletchall struggling vainly in the grasp of the giant, quite purple in the face, while his captor, flourishing a huge knife before his eyes, cried out, at the top of his voice:

"If that's to be the game, boys, then every man to his bird!"

The choking scream of Fletchall—his evident danger—the resolute front put on by Drayton's friends and followers, and the large proportion of them present—had the proper effect with the loyalist leaders, who now addressed themselves more earnestly than ever to the task of taking off Browne and Kirkland.

"Madman!" said Robinson to Kirkland, "do you not see that they are three to one against us?"

"And whose fault is that? But for the stupid policy of Fletchall, in keeping the men away from the gathering, we should have had men enough—might have taken all these fellows at one cast of the net, and struck such a blow as would have rung from the mountains to the seaboard."

"The sun will rise to-morrow," replied Robinson, as he withdrew Kirkland from the crowd into the woods.

Browne was not so easily managed. He had so nearly approached the consummation of one stroke of bloody vengeance, that he raged furiously against those who, after a fierce struggle, succeeded in disarming and bearing him away from the scene. Still raving and struggling as he went, he deplored his disappointment, denounced the party as faithless to their sovereign, weak, cowardly, and wanting in the wisdom to strike the first blow when all the signs were auspicious.

They consoled him with assurances that the time would come—that it was the especial counsel of Lord Campbell that they were not to strike until the arrival of the British army, which, according to his secret dispatches to Fletchall (which had determined the course pursued by the latter), was already on its way for the coasts of Carolina.

"And what am I to do with my bird?" demanded O'Brien, as he still held Fletchall tenaciously by the throat, threatening him occasionally with his knife.

"Oh! let him go," said one of the company; "he's nothing but a barn-door fowl."

"And, therefore, the more proper for the spit! But be off!" said the Irishman, and giving the crestfallen colonel a kick—"Be off, and thank the color of your feathers for saving you from my tender mercies!"

Fletchall disappeared with all expedition, followed shortly by Browne, Cunningham, Kirkland and the rest of the chiefs. These all sought Fletchall's quarters, the better for their future conferences.

That night Orrin O'Brien was made happy by receiving from Drayton a lieutenant's commission, with instructions to report to Colonel Hammond, at Snow Hill.

The party of Drayton had escaped a great danger. But for the policy of Fletchall, in preventing the appearance of his whole regiment upon the ground, and but for the timely attendance of so many of the associated Whigs, the pernicious and wild eloquence of Browne, enforced by the miserable exhibition which he made of the treatment he had received, would have prompted to a general massacre. It was yet to have its effect, and the savage temper of Browne was yet to find a fitting auditory, prepared to follow his insane, but still wonderfully capable guidance. He would yet have a command of his own, despite of the Fletchalls and others, whom he held to be but phlegmatic workers in the pious mission which he kept before his eyes. But we need not anticipate.

The crowd dispersed, after hearing an exhortation from Drayton to be vigilant and active. He had brought over several of the officers of Fletchall's regiment, and distributed commissions among them. He urged upon them a speedy organization, being now satisfied that the highland country, under its present leaders, and with its existing prejudices, was not to be conciliated till after a blow, or many blows, had been struck, and much precious blood spilled unnecessarily.

Nor were his apprehensions limited to himself. The crowd that heard his voice, proceeding in groups to their several homes, discussed the prospect from their own points of view, and by their instincts, perhaps, rather than their reason, came to a like conclusion with himself. They were an excited people—somewhat bewildered, but now, for the first time, realizing in mind the prospect of terrible civil commotions, to say nothing of a foreign war.

It was now clear to them, as to Drayton, that the loyalist leaders were fully possessed of the idea of both—nay, that the secret thought of several among them was of the importance which they were to derive from it socially, and possibly of the profits which it would ultimately bring. He and his party, which increased in numbers as it went, now took the route again towards the Savannah river; Drayton and Tennent dividing their labors between the people of Augusta, the neighborhood of Snow Hill, Colonel Hammond's residence, the Ridge, and what was then called the Long Cane Settlement. They had still a great deal of work before them in the effort to mould the opinions of a population so sparsely settled, and so little possessed of the means of information. Drayton was soon to hear tidings which would render it necessary that he should put off the civilian, and put on the soldier. In a brief period Kirkland was at the head of an army of nearly two thousand men. But of this hereafter.

# CHAPTER XIV.

## BROTHER AND SISTER.

While these events were occurring in the highland country, the convalescence of Walter Dunbar had been steadily going on. He is no longer the occupant of the bachelor lodgings of his friend, Martin Joscelyn. He is restored to his father's house, if not to his affections. There he finds Mr. Alison installed in place, almost as one of the family.

This guest does not please him, nor, indeed, does he please Mr. Alison. The latter is a very good looking gentleman, a few years older than Walter, and carries himself with a degree of complacency which would seem to indicate his own conviction that he is also by many years the wiser man of the two. He has a cool, composed and patronizing way about him, which is particularly annoying to Walter. He is already quite at home in the family—spends much time in conference with old Dunbar, from which the son is excluded; disposes himself at length along the sofa, even in the presence of the ladies, and discourses to the ears of these, both aunt and niece, in the style of an ancient intimate or connexion of the family, dropping most of the usual ceremonial forms of address in speaking to or with them, and placidly assuming for himself a position in the household which hourly makes Walter more and more distrustful of his own. He bears with these things as well as he can, in deference to the guest whom his father seems greatly to favor; but he writhes under the annoyance, and will probably break out in wrath under some future provocation.

But, in regard to *his* feelings, Mr. Alison gives himself but little concern. He is a tall, well made, and rather handsome person, of dark complexion, but good features, with fine dark eyes, and an expansive profusion of whiskers and moustache. But there is a something sinister in the expression of his face, and especially in his eyes.

His countenance rather repels confidence and provokes suspicion. But his manners withal are soft and soliciting. He speaks in low tones, and always with the air of one whose relations with you are especially confidential. It was this peculiarity of the man which caused Walter to dislike him from the first; especially when he found him sitting closely beside his sister, Annie, on the sofa, his head half inclined towards her as he spoke, and his tones so subdued as to reach no other ears in the apartment.

Walter thought of his friend, Martin Joscelyn, and grew jealous, at once, on *his account*, nay, he grew jealous of his sister—jealous and angry—and summoned her to a private reckoning, on the strangeness, if not significance, of this newly-born intimacy with a stranger, and one, too, who seemed so very willing to presume upon it.

"And what would you have me do, Walter? He is the guest of our father, and seems to possess his confidence."

"But that is no good reason, Annie, why he should have yours."

"And who says that he has?"

"It looks very like it!"

"Perhaps so; and I confess I do not like that it should wear this appearance, but—"

"Ah! you do not?"

"No! it distresses me at times. But I see not well, so long as he forbears offence—"

"But this *is* offence!"

"Not so, my dear brother. It is, perhaps, not good manners, and it may argue presumption; but, on the other hand, it may be simply a way that he has."

"Gentlemen, in society, are required to have *good* ways and good manners, and it is no excuse for presumption or impertinence to say that it is only a person's way."

"Very true, Walter; but it would be an error to describe this person's conduct either as impertinent or presumptuous. It is a little too free and familiar for my taste, I confess; but does not actually pass beyond the bounds of propriety."

"I will take him to task on the subject! I will set him right!"

"You will do no such thing, my good brother," answered the girl, now very earnestly, and with something like alarm in her manner; putting her hand on her brother's arm, and fixing upon him a steadfast and commanding look, which became her fine countenance well, as indicative of a degree of character which her very feminine style of beauty would hardly lead the spectator to expect. "You will do no such thing, my good brother, for mischief would follow."

"What! do you fear for me?" he demanded, impatiently.

"I am not talking of fear or thinking of yours. But this man is our father's guest, and comes here, as I take it, on business of importance. Any step of the kind that you propose would drive him from the house."

"And that's what I want to do!" the young man vehemently exclaimed.

"Oh! Walter! how can you think of such a thing? Drive him from the house."

"Yes, I tell you—drive him from the house, on my father's account, if not on yours."

"Do not give yourself any anxiety on my account, Walter, and really I do not see why you should be apprehensive on account of father."

"This fellow is here on business of mischief! I know it! He comes from Cameron. He is an emissary from the up-country, where they are brewing more mischief than the country can swallow with safety, and heaven knows what will be the end of it! This man makes our father's house a place of rendezvous for all sorts of people. He and they come and go almost at pleasure, and they come and go altogether by night. They will involve our father in their meshes of mischief—involve him, at his time of life, in political entanglements which may bring down ruin on his head and ours. I tell you, I am very apprehensive of the consequences of this man's presence in our dwelling."

"And I confess, Walter, I share in all your apprehensions and anxieties. It is as you say; but I do not see how *your* interference, or mine, can help the matter. You know our father's passionate nature too well to suppose that either of us can guide or influence him in any respect, where his will is once finally settled; and any attempt on your part to drive this stranger from the house, would end in you yourself being driven out! Nothing could possibly enrage our father more than that he should fancy you entertain any such purpose. Our policy is to treat this guest as civilly as possible."

"And so you are to entertain him, when he pleases to seat himself beside you on the sofa—his head inclining towards you, as if the next moment he would lay it on your lap—"

"Hush, Walter, don't be silly now."

"Ay, but it does look so sometimes, Annie; and then his whispering conversation in your ears alone."

"And how can I help that? You men are all so conceited, that it seems to be taken for granted among you that any and every earnest attention to a woman is sure to be successful in snaring her fancy."

"And, by Jupiter, there is but too much truth in the notion,—certainly it is a very common secret of success."

"Perhaps so, Walter; but please do not suffer your dislike of this man to possess you with the notion that he either likes me or I him, or that—"

"But I half suspect, Annie, that you do."

"You should know, Walter, better than anybody else, where, and upon whom, my liking is placed, and should think better of your sister—should, by this time, know her better, than to indulge in any such unjust suspicions."

"Ah! poor Martin! How would he relish to see this impudent fellow sitting beside you on the sofa—half reclining on it, his head bent sideways, looking upwards in your face, and speaking in those soft, subdued tones which are so pleasant in a woman's ears and fancies, as so expressive of the humility in a lover's heart! How do you think Martin would feel at beholding such a picture—a picture that I myself am forced but too frequently to see!"

"And to which I find it very painful to submit. But, as my father beholds it, Walter, I do submit; and I trust that Martin's confidence in me would not be lessened, were he even to behold it. One thing I will say to you—this relation between Mr. Alison and myself never occurs except in the presence of the family, and it is never suffered by me to continue very long. You will have remarked that, when he assumes this attitude and manner, I very soon contrive, not only to leave him, but to leave the room. Let this content you. You may take for granted that I will not suffer any trespass on the part of any guest, and shall be quite able, without your interference, to protect myself against Major Alison's freedoms, whenever they shall become impertinences."

"What! he is a major, is he?"

"So father styled him only yesterday, and complimented him on his commission."

"Then it has only just reached him. My father's compliments could only be given, in that case, to an open loyalist—so that we know where he is in this struggle."

"And where my father assumes *you* to be also, Walter."

"Ah, my dear Annie, *there* is my black dog! It is that trouble that haunts me, day and night, and takes from me strength and courage! I know not *where* I am! I doubt! I doubt! I cannot free myself of the doubts that assail me on every side. There is right and wrong on both sides; neither seems to be unmixed of good and evil. My sympathies are with my friends, rather than my father; and he would coerce me by his authority, regardless of all argument. My opinions are fully with neither party, and in some degree I concur with both. The colonies—our people, surely have their rights, but the crown has its rights also; and I hold these rights to be the stronger, for that I doubt if the colonies are yet quite strong enough to go alone; and what is to bind these colonies together when the cohesive influence of the crown shall be withdrawn?"

"But, Walter, the leaders in this popular movement do not meditate separation from the crown."

"So they say; but it must come to that finally, should the first step be taken, and should their united force be sufficient to resist the arms of the crown in the event of war."

"But, is it likely that war will follow?"

"I fear it; indeed it has begun already. King and Parliament have both declared for coercion—pride and interest, in them, unite to make coercion seem the proper policy. There will be no effort at conciliation, where one of the parties assumes its own strength to be supreme and *knows* the other party to be feeble. In all such cases, pride becomes passion—passion puts on the worst form of arrogance, and turns a deaf ear to right, justice, reason, law—all the securities of states and empires. I know not where to turn and how to decide, and my father leaves me no choice. His will—"

"Have you none of your own, my dear brother?" and she looked with eyes of intent inquiry into his own, as she asked the question.

"Has he ever allowed us any, my dear sister? Does he not still rule us as mere children, to whom he can say now, as he did when we were so: 'Go there and come hither'? It is this conflict in my heart, between my sympathies and my father's authority, to say nothing of my own conflicts of opinion, that crushes the very life of manhood out of me —that caused me to discredit my manhood on that miserable day— ah!"

And, with his whole form writhing under the bitter memory, while the big, hot, scalding tear drops dilated in his eyes, he turned away from her, and paced rapidly the chamber.

She followed him—she put her arms around his neck, and while her own eyes filled with tears, like his own, she said:—

"Alas! my poor brother! You are not yet strong enough for thought. Your strength will come back to you in season. But, *go from hence for a while.* Here, you have too many associations calculated to embitter thought and to enfeeble will. Go down, and visit Angelica, and forget these miserable politics, and lose the memory of your defeat, as you call it, which Martin, by the way, says you most strangely exaggerate. He says you spoke as well as any man could, whose heart was not in his speech."

"Aye, he was right! My heart was not in my speech, Annie; but the worst is, I know not where my heart is, or whether I could do justice to either argument. My father stands between me and all thinking; and even though he be right, in his opinions, yet I feel that I should never heartily adopt the same conclusion, so long as the denial is made of my own right to work out the problem freely for myself. Do you see—do you comprehend, Annie?"

"I do—I do, my brother! But go and visit Angelica. Spend a week or two on Beach Island. She will show you where your heart is, I fancy, and will so nourish it, on wholesome food, that you will come back with a better *will,* working finally to a right conclusion. I do wish that you *could* think fully with Martin. I am sure that *his* heart is in the right place, for his head goes fully with it."

"You and your Martin! That swallow! And your perfect faith in the wisdom of his twitter!"

"Do not laugh at Martin, Walter. He is a good friend of yours."

"Do I not know it? I love the dog as if he were my own brother. I believe that but for him and you, I should not now be a living man."

"And Aunt Janet, Walter. Do not forget her, and her good nursing."

"Dear old aunty! But I must consult her about this visit to Angelica."

"Why consult anybody in respect to a matter which your own feelings ought to decide upon in an instant?"

"True!—very true! What was I thinking of?"

"There is your error, Walter! It is your weakness. You are too apt to consult—your books—and other people; and you deliberate so long—you have such a habit of deliberating—you know—"

"That the day escapes me, you would say, while I speculate upon the sunshine. And there is too much truth in what you say!"

"Go and see Angelica! You are now quite strong enough for that, and with her for a while, and a little birding and fishing, when love-making becomes insipid, you will relieve it from all monotony."

"And I am to abandon the field wholly to this fellow, Annie? Is that what you are after?"

"What field—what fellow?"

"This Alison, who threatens to usurp all the rights of our poor Martin."

"Pooh!—for a grown man, Walter, you are a great blockhead! Martin can take care of himself—"

"And you, too."

"I hope so, when the time comes. Meanwhile, be sure of this—I shall amply protect his rights, in the assertion of my own. Have no fears of this visitor, and beware of any collision with him, if only on our father's account. Make your preparations, and set off for Beach Island as soon as possible. You are now well enough, and will hardly be excused if you delay your visit much longer."

"I will try horseback riding to-morrow," said he; "a few days of exercise, in an hour's canter at a time, will find me again at home in the saddle, and, somewhere about the close of the week, I will ride over to Beach Island. By the way, the last note from Angelica had something in it like a reproach of yourself, Annie. It exhibited some pique. What is it?"

"Ah! you must put that matter right. Mrs. Kirkland and Angelica came to see you when you were in the crisis of your sickness. We did not dare to admit them, and they were quite angry at the time. You can easily explain everything. What we did was solely done under the necessity of the case, and with the positive orders of the doctors. Even father was not allowed to see you, and he came, too, on the very same day with them."

"If there be nothing more than that, Annie—"

"There is nothing more, I am certain. But your Angelica is not so much the angel, Walter, as not to find, even in this, a sufficient cause of complaint. It will be for you to see that she has no worse, in your long delay to visit her. With an effort, you might have gone down several days ago. In any case, I should certainly have expected it of you. The truth is, brother, I am of the notion that you are rather too cold as a lover."

"Philosophy, Annie—pure philosophy! The wooing of a man, and a gentleman, must never lack in dignity, and hurry is as adverse to gentility as it is to wisdom. Never you fear that she will be satisfied with me, and if your offence is only what you think it, I fancy I can soon put you right with her."

"You are something of the puppy, Walter, in your conceit, like all your sex."

# CHAPTER XV.

## MAJOR ALISON—THE ORCHARD SCENE.

The person who furnished us the chief subject of conversation in the preceding dialogue of brother and sister, was not insensible to the prejudice against him which he had inspired in the mind, the blood, or the brain of Walter Dunbar. His vanity had saved him, however, from any suspicion of a like prejudice in the bosom of the sister. Nor was he aware, nor did he suspect, that there existed any tender relations between the fair Annie and her modest lover, Martin Joscelyn, or any other person. He had not seen that young man at Dunbar's on any of the occasions when the latter had visited the house; and had every reason to suppose—unless an exception was to be made in his own favor—that her "maiden meditations" were all "fancy free."

But he had no sort of doubt in regard to the feelings of Walter Dunbar. He judged, in some degree, of the moods of the latter, by the feelings in his own breast. These young men, at their very first meeting, had, by infallible instincts, been made conscious of a certain moral antagonism, which no subsequent experience could lessen or remove.

Walter Dunbar found something in the self-complacency of Alison which was enough to offend his own self-esteem, at a single glance. Besides, he found him a familiar guest, in possession of his father's house, and making himself as perfectly at home in it as if his rights were paramount. He appeared, also, to be in possession of the confidence of that father, who had shown himself none. And these were sufficient grounds for annoyance. They kept him moody, if not fretful.

Alison beheld in young Dunbar quite a rival to himself in all personal respects—a goodly figure, a graceful carriage, an easy manner, and a fine, intelligent and expressive face. But these were dashed, in his eyes, by a coldness, distance, and reserve, amounting almost to repugnance, which, without violating any social courtesy or propriety, bade him, at least, to remain at a distance. And, after a few slight attempts at conciliation, which were civilly ignored, he did not repeat his efforts. They met, bowed, exchanged these civilities which were essentials of good breeding while they were in the same household, but had no intercourse beyond.

The ladies of the house, with that nice instinct which informs all well-bred women, beheld, at a glance, the true character of the relations between the two—a discovery, by the way, which led to that greater degree of solicitude, which they both displayed, to minister to their guest with that delicate grace which is the chief charm of hospitality. And this solicitude it was which, in some degree, persuaded Alison that Annie Dunbar by no means shared in the prejudices of her cold, repulsive brother. Nay, he beheld in them a higher significance of meaning, which greatly gratified his self-esteem. The fact that she listened to him submissively, was assumed to signify pleasurable listening. That she replied briefly, only argued a timidity, the result of her consciousness of inferiority. Satisfied that he could talk well, he, like too many others having this "gift of the gab," persuaded himself that he talked *irresistibly;* and, at the very time when Annie Dunbar showed herself most reserved and most languidly indifferent, he grew more and more earnest, and, in his secret heart, felt most confident.

This curious self-complacency, which works so much self-deception in the case of vain persons, possesses a wonderful ingenuity in arguing, from all things, to favorable self-conclusions. A remarkable instance of this occurs in this very connection, and may be given in the very words of Alison himself:

"She *fears* me!" said he to himself, one night, after he had reached his room, and while preparing his toilet for the night.

"She *fears* me! that is certain! She is already conscious of my power over her. She is awed. Humility grows with love. It prefaces the way for love. At first, there is a sense of oppression. The heart trembles, as if under a weight, in the first moment of consciousness, when the assailant approaches—a delicious thrill, that feels like a terror, it is so strange and new, penetrates it to the core. The very tones, soft and low, which are yet so delicious in her case, are yet calculated to affright. Nay, the first burden of the growing feeling becomes almost insupportable. Thus, when I approach her on the sofa, she leaves me; she flies the room; she retires for the night; no doubt to conceal her agitating emotions—perhaps to weep in secret over the strangely delicious feeling of her bliss! It must be so! She has hitherto had no experience, and she flutters, like the bird, for the first time in the snares of the fowler. I know the sex! I know all her symptoms. She will be mine! She is eligible—very beautiful indeed! —as fine a looking creature as I ever saw; of good blood and breed, and very comfortable havings. What more! John Alison!"—here he apostrophized himself—"John Alison, it is high time that you were comfortably settled! Thou hast been too long a rover! Thou must wive! It is the fate which we must arrive at, soon or late, and what better can'st thou do than accept this damsel, who loves thee, or will soon do so; who hath incomparable beauty; a goodly name, and such havings as are calculated to render life passable, even when in bad company? It must be so! It is settled. The question is one of time only, and we are making progress daily."

He combed his long hair, beard and whiskers with much care, and proceeded to bind them up for the night in a copious silken bandanna of many folds.

"Yes," said he, "it is settled! The die is cast. I am decided!—and yet it makes one feel monstrous queer emotions, the idea of making a change so complete in all one's habits and relations. What! surrender one's liberty; become bound only to one household; one woman; to need to consider another before you can pass out of your own dwelling; go upon a journey; dine with a friend; fight a duel; engage in a flirtation! Very queer, indeed! Had I not better consider of this sacrifice a little longer? There need be no hurry, of course. She will keep; and, knowing *me* by this time, it is very certain she will wait! As for the old fellow, I have him under my thumb! The old aunt is something of a puzzle; very civil, yes; very kind and considerate; but she sometimes has a d——d suspicious twinkle in her grey eye, as if she was peeping over at my cards, and knew exactly how many trumps I had left. I must take care to keep my hand in the shadow! As for this youngster, it is clear we are not the men for each other; we shall never get on together. But, as I shall not marry *him*, when I take his sister, I shall see, when I have got *her*, that he mars not me, nor meddles with her! In the meantime, however, it will be well to get him out of the way. He may have a power for evil if not for good; may check a wheel which he cannot himself put in motion. His father doubts him—holds him to be purposeless and feeble—and so, in truth, it would seem that he is. To faint in making a speech!—what a ridiculous affair! He is hardly man enough to do much mischief anywhere; but if I can get him off, out of the way, anywhere, I shall be better able, with less interruption, to carry out my plans. To-morrow—yes! to-morrow! It will come, no doubt, and I shall throw out a feeler on this subject. I have a plan—the very thing! Truly, it is astonishing how quick are my conceptions! I no sooner feel the difficulty than I discover the means of getting over it! That, indeed, is my great virtue. Cameron knows it, and McLeod, and McLaurin. As for Fletchall, you can teach him nothing but obedience. Kirkland, now—but no! he will go off at half-cock, and recoil from his piece the moment he fires! He does not comprehend me; and the great difficulty is to keep him from doing mischief. But I have schooled Cameron sufficiently, and Cunningham has got a head of his own. A little time—a little time—and—the game will be in our hands! We shall then see who will have the mastery in this goodly little colony!"

Successive yawns completed his soliloquy; and, extinguishing his light, after re-adjusting the handkerchief about his cheeks, he threw himself upon the bed.

But he did not sleep, though wearied. There were busy thoughts to keep him wakeful, and a large amount of business on his hands, which thought was yet to methodize and adjust.

While thus engaged in meditation, all his windows being open, he heard a signal whistle without, which so nearly resembled that which had been concerted between himself and certain of his associates, that he was on the point of rising from his bed and attending to it, as he had more than once before had occasion to do, even at midnight. His proceedings, by the way, were, by instructions of old Dunbar, to be neither watched nor questioned.

But he paused. The signal, after a few moments, was repeated; and he then perceived that there was a difference between his own and that to which he now listened, and it was now evident to him that the sounds were produced *from an instrument*, which none of his agents employed. They were too full and sharp to be produced by the mouth or through the fingers. There was one way by which to decide any doubt which he might have. In his arrangements with his friends, if the signal, *thrice* sounded, failed to reach his ears, the party making it was to fling a handful of sand against his window shutters. For this he waited; but in vain. No sand was thrown.

Twice had the signal been given, when he heard the lower back door of the house, which opened upon the southern piazza, cautiously opened. He knew, accordingly, that this signal was not made for him, since it was about to be answered by another party.

Who was that other party? That was a question deserving of inquiry, and, if possible, solution. In those times, when the whole country was in a state of the liveliest agitation; when men and parties were all engaged in secret operations, which demanded every precaution, and when he, Alison, was in a situation so equivocal, and which involved no little danger, he felt the necessity of probing this mystery, even though it might not directly concern himself. His windows, on the southern quarter of the house, overlooked a part of the grounds, the orchard and the garden. He rose cautiously and stole to the window. Very soon after, he discerned a female figure stealing from the house, in the direction of the garden. It was a bright, starlight night—there was no moon; but the light was quite sufficient to see objects in motion, especially where white garments were worn. This was the case in the present instance. Alison soon decided that this figure was that of a woman. In another moment she was hidden from sight in the shrubbery of the orchard.

Scarcely had she disappeared when the figure of a man was seen to follow her, also seemingly emerging from the house. He, too, in a moment after, disappeared from sight.

Here was a mystery. It was now quite eleven o'clock. Who were those persons? What could they be about? The family, like himself, had *appeared* to retire fully two hours before. All had been silent in the dwelling for more than an hour. What could be the meaning of these proceedings? Could they concern him? It must be so! Such was Alison's conclusion, as, hastily dressing himself, as well as he could, in the darkness of his chamber, he muttered to himself:

"This youngster has disappointed his father. He is supposed to be secretly inclined to the rebel party. Can it be that he aims at *me* now, and has he brought his emissaries here? But how about the woman? What hand hath she in it?—and is it the old one or the young one—the stately, withered Miss Janet, or my beautiful, budding Annie? She, too! It is just possible! These women are mostly pestilent rebels, and encourage the men to rebellion. It behooves that I should take watch of these parties and ferret them out! Where lies the fox? We shall see!"

And so soliloquizing, having now dressed himself, he stole quietly into the great passage, down the stairway, and finally to the rear door, opening upon the piazza. The door was unlocked—simply on the latch.

"Yes!" quoth Alison, "they have come out of the house, as I thought."

He made his way out also, but paused to survey the route, to the gate of the orchard; noted that there were certain peach-trees about the area, under whose shadow he might, in all probability, with a little caution, approach the party unseen; and then promptly proceeded on the path.

Suddenly, as he neared the orchard, in which he fancied he already detected several shadowy forms, he came upon a female figure, concealed from him behind a tree, until the moment when he was almost in contact with her person.

It was the action of his merest instinct, to grasp this person by the arm. She immediately gave a slight scream of alarm, wheeled about, confronting the assailant, and disclosed to him—neither the stately Miss Janet, nor the blooming and fair Annie, but the ebony complexion, and African features, and sturdy person of Flora, the sable waiting-maid of the young lady.

Alison dropped her arm, or rather flung it from him, the moment he discovered who she was. He heard a movement in the orchard, and now caught a glimpse of a figure, making quickly towards its deeper recesses. Without pausing to think upon what he was doing, he darted in the direction of the orchard, at the gate of which he found himself, before perceiving that the tall figure of a man stood beside it, quietly resting one arm against the post, and apparently awaiting his approach.

This was Walter Dunbar. In stern accents, the latter asked the intruder:

"Who is this? What do you wish here?"

The position of Alison was now rather an awkward one, and he felt it; but he was not easily abashed, and he replied promptly enough:

"Is it Mr. Walter Dunbar? Ah! I see! I am satisfied, sir."

"And what has satisfied you, sir?—what have been the doubts which have brought you from your bed, sir?"

The subtle man knows that frankness, on certain occasions, is the profoundest policy; and Alison having recovered himself from his first surprise, his ready wit prompted the only reply which could have answered, by way of excuse for his appearance in a scene to which he had not been invited.

"Pardon me, Mr. Dunbar, for this unwitting interview, but, having heard signals which I deemed to be meant for my own ears especially, I obeyed them. This will answer to you for my presence now. You are probably not unaware of the fact that I am here, subject to a summons, at any hour, on matters of equal importance to your father and myself."

The apologetic statement was received in silence. Alison, however, lingered still; his eyes straining in the direction of the orchard thickets. For, by this time, his quick wit had conceived the strong probability that some one, or both of the ladies, were still within the orchard, from the presence of the servant girl, who had evidently been placed as a watcher against surprise or intrusion from the dwelling.

"Well, sir," said Walter, quietly, and with great coolness of manner, "you perceive, sir, that you were mistaken, and that these signals were meant for my ears, and not for yours. If you will oblige me by letting me know what yours are, I shall take care, in future, that mine shall not be confounded with them."

"I am not disposed to trespass, Mr. Dunbar. Good night!"

"Good night, sir."

And, cursing Walter in his heart, chafing bitterly at the necessity of having to apologize, and through the medium of a falsehood, Alison slowly made his way to his chamber.

But not to bed; not to sleep, at all events. Concealed behind one of the latticed blinds, he established a watch upon the area between the house and the orchard, resolved to see what parties should return to the dwelling. Long and wearisome was his watch, and full of bitterness his soul.

"This youngster!" said he, shaking his fist, and clenching his teeth together as he spoke. "This youngster would brave me, if he dared! He shall feel me ere he knows! I will pluck his sting some day! It is clear that he is in my way, and it is probable he thinks me in his. Well!—well! Perhaps! I shall work a traverse for him before long which will square the account, some way, between us. We shall see which is the wiser, if not the better man!"

Meanwhile, what of the party in the garden?

As Alison returned towards the dwelling, Walter followed him till he beheld him re-enter and close the door. Alison was conscious of this proceeding, and it added to his feeling of bitterness and mortification.

Returning to the orchard, Walter called the girl Flora, and motioned her to go before him into the orchard, saying, as she went:

"A pretty sentinel, i'faith!—and, but for her timely squeal, that rascal would have been upon us! But we are safe for the rest of the night. Ho! there, where are you?"

Here he was joined by his sister and Martin Joscelyn, Flora remaining in the background. He reported the nature and source of the interruption, with the excuse for it given by Alison; but while admitting its plausibility, he decidedly declared his doubts of its honesty.

"And now," said he, "it is not to be supposed that this fellow has gone to bed. He is watching for our return to the dwelling. Annie must return by way of the garden and kitchen. She can make her way unseen from any of his windows. Flora shall return from hence over the open court, and I shall follow her, after a certain interval. What say you, Martin?"

"Very good, so far as it goes; but something further may be done towards mystifying, if not scaring, this fellow. The clump of peach and pear trees, near the gate, are all visible from his windows. We can easily wind around these trees, imperfectly seen from the house, simply as human beings, go into shade, wind again around them several times, so as to give him the impression of ten or twenty different persons. This will go far, not only to relieve all suspicions about Annie, but to awaken his mind to a new train of thought, and possibly to a sense of his growing danger, of which I suspect he has had some intimations already."

"A good notion that! The thing can be very easily managed, even with one or two of us. Now, Flora, do you go back to your tree, and see that nobody catches you again. As for you, Annie, I will go with you through the garden and see you safe; so take your farewells at once. And you, Martin, while I am gone, move rapidly around the tree, as soon as you hear my signal, then show yourself as moving down to the thicket where I found you. You must be sure and make your way round by the apple tree but once only, then disappear immediately after. Another signal will announce my return, and, when I reach you, after following your route, we shall be ready, both of us, to repeat the march."

Very soon after this, Alison pricked up his ears, as he heard the former signals repeated, seemingly from the woods beyond, and answered deliberately from the orchard. After a while, he discovered the figure of a man passing quickly across an open space, at the entrance of the orchard, and disappearing immediately. Another, and soon another followed, moving with more or less rapidity. Successive signals, pitched upon different key-notes, reached his senses at certain intervals, and, at length, all was silent.

Next, and not long after, he discovered the figure of a woman emerge from the apple tree under which he had grappled with the maid-servant, and slowly approach the dwelling. She disappeared in the shadow of the piazza.

It was fully an hour after this before he saw any other object, and then came, slowly walking, the figure of a man, whom he took to be Walter Dunbar, who crossed the area as Flora had done. A few moments after, he heard the closing bolts of the door lock shot home, without any precautions taken for deadening the sound.

He was in a fever of anxiety.

"What can it be? What can it mean?" he demanded of himself. "There must have been twenty-five of them, or more! Can it be that this youngster is getting up a troop? I heard nothing of this—and without his father's knowledge or confidence? If so, it must belong to the rebel party. And what daring to have it gather *here*, under his father's very nose! I must work it out! Must get at the secret! If money can buy a negro, I shall get it out of this servant wench!"

There were some further reflections on the part of Alison, before he could close his eyes that night—the conclusion of which we may comprise in a couple of sentences:

"I am evidently no longer safe here. I must change my quarters."

# CHAPTER XVI.

## FOOT PRINTS.

The next morning Walter Dunbar failed to make his appearance at breakfast. He had ridden forth at day light, and his absence occasioned no inquiry, and remained unaccounted for. Mr.—as we shall henceforth distinguish him—Major Alison was in the breakfast room ere the advent of the old Baron. There he encountered Annie, alone, preparing the table. He scanned her countenance with keen glances of inquiry, but without effect. Her face, in this instance, was no telltale. Nothing could be more calm, artless and dignified. There was no troubling consciousness in her eyes, significant of concealment, or of the possession of any secret, and the tones of her voice were as smooth and unbroken as if she had slept through the night on a pillow of the most placid and pleasant dreams.

Alison was baffled in his scrutiny. He claimed to know much about women; and, having his vanity on this head, could not easily persuade himself that so young a creature should contrive to escape or defeat his analysis. He was not content, however, merely to look with eyes of keenest vigilance, or listen with ears of the most lively suspicion. He glimpsed at the events of the night. He frankly told the lady that he had been aroused by signals which he had deemed intended for his own ears, and which, at first, he considered as meant to warn him of danger.

"And I need not tell you, Miss Annie, that your father's interests, as well as my own, require our utmost vigilance while I am here."

The lady expressed some natural surprise. She could not exactly see in what respect her father's interests could be comprised in the business of Major Alison. She hoped, indeed, that he was mistaken. At all events, she was not willing to infer that any danger was implied to her father, at least, though, from the language of Major

Alison, it would seem to suggest so much. She expressed herself as anxious for an explanation.

"Too cool by half!" was the inward soliloquy of the Major. "The girl is no fool, by Jupiter! She has had some experience—has been taught her lesson. She still needs to be watched."

His suspicions were enlivened. But the entrance of Miss Janet, and the subsequent appearance of old Dunbar, arrested the conversation, though it did not lessen the keen scrutiny which the Major maintained upon both of the ladies during the repast.

"Where's your brother, Annie?" was the abrupt question of her father.

"He rode out early this morning, sir. He proposes exercise on horseback at present, the better to recover his strength."

The old man muttered something querulous in reply, and the breakfast hour passed off in the talk of the ordinary nothings.

After breakfast the two gentlemen walked out into the grounds, the Major leading the host in the direction of the orchard. While they walked, he told him of the adventure of the night. The Baron was astonished.

"What could it mean?"

The Major revealed his suspicions.

"What!—my own son!—and under my very nose, too! It is monstrous! It is impossible, Major Alison. No, sir!—no! Walter has not answered my expectations. That is true. He has disappointed me, woefully disappointed me, as I said to you before. But he is not treacherous, Major Alison. If he is too cold for the King's cause, be sure that he does not sympathize with the rebels. He is too slow, too indecisive, I know! It is the trait in his character which I dislike and distrust—that which mars his otherwise good parts. But I am well satisfied that he has taken no part with these men. We must find some other clue to this mystery."

"Perhaps so; but how do you account for his presence among these men, for the watch he kept, and—"

"You say that there were many of them?"

"I counted no less than twenty of them, at different times, moving to and fro; and see here to the numerous tracks, all of men's feet, under the trees—see here—there—"

"By Jove, there are also the tracks of a woman."

"So there are!" exclaimed Alison, with well-acted surprise; then added quickly—"and, by the way, I did distinguish the servant girl, Flora. I saw her, apparently on the watch, under the apple tree, just before the gate."

"The Jezabel! I must see to her! She shall answer! What! Treachery in my own household! Walter Dunbar shall answer this—shall tell me all, and so shall the wench. I will have it out of them, though I have to tear it out of their very hearts."

"Softly, softly, my dear sir. This will never do. It is the worst policy to let those parties know that they are suspected. It is better that we should discover their game, without seeming to overlook their hands. More of this hereafter. In the meanwhile, it is my policy to change my quarters as soon as possible. I shall do so this very night, taking a trip down to the heads of Ashley, where I shall hope to see or hear from Lord William."

"Don't forget the commission."

"Do you persist, sir, in that?"

"Do I live? Will I eat, drink, sup, sleep, swear, fight when the need calls for it?"

"But you will not be needed, sir. Your age——"

"It is not infirmity, Major Alison. Do not fear for me, Major. I can ride as well as ever. You do what I request—what, indeed, I have the right to demand. It is, perhaps, proper that you should go from hence for a while, especially if the rebels are really busied in my own household. But I will see to them."

"Do nothing rashly! Our fruit is not yet ripe. We must not move till his Majesty's fleet is known to be upon the coast, and his armies prepared to effect a landing. A blow then, simultaneously struck, in the highlands, the middle country and the seaboard, will strike off at once all the heads of the hydra!"

"It is an admirable arrangement!"

"Keep watch here; discover what you can, but do not suffer your watch to be suspected. One thing, however, you can do, as regards your son."

"Ah! yes!—my son! I should like to have your counsels about him! I confess he puzzles me."

"Send him hence! Send him up to your kinsman, Kirkland. There he will be in good hands. He is here under evil influences. I am told that his chief associates are the men, Joscelyn, that brigand Hamilton —he is no better than a brigand—and that arch-rebel, Hammond, of Snow Hill. From such associates, what can you expect? You say that he is indecisive of character?"

"No! I meant not exactly that. He is, I may say, as yet undecided in his opinions—that is to say, he has not yet made up his mind upon the argument, and believes that there are certain inherent rights in the colonies, as colonies, and in the people themselves, and that, in some measure, the crown and Parliament have been the aggressors."

"And who is to decide between them? That is the very plea of the rebels. Be sure that, with these notions, if he still remains undecided, he will not remain so long if he continues to associate with these men. You must separate him from their malign counsels. You must give him safer associates. In the highland country, associating with Cameron, Kirkland, the Cunninghams, Pearis, Fletchall, and our other leaders of the back settlements, most of whom are British, they will bring him right. Send him off to Kirkland with despatches. Take care to write nothing that would commit yourself or the cause."

"What, sir! Do you think that my son would basely steal my secrets?"

"By no means, sir. But he may lose his despatches. They may be stolen, or taken from him by the way——"

"True—true!"

"And you know that, while in his present state of mind, we cannot trust him with our pass-words, our secrets—cannot tell him who are the friends to be trusted on the route—must simply indicate the route, and leave him to his own prudence. I can communicate with Kirkland, and put him in possession of the facts of the case, and of your objects in so disposing of your son. You have one good plea for sending him away in the necessity of changing the air for his more rapid recovery; another in the necessity of sending your despatches by a safe hand; and if his sister should accompany him, it would not be amiss. There, among our friends, and where we are strong, your family would have much better securities than here, where, I am sorry to say it, we are rather feeble. Should your commission reach you also, it is very certain that your chief employment, for a season at least, would be in that quarter."

There was something hesitating in the manner of Alison as he made these last suggestions.

"These are things to be thought of," answered the old man gravely. "In the meantime, Major, will you do me the kindness to take the measure of these *female* shoes? My back was ever too stiff for stooping, and it grows less and less flexible every year."

There were two distinct tracks of female shoes. The old man received the measures in silence, and put them in his pocket. In two hours after, having continued their conference in the chamber of the Baron, Alison retired to his own room, destroyed a pile of MS. notes and correspondence, then packed his valise, had his horse brought forth, and rode off without further seeking to see any of the family.

It may be well to hint that the anxieties of Annie, when she saw the course which the two men had taken, towards the orchard, after leaving the breakfast table, became exceedingly lively. Flora was summoned to her, and the young lady simply pointed them out to the eyes of the negress, where they stood, at the entrance of the orchard.

This was quite enough. Flora disappeared, in what direction none could say. But she, no doubt, satisfied her curiosity, as far as this was possible; for, under Alison's management, the proceedings of Old Dunbar and himself were tolerably circumspect. But at the close, she suffered herself to be caught, crossing the course of the two, as they made their way back from the orchard to the dwelling.

"What have you been dodging about here, young woman?" demanded Dunbar, seizing her by the shoulder, and subjecting her to a sound shaking.

"Oh! maussa, I ain't been dodging at all! wha I had for do tree day in ebbry week?—bin hang out de clothes, for dry 'em."

"You've been in the orchard then, you blasted ——, all the time?" giving her another shake.

"Das de berry place, maussa, where I hang de clothes! Hab for hang 'em dare, 'mong de trees. I ax you for plough-line dozens o' times, for hang de clothes on, but you ain't gi' one!"

Another rough shake, and, with an oath, he dismissed her to her mistress.

In ten minutes after, Annie had possessed herself of an old pair of Miss Janet's shoes, two sizes larger than her own, while the latter she hid from sight. These she put on, walking in them with some difficulty; but she was rewarded for her pains-taking precaution. Hardly had Alison ridden off, before the old man came to her chamber, and, with stupendous cunning, in the sweetest-tempered voice of the wolf, with his claws carefully covered with the fur, he said to her:

"Annie, my child, I am about to ride down to town, and will bring you a pair of shoes. I know you need them."

"Certainly, I do, papa! Thank you! You remember, I begged you to get me a pair fully a week ago"—and, so speaking, she pulled off the capacious shoes of Aunt Janet, which were certainly worn enough to justify the desire for a new pair, and handed one of them to him in the most careless, confident manner. He took the shoe, and put it into his pocket. He was too prudent to apply the measure at the moment, though so eager to do so, that he hurried at once to his own chamber for this single purpose. The result was a not ungrateful disappointment.

"I am glad she was not there!" he exclaimed, with a sense of relief. "It would be terrible if I could no longer trust her!—if both my children should be false to me!"

It was with a little sense of loss to herself, when the shoes were brought home that day, that Annie found herself compelled to consign them to Aunt Janet. That good lady admired them, as a good fit, as well as a neat shoe, put them carefully away in her drawer, and forgot all about them for a month, until, indeed, it became absolutely necessary to throw away the old ones. And the good old Baron, satisfied, himself, in the first instance, gave no more heed to so small a matter.

## CHAPTER XVII.

### APRIL CONTRASTS—SMILES AND TEARS.

Walter Dunbar did not return home that day, nor the next, nor the day after. He had found his canter so pleasant, and so little fatigueing, that he continued on his way to Beach Island. He had, no doubt, purposed the visit to his *fiancée* before starting, as he took the precaution to carry with him his valise, stored with sufficient changes of clothing for a few days. His father—a thing very unusual with him of late—was curious in respect to his prolonged absence, which it was easy for his daughter to account for. The old man was aware of his son's engagement with Angelica Kirkland, of which he did not disapprove. He only said, grimly, when he heard of it:

"Well, if she is a fool, she's a beauty, and a good-natured creature enough. I suppose she will answer as well as any other."

The stern old Baron entertained no very profound, though some natural, opinions of the uses of women.

Walter met with something more than a cordial welcome from Angelica. That young lady was not the person to suffer her sense of female dignity to silence the expression of her feelings or humors. She was all delight, and all reproaches—the reproaches so seasoned with delight as to render them grateful to the ears which they yet appeared to assail. She hung upon Walter's arm; she leaned upon his shoulder; she wept, and laughed and sang, in the midst of her reproaches.

"And you are come at last; and you could keep away from me so long. Oh! Walter, how could you have the heart! And there was that stiff, old, grumpy aunt, and that cold-hearted sister of yours—and the old Turk, your father—to think that they should drive mamma and me away from your very doors, when we came to nurse you! It was so mean of them, Walter—so cruel!—and you were so ill! I thought I should have died when I heard it! I was so miserable! I couldn't rest, until mamma took me up to town; and, after we got there—got to the very door—to be turned away, and not let to see you! It was shocking, Walter! Mamma was very much insulted, and so was I, Walter! I really felt as if I could have slapped the face of that crumpsey old maid; and if *he* had not been your father, Walter, I'd have——"

"Pulled his hair, of course!"

"Yes, indeed! I was very much provoked to do so, anyhow!"

"But you'll forgive them all, Angey, since they have made me well?"

"No, I won't!—not in a hurry, at least; for why should I and mamma not be permitted to make you well? I had as much right to be with you as any aunt and sister in the world; and everybody knows that mamma's one of the best nurses in all the country! No; it was their own jealousy and spite, Walter; they are jealous of me, Walter. They know that they don't and can't love you as much as I do, and they hate me for it, Walter. That they do!"

And she mingled these reproaches with alternate tears and laughter, and pretty petty changes of manner—a child caprice of poutings and endearments, which men of sense will always tolerate in a beauty of eighteen.

"Hate you! Pooh! pooh! Angey, what nonsense are you talking? There never were more loving aunt and sister in the world. They love you almost as much as I do."

"No, indeed, they love *you!* but they're jealous, too, because *you* love *me*. They think you love me better than you love anybody besides; and, is it not so, Walter? Now, tell me, is it not so? Don't you love me more than anything in the world besides? Now tell me so, if you wouldn't have me hate you, you great bear of a man."

She had her arms about his neck the while she spoke.

"Let go, you monkey! You'll choke me!"

"I mean to do it, if you don't say what I tell you!"

"Oh! I'll say anything to get free from such a monkey! There, take *that* for your answer—and *that!*—and *that!*—and *that!*"

It became her turn to cry out against suffocation, since his kisses, for a brief space, completely silenced her prolonged strain of girlish eloquence, by the simple stoppage of her mouth.

"Oh! you creature! You will kill me! And see what you've done with my beautiful ruff and neckerchief! You'll have to give me another, Walter, and it must be a beauty."

"Oh! you shall have a dozen, only no more reproaches of Annie and Aunt Janet. I tell you, foolish girl, it was their nursing that saved my life."

"And I tell you mine would have done the same thing—mine and mamma's."

"No! no! You'd have killed me. You couldn't have kept that little Italian tongue of yours still for a moment, and I couldn't have borne any excitement, Angey. Why, child, I had brain fever!"

"Oh! that was all pretence, Walter. How could you have had brain fever, only from making a speech, and you a lawyer, too, whose business it is to make speeches?"

His face became white, then purple! That allusion to his luckless speech was not calculated to call up pleasant memories. He put her from him, and she beheld the sudden grave change in his countenance; but, with that levity of habit, which was so much her girlish characteristic, she would still harp upon the one offensive string.

"Oh! it bothers you, does it? You don't like to hear of it! You want me to think you a very great man, that can't fail in anything! But, you are not perfect, Master Walter; you are not the very great man you think yourself."

He still looked annoyed. His self-esteem made him uneasy; and, seeking to change the subject, he asked abruptly:

"Where's your mother and Grace, Angey?"

"What! You're tired of me already? What do you want with them? They'll come in when it suits them; and, let me tell you, mother will be in no hurry to see you. She was terribly vexed with Miss Janet and Papa Dunbar, when they turned us from the door, and I was vexed, too, and so broken-hearted that I vowed never to speak to you again. Never!—never!—never!"

"Pretty Poll!" said he, caressing her.

"Now, don't you be laughing at me, Walter."

"Do I look like laughing?"

"No! you are looking like the great bear which you are. I don't believe you, Walter. I don't believe you have as much love for me as would lie on the point of a needle."

"Let it be a large one, Angey."

"Get along! since you don't love me! Here, it's been more than three weeks that you've been well, and you haven't been to see me in all that time. What do you say to that?"

And pouts and smiles were the natural accompaniments of this speech, to be hushed and stimulated by kisses.

Oh! this child-play of lovers! Angelica was just as silly a sweetheart as Shakspeare's Juliet, without her delicate sensibility. She had something more of the hoyden about her. She had more flesh and blood than Juliet, and a more solid physique, without that refinement of heart and manners in Juliet, which depends equally upon organization and the superior training of society. Angelica was not the woman to rise above her training, or to find the fancies which lie latent in the affections.

The scene was interrupted by the entrance of Mrs. Kirkland, who, rather cold and stately at first, was, however, too kind-hearted to nurse an angry feeling. She, too, had her complaints about the rudeness of old Dunbar and Miss Janet, but the stress of her anger fell chiefly upon the latter.

Women rarely forgive each other. For men, usually, there is a secret ally in the heart of all the sex, which makes them tolerate, in the case of the tougher gender, what they can never forgive thoroughly in their own. Walter, himself, was soon excused, as being wholly ignorant of the mortifying denial to which they had been subjected. He pleaded for the forgiveness of his aunt and father, by referring to his own extreme condition, and to the imperative orders of the physicians, but the old lady had her reply to all this.

"Your father had to do what was told him, of course," said she, "and they scared him about you, Walter—"

"But I *was*, really, in a bad way, my dear madam; Dr. Ford says it was touch and go with me. Even my father was not suffered to see me."

"Of course, you were in a bad way, but not so as to need that *we* should be kept from you. That was all your aunt's doings, Walter. She has such a conceit of herself as a doctoress and nurse, that she thinks nobody can do anything in a sick room so well as herself."

He replied gravely:

"She certainly did the best for me, Mrs. Kirkland, and so did little Annie. Never were persons more devoted. Day and night——"

"Oh! of course! They deserve great credit, Walter; and we ought certainly to be grateful to them, and to God, that you are well now."

"I am not yet strong enough," he said, "to be considered well; and, if you will permit me, I will throw myself down upon your sofa for a while. I feel myself quite tired."

"Oh! do so! I had forgot. And you rode over here since breakfast."

"Before breakfast, ma'am."

"And you have eaten nothing? Bless me! How thoughtless I have been—and you, too, Angelica! How could you keep Walter so long, listening to your nonsense, and never once think of asking him if he had had any breakfast?"

"Oh! I never thought of it, mamma. How foolish it was to start before breakfast, Walter."

"Well, don't reproach him, since, I suppose, it was his anxiety to see you that made him forget whether he had eaten or not. And now, why don't you go and get him something?"

"Why, what shall I get him, mamma? What will you have, Walter? I really don't know, Walter, what we've got in the house."

"Oh! you good for nothing! I shall have to get Grace to see to it, after all. You must have a biscuit, Walter, and some of Grace's blackberry wine. Grace!"

And, at this very moment, Grace presented herself, unsummoned, preceded by a servant, bringing in a salver, with biscuits and the wine.

Gently and affectionately Grace came to him, and took his hand.

"Dear Walter, I am so glad to see you again. How do you feel?"

"Thank you, Grace, better. But do not expect me to rise for awhile. I feel temporarily exhausted by my ride."

"Do not rise! Take a cracker and swallow a cup of blackberry. It is of my own making, but it is pretty good."

He drank the wine, approved of it, and took a biscuit. Grace suddenly left the room, returning, a few minutes after, with a couple of pillows.

"Put these under your head, Walter. There are no cushions to this sofa."

He raised his head, and she disposed the cushions under it.

"Ah!" said the mother, thoughtfully. "Grace is so thoughtful! She is worth a dozen of *you*, Angelica!"

Walter did not exactly think with the mother; but he had a dim consciousness, at that moment, that it would be much the better for him could the two girls be blended into one.

Grace blushed at her mother's compliment, and, as Walter beheld it, he fancied that there was something now of Angelica's beauty in the sad, plain, pale face of her sister at the moment.

"I never thought of it, mamma," said Angelica, excusing herself.

Walter recollected a maxim of Miss Janet, his aunt—it was an awkward recollection:

"True love is the most *thoughtful* of all things! It loses half in its consideration of the thing it loves."

It was agreed that Walter needed rest, and Angelica was with difficulty persuaded that she, as well as her mother and sister, had better leave him where he lay. It was pleasant summer weather still, though cooling gradually into autumn.

When Walter awakened from his sleep, he discovered that some thoughtful hand had spread a shawl over him while he slept. He wished it might have been Angelica. He feared that it was Grace who had done it; and he was right.

How frequently, in absolute conflict with the passions and the sympathies of men, are the righteous instincts of their minds. This conflict between the two—when shall it be reconciled for the promotion of human happiness?

Had Walter but heard the few sentences that passed between his sweetheart and her sister, as they left the room together—with flashing eyes, said Angelica:

"You are quite too officious, Grace. If you hadn't been so forward, I should have got the biscuits and the wine, in a few minutes more; and surely there was no just need of hurry; and why couldn't you tell me, in a whisper, and let me get the pillows for him? Then mamma wouldn't have found fault with me in his hearing."

"I am sorry, Angey, that I did not think of it, or I would have done so," was the meek reply. "But you had been for some time alone with Walter, and I prepared the waiter with the wine and the biscuit, to be sent with you, long before I went in myself."

"You are not always so thoughtless, Miss Grace," said the other, glancing sharply at the unconsciously offending sister, and hurrying up to her own chamber, where, for an hour she will sit, hand in lap, looking out upon the pleasant landscape, while brooding over the prettiest butterfly fancies that were ever engendered in the sunshine of a thoughtless brain. And so brooding, as the soft, mild airs of the south float in through the lattice, she will gradually sink into a muse, which shall become a slumber, from which she will awaken only to be disturbed with the difficulty of choosing the most charming costume with which to please the eye of a lover.

Meanwhile, Walter, too, will have slept—needing sleep, indeed, not only because of the fatigue of his morning canter, but because of the few hours which he could appropriate to sleep during the previous night.

He awakens to find Mrs. Kirkland quietly sitting in her oaken rocking-chair, and busied, spectacles on nose, with her basket of work beside her, and the half knitted stocking growing beneath her hands. Grace next will enter, in garments as homely as her face, but neat and well made; and she will pass to and fro, from one room to the other, while she attends to the affairs of the household, and duly prepares all things for dinner. She mingles, while passing, in the chat which goes on between her mother and Walter; but with stray sentences only. It is only when the hour of dinner is approaching, that Angelica reappears upon the scene; gliding in like a sylph, with all her charms in full color, and showing in the brightest vestments of her wardrobe. She is all smiles, and she glides at once to the sofa, takes her seat beside Walter, puts her hand upon his shoulder, looks lovingly into his face, hopes that he has recovered from his fatigue, and assures him that she would not have left him for the world, and would have been with him long before, but that she would not disturb his slumbers! Dear little thing—she said nothing of her own!

And, as he gazed upon her exquisite beauty of face, and grace of person, he had no misgivings. His eye was a false medium to his mind, and his judgment was blinded by his sense of the beautiful. He surrendered himself to his fancies,—to the sensuously susceptible of his nature, and the warm, fond kiss, from her exquisitely fashioned mouth, bestowed with a fairy laughter, the moment her mother had left the room, seemed to set the seal of perfect security upon his bonded bliss.

The call to dinner brought back the dreaming pair from elysium to earth. We are sorry to say that Angelica had a better appetite than Walter. We do not know that he observed it. Grace, the quiet house-keeper, had done her best, with the few resources of the simple world in which the family lived, to show to their guest how welcome was his visit; and, though Walter showed but little appetite, yet he was in the best of spirits, and so behaved as to make it seem that he felt himself happily at home. From the dinner table to the parlor, from the parlor to the garden, from the garden to the grove, Walter and Angelica wandered through the long sweet hours of the summer afternoon; and sitting, with hands clasped together, upon a fallen trunk of the forest, they counted nothing of the fleeting moments, until the sun suddenly confronting them with his rays, full on the line with their eyes, stared boldly in their eyes for a moment, ere he sank out of sight beyond the long range of forest-crowned hills, that makes, from the Carolina side, the loveliest of landscape hedges, skirting the yellow waters of the Savannah a wide stretch, along the prolific plains of Georgia.

What they said, of what they thought, in how much idle and pretty matter they indulged, what need we repeat? The subject matter of speech, and modes of thought and feeling, among young lovers, of the Italian type, are sufficiently well comprehended by all classes of readers, and it will suffice if we refer them to the proper manner and mode, in the love-play *par excellence* of the great master, which gives us the pathetic tragedy of the rival houses of Montague and Capulet.

This sort of child's prattle rarely interests or satisfies third parties —reader or spectator. With cool heads, and hearts but little inflamed by sympathy, we see, as spectators, the singular childishness, which is yet the peculiar charm to the parties, in an early or first attachment. It commends itself to the masculine heart, whose fancies have already been beguiled by its very childishness. This argues for simplicity, for truth, and nature, and a trusting confidence which appeals always successfully to the masculine, or the more powerful mind, wherever it is magnanimous. And so the grave man listens gratefully to the simple prattle of the child, who looks up to him appealingly for the satisfaction of a juvenile curiosity. It is not difficult to understand, therefore, why it is that the affections of the grave and wise are so frequently won by the simple and unintelligent. The very play and caprice of the beautiful child is a charm in itself, as it argues for confidence in the sterner nature before whom it may wanton, and remain unbidden and unchecked. If the child-talk of Angelica, beautiful idiot as she was, was a pleasure to the ears of Walter Dunbar, it was because of the tacit avowal which it made of equal confidence and dependence. He might smile sometimes at its simplicity, even when that became silliness, but it was the simplicity or silliness of a heart which, like a shallow fountain, prattles sweetly of its innocence, without requiring that you should sound its depths. The shallowness of the fountain does not lessen the charm of its song, which delivers itself freely, keeping none of its secrets hidden from your eyes or ears. In like manner were the sterner nature, and deeper thought, and more earnest passions of Stephen Joscelyn beguiled by the same transparent prattler, even though it sometimes vexed his intellect, that it should find itself so completely enthralled by so shallow a charmer.

But the spoiled beauty was not simply satisfied to prattle and to charm by the pretty petty play of the child, as expressive in its play as it is lovely in its grace of form and feature. Like most spoiled children, her caprice was too apt to show itself mischievously. It was lacking in the essentials of prudence, and its vanity vexed, or its will opposed, it could exhibit some qualities of evil, which were very easily aroused, showing the reptile, however startlingly beautiful. The very thoughtlessness of a childish nature, unless restrained by judicious training, long continued, will finally egg it on to a mischievous restlessness of mood, in which, having no regard to consequences, it will fire the powder magazine, without ever dreaming of the explosion which is to follow, and once aroused with this mischievous passion of unrest, it will listen to no counsel, and only awake to the truth, to wail over the catastrophe, but not to grow wiser from it.

We are soon to have an instance of this wanton, if not wicked, levity of mood, in the case of the capricious beauty, whose empty prattle was to prove itself not less full of danger than emptiness.

It happened that the next day was the one chosen by Stephen Joscelyn to send for his chamber furniture. He had transferred himself, as we already know, from the house of Mrs. Kirkland, to lodgings at the dwelling of his rustic friend, Dick Marvin. He had, only the day before, written briefly, but kindly and respectfully, to Mrs. Kirkland, to say that Dick's wagon would come, on the second day following, for his goods and chattels. Accordingly, Marvin himself appeared, soon after breakfast, and his wagon was drawn into the court.

It was with sad eyes and a sinking heart that poor Grace attended Marvin to the chamber which she had learned to venerate, and pointed out those articles for removal, belonging to Stephen, each of which, as she beheld it borne forth, filled her heart with a pang, as if at the departure of some precious friend. And there were the books —his little library—how precious to her, as to their owner. From these books he read, almost nightly, to their little circle. From his melodious readings she had imbibed her first sense of the wonderful and various powers and graces of the grand orchestra maestro, Shakspeare. So the notes of the cathedral organ, as struck by the hands of the heaven-inspired Milton, had been made first to reach her soul; and next to him was the Gothic harp, of blended chivalry and nature, which owned its master in the stately and sedate, yet fancy-loving muse of Edmund Spenser.

And these were all gone! And he who had taught her where the true charm lay in the strains of each of these sovereign singers, he, too, was gone; driven cruelly from the house which he had made to her so delicious, and which, in her secret heart, she felt devoutly that she might have made to him so happy. Alas! alas! for that heart-blindness of man, which seeks for its food in a bird song, and wanders off, following a will-of-the-wisp, in the fancied conquest of a star. Alas! for poor Grace, and doubly alas! for the big heart and the crippled spirit, as well as form of poor Stephen Joscelyn!

When all the things were gone, meted out to Marvin, by the girl's own hands, book by book, with sometimes a tear falling upon the almost sainted cover, she hurried to her chamber, and locking the door, threw herself upon the couch, and gave full freedom to the tearful flood that would no longer be suppressed.

There was a knock at the door, she wiped her eyes hastily, choked down the suffocating sobs, and opened to admit her mother. A quick glance of the eye revealed to the mother the tears that still would show themselves in the eyes of the daughter. The mother said nothing, but sadly kissed her, and the sobs of the young woman grew into words.

"Oh! mother, he is gone from us forever! That cruel speech! That cruel speech! It has pierced his noble heart like a sword!"

"No more, my child! I have that faith in Stephen which tells me that he will forgive—that he has forgiven—that all will be made up again between us."

The girl shook her head mournfully, and as the sudden roll of the wagon wheels, now moving off, came to her senses, the sobs were renewed, the tears began again to flow, and, throwing herself again upon the bed, she buried her face in its pillows.

The mother sat beside her for a few moments, caressing her in silence, then, as she rose to leave the room, Grace lifted herself partially, kissed her, and said:

"See to the house to-day, dear mother. I had rather keep my chamber. Let me not be seen. I am sick—yes, I feel, mother, that I am very sick—here—here!"

And she pressed her hand upon her heart, as if because of some keen shaft which had just entered it, while her wan face betrayed the expression of an agony, which found its sufficient speech in the deep silence which followed, as the two separated, both in tears.

## CHAPTER XVIII.

### PRETTY, BUT PERNICIOUS PRATTLE.

Walter and Angelica came out on the piazza, preparing for a ramble, just at the moment when the wagon, with Stephen Joscelyn's chattels, was moving off. Walter knew Marvin, and the two had some talk together, which it is not essential to our progress to report. We must say, however, that the young lawyer was seemingly much more cordial than the young farmer. Marvin was rather shy of speech, and indifferent of manner—a matter which seemed equally to surprise and affect Dunbar, who, at length, bade him good morning, and turned abruptly away, rejoining Angelica, who awaited him at the steps of the piazza.

Small things of this sort usually discomposed Walter. He was painfully sensitive to neglect or indifference, and a jealous self-esteem naturally referred such exhibitions to some decline in his own position. It was natural enough that he should be reminded, on this occasion, of the unlucky argument at the public meeting at Augusta. His brow was grave accordingly as he rejoined Angelica, and, half soliloquizing, he said:

"I wonder what can be the matter with the fellow?"

"What fellow?" asked Angelica, as she took his arm.

"Marvin! He was always a good friend, and something of an admirer of mine, and he now seems unwilling to give me even the time of day."

"It's all owing to that hateful creature, Stephen Joscelyn."

"Stephen Joscelyn? Why, what has he to do with it?"

"Everything, no doubt. You see Marvin is hauling away his things now; he lives with Marvin, you know."

"No! I did not know, and I was just about to ask what had become of him, not seeing him, and should have done so, but that I had so much to ask about yourself. When did he leave you, and why? I thought he was your mother's right hand man, and one of the best friends of the family."

"Well, so, indeed, she thought him; but we couldn't well agree, somehow."

"And why do you call him hateful, Angelica? That is a very strong word."

"It's what he deserves. He's hateful and spiteful, and I don't like him."

"Was there a blow up—a quarrel among you—that caused him to leave you?"

"Well, not exactly. Mother and Grace had nothing to do with it, and they blame me for it. You see, Walter, the man is odious to me —a hateful cripple—and he had the impudence to make eyes at me, and follow me about, and talk love talk to me, and all that sort of thing."

"Surely no harm in all that, if he was not impertinent."

"Oh! but he was impertinent. What right had he to think of me?"

"Right? Well! That may be a question, Angey. But did he propose to you?"

"No, indeed! I never let it come to that. I couldn't abide him from the first—he was so consequential, and always spoke to mamma and Grace as if he was laying down the law. And then he would come and sit beside me, and he would read to me love poetry, and look so into my very eyes, like a dying duck in a thunder-storm, until I sickened at the very sight of him."

"But it does not appear to me, Angey, that these were very serious offences on the part of the poor fellow. If men were always to be hated, simply because they loved, pretty women would themselves become the most hateful monsters in creation. You must beware of that danger. You need not have been angry with him for loving you, surely. It was only a gentleman's tribute to your beauty!"

"He a gentleman! And what makes him a gentleman?—a poor deformity; why, it was dreadful, Walter, to see him hobbling after me, from room to room, and into the piazza, and down to the summer-house, always bringing some book in his hand, as if he thought I cared to hear him read. Why hadn't he the sense to see, from the first, that I didn't like him? It was great impudence, Walter, that he should pretend to me, and follow me about just as if I was some of his own property, and I engaged to you all the time."

"But he did not know that, Angey. You know how long it was our secret, even from your mamma and Grace."

"That's true, Walter. But whether he knew it or not, what was his love to me? How should I think of such a creature? How should he dare to think of me, or to suppose that I should care for such as he?"

There was much in all this miserable egotism that revolted what there was of humanity and good sense in the bosom and the brain of Walter Dunbar; but man rarely questions too closely that nature in woman, which, however unjust to other men, still utters itself warmly in his own behalf, and, when beholding her lover look with sad gravity upon her, Angelica put her arms about his neck, and murmured:

"Yes, Walter, how impudent of him to suppose, that, loved by you, I should ever think of him?"—

He replied to her with a kiss and a smile, and the twain walked away together, musing sweet things, into the shadows of the woods, and took their seats beside each other upon the familiar trunk of the fallen tree.

But the thought of Walter was still in a state of unrest, and unsatisfied. He resumed the subject:

"Stephen Joscelyn," said he, "though a cripple, is yet a very remarkable man, Angey; and, though he may err in loving you, yet I do not see that there is cause of complaint in that. That his tastes and fancies should spring like mine, and take a like direction, would argue, Angey, that there was much sympathy between us. I should not count it arrogance or presumption that he should love and even seek you, Angey; and surely there is penalty sufficient for the offence, if offence it be, that he has failed to win your person. If you will permit me, my love, I will say that I think you speak of him quite too harshly. That he is a cripple, is sufficient reason why you should speak of him tenderly, with pity, if not sympathy. The people all speak of him in terms not only of respect, but endearment. He is doing good service to the young of this region. He is known to be a man of talents; your mother, too, thinks highly of him."

"Yes, indeed; she and Grace almost worship him, and they have scolded me, dozens of times, for my treatment of him. But, because my father employed him, and he settled the estate, is that a reason I should love him?"

"Perhaps not! But it is surely a reason why you should treat him with respect and gratitude."

"Gratitude! Why, what has he done, which you would not have done—which any lawyer would not have done? He expected too much for his services; and, the long and short of it is, Walter, that I, at least, told him a piece of my mind, and that was the way we got rid of him at last."

"And it was you and he, then, that had the quarrel?" asked Walter, now looking more gravely than ever. "Angey," said he, "Martin Joscelyn, his brother, is one of the best friends I have, and, though I do not know much of Stephen, I would not, for the world, that *you* should deal harshly with him. For my sake, I would rather you would submit to some annoyances. It was easy to dismiss his pretensions to your hand, without offence or quarrel."

It is possible that but for the earnest tone of Walter's speech, Angelica would have forborne the revelation of the true grounds of her quarrel with Stephen, and the exposure of her own conduct on that occasion. But she was forced to make her defence; and, warmed by the excitement of doing so, especially as she was not unconscious of the weakness of her argument, she proceeded to make her case as strong as possible, without any heed of the consequences to others, and governed only by her own selfish instincts of vanity and passion. The grave tones of Walter's voice were sounding unpleasantly and rebukingly in her ears, and his grave looks were fastened upon her face inquiringly. Including all of Stephen's alliances or sympathies within the sphere of her dislike, she was vexed to learn that Martin Joscelyn was so much and intimately regarded as Walter's friend, and she began her justification in a manner which was greatly calculated to increase his gravity of aspect.

"I'm sure, Walter, I do not see how Martin Joscelyn should be such a friend of yours, or why you should need his friendship."

"But *I* see, Angelica."

"What is he?—what has he got?—what has he done, Walter?"

"He is a *true* man, Angey; he has the virtue of *fidelity;* he has been true to me; he loves me."

"Oh! what is the love of man for man, Walter?"

"It is life over death, in death, through death! It is always a living thing. It is a possession which I would not willingly lose."

"Well, if Martin Joscelyn does really love you so, I'm very sure that Stephen does not."

"How is it sure? I have no reason to doubt that, though Stephen may not love me, as Martin does, for there has never been any intimacy between us, he can have no unkind feeling for me—is friendly, though not intimate."

"But I know better, Walter! I think my first dislike to him arose from what he said about you."

"Ah! what did he say?"

"It was one night, when Martin spent the night with us and Stephen. We were all talking about the people in Augusta, and Martin brought up your name, and spoke well of you."

"I'm sure of that, if he spoke of me at all."

"But Stephen shook his head, and compared you to Macbeth in the play."

"To Macbeth!"

He might well be astonished.

"Yes, he said, like Macbeth, or, as Lady Macbeth said of her husband: 'He is infirm of purpose; he can never succeed in anything.' "

Walter now looked graver than ever. Angelica went on.

"Oh! I was so vexed! I didn't know what to answer, so I said nothing; but the next day, when Stephen was at the school-house, I searched his library, and found the play, and there I read it all, and I found that Macbeth was a murderer and a monster of wickedness. And to compare *you* to such a wretch!"

Walter could not help but smile, though he was somehow very much saddened by what he heard.

"Well! well!—what then?"

"I could see that he did not like you, from that, and to compare you with such a monster, put me in a great rage. I longed to tell him about it; but I did not—and then—"

Here she paused, as if doubtful how to proceed.

"Well?" he enquired, "what next? Is there anything more, Angey?"

"Yes; several times he spoke of you afterwards, and always, it seemed to me, slightingly. But at length he came home from the great meeting at Augusta, and when mamma asked about the speaking, he told that you spoke, and he made fun of your speech, and spoke of you contemptuously, and called you a pitiful fellow."

"Ha! said he that?"

"That he did; and I could stand it no longer. Then I up and gave him a piece of my mind. And so he moved off the very next day, and a good riddance of bad rubbish. I don't care if I never see him again."

The love-making was all over for that day.

The facts reported by Angelica were undoubtedly facts. The conversation had taken place, and the language had been used, with some exceptions, very nearly as reported. But the *suppressio veri*—the absence of those details which would have made all these facts innocuous—had necessarily the full effect of the *suggestio falsi*. The *suggestio falsi* was also there, in the narrative, but it was hardly designed by the speaker. In her passion, at the time, when she heard the last conversation, she had confounded "poor fellow," and "it was a pitiable exhibition," as used by Stephen, as with merely "pitiful fellow," and her jealousy had construed the tone of sympathy and commiseration, with that of scorn and contempt. This was all due, not to any deliberate purpose to misrepresent, but simply because of her prejudice against Stephen, which, wrongheadedly, but naturally enough, in the case of a silly creature like herself, looking on her lover as a miracle, was impatient of the superiority apparent in the language of the speaker, and under the influence of these blinding prejudices, she had failed to note, in the first conversation, that Stephen had spoken favorably of Walter's abilities, though he had added: "I fear, from what I have seen of him, that he labors under that 'infirmity of purpose' with which Lady Macbeth reproaches her lord; and that he will never do anything at the right moment, in the right place, and under the right inspiration."

It was easy for the silly girl, thus blinded by her prejudices and passions, to fall into the errors which she made, and to reverse the truth in the whole character of her relation.*

---

* This is no fiction. The facts, as reported, are of real occurrence, within my own period and circle of acquaintance. The result had nearly been a duel, *à l'outrance*, which was, with difficulty, arrested. It required but an opportunity for explanation to put all the parties *rectus in curia*. The difficulties in the way of an explanation are very great usually, where a lady is in the case, it being a point of honor among gentlemen not to suffer the names of ladies to be involved in any such controversies. It may safely be presumed that one half of the murderous duels fought among men are due to just such miserable representations by silly or malicious people.

She did not design this—she was simply a—fool!

Had she not been such, she would have seen the instant effect which her revelations had produced upon her lover.

As we have said, the love-making was all over for that day; and that was what she could not comprehend. With her, what she had to prattle about, was speedily dismissed from her mind as soon as her own string of prattle was finished.

But not so with Walter Dunbar. He was wounded to the quick. His self-esteem, always doubly sensitive, in the case of one who is conscious of infirmity of any sort, was savagely eager and passionately resentful. To be spoken of in language of contempt, was not to be forgiven or forgotten. In due degree, with the consciousness of defect, will be the virulence with which we visit those who discover the defect; and where our own consciousness is an ally of the discovery, our anger at the discoverer is proportionately great.

Walter Dunbar, as we have said, had no more love-making for the day. The silly girl at his side could not appreciate the result of her own revelations. A creature, herself, of the merest impulse, things went and came, transiently, without making much, if any, impression upon her thoughts, though they did upon her feelings. She had to justify herself, and she did so, without respect to any other considerations.

Not so he.

Walter Dunbar was no fool. He was a man really of considerable talents. He lacked, in some respects, of mind; but he was sensitive, of delicate organization, and, but for a deficiency of *will*, would have been a strong man. Of nervolymphatic temperament, he could arrive at conclusions rightly, *but never in time*, and, with a certain consciousness of this, he was apt to be equally slow and precipitate in action; to hesitate where he should have leapt, and to rush headlong just where he should pause to survey and consider. He was never just where he should be in the moment of action. His training had somewhat conducted to this condition—a different training might have had different results. But there was an inherent defect of character, arising from an undue development of the feminine element in his composition, which no education, perhaps, could have ever wholly overcome; and, deficient in will, his self-esteem lacked that support which would have rendered him less sensitive to the opinion of others. Much of his weakness lay in this respect; hence the terrible mortification under which he succumbed because of his failure at the Augusta meeting. When Sheridan failed in the House of Commons, he exclaimed, with an oath—"I have it in me, and by ——! it shall come out!" The consciousness of intellectual resource, in his case, was sustained by a will, commencing with his self-esteem, and stimulating to new effort. The failure of Walter Dunbar had the opposite effect in depressing his energies, making him doubtful of his own future, and distrustful of every effort which he should hereafter make to retrieve his reputation. He now absolutely shrunk from and shuddered at the idea of boldly facing the multitude, at the Court House, or at the hustings, in the renewal of a practice which had been once his pride, as most successfully begun.

The effect of Angelica's revelations upon him was to bring up again, in full array before his memory and imagination, the painful experiences of the few past months—the complications in his political moral; the failure of his speech; the harsh and cruel denunciations of his father; the disappointment of his friends; the supposed exultations of his enemies; in brief, the thousand humiliations which the thought of a morbid and ambitious mind will conjure up under such circumstances, all tending to the same result, that of keeping down his hope, depressing his energies, and holding ever before him the mortifying suggestion that he had deceived himself with regard to his powers, and that the little world in which he lived had lost all faith in his capacity for performance in the exacting and ambitious profession which he had chosen. He was no longer an authority among men; he shuddered at the idea that he had been a fraud upon himself, as upon them—a mere pretender—a self-deluded imposition.

It was with the greatest effort that he was enabled to preserve something like calmness of face and temper, in the presence of Angelica. He writhed beneath the torture which she so unconsciously inflicted. Before his mind's eye now stood forth prominent, as the embodiment of all his mortification, the form of Stephen Joscelyn. He recalled the unwieldy movements of the cripple; his herculean shoulders; the calm dignity of his face; his noble head and aspect; his dignified bearing, in spite of his deformity; and he cursed, in the bitterness of his soul, that tacit assumption and assertion of superiority which Stephen was described to have made, in his manner and language of contempt and scorn.

Angelica, still prattling, and passing to scores of small topics of the city and the neighborhood, did not see the effect of her revelations. The closely compressed lips, the clenched teeth, the savage glare of eye, all of which denoted the workings within him of the demon which she had so thoughtlessly roused, and which he could not entirely subdue or repress, yet in great degree escaped her attention. It is astonishing how blind a thing is satisfied vanity; how it will, in the exultation of its instincts, continue to goad the sufferings of others, even those whom it would fain soothe and conciliate. To look out from self, and see what eye it is that weeps; to open the ear, and hearken to the moan or the groan of the spirit which it wounds mortally at every look or utterance; to think *from* the necessities of other hearts, and to feel from the inevitable pain in other bosoms; these powers are self-denied to that miserable child, vanity, which is at once the progeny of a sensuous and selfish nature, and a feeble intellect. She could see that Walter Dunbar no longer abandoned himself to that play of the passions which belongs to the intercourse of young people so related as were they, was no longer pleased "to sport with Amaryllis in the shade," and twine "the tangles of Næra's hair," but she could ascribe the change to nothing that she had said; could ascribe it only to coldness, caprice, and the love of change, so natural, as she said, to men; could only repeat her cuckoo note of reproach—the common-places of such a child on such a topic.

"Oh! Walter, you love me no longer. I see it; I feel it. You are so cold; so changeable; just like all your cruel sex, that don't know and don't care what heart you are breaking."

And Walter would make a desperate effort to soothe and satisfy the pretty puppet at his side; would fold her in his arms, and reassure her with reluctant words of homage, coldly uttered, and seal the empty assurance with his repeated kisses; and the silly thing would take the false counters as good coin, and still see nothing of the bitterness that kept working in that soul, which was yet required to pour forth speeches of sweetness, nor the fever burning in those lips, the kisses of which were yet supposed to be those only which contained the honey-dews of love! No; there was no more love-making that day—such as had been before.

## CHAPTER XIX.

### THE BLACK DOG.

No! nor that night. But let us not anticipate.

Fortunately, to relieve the weight of the scene upon the brain of Walter, Angelica suddenly remembered that it was lunch-time. She never forgot lunch-time. She knew when twelve o'clock came, as truly as does the mule, who will, of himself, stop at that hour in the plough. Thoughtless people are generally great feeders. They devolve upon the animal the duties of the intellectual. They take their stimulus for life from the pantry. They brood over cates and meditate dulcas; and with such people, love is simply a form of blended appetite and vanity. Alas! for the hapless wooer, having an active brain of his own, who is beguiled through his merest fancies by a pretty play-thing! Such creatures as Angelica Kirkland are but the play-things of men. Happy for them when, in the lover, they can find the lord, the master—who, with a purpose of his own, having survived his fancies, shall subdue them to some legitimate uses, in the development of which it is possible that each shall find a soul.

They went home together, Angelica still prattling by the way. She had to *do* the whole country. She was one of those creatures who pick up all the local scandal, who find out all the weak places and the sore spots, in the neighboring household—who know just where your shoe pinches—what resources you have in lands, negroes, stock and money—how you have portioned off your children—what you are to expect on the death of your Aunt Jones, or your cousin Thompson, and what were the influences that prevailed upon Susannah Smith, to marry the old widower, Elijah Perkins—she a young girl of seventeen, and he an old fool of sixty-six.

"But he had his carriage, you know, and he could give her all that she wanted; and, may be, she isn't making his money fly. Such a sight as she makes of herself every Sunday in church, with her flowers and her flounces, and her feathers, makes everybody laugh!"

But Walter Dunbar did *not* laugh. He did not even hear. It was lucky for him, in the present state of his mind, that she said nothing which demanded his attention; and she was one of those vain prattlers who are sufficiently well satisfied if there be an audience, whether the parties present be listeners or not.

And so, Angelica, quite satisfied, they reached the house, and found the lunch in waiting. Grace, poor, dutiful girl, had made all the preparations for all other parties, during their absence, and had then retired once more to her own room, and to that solitude in which she could find no relief, but in which she could hope for security.

Walter Dunbar had no appetite. He ate nothing. Angelica had lost nothing of her's; and it was only after pacifying the first demands of the wolf that she discovered the short-comings of Walter—his slowness to discover the virtues in Grace's biscuit; the excellence of Grace's preserved damsons; the merits in Grace's marvels; and the marvelous perfection of Grace's blackberry wine. But though saying grace over all these edibles, while commending them to the appetite of her lover, she was careful not to say the name of Grace once. Vanity, the very silliest, has yet a peculiar cunning of its own. And so again, Angelica, after lunch, persuaded Walter that he needed rest, that his walk must have fatigued him, and, gratified for the suggestion, as a means of escape, he gladly seized upon the chance afforded him to retire to his chamber.

His departure was the signal to Angelica to seek her's also.

Lunch implies sleep, at least in summer—the one succeeds the other as the sparks fly upward—and dinner succeeds the *siesta;* and, after that, by way of sentiment, the love-making follows as a course, properly rounding off the solids. Alas! for the sentiment, when such are the ordinary entertainments in the rounds of life.

Walter Dunbar did not sleep. For two hours previously he had been conscious of an unvarying buzzing in his ears, to which he had to yield them, under a social necessity; but he had found it a terrible task to do so. But Angelica, having much to say, was quite satisfied with a companion who exacted no attention in return.

Now that he was alone, with no drumming or buzzing in his ears, his memory and thoughts became concentrated upon those portions of the prattle of Angelica which so keenly touched upon his self-esteem. It was easy to conceive that Stephen Joscelyn, having discovered Angelica's preference for himself, had sought to lessen him in her regards, the better to make a progress of his own. But, in doing so, Stephen had made a mistake—had put himself *hors des régles*, and was liable, in the courts of chivalry, in an *action on the case*.

Walter, following this miserable conjecture, went over the details of the case, thus grounded in his merest fancies, with all the eagerness of passion. He drew up, in his mind, *seriatim*, all the counts in the declaration. He elaborated them, in imagination, till each became a damnable crime; until—the case fully summed up—Stephen Joscelyn stood before him, in the dock, one of the most atrocious criminals that ever disgraced humanity—as one who, passing between his brother's best friend, and that friend's best hope, had sought to supplant him in his best affections; and, failing in that attempt, had basely sought to vilify and slander him in the estimation of the woman whom he loved!

It was a very shocking case—it will always be a very shocking case, where a morbid vanity and a headstrong passion are the parties to prepare the indictment.

The brain of Walter Dunbar was intensely excited while he revolved all the counts in this his declaration against Stephen Joscelyn. He, Stephen, was the embodied representative of all who had done him wrong; of the orator whose competition had been fatal to him; of the people whose admiration he assumed himself to have lost; of the father whose scorn had spurned him; of the woman whose affections were only not lost to him, by these arts of the offender, because of her unquestionable affection and fidelity.

Beautiful case—very beautiful—and in its preparation Walter grew savagely thoughtful of the extent of the damages.

It is true that, more than once, in reciting his wrongs to himself, the image of the brother of the defendant, Martin Joscelyn, would thrust itself between them, and endeavor to reconcile the parties. *His* devotion to Walter would plead to him, and there would be a momentary misgiving, whether he was doing right; and the question would occur, again and again, whether he had not better let the action drop? But the demon was too strong for the angel, and, before the argument was quite adjusted in his mind, his good friend, Martin Joscelyn, had disappeared wholly from the scene, leaving the case as at first, "Walter Dunbar *v.* Stephen Joscelyn—Slander," &c.

It was remarked by Mrs. Kirkland that Walter ate no dinner. It was remarked that he had eaten no lunch. It was concluded that he was ill; and the solicitude of all parties was aroused to sympathy. Angelica reproached him that he was sick, yet pressed the favorite viands upon him. In order to escape the annoyance of her attentions, and silence the anxieties of Mrs. Kirkland, Walter made a desperate effort at composure; and, as is usually the case with persons who suffer mentally, and would conceal it, he rushed to the opposite extreme, became very gay, very flippant, rather; affected the joyous, and became the noisy, and, through grimace, persuaded himself that he had disarmed suspicion.

He was not a very good actor; but his audience was not very critical. Angelica was easily deceived, and laughed with her lover; her good old mother naturally ascribed the previous gravity of the young man, and his want of appetite, to his late sickness, and continued feebleness; and that he could become the Merry-Andrew was a sufficient proof of improvement. He would be better, no doubt, the next day—only he must not suffer Angelica to beguile him to any more of her long walks. "Angelica is so fond of those long rambles in the woods, especially when she had company that she liked."

He said nothing about the long talks, in which all the mischief lay.

The warning served as a hint to the pretty damsel. She started up for an evening walk. It was so beautiful an afternoon, and the weather was so pleasantly cool, now that the sun was wheeling down upon his last groove in the west.

"Come, Walter, what say you to a walk? We will go to the Indian Spring."

Walter was willing. He professed to be so at least; but he answered vaguely, with an abstracted air. He had already forgotten his *rôle* of the humorist and funster, and had gotten back to his grave face, and gloomy moods.

Grace watched his features earnestly, and saw that something had gone wrong. He had undergone a material change for the worse, since the first few hours after his arrival; and this change had been the result of his long ramble with Angelica that day. Grace was troubled. She could see that Walter's trouble was of the brain, the thought, not of the mere body. That seemed without ailment, for, though less vigorous than formerly, and somewhat thinner, his convalescence, from his recent attack, might be considered complete.

It was then a trouble of the mind, and its growth was of the last few hours, and these had been spent mostly with Angelica, and the inference was a reasonable one, that it had its birth in some communication which Angelica had made to him.

What could be the nature of that communication, which could produce so sudden and striking an effect?

Grace's logic brought her to this question; but there it was graveled. That she could conjecture nothing beyond, increased the troubles of her own thoughts. She knew the silliness of her sister; her childish and thoughtless vanity; and the only conclusion which she could reach was that Walter was becoming tired of the prattle of his pretty puppet—that she had somehow exposed herself—and that his gravity and uneasiness originated in his vexation at an engagement from which he desired to be free.

This conclusion was matter of disquiet enough to the good sister, who, whatever the follies of Angelica—and they occasioned her constant annoyances—was yet her sister, the beautiful child whom they had all so unwisely petted, because of her beauty. As the youngest, too, she had been the nursling of Grace herself, as well as of the mother.

Grace saw the two young people leave the house for their evening ramble, with many misgivings. The uncertainties of her thoughts—for all these conjectures had passed through her brain without settling, or taking definite feature—were so many additional sources of disquiet, that they could fix no where, for it never once occurred to the poor girl that her sister could be so foolish, so wickedly foolish, as to breathe to her lover a syllable of that most unfortunate passage between herself and Stephen, in which she had been the sole offender. Grace could only retire to the solitude of her chamber once more, and lose, in her own heart-sorrows the anxieties which she felt for the two *happy* lovers. They *ought* to be happy, for had not the course of true love run thus far smoothly? Alas! even Grace could understand how it is that thousands, give them all that they desire, will yet not suffer themselves—because of their own perverse vanities—to be made happy, either by gods or men.

The lovers this time changed their route of ramble. Angelica guided the movements of both. They traversed for a while the main road, then entered the large domain of Galphen, the great Indian trader of Carolina, sped along the heights of Redclyffe, and wound down its gorges into a beautiful amphitheatre, scooped out, as it were, from the surrounding hills, at the bottom of which, shaded by the loveliest of groves, bubbled forth a fountain called Indian Spring, the waters of which, cold and clear, were daily visited by the wayfarer, who slaked his thirst from the rude wooden basin, which received the waters, drinking from the *calabash*, or gourd, which hung above it in the wind, depending from the branch of a shady oak. Here, sitting beside the fountain, hearkening its undersong the while, the traveler rested, while he drew forth and fed from his little wallet of biscuit and smoked venison. There is a charm in thus feeding, in such a scene, which sweetens appetite, and wakens up an Oriental fancy in the most sterile brains.

For such pilgrims, so seeking this gracious fountain, rude seats had been provided. But nothing had yet been done by art for the full development of the susceptibilities in nature. The scene sufficed of itself, and the eye naturally beheld it with satisfaction; and, in the coolness, the shade, the quiet, the simple song of the bubbling waters—a pleasant monotone—the rustling of leaves, as the rising breezes swept down the gorges, the sad cooing of doves in the neighboring thickets, or the occasional carol of the mockbird, making sudden gyrations in air in correspondence with the gush of music from his throat—the heart grew soothed, while all the fancies, awaking together, furnished for the scene the crowning halo of romance!

In such a scene the thoughtful person does not speak. We take for granted that each feels for himself as we feel, and do not need that either should cry out his raptures. The mere exclamation: "How sweet—how beautiful!" seems to mar the sense of enjoyment. We leave the scene itself to speak for itself, and the sufficient utterance for thought lies in our own consciousness of feeling. The falling of the "Indian Spring" might have had some soothing influence even upon the morbid and vexed spirit of Walter Dunbar, but it was not allowed to appeal to his eyes, nor sing from its waters to his breast.

The tongue of Angelica became eloquent in pretty prattle, in its praise, and the face of Walter, as he threw himself languidly back against a tree, expressed nothing but a sense of weariness, the evidence of the unrest laboring within his bosom.

At that moment the trampling of several horses' feet was heard sounding along the ridges above; and, looking upward, the two beheld, glimpsing through the woods, at a smart canter along the heights, a troop of horse. Dunbar was roused.

"What can it be?"

"It's a troop of horse," answered Angelica. "They're raising troops of horse and companies of infantry all about the island."

Walter seemed to be counting the troopers as they came in sight.

"There must be from twenty-five to thirty," he muttered.

"And would you believe it," she continued, "that miserable, hateful cripple, Stephen Joscelyn, he, too, is one of them; he's raised a troop of his own, and they've made him a Captain—think of it! He, a Captain!—and he's as proud of it, they say, as if he was born to be a General; and he marches them, and teaches them, three evenings every week, and on Saturdays they're out all day, galloping over the country, and picking up recruits. Only to think of *him* as a Captain of troopers!—and how should he know how to teach 'em and drill 'em, and all that sort of thing? I do believe this is his troop now, though there are several of them. I should not wonder!"

While she was speaking, Walter had raised himself from the ground, and strode, or rather staggered, forward, shading his eyes, and trying to distinguish the parties. The troop, meanwhile, following the road along the ridge, wound half way about the amphitheatre, so that, at intervals, every individual trooper loomed out distinctly to the eyes of the two looking upward from below.

Walter's face suddenly became deadly pale for an instant, then, as quickly, darkly savage.

Yes! It was he! It was Stephen Joscelyn himself, who rode at the head of the troop! There was no mistaking that stalwart person, that erect form, that graceful and stately horseman, who, blending completely, to the eye, the man and the horse, realized to the fancy that brave conception of the Greek, which gives the Centaur to undying fiction! Who, in that perfect horseman, would suspect the deformity which made it painful to behold the same person as he walked? And as he rode by, little dreaming of those who watched him with such bitter feelings from below, and, as his full, sonorous voice rang out the word of command, calling up all the echoes of the hills, Angelica grasped the wrist of her lover, and exclaimed:

"Oh! how I should like to pull the hateful creature from his horse, and choke him on the ground!"

And could Walter at that instant have seen her visage, fiery red with passion, and with eyes that shot out lightnings, he would have acknowledged the presence of a Medea, prepared to enact the murderess. It was just such a spectacle as she exhibited on that fatal day when the long-suppressed passion poured out all its bitterness in the very teeth of the man whom she so madly hated! How to account for this passion in one so feeble! Blind antipathies on the part of the weakly, are the modes by which they resent all superiority.

Walter Dunbar did not see the tiger expression of that young and otherwise lovely face. He did not hear fully to comprehend the savage speech which fell from that envenomed tongue. All his senses were concentrated upon that passing vision of his own hate, and possibly his fate!

Yes! there above the peaceful fountain—a fascinating spectacle of the hateful and the loathsome—stood *his* Black Dog!—a monstrous form, bearing the head and front of Stephen Joscelyn! The young man literally gasped for breath, in the choking sensations of his swelling heart.

Yes! without hearing what is spoken by the child-woman beside him, his thought—his fierce desire—responded to her's, and he half started forward, as he fairly beheld the person of the leading trooper, with the will and purpose to tear him from his horse, and grapple with his throat in a mortal wrestle of life and death.

In a moment more the troop had disappeared. One faint blast of a distant bugle reached their senses, and all again was silence. The fountain resumed its innocent prattle, but it was not suffered to continue. Angelica resumed her prattle also, which unhappily was not so innocent.

"Now, is it not monstrous that such a creature as *that* should presume to be a trooper!—to be a Captain of cavalry!—the miserable, crooked, hobbling!—"

Walter silenced her by a groan, sinking back again upon the bank.

"What's the matter, Walter?" she demanded.

"Hush!" he murmured. "Not a word! Let me sleep a little!"

"Sleep!" she exclaimed. "Why, Walter, what can you be thinking about? Sleep here, and the sun just going down? Come! It is time to be going home. It will be quite dark before we get there."

He rose, but as one half stunned and stupid—weakly, with an effort, and turned a vacant face upon her. She was now, for the first time, startled by its expression, or rather lack of expression—its chalky whiteness, and the *doze* that was conspicuous in his eyes.

"You are sick, Walter!"

He groaned—then, immediately, as it were, he answered with a *ghastly* laugh—

"Sick! What should make you think so? Ha! ha! No, indeed—not sick, Angey."

"Oh! but you are sick, Walter!"

"Pooh! pooh! it is only want of sleep. If I could sleep now!"

And he turned his eyes, with apparent longing, to the bank side against which he had lain.

She took his arm. Just then the singing of the fountain seemed to take his ear, and he turned to it, filled the gourd, and drank freely of the water. Then, shaking himself, as if to free himself from drowsiness, he said:

"Come!" and, with her arm in his, the two silently ascended from the valley.

When they had reached the elevated ridge, and stood upon the public road, Walter stopped and scanned the track which had been beaten up by the passage of the troopers. While he did so, he muttered loudly enough for her to hear, but still as in soliloquy:

"Monstrous, indeed! That *he* should be a trooper!—a Captain of cavalry!—he, the pedagogue!—the deformed! whom men do not seek!—whom women scorn!"

He had evidently caught some of these words from her speech, but he was prepared to put them to a different use. The monstrousness of the thing lay elsewhere than in the vanity or presumption of Stephen Joscelyn. Walter continued:

"It is monstrous! The world expects nothing from him; satisfied that he plays his proper part as the pedagogue, men are not envious of him, because of his deformity; women despise him for the same reason."

"Yes, indeed!" interposed Angelica.

"Hush!" said he. "You know not what you say. He is all this, and this is nothing.

"But I!——"

"What's it, Walter?" as he squared himself round, and faced her.

"I! Look at me, Angelica Kirkland."

"Really, Walter, you scare me."

"I would not scare you," he said gently—

"But, look at me!"

"Well!——"

"Do you see any deformity in me!"

"Deformity in you, Walter. No! How should I? You are perfect. You are the handsomest man in all the country."

"Ha! ha! ha!"

"Why do you laugh so!"

"That you should be so blind! Me handsome! I tell you, girl, I am terribly deformed—in my own eyes, at least! Here now is this person whom you scorn, whose love for you you felt to be an insult, from whom the whole country has no expectations; yet this man, crippled as he is—loathed by women, and unloved by men—is at once schoolmaster, by which he frames the minds of future generations—lawyer, by which he retrieves the fortunes of widows—orator, by which he wins the applauses of the multitude, and *he* also, it seems, can decide promptly in affairs of State; and *he*, a cripple, can muster a troop of horse, performing, even for the emergencies of war. Great God! what then am I? who can do nothing—decide nothing, satisfy nobody—not even a father—and yet, a most perfect man! Have I not a right to *hate him!* Aye, and he shall feel my hate! I have the power and the will, at least, for that! Should he not have been satisfied with what he is, and may be, not sought to rob me of that which is mine! Yes! yes! Angelica, I am willing to believe as you do! I am a very—nay, as you say it—I am certainly a most perfect man! Come!"

"Walter, you do sometimes speak the strangest things! Something's the matter with your head still."

"Yes! yes! I think it likely," with a wild laugh. "The head seems to me in the wrong place. The eyes seem to me to be always looking backward. The back of the head is in front!"

"You frighten me, Walter. I never knew you to speak so strangely before. Come, let us go home. It is getting quite dark; and I feel scary."

"Dark, and what of that, my beauty! You that have eyes able to see any perfections, can surely find the way in spite of the dark."

For the rest of the way the silence was scarcely broken between them. Walter had shaken himself free of Angelica's arm, and went forward, in moody silence, as if he were entirely alone.

With difficulty she kept up with him. She had now no impulse to speak. She was really terrified, and vague notions that he might be mad began to trouble her own little brain. She little knew how much of all this was due to her own pretty, petty—and, as the world is apt to call it, in the case of pretty damsels—innocent prattle.

## CHAPTER XX.

### GRACE'S DISCOVERY, AND WHAT SHE GOT BY IT.

Well might Walter Dunbar wonder, when he thought of Stephen Joscelyn, and the energy and activity of that brain, which, rising superior to the physical deformity, or seeming disability, from which he suffered, could address itself with so much ease and flexibility to such a variety of occupations; and this last, that of a Captain of dragoons, apparently so greatly in conflict with his physical condition! But a rare vitality, a wonderfully active mind, a will superior to all conditions, and resolute against opposition, constituted the secret of Stephen Joscelyn.

Nothing could surpass his activity in his new vocation in the cavalry. He now rode incessantly, in the prosecution of his present enterprise. All the intervals of his time from school-keeping were thus employed. In the course of three weeks, he had organized a corps of no less than thirty light horse. He had infused the military spirit among all his neighbors. He picked his men with care, and such was his popularity, such the confidence of the people in his honor and good sense, that he was permitted to make his own appointment of officers.

These he drilled with care. Dick Marvin became one of his Lieutenants, and little Dick, his son, was, to his great delight, promoted —as he could wind the horn with good effect—to be the bugler of the corps. Several of the taller school-boys of sixteen, seventeen and eighteen, were permitted, with the sanction of their parents, to enter the troop. And there were no better or braver troopers in it. We shall probably hear of them in times to come. Stephen's practice was thus continued day by day, almost as soon as school hours were over. By night, he himself studied in such military manuals as could then be procured. Where books failed him, he strove, by dint of thinking, to work out the processes for himself. He communicated with, and received instructions from, Capt. Samuel Hammond, then one of the best military leaders in that neighborhood; and he put himself in correspondence also with other parties in Charleston, through whom he procured a few common sabres, and a collection of horseman's pistols. The letters of Drayton finally secured him promises from the Council of Safety in the metropolis, of ample supplies at an early period.

His vigilance, activity and zeal, bringing him still more into notice, he received the appointment as a member of the "Secret Committee" of the precinct of country in which he dwelt. His life had been the busiest, ever since the great meeting in Augusta; or rather, perhaps, we should make it date from the period when he left the house of Mrs. Kirkland. The blow he had on that occasion received from the tongue of the fair, foolish woman, whom he had so unwisely fancied, seemed to have stung him to a concentration of all his energies and powers, in such a direction as would take him away from all thought of that unhappy passion in which he was denied to hope.

Well might Walter Dunbar wonder! Stephen Joscelyn was a wonder to all who knew him—to scores of men who knew him much better than Dunbar. The latter knew Martin, his brother, to be a man of great energies also; but even he could not compare with Stephen. Well might Walter feel all the pangs of a wounded self-esteem, in making the enforced comparison between his own feebleness of purpose and deficient performance, and the powers of that really strong man, thus developing resources of might and character, seemingly so inconsistent with his obvious defects and disadvantages.

The sense of shame, the agonies of envy, that followed the comparison thus forced upon his thought, even by the witless speaking of Angelica, made him writhe, in the bitterness of his heart, when in his own chamber; his mind ever recurring to the supposed crime of Stephen against himself. Brooding thus alone, only served to confirm, in his bosom, every sentiment of hate and bitterness which had been provoked by the revelations made him. That these sentiments should finally prompt him to some mode of expressing them, may reasonably be conjectured.

Though he had subdued himself, on returning home with Angelica, to a proper social deportment, it was yet evident to all the ladies of the household, not excepting Angelica herself, that something had seriously gone wrong with him. When questioned by Mrs. Kirkland, he himself was now not unwilling to profit by the evasive suggestion which the good lady made, that he had overtasked his strength—that he had assumed his convalescence to be complete, when much more time and self-nursing were essential to his perfect restoration; and having arrived at this satisfactory conclusion, she again protested against further exercise, insisting that there should be no long walks taken any more, no matter how love should plead, until *she* should *decide* upon his ability to encounter physical fatigue. She, too, like Aunt Janet, had her vanity as a nurse.

Grace was not so easily deceived as her mother, and Walter felt that her eyes scanned his countenance with glances of keenest inquiry, mingled with doubt, when he thus accounted for his deportment by connivance with her mother's opinion. Angelica was easily persuaded to adopt the opinion of Mrs. Kirkland, though she insisted that their walks had not been very long, and were by no means fatiguing. Grace sagaciously thought again of the long *talks*, and rightly guessed that in them, rather than in the *walks*, lay the true difficulty. But as yet she never once, even in her own thoughts, referred to Stephen Joscelyn, as having any, the slightest concern in the matter. Poor girl! she thought of him only as being *her* concern.

She was soon to be enlightened. That night, when she and Angelica had retired—and they slept together—the latter, who was one of those persons who must be talking, mentioned casually their meeting with, or rather their sight of, Stephen, at the head of his cavalry.

She spoke in her usual flippant and harsh manner, when he was the subject. The light seemed all at once to break in upon her sister, and Grace said quickly:

"I hope, Angey, you did not speak of *him* in these terms to Walter."

"Indeed, but I did."

"Good Heavens! Angelica!"

"And why not, I want to know?"

"Why not? when he is the brother of Martin, who is the best friend of Walter."

"A fig for his friendship! Why should Walter care a straw for the friendship of any of these Joscelyns?"

"But he *does* care, and to hear the woman who is to be his wife speak in such terms of the brother of his friend, must make him very uncomfortable, to say the least. Take care that Walter does not discover that Martin Joscelyn is quite as dear to him, as a friend, as Angelica Kirkland is to him as a wife or sweetheart."

"I've no fear of that; and I had good reasons, too, for speaking as I did, and I showed Walter that if Martin Joscelyn was his friend, such was not the case with Stephen, who was his bitter enemy."

"But how *could* you say that, Angelica? How *dared* you say a thing that you do not know to be true?"

"Dared! that's a pretty word for you to use to me, Grace, and I won't suffer you to say it. Don't you say it again. Dare, indeed!"

"Certainly it is evil doing, Angelica, that you should say to Walter what you know to be untrue."

"Ha! you call me a liar!" The attitude which accompanied these words was sufficiently threatening. Grace said quickly—

"Do not *strike* me, Angelica, my sister! Do not, I implore you! It is sad enough for me to know that you will heed no counsels of mine, and that I rarely address you, even in the language of sisterly love, without provoking you to anger. Do not do a worse thing, and one that you will one day regret in tears and bitterness."

"I have half a mind to do it."

"If you do, Angelica, I shall certainly tell Walter."

The threat seemed to have its effect; the uplifted hand was lowered, and, in more subdued tones, Angelica answered:

"And would *he* believe you, do you think, Miss Tell-tale?"

"Would you dare to deny it?"

"Dare again!" And she advanced threateningly, and her hand was again uplifted.

Grace folded her hands upon her bosom meekly, and said:

"Even though you should strike me, I must speak, Angelica, and you must hear me, my sister. I would save you from yourself. It is now painfully apparent to me that the present melancholy condition of Walter's mind is due to *your* influence in some way, and not to the effect of his late sickness. If you have told him any untruth, Angelica, about Stephen Joscelyn, you have been guilty of a great sin, and will be grievously punished for it. You will make mischief between these men; and God knows what may come of it. Walter is rash and hot-headed, and Stephen is a man with too much fire in his own brain to submit to insult or injury."

"Why, what should that poor cripple do to Walter Dunbar?"

"Do!—and is it possible, Angelica, that you would have Walter Dunbar presume on the condition of the cripple to use violence? For shame! for shame! Hear me, and say, tell me, my sister, tell me that you have not been guilty of this sin of reporting to Walter the wretched quarrel which you had with Stephen."

"That was the very thing I did tell him! And what have you to say?"

"Great Heaven have mercy upon us. What can be done?"

"Yes,"—exultingly—"I told him how the vile and hateful creature had called him a pitiful fellow, and spoke of him with contempt."

"Then may God have mercy on your soul, Angelica, for you told him a most horrid falsehood."

Hardly had she spoken, when the closed hand of the sister smote her upon the mouth. The blood flowed on the instant, a low moan, that of a wounded spirit, broke from the lips of Grace, as she covered them with her 'kerchief; and such a look as went out from her eyes upon the offender—so sad, so full of pity—so very sorrowful, that even the heart of the passionate fury seemed to be touched. Grasping Grace by the wrist, as she was about to leave the room, she said quickly, in low, husky tones—

"I did not wish to do it, Grace; I did not mean it—I did not. You will not tell, Grace."

"You have effectually closed my lips," was the answer. "Would to God you had always been able to close your own. I fear, Angelica, greatly fear, my sister, that you have done such work this day as may require much better blood than either yours or mine to wash out. I will sleep with mother to-night. May God forgive you, my sister, as I do."

"Grace! Grace!"

Calling, as the other was retiring, she darted after her, and seizing her about the neck, was about to kiss her, when Grace interposed her hand.

"It cannot be just now, Angelica; the caress following the blow would be much harder to be borne."

"Then you do not forgive me."

"I forgive you, my poor sister, from the bottom of my heart. It will be well for you if you ever can forgive yourself."

"You will not tell our mother?"

"To our mother, Angelica, I must speak the truth, which I may not yet confide to any other person."

"Go, then, you spiteful thing. I always knew that you had no heart."

To this there was no answer. Grace left the room in silence. There was a difference that night in the sleep of the two sisters, if they slept at all. The psychologist must conjecture for himself the character of those dreams which visited the sleeping brain of the Sleeping Beauty.

## CHAPTER XXI.

### GRACE'S BILLET.

The revelation of what had taken place between the sisters, was made by Grace to her mother, as a reason for claiming to share her bed with her that night. We need not dwell upon the painful scene between the two. Mrs. Kirkland was a loving mother to her children. She *knew* the value of Grace; but she also *felt* the beauty of Angelica. The one might be, in a *household* sense, her *pride*, but the other was her *pet* as well as pride; and though not blind to this erring nature of the girl, at once passionate and feeble, she had never been able to find the heart to check or chide her, in any proper manner, so that the correction might prove adequate to the cure of her infirmities of mind and temper. She was a kind mother, but not always a wise one.

Grace had not dilated in her narrative of the quarrel; she had not used any epithet in describing its details. She had, on the contrary, softened everything that could tell against her sister. Still, the mother thought that Grace *might* be to blame. She had spoken, perhaps, too harshly to the child.

But the broken mouth, the still bleeding lips, spoke also, and told their own story more emphatically than any words; and the old lady groaned at the miserable signs of strife between her children. But she could only groan. How to reach the evil? For the cure of this, she could only pathetically wish that the time would come when Walter Dunbar would find himself prepared to marry. Circumstances, as yet, did not suffer him to decide when the happy event might be permitted to take place.

But the subject of greatest anxiety with Grace, was the possibility of a scene of violence between Walter and Stephen. The mother, however, could not see with her eyes, or feel any of the apprehensions which oppressed her daughter's heart. There might be words between them—that she thought possible—but blows—surely not!

In the first place, "Walter would never lift his hand against a cripple." But Grace suggested that a challenge might pass, and a duel with pistols follow, the use of this weapon being suggested to put the cripple on an equal footing with any man.

But Mrs. Kirkland had an answer for this also. She believed that Stephen Joscelyn was too pious to resort to any such murderous practice, even though Walter should invite him to the field. And, finding her mother somewhat disposed to yawn over the farther controversy, Grace retired back upon her own sad heart, weaving apprehensive fancies in her brain, which kept her wakeful all night.

With early dawn she was up and stirring. She was not likely to be disturbed for some hours. She took her writing materials, penned several little notes, destroyed them as fast as she penned them, and left the table unsatisfied.

Then, listening and watchful that no one should surprise her, she resumed her efforts at the desk; and, after several more experiments in writing, she appeared satisfied, swept the mutilated papers out of sight, but hid one selected slip carefully away in her bosom.

It was a mere slip of paper, upon which she had written but a single sentence, a small result from such labor and anxiety. But she carefully folded and sealed it, and as we have said, hid it away in that bosom, where lay harbored some other sad secrets of her own, about which she dared neither to write nor speak.

She next proceeded, but very wearily, and with frequent signs of forgetfulness, to her usual housekeeping duties. Arrangements were made for the usual breakfast. Betty, the housemaid, was summoned; the table spread out as usual, and when everything was ready, Grace went up again to her mother's room, where she renewed the subject of the last night.

The apprehensions which she felt were totally unrelieved.

But what to do?

Her mother was by no means the counsellor for such a case. Yet, who else could she consult? Again the subject was discussed between them, but nothing that the girl could say to the mother sufficed to make her share in her anxiety. She had no fears of Stephen, even if she could doubt Walter.

A desperate suggestion occurred to Grace.

"Why not explain the whole affair to Walter himself, and disabuse him of the false and foolish impressions which he had received from Angelica."

"And make your own sister out a liar!" retorted the mother, sharply. "Expose her to the man that's to be her husband! Grace, Grace! I'm astonished that you've got so little affection for your own flesh and blood."

Poor Grace! She was confounded.

Still, what was to be done? Something, it is true, she *had* done, but would it avail? It might; for the safety of one of the parties, but in no wise for the other. And she had not yet completed even that one thing, upon which she had grounded some portion of her hope to keep the peace between the parties, and arrest the incipient evil in the bud.

Worried, wearied, discomfited, she hurried down stairs, and passed the piazza, looking forth eagerly, up and down the road. The clock struck; she counted each stroke unconsciously aloud.

"Seven!

"It is too soon," she murmured to herself. "He will hardly come along before eight, or after. But he *may* come along sooner than usual. It is uncertain. That is my only chance, and I must not miss him."

So speaking, she went out, and called up Billy, the negro boy, who tended upon the horses, drove the carriage, at times, and worked in the garden. In low tones, looking to the dwelling all the while, as if fearing to be observed, she said to him hastily:

"Billy, have you seen little Tom Watts going to school this morning?"

" 'Taint time for 'em yet, Miss Grace. 'Speck he'll be coming along by breckfus (breakfast) time."

"Well, go out to the road, Billy, and watch for him. Don't let him pass. Stop him when he comes, and bring him up to the gate. Let him wait for me. I won't keep him long. I'll be on the watch for you, and be ready. Tell him I must see him."

She appeared a little easier of mind when this arrangement had been made, and she beheld Billy trotting out to take his station by the road side.

She was fortunate in her plan. The breakfast was much later than usual. Not one of the family had yet descended from their chambers, when Billy reappeared, conducting the school-boy, little Tom Watts, then on his way, with his satchel of well-thumbed, dilapidated and greasy books, harbored in close propinquity with half a dozen sweet potatoes, a good round of hoe-cake, and the leg of a chicken. Such was the dinner assigned him for the day—such as most of the boys took with them to school, and which, eaten beside a branch of clear, bright running water, was a thousand times more grateful to appetite and health than the costly dinners of the rich at formal sittings.

Grace added something to the contents of the urchin's wallet, which made him show his white teeth in delight. Some hot rolls of wheat flour, and a few slices of delicious ham, opened to his mental vision the felicitous dream of a supper with the Barmecide.

"Tommy," said Grace, "I want you to do me a favor."

Tommy was quite willing to do favors where the compensation was not only so liberal, but made in advance of the service. He grinned his assent. She handed him her billet.

"Give this to the master, Mr. Joscelyn, just as soon as you get to school. Will you remember to do it, Tommy?"

He promised.

"And, Tommy,——"

She paused.

"What's it, Miss Grace?"

"Ah! Tommy, you need not say who sent it. Remember that, will you, Tommy? Don't say I sent it!"

Tommy promised.

"And, Tommy, when you come back from school, stop, and I will give you a nice piece of potato-pone. Be sure and come for it."

Tommy went on his way, and found himself thinking of the angels, and of the stuff that they are, or should be made of; and he muttered as he went along—not deluded, it seems, as older people were, and are apt to be.

"Mother and all of them says as how Miss Angelica is an angel, and a beauty; but I do think Miss Grace is a hundred, hundred times more beautiful an angel than all the Miss Angelicas I ever seed."

And Tommy was right.

And Tommy was off, and never did he reach school half so rapidly as he did that day, for he was thinking of angels all the way, and he seemed to have borrowed their wings. And when he reached the school-house, he found the master just arriving on horseback; and the urchin took the horse (though not one of the troop) and hitched him to a swinging limb, but, ere he did so, and when about to lead the horse away with one hand, having dropped his wallet from the other, he held up the little mysterious billet, and shook it full before the face of the master.

Stephen Joscelyn took the note, opened and read. He called the boy back.

"Who gave you this, Tommy?"

"Miss Grace told me not to tell you, sir."

"Well—very well, Tommy. Tell Miss Grace that you did not tell me; for you did not tell me, you know."

"To be sure, sir, I didn't."

"That's right, Tommy! Always do as Miss Grace—as the young ladies tell you."

And the boy went off with the horse perfectly satisfied with himself; and the master entered the school, and took the chair of authority, and, while the children came tumbling in, one by one, or in groups, Stephen Joscelyn read and reread the mysterious little billet, which he kept turning over and over in his hand, apparently much puzzled by its contents. And yet these were sufficiently brief, sufficiently simple, as we read over his shoulder, and not seemingly designed for a puzzle. The note consisted of a single sentence only. It ran thus, and in a disguised hand:

"Be on your guard, Stephen."

"Poor Grace—the good girl—but what can she mean? What can be the matter? She has disguised the hand, but the name, Stephen, tells it all."

He mused for a while; but, as if unable to make anything of it, he laid the paper aside, looked at his round, silver watch, brought his little mallet down with a sharp stroke upon the table which hushed in a moment all the bedlam clatter of the boys—books were immediately opened, and the business of the school at once begun.

By this time all the family at Mrs. Kirkland's were astir. Walter was the last to leave his chamber. He made his appearance in the breakfast-room, where the ladies had already assembled, and was met at the entrance by the beautiful Angelica, looking like the buxom, but innocent May, just descended in a shower of roses. Who, in that gay child-aspect and sunny, bright demeanor, could conceive the possibility of such demoniac passions in her bosom as could so deform her visage the night before?

For a moment his own countenance lighted up as he beheld her. But only for a moment. A settled gravity soon resumed its sway over all his features, and there was a stern rigidity about his mouth, which prevented any play of the muscles in that always most speaking member of the face.

The usual salutations were cordially enough exchanged between him and the rest of the family, but even he could see that there was something cloudy in all features save those of Angelica.

And there were the broken mouth and swollen lips of Grace, not contributing in any degree to render her sad, wan face attractive to the lover of the beautiful.

He was not so absorbed in self as not to see the wound; and, while inwardly contrasting the face with that of Angelica, to remark upon it. It was natural enough that he should do so, and the heightened color on the cheeks of his betrothed, as he asked the question, tended still more to increase the gratifying contrast, which his thought had made between her charms and the want of charm in the countenance of Grace.

"Why, Grace, what have you been doing to your mouth? What has done it?"

"Only a trifling hurt, Walter. My own folly."

"It is an ugly cut, Grace, not a trifling hurt, by any means. One would almost suspect you of having been engaged in a bruizing match. It is just such a wound as a good fist, by a skillful boxer, is very apt to make. The upper lip seems to be divided."

It was now Grace's turn to become red in the face, while that of Angelica grew as suddenly pale. Mrs. Kirkland was all in a fidget, and, by a very awkward movement of her arm, overthrew the teapot, with all its contents, upon the floor. There was a grand smash.

It was a most happy diversion.

Grace cried out:

"Have you scalded yourself, mother?"

The object of Walter's solicitude was changed at once, and the divided lip of Grace was no longer the subject of discussion. She busied herself in picking up the fragments of the teapot, then disappeared to draw another pot of tea. This still farther delayed the breakfast, and the fate of the teapot, and the alarm of Mrs. Kirkland, when it was found she was not scalded, became a topic of playful remark, in which all parties were relieved from their previous anxieties. Angelica got over her terrors, and the paleness passed away from her cheek.

After breakfast, Walter Dunbar retired to his chamber.

Grace seized the opportunity afforded by his absence to say to her mother, in the presence of Angelica:

"Whether you fear as I do or not, it will be well to take such precautions as we can to prevent the mischief, which I, at least, still apprehend. You can see that Walter meditates something very seriously. You can see it in the sudden change which has come over him—in his reluctance to talk as usual—in his absence of manner—in his compressed lips, and in the wandering expression of his eyes. I see it, at least. It will be well to keep close watch upon him, and prevent him, if possible, from leaving the house to-day. You, mother, must do your best to interest and engage his attention. Show him everything about the grounds and garden; consult him about that question between you and old Mr. Mercer—about the titles to the land, I mean—the old parson's tract; and there are several other things about which you will have need to talk with him as a lawyer. Nor must you, Angelica,——"

Here she turned to her sister, and spoke with a changed manner. Now she is just as earnest as in speaking to her mother, but there is in the voice, and look, and gesture, a dignity such as a just authority should ever impart, but which, in the meekness of her nature, she had hitherto forborne, whenever she had occasion to speak to Angelica. The latter *felt* the change, and instinctively seemed to succumb before it, while Grace proceeded:

"You, Angelica, must now do your best, using all the attractions you can command, to keep Walter here at home until his mood changes for the better. It will need all your efforts to undo that mischief which I am satisfied your thoughtless speaking has already done. Do not suffer him from your sight to-day, if you can help it.

To gain time is a great deal towards the cooling off the passions. A day or two, and the angry feelings will subside, and more prudent thoughts will arise, to arrest any rash conduct which he may now meditate. Nay, do not answer me, Angelica! I am not able, it seems, to persuade our mother or yourself that there is anything to be apprehended between Walter and Stephen Joscelyn. But I am sure that there is trouble, if not danger, to grow from what you have said to Walter. I know it must be so from what I know of these men, and I warn you that it will need all our woman's wit to keep them from quarreling, if not fighting. Heed my words! There is no harm in taking proper precautions, at least for a day or two, so that we can keep the parties from meeting. See to it, then! You have sufficient *right* to be with Walter continually, and hitherto it has been your pleasure and his that you should be so. Let it so continue. Your own report of his conduct yesterday evening, coming home from 'Indian Spring,' ought to be enough for you. I tell you that he is fighting with himself now, every hour, to keep down from our sight those passions which are raging in his breast, and which you, my sister, have so foolishly enkindled. I speak to you now in the presence of our mother. From this time forth I shall never seek to counsel you *except* in her presence. On *this* particular subject you shall never be taxed to listen to my words again."

She then left the room, and retired to her mother's chamber.

The solemnity of her speech, its earnestness, the loftiness of her manner, so unusual with her, so seldom if ever seen by either of them before, now deeply impressed them both. The mother hearkened with surprise, and in utter silence. Angelica was absolutely awed. She had, more than once, endeavored to interpose, and reply to Grace, but the uplifted finger of the latter sufficed to keep her silent; and the silence continued for some little while after Grace had gone, neither well knowing what to say. When, at length, the mother spoke, she did so in language which was rather new from her to the ears of Angelica.

"You have been a very bad girl, Angey. You have acted very foolishly in telling Walter about your quarrel with Stephen, and you have not told him the truth! Grace is right! Stephen never said a word against Walter or his speech!"

"But, mother,——"

"Hush! I will not hear a word from you—not till I am done, at least. I say that you have told falsehoods upon Stephen! *You* may not think so, but *I know* so. You were told, both by Grace and myself, that you were mistaken in what Stephen had said, and about his manner of saying it; and, the truth is, your foolish, headstrong passions have made you deaf to all good and right hearing. It ought to be enough for you that your mother and your sister both give evidence against you; and when you persist in your statement, it is giving us both the lie. I ought to have told you of this before, even as I am doing now, but I thought it would all pass off in a little while, and I never dreamed that you could be so foolish, and so wicked, as to go off and blab all this stuff to Walter. Mark you now, if he ever comes to think of it soberly, and in cool moments, he will set you down as a greater fool than you are; that is, if he does not think worse of you for it still! It will be well, indeed, if he does not happen to think you as wicked as I do!"

Angelica pouted, and was about to fling herself out of the room, when her mother called her back.

"Come back, Angelica, and none of your foolish airs with me! Is this a time for you to get into passions? It is your passions that brought us this trouble—your headstrong violence—and it will bring you to worse trouble yet before you are done. Grace speaks what's right to you; and, instead of your pouting now, and flinging about you, treating your own mother with impudence, you ought to be trying your best to do as she advises. See to it now, and don't be a fool any longer! Hush! I hear Walter moving on the stairs. Make your face smooth, and meet him, and do your best to keep with him all day, if you can. I will join you directly."

## CHAPTER XXII.

### ESCAPE.

In a surprisingly short moment, Angelica had put on the sweetest face in the world, and joined Walter at the foot of the stairs, with the smiling of an angel. She was not without her cleverness. In place of wisdom, she had a plentiful supply of cunning, and was a mistress of that ready art which can veil its secrets promptly, keep its utterance, at all events, from the tell-tale countenance, and substitute, at a moment's warning, for the demoniac glare of hate, the sweet, wooing solicitude of an expression which beams only with love. Happy art, in a world where society itself imposes upon most persons the necessity of walking in a mask, and making of fashion a disguise for falsehood.

The two went forth together into the garden, where they were joined, after awhile, by good Mrs. Kirkland.

Grace, meanwhile, was in her chamber, suffering somewhat from a little case of conscience which compelled her to self-examinings, which did not seem to result satisfactorily to herself. Had she not conveyed a falsehood, purposely, to Walter Dunbar, when she referred, for the condition of her mouth, to her *own fault?* That was the question. She was guilty of evasion, doubtless. But was it not *really* her own fault that the mouth was broken? Had she not provoked her sister to violence? Had she not used strong and offensive language? Had she not charged her with false-speaking and slander, and though the charge was justified by the truth, was it proper and becoming in her to make it?

These were the questions.

Was she not taught to beware that offence should not arise from her?—and was not the provocation which she gave to her sister, offence?—and did not that offence prompt her to strike the blow, and, consequently, was not the blow, so given, the fruit of her own fault—unjustifiable, no doubt, in Angelica, but properly incurred by her?

The sweet creature was not a very subtle casuist, perhaps, but in her very meekness she justified herself for the seeming evasion of the truth of which she had been guilty. It was no evasion of the truth. It *was* her offence that occasioned the blow, and so the blow came of her own fault.

This question of conscience having been settled in her mind, she addressed herself to the household avocations, which the present cares of her mother and sister, in occupying the attention of their guest, had devolved almost entirely upon herself. But she did not the less give an eye to them also. She beheld the lovers go forth into the garden; she saw them, at length, joined by her mother, and became comparatively easy in mind on the subject of her previous fears, especially as Walter did not seem to betray any restiveness, or desire to leave the premises.

Meanwhile, Mrs. Kirkland, adopting all the suggestions of Grace, even though she might have thought them useless and unnecessary precautions, engaged the ears of Walter, now with her peach and apple orchards, and the varieties of wild grapes, to which her late husband had given special attention. Her peaches, in particular, were subjects of endless details. How to graft, bud, top and twine; how to protect from the "borer;" by what process to persuade the fruit to grow large enough to fill a saucer; and a thousand secrets of art and culture, not forgetting some mysterious modes of operation, which argued much more of sorcery than science. Vegetables next, the squash, green peas, potatoes, the gardens and the fields; upon all these she could and did expatiate, with all the enthusiasm of a successful country wife. Her dome, the wines of grape and blackberry; her brandies of plum, and percimmon; these, next in order, underwent due representation and consideration. To pass to the dairy was but a natural progress. Her milk, cream, butter, and even cheeses, were among the best of the country—none superior.

But further detail is unnecessary. Enough, that, in dilating upon all these successive topics, she necessarily conducted her guest to the various scenes in which these constituted her *dramatis personæ*. From the garden to the orchard, from the orchard to the potato patch, from this to the cow-pen, from the cow-pen to the dairy, the good old lady led the unresisting and seemingly well satisfied, but very silent Walter. She said apologetically, at length, as if to justify her exactions:

"You see, you young people will have to learn to see and know how to do all these things for yourselves, and who can better teach you than Grace and myself, who have been doing and seeing to them all our lives? Angelica, you see, Walter, knows little or nothing of them, as I may say. It all falls upon Grace. She is my right hand, and sometimes my left hand too. I don't know what I could do without her; and it's well for you, Walter, that Angey took your fancy, and not Grace, for I could never have given Grace to anybody that might take her from me."

Angelica found much to vex her in this very natural speech. Several times during the talk of the old lady, her compliments to Grace as a dutiful daughter, and an admirable housekeeper, had grated harshly on her ears, though it is quite probable they had made but little impression upon those of her lover.

Walter did not show himself impatient—only languid. He did not seem sullen, but he was mostly silent.

To Grace, had she been present, it would have been evident that his thoughts were wandering off, all the while, from the sphere of his companions, and that the same melancholy, or savage brooding, over one intensely working idea, which had been apparent to her before, argued still for those fears, in her mind, which we have heard her so urgently express.

At length, as if somewhat exhausted with her own eloquence, and, perhaps, somewhat fatigued with her ramble, Mrs. Kirkland led the way to the dwelling, quietly followed by the young couple. As Walter had shown no impatience, both Angelica and herself had come to the conclusion that the fears of Grace were groundless. They both accordingly relaxed in their vigilance; and though, for some little while after, the good mother continued to challenge the attention of Walter, having brought up the subject of the land-title in dispute, and some other law matters, she yet finally forgot altogether the mission which she had undertaken, and fell to dozing in her oaken arm-chair over the half-finished stockings in her lap.

Grace had watched, at intervals, the several progresses of the party. She had witnessed their quiet return, all together, to the house. She had heard no movement below stairs which could indicate the departure of any one, and was quite satisfied until she heard Angelica singing gaily, as she darted up the stairway.

At that moment Grace happened to look out from the window, and, with a slight scream, she hurried out to the encounter with Angelica, who had not yet reached the platform at the head of the stairway.

"Go," she cried to Angelica, hurriedly, but with a voice of command; "go, hasten out, and stop him if you can! He is now bringing his horse from the stable. Stop him by all means! Say that you wish him to drive you in the chaise, over to Mrs.——, Mrs.——. Oh! anywhere, only stop him!"

It was surprising how rapidly Angelica obeyed. That voice of authority, so suddenly speaking, was not to be gainsayed. She darted down the steps, was in the piazza, in the yard, in a few moments, while Grace, with hardly less speed, made her way down to her mother, to whom she cried at the door:

"You have suffered him to escape!"

Starting up from her sleep, the old lady dropped stocking and knitting needles, and wildly asked:

"Where's Walter—where's Angey? They were here but a moment ago!"

"Gone! And you, mother—you could forget—could not keep awake for a few hours!"

"Was I asleep, child? I did not think it, I declare; but I felt drowsy—it was so warm in the sun, and we walked, you know, a good deal. And, Lord bless me, how could Angey let him go? And it seems but a moment ago that I saw them both there, sitting at that very table, and playing domino together!"

"Domino!"

Grace spoke the word with as much emphasis as if it had been an oath. She went forth into the piazza, and saw the scene to its close.

Angelica had ran forth shrieking:

"Walter!—Walter!"

She was answered by the heavy clatter of his horse's feet, as he darted, at full gallop, up the road; aye, and in the very direction of the school-house of Stephen Joscelyn.

Grace groaned bitterly. She turned away from the drowsy mother and the butterfly daughter, leaving them to those mutual reproaches, which they were both very ready to utter, now that the warnings of Grace, which they had treated so heedlessly, seemed about to prove themselves justly founded in her fears.

"What are we to do, Grace?" demanded the mother, hurrying up to the chamber where the elder girl sat moodily brooding over her apprehensions.

"Do! What can we now do, mother, but fold our hands in patience, and wait upon God?"

"But, oh! Grace, it's impossible that there should be fighting between them. Surely, surely, Walter would not strike a crippled man like Stephen."

"She has maddened him with her false and foolish talk. He will not see that the man is a cripple. He will hear and listen to no explanation. He will obey no voice but that of the passion singing violence to all his senses."

"Oh! something should still be done."

"Yes, mother; make Billy get out the chaise, harness the horse, and you and Angelica drive as fast as you can to the school-house. You may be in time."

"But why not you go, Grace?"

"No! I could do nothing with either party. You must go, even though you go alone!"

"It won't do to take Angey."

"As you please, mother, but go at once."

And so it was finally arranged.

# CHAPTER XXIII.

## GULLIVER IN LILLIPUT.

Calm as the summer atmosphere which he was breathing, Stephen Joscelyn sate in his chair of authority, pursuing his wonted drudgeries of the "Oldfield School" master. His thoughts sometimes reverted to the little billet of warning which he had received, and he occasionally read and re-read it, as if with the hope to discover something more from its meagre sentence—something of latent meaning—which had before escaped him. But in vain; and, unable to discover anything definite in the warning, he laid it down, aside—only to muse upon Angelica! Very sad and bitter were his musings. How much more bitter they were to become, when all should be known of the performances of that lovely damsel!

Suddenly, the thundering tread of a horse is heard along the highway. It leaves the highway, and the next moment is at the school-house door. In another moment the door is thrown open, wide, and Walter Dunbar stalks in, lofty, large, wearing a high head. In his right hand he carries a horse-whip. In his countenance there is the expression of a deeply-seated wrath. In his air and manner are dogged determination, and a fury which is but imperfectly hidden beneath a studied effort to appear cool and scornful.

These expressions of countenance, air and manner, were not at first visible to Stephen, who sat at the opposite extremity of the room. He had simply discovered who was the visitor, but without yet noticing the written language of his features; accordingly, Stephen Joscelyn called out in hearty tones:

"Welcome, Mr. Dunbar. I am glad to see you."

He could use no other language to the close friend of his brother. He could conceive of no reason why he should employ other terms of speech, and though not intimate with Walter, and not, perhaps, esteeming him so greatly as did his brother, he had certainly no unkindly feelings towards him, nor could he imagine the existence of any such, in the bosom of Walter, towards himself. He was soon taught otherwise by the prompt reply of his visitor, to the welcome which he had thus given.

"That is to be seen, sir," said Walter, striding forward.

"Ah!" and the memory of Stephen now recurred to the little billet of Grace; and as he beheld the flushed face, and the wrathful expression in his eyes, he began to discover the clue to its meaning. He could now conceive that he was to "beware" of Walter Dunbar, though why this should be necessary was yet a perplexing puzzle.

"Yes, sir, it is to be seen, when you have heard me, how far my visit will be welcome to you—in what degree you will be glad to see me."

"Go on, sir; let us hear what you have to say which renders necessary so impressive an introduction. I should, indeed, be sorry to think that any conduct of my brother's friend should make him less than welcome to Stephen Joscelyn."

"You have nothing to do, sir, with my friendship for your brother. You have no share in it. That shall not protect you!"

"Protect *me!*" said Stephen, rising from his seat. "Protect me! I am not in the habit, Mr. Dunbar, of calling upon any body for *my* protection, or appealing to any name, however sacred, for such a purpose. Speak, sir, what you have to say, and begone, as quickly as you can. I do not long suffer the insolence of any man."

"What! braggart as well as slanderer!"

"Slanderer!"

"Ay, sir, slanderer! I come here to pronounce you, to your very teeth, a slanderer. You have dared to speak insolently of me behind my back; to seek to disparage me to my best friends; to vilify me with offensive epithets; to do me injury, so far as your foul and treacherous tongue could do it."

"You are mad—mad as a March hare, or a more consummate block-head than I thought you! *I* slander *you!* It is false! I pity you too much, just now especially, to do you harm in any way. You are either the inventor, or the repeater of a falsehood. Your informant, if, indeed, you have one, is simply a liar!"

"Scoundrel! do not dare to say it! Do not defame one who is of angel purity, by your cowardly denial of the truth. Say but that word again, and I will lay my horsewhip over your shoulders!"

Stephen Joscelyn now deliberately took up the heavy, black mahogany rule which lay upon his desk, and advanced with his hobbling pace, over from behind the little barriers of desk and table which stood between himself and his assailant.

Up to this moment, a dead silence had prevailed among the boys of the school. They had been taken aback with surprise, and confounded by the unanticipated scene. They had been the first to discern the angry, the almost demoniac expression in Walter's face, and had awaited events for its explanation. But, when the affair, by the threat of the latter, appeared to be reaching its crisis—when they saw the uplifted whip in his hands, and beheld the master, with his awkward, scrambling, sidelong movement, advancing, as it were, to the encounter, there was an audible murmur among the bigger boys, several of whom now arose and stood up in their places. Sturdy fellows they were, too, and some few of them, as we have heard, had been admitted among Stephen's troopers. The passions of Walter Dunbar had suffered him to see none of these movements, or even to hear their murmurs; nor, perhaps, was Stephen Joscelyn more observant, under the excitement of the moment.

When, by the last speech of Walter, he was forced to believe that he referred to Angelica Kirkland, as his informant, the tears nearly forced themselves into his eyes; but, at such a moment, and in the face of such an assailant, he must show no sign of weakness! He quietly, but resolutely advanced, till he stood confronting Dunbar, with only a few steps between them.

"Mr. Dunbar," he said, very quietly, "I gather from what you have said that there is a lady in the case. I shall be as scrupulous as yourself in forbearing even to conjecture who she is. I prefer to assume that *you* assume the responsibility of the whole affair, of your own words and actions, and do not wish that either of us should involve anybody in our controversy."

"Precisely so, sir; I am responsible for all I say, and for everything I do."

"Then, sir, let me say that you should have been sufficiently scrupulous to execute your mission with more privacy, and not before such an assembly."

"No, sir; here! Here, before your whole school, I prefer to expose you to the scorn of the country, as a vile slanderer and defamer."

"Your epithets and declamation are hardly wise. You have chosen, sir, and I accept your choice. You have chosen to assert the falsehood as your own, and I accordingly, deliberately brand and denounce *you* —you—as the fabricator of the lie! Do you understand that, sir?"

The demon was fully unloosed. With a yell, Walter cried out:

"Take that, scoundrel!"—and the uplifted whip was about to descend; and the rule, in the hands of Stephen, was just as ready to fall; and, with such a weapon, in such hands, the blow must have crushed through hat, scull, and brain, when the weapons of both parties were arrested by an unexpected interruption—by the appearance of new parties to the conflict.

Heated and influenced by what they had heard, a concerted movement took place among the boys. Had Walter, or Stephen, but hearkened to the few murmured words in a little group of four or five among them, it might possibly have kept the chief belligerents in more sober paces.

"I'll jump upon him first," whispered little Dick Marvin to his comrades; "then you pitch in."

And, true to his word, the moment the whip was uplifted in the hands of Walter, the urchin, agile as a monkey, with a single bound planted himself upon the shoulders of Dunbar, grappling him tightly with one arm around his neck, while with the other hand he suddenly snatched the whip from the grasp of the assailant. This was the work of an instant. The signal, once given, Walter was grappled by three others. The whole school was in arms, and all was uproar. Walter was surrounded, and in spite of the most desperate struggles, he was borne to the floor, flat upon his face, with half a score of the young athletes squat upon his body from head to feet. It was Gulliver, prostrate under the bonds of the Lilliputians.

"Let him rise, boys. He has had enough. He can do no harm. God knows, this is humiliation enough!"

The words of authority from Stephen, calmly judicial of expression, were immediately obeyed. But, even though relieved of the pressure of his puny antagonists, Walter Dunbar did not rise from the floor.

"Lift him up," said the master.

They did so. They raised him to his feet, and he stood up at length, not erect, but with the aspect of one ready to drop again. His hurts, his previous illness, these, together, might have produced his present drooping and prostrate condition. But the deep sense of his humiliation was upon him, and was, perhaps, the more sufficient cause. He groaned beneath it. He presented a pitiable spectacle. The blood still trickled from his nostrils. It had already streamed over his bosom. His clothes were stained with it, and some rents in his face, as well as his garments, betrayed the free use of the claws of the young tigers that had brought him to the ground.

For a few moments he stood, vacantly gazing around him. Then his eyes fastened upon Stephen, who stood before him still in the very spot which he had occupied when, in the violence of his wrath, his assailant had lifted his whip to strike. A savage glare of Walter's eyes, as he became conscious of the presence of Joscelyn, declared his unabated hate. He smiled bitterly, as he said:

"Your myrmidons are too many."

"I did not need their help, Walter Dunbar. Their interposition saved you. Had your whip once smitten me, I should have brained you with a blow. Go, sir; go now. I am sorry for you. I pity you from the bottom of my soul."

Another hateful glance from Walter's eyes upon the speaker, and the humbled assailant wheeled about, and half tottering as he went, made his way out of the building.

"Boys," said Stephen, after Walter had gone, "boys, I thank you. I had thought to scold you for coming between me and my enemy. What! Did you think that *he* could hurt *me?* and did you think that I, who have kept *you* all in order—stout fellows as you are—was not a sufficient match for *him?* But I thank you, now that I think of it. But for *your* timely putting in, Walter Dunbar would be now lying a corpse before your eyes. I thank you."

And he waved the heavy rule in his hand with such a grasp and such a swing, that all present readily believed that, even as he had said, he could have crushed his assailant at a single blow!

## CHAPTER XXIV.

### AFTER THE STORM.

It is difficult to conceive how Walter Dunbar made his way to his horse, found and remounted him. He walked forth from the schoolhouse, and out to the tree where the horse had been fastened, in a sort of doze, with the uncertain step of one who had been stunned, and still continued stupefied. And when mounted, he rode off, with bent figure, like that of a man in years. It was the humiliation in heart and head which thus bowed and weakened him—robbing him seemingly of all will and purpose—and not the physical injury which he had received. This was slight, consisting of bruizes simply; but the blood upon his face and garments would seem, to a mere observer, to argue much more serious damage.

He did not depart in the hot haste or at the swift gallop with which he came. The steed was suffered now to walk, and continued to do so until the rider was roused out of his lethargy by the sudden scream of a woman.

He had met, unexpectedly, with the chaise of Mrs. Kirkland, who was driving, with Angelica sitting beside her.

The scream came from the lips of the latter.

In his stupor, seeing and hearing nothing but the aspect and the voice of his own humiliation, he had been awakened to the consciousness of their presence, only by the scream of his betrothed, and this was uttered only when the chaise had so nearly approached him, as to suffer the ladies to discern the bloodied and torn condition of his garments.

Instinctively, at the first sight of them, Walter clapped spurs to his horse, which darted by them at once in a smart gallop. Angelica screamed after him.

"Walter! Walter!"

He answered with a half idiotic laugh, but continued on, still plying the spur, and seemingly anxious to make his escape.

Mrs. Kirkland immediately wheeled about, applying the whip to her own horse, which was one of those good old sedate beasts, to which we give the name of a family horse, meaning by that such a well-bred domestic animal as anybody can drive. The whip did not materially accelerate the movement of "old Bob." His flanks were inaccessible to persuasion of this sort, at least when administered only by a female hand; and he continued to jog on, at an even pace, philosophically slow, while the steed of Walter was going forward at a topping pace, almost amounting to a run. He had no guidance from his rider, but naturally took the route back to the stables where he had been sumptuously fed the previous night. He reached home, accordingly, a considerable time before the ladies in the chaise.

Grace Kirkland, whose feverish anxieties had kept her on the lookout, happened to be in the piazza at the moment of Walter's arrival.

Her terrors were heightened as she beheld his condition. He was there—he was safe. But the blood upon his garments showed that there had been a violent conflict. Was it his blood or that of Stephen Joscelyn? The appearance was natural, as the former had returned in safety, that the blood was that of the latter.

She could not speak. Her limbs tottered beneath her. Yet a fearful fascination kept her in the piazza, watching the person of Walter, who seemed disposed to linger, with his steed, in the stable whither he had ridden him at once.

She could no longer endure the shocking doubts, fears and anxieties, which kept crowding upon brain and soul, a formidable host, more terrible than an army with banners.

She went forth towards the stable. As he saw her approaching, he advanced to meet her. He had probably hoped, in her withdrawal from the piazza, to make his way to his chamber without being encountered and questioned on his way. The agony was before him of making known his own defeat, and confessing to others the secret of his humiliations. He could not escape it now.

Shocked at the spectacle which his person and dress presented to her eyes, and which was infinitely more significant of strife as she approached, than it had been at a distance, she exclaimed, as they met:

"Oh! Walter Dunbar, what has happened? What have you done? What means this blood upon you? Whose blood? Have you, Walter —oh! Walter—have you forgotten the commandment, 'Thou shalt not kill'?"

"It is my own blood, Grace!" he answered, gloomily; "I have killed nobody!"

"God be thanked that it is so. But there has been strife, violence, and with no cause."

"No cause! But do not speak to me, Grace—let me pass—let me get out of sight! Oh! if I could bury myself out of sight forever! My God!—my God! Oh! Grace, I have suffered to-day the greatest humiliation of my life! I would to God that he had taken it! It would have been a mercy!"

"He! Who? Stephen——!"

"Aye! Stephen Joscelyn! My enemy! My fate! He has triumphed over me. His foot is even now upon my neck!"

"Stephen your enemy, Walter? What a delusion!"

"Delusion!—with this evidence before you."

And he smote his bloody vestments. Before she could answer—

"But they come!" he cried, starting and hurrying forward.

The rattling of the chaise was heard along the highway.

"She must not see me thus, Grace! Let me pass to my chamber."

He was gone, and a few moments after Angelica arrived with her mother.

"But where is Walter?" demanded the mother and Angelica in the same breath. They were both in a whirlwind of excitement.

"He has gone to his chamber," said Grace.

Mrs. Kirkland was about to seek him there when Grace interposed.

"Let him change his clothes, mother. Besides, it will not do to ask him anything. He talks like a madman."

"What could have happened?" cried Mrs. Kirkland. "He was all over blood!"

"And he looked so wild, and laughed when I called to him. Oh! that terrible laugh! It made my blood curdle in my veins. He must be wounded, mother; you must go to him! Don't mind what Grace says."

"I don't think him much hurt," said Grace, "though he says the blood is his own."

"Of course, *you* don't think him much hurt, and don't care. They must have had a terrible fight. That Stephen Joscelyn must have stabbed him with a knife!"

"He did not say so!" replied Grace.

"Maybe Walter has killed him!"

"God forbid!" cried the mother. "Oh! Angey, if such a thing has happened, it will all be your doing! And Walter will be tried for murder,——"

"Stop, mother!" said Grace. "You and Angelica be calm, I pray you. From what Walter said to me, I'm sure there's not much harm done on either side. He told me that he had killed nobody—that the blood on his clothes is his own blood."

"Then, to be sure, he must have been wounded. It's cruel of you, mother, to let him go to his room, and bleed to death by himself."

The mother was in a terrible bewilderment.

"What shall I do, Grace? There's reason in what Angey says."

"No, mother. I tell you that Walter has no serious hurt. He walks and talks pretty much as ever, and went to his room, not only without help, but rapidly; he even ran up the stairs, as he did not want you and Angey to see him in his bloodied and torn garments."

"But we did see him, you know, and he looked as if he were mortally wounded! Oh! how dreadful he looked!"

"I tell you, Angelica, he is not much hurt. Mother, be quiet, and wait on his movements. How could he be mortally wounded, to gallop home at full speed; then to hurry up to his chamber, taking two steps at a time?"

"Oh! but I've heard of a man walking a full mile, with a bayonet stuck right through his heart! Grace don't care if he should die. You must go to him, I tell you, mother, and send for Dr. Moore. I shall die, mother, if you don't. I feel so faint already."

And the young lady threw herself down upon the sofa, falling back, not ungracefully, with an air of faintness.

"Give her some blackberry wine, Grace; and, Grace, don't you think if I carried some of the wine up to Walter, it might settle his nerves, and then I could talk to him?"

Grace, who had recovered her own firmness, in the full faith, not only that Walter was unwounded, but that Stephen also had escaped all serious hurt, now said, authoritatively:

"And why would you talk to him just now, and what would you say? That's the very thing that he would dislike most of all. He does not wish to be talked to, and to speak to him of this affair would be the greatest mistake which you could make, either of you. No! Let him talk to you about it, if he will. He will owe it to you, Angey, at least to do so. He will feel the necessity of making some explanation; and, till he does so, you will take my advice and say not a word on the subject. From what he has said to me, I can see that his worst wound is in his soul, not in his body. He has evidently got the worst of it in this affair, whatever it may have been, and he feels all its humiliations."

"Humiliations!" cried Angelica, starting up; "you don't mean to insinuate that *my* Walter has suffered any humiliations at the hands of *your* Joscelyn!"

The ancient devil of vanity was again in arms. The speech of Angelica sent all the woman blood of Grace into her cheek.

At that moment, to the surprise of all parties, Walter Dunbar silently entered the room.

"Had he heard anything?" was the question of each of the ladies to herself.

His dress had been changed. The bloody proofs of his late struggle had been cast off, and his ablutions in cold water had lessened somewhat the further evidence of violence, which was still sufficiently apparent in the face; but his step was free and firm—his person was erect—there was no sign of wound or maim about him; and, after no little effort, he had been able so to compose his features as to appear with a half smile, laboring, struggling, and hardly grateful to the spectator, faintly showing itself in mouth and eye. He had made a great effort at ease, if not *nonchalance,* in the brief time which had been allowed him to dress.

His entrance silenced all the speakers. But every countenance expressed a natural curiosity, saving that of Grace. She was about to leave the room.

"Stay, Grace!" said Walter. "Stay, and hear what I have to say. You all naturally need some explanation of the spectacle which I have exhibited to you all to-day. It is very mortifying to me to say what I have to say, but it must be done. Once said, I trust, for my sake, that it will be no more a subject of remark among us. You must know, then, that, under a sense of injury, I attempted an act of violence to-day, and got the worst of it! I cannot give you particulars, nor enter upon details which have been most humiliating to me. I have been rash, perhaps, and erring. I may have been misled" —here he looked significantly at Angelica—"but if so, I have been sufficiently punished for my error. Enough, that the affair has ended thus far without the commission of any crime! I have been the only sufferer, and you see in what small degree."

"Will it go no further, my son?" demanded Mrs. Kirkland, earnestly, laying her hand upon his arm.

"*I* do not desire that it should," he replied. "In fact, there is one consideration, especially, which makes me regret the course which I have taken. I did not design, I assure you, anything beyond the mere expression of my anger and resentment, and the exposure to himself of a dishonorable proceeding on the part of another. But there was new provocation given me, and, under the passions roused by the new provocation, I forgot my own previous resolution of forbearance. Enough now. If you will permit me, we shall hereafter avoid the subject."

Grace looked at him very earnestly when he spoke of the dishonorable proceedings of another. She looked then at Angelica. Oh! how she longed to speak, and defend the absent and the injured! But there stood her sister—the truly guilty one—already white in the face, from that portion of the speech of Walter—inadvertently made, perhaps—in which he spoke of having been *misled*. Grace, as well as the mother, trembled quite as much as Angelica, at the utterance of this sentence. All were silent, and, having made his explanation, brief as it was, Walter again left the room quite as suddenly as he had entered it, returning again to his chamber.

His effort at composure was short-lived. He had performed his part with sufficient dignity; and this done, in compliance with what he owed to society, as a gentleman, he relapsed into his former moodiness. But he was outwardly composed. The very sense of humiliation under which he labored, had the effect of subduing his conduct, if not his mind, to the soberest paces. He appeared at dinner and at supper, talked a little, but not freely, and evidently under great mental effort at self-restraint. Sometimes, in the midst of the conversation, he would start up and walk the room in silence. He did not trust himself with Angelica alone, nor, at present, did she desire that he should. Both, for reasons of their own, were unwilling to be alone together. She feared his questioning. He did not distrust her, though, had he better known Stephen Joscelyn—had he not been persuaded that Stephen had played a viperous and treacherous part—he might have been startled at his solemn and stern denial of the charge made against him, and of the manly forbearance he had shown, when taught that a lady's name was involved in the slander which he yet so solemnly denied. It was the keen sense of humiliation, in the heart of the lover, that made him shrink from every exposure of his weaknesses or humiliation, to the eye of Angelica. They had a brief interview that night, and, silly as ever, she would fain have gratified her curiosity, at the expense of his sensibilities. She forgot his entreaties, as well as the counsels of Grace, so far as to say:

"But tell me, Walter, what did take place between you?"

Then, sternly looking at her, he answered:

"Have I not implored of you all, that you would not refer any more to this subject?"

"But that was before them all, Walter. Surely, it is different when you are alone with me?"

"Were you wise, Angelica, you would know that *our* policy is to discourse of things only which are grateful. Enough for you to know that the result of the affair this day has put my mind in such a frame, that I know not if the things which have pleased me once will ever please me again. I know not that even *your* love will ever be to me the precious thing that it was before."

"Oh! don't you say so, Walter."

"My heart has grown old in the last few hours. I feel it withering within me. Ay, Angelica, I think it would be better for you, if yours would close against me, and open only to some more happy suitor—one upon whom the Fates do not always frown! I am a doomed man. Every step I take, even in the flush of hope, youth, ambition and pride, conducts me only to new humiliation. Better for you, perhaps, than wedding such a lover, forswear our sex forever, and live a life of maiden solitude, never looking out upon the sun."

She was not the woman to comprehend this speech.

"But I won't, Walter, not while I live, and while you live. Never, never, never!"

And she wound her arms about his neck, and hung upon him fondly; but her kisses might as well have been pressed upon lips of marble. He felt them not—he did not requite them, but very quickly unclasped her arms from about his neck, and paced the floor with his own arms crossed upon his bosom, his chin drooping down, as if seeking rest also, and his eyes communing only with the floor.

"Doomed!" he exclaimed, bitterly; "doomed!—with every forward step taken only towards some mocking humiliation! Oh! God, what jibes, what mockings will follow upon this last most bitter action. Fool! fool that I am, to learn no wiser lessons from the past—not to see that my true wisdom is to crawl out of the sun's eye, and hide myself from a world, in whose fields I can only reap humiliation."

She followed his steps—she again clung about his neck. She longed to tell him of her crime and error; but her feeble and vain nature was too much for her courage, her truthfulness, or magnanimity and sense of justice. She felt that she ought to relieve his self-reproach by her own—by self-accusation and repentance; but her nature was too little earnest for even this small degree of self-sacrifice. And while she hung upon him, seeking by fondness to reconcile him to himself, there was a rap at the outer door. Then both remembered that the tread of a horse had been heard, from the road, but a few moments before.

The rap was repeated.

It was late. All the servants had gone to bed.

Walter went to the door, and the surprise which he felt was natural enough, when he found himself face to face with no less a person than Major Alison.

He was, as we well know, no admirer of Major Alison. There was no cordiality between them. But common courtesy compelled Walter to be civil; and then, Major Alison took an early moment to say that he brought letters from his (Walter's) father, which required instant attention.

He was conducted into the parlor, introduced to Miss Angelica, and soon Mrs. Kirkland, who had not retired for the night, was summoned to receive one of these letters.

That to Walter summoned him home, in very imperative language. The father wrote:

"I have important business which you must attend to. I can confide to no person but yourself. It is desirable that Major Alison should spend a part of his time on the river, a part of it on Beach Island, from whence he will need to go into the contiguous country. I could desire that our cousin Mary (Mrs. Kirkland,) would give him a welcome to her dwelling, for a brief period, and thus serve one who is, even now, busied in the service of her kinsman. I have written to her on this subject. It is desirable that the presence of Major Alison, at her residence, should remain unknown and unsuspected, as long as possible. He will adopt and continue such precautions as he may deem necessary for security."

The letter to Mrs. Kirkland was to the same effect. That good lady, though she had not forgotten that she had a quarrel, or, as she phrased it, "a crow to pluck," with her cousin Dunbar, was sufficiently prompt and courteous in her welcome to Major Alison, who began, accordingly, to play the courtier, with his wonted grace and subtlety.

He made himself very soon quite at home, and Angelica very quickly displayed her satisfaction, in a prolonged conversation with so charming a guest.

Walter was astounded at the facility with which, in a few moments, she had thrown off all the signs of that passionate anxiety which had made her cling to his neck with such fervid professions. But he was not displeased with any influence which could divert the keen eye of Alison from his own mental distraction.

Having done the honors to her new guest, provided refreshments, roused up Billy to see to and feed the horse of the stranger, the good lady, followed by her daughter, retired to rest. She had previously indicated to Walter the chamber she had designed for Alison, and he was left to "do the honors."

The two gentlemen were left together. Alison showed himself disposed to be flexible, and was talkative enough, if not communicative. Walter was as stately and reserved as usual. The only subject upon which he could have desired that the other should speak, namely, the object for which his father so peremptorily desired his speedy return, was one which he did not touch upon at all; and the pride of Walter did not suffer him to ask any questions.

Very soon the dialogue, such as it was, came to a dead pause between them, and Walter, professing to be fatigued himself, and assuming that the new comer was in like condition, took up a candle, and proposed to show him the way to his chamber; and so the pair withdrew for the night.

## CHAPTER XXV.

### A TOUCH OF GOUT.

The next day, after a sleepless and miserable night, Walter took his departure from Beach Island, for Augusta, leaving Major Alison in possession of the field. But this consideration gave him no concern. He seemed to have no apprehension from the gallantries of that courtier-like gentleman, and had no reason to question the fidelity of Angelica, however much he might be surprised at her flexibility.

We may take for granted that the Major was not the person to forbear any of the privileges to which his graces of manner and social resources might prompt him to pretend; and we may assume that he soon became quite as marked in his attentions to the beauty of Beach Island as he had been to her of the "Sand Hills" of Augusta. His approaches were destined to be quite as familiar, to Angelica, as they had been to Annie Dunbar; and, with this advantage, that they were scarcely received with so much coldness and *hauteur*. Youthful gallantry needs to be kept in frequent exercise, if only to make its right hand perfect in its cunning; and gay young gentlemen are very apt to play the lover, if only that they may pleasantly pass the time. It forms no subject of scruple, or even thought, with cavaliers of the ballroom, that young damsels are liable to deceive themselves as to the quality or character of the courtesies which they receive; and it is, perhaps, quite as fortunate for the damsels that so many of them can, with such facility, learn the secret of requiting the suitor in his own coin.

Angelica was gay enough in spirit to welcome the cavalier with smiles, without deigning him any further favors. Her vanity liked homage, while her cunning disarmed it mostly of the power of harm. Besides, what degree of love she *could* feel, was really enlisted in behalf of Walter, who, with quite as fine a person as any which she knew, was of a good house, with very fair prospects, had high reputation for morals as well as talents, and was generally considered—to use the elegant language so frequently employed by those who do not suffer from much ardency of temperament—as being "as good a catch" as any in the country.

Major Alison, lying *under* all day in the house, and sallying forth only by night, had sufficient opportunities for the exercise of his gallantries, and testing the quality of hers. We shall leave them thus related, for the day at least, taking for granted that, without disturbing the old match, they will be found a sufficient match for one another. So mote it be.

Walter was received very coolly by his father, who soon let him know the business for which he had required his presence. The scheme of Alison, which he had suggested to the old man, for sending Walter up to the highlands, the better to wean him from old and dangerous associates, and bring him into contact with those who might succeed in bringing him into the right political fold, had ripened to maturity during his absence at Beach Island. Walter was to be the bearer of "*dispatches*" to certain leading men among the highland gentry, which he was taught to believe were of vast importance to his father's interests and the public good. He was instructed to treasure them as sacred, and to deliver them only into the hands of those to whom they were severally addressed. There were letters to his kinsman, Moses Kirkland, to Colonel Robinson, Robert Cunningham, Richard Pearis, and others, all of whom were engaged in the work of subsidizing the common population in behalf of the royal cause.

Now, these letters were really only shams—they were little more than letters of introduction. Old Dunbar and Alison had sent their real dispatches by a very different hand, anticipating the departure of Walter, but announcing his coming, and revealing to all these persons, the plot against his supposed political preferences; requesting that he be kept among them for a season, until his latent loyalty should be developed, by their influence upon him, into some activity. He was to be persuaded to commit himself to the cause, and a Captain's commission, already filled out, and signed by the royal Governor in South Carolina, was to be employed as one of the lures by which to beguile him into the royal ranks. It was well known to them that he had not yet, in any way, committed himself to what they facetiously called the "rebel" cause. His indecision of character was what they had to correct; and, to decide his course, they very well conceived that the processes employed should be to give him a proper bias, under leading minds; assail his virtues through his impulses and passions; minister to his self-esteem as much as possible, and when once committed to some overt act or speech, it was felt, and believed, that his self-esteem, or, if you will so call it, his sense of honor, would keep him faithful to the cause. They were to keep him among them in constant intercourse with the chief men, and unapproachable by persons of adverse sentiments; and thus, from hearkening only to one mode of speech, argument, and opinion, they reasonably calculated on giving the necessary direction to a mind, the great defect of which was the absence of that wit which is so essential to the manly virtues in any character.

Verily, a very pretty plot, which old Dunbar persuaded himself was quite justifiable, though his son was the subject of it.

We have said that he received his son coldly. Perhaps it would have been better to have said that he received him without any show of affection or sympathy. For he was not cold, but irritable, and even passionate. Naturally of impatient and irritable temperament, he was now suffering from an attack of the gout, which kept him from his daily practice upon his war horse. For his son, he had few words, and these were simply commands.

"You will go," said he, "to-morrow?"

"I will go," was the answer.

"Start at daylight."

"At daylight."

"Very good! I will not see you then again till your return."

The young man bowed his head in silence. The father gazed at him sternly and steadfastly for a few moments. Their eyes met. The stern coldness of glance in the one, was encountered by a sort of vacant, apathetic, unmeaning stare in the other.

The submission of the young man—the passive, soulless, lifeless, indifferent air and manner—so full, as it seemed, of utter hopelessness, suddenly touched the father's heart. He fancied that this condition was the result of the exercise of his own authority. He could not otherwise understand it. He little knew, had not as yet heard of that recent humiliation on Beach Island, super-added to those which had gone before, which had been as the last feather on the back of the overburdened camel. And he knew nothing of those psychological characteristics of the youth—a mother's gift, perhaps—which were so very unlike his own.

Enough, that he was touched. Rising with difficulty from his cushioned chair, he said, in softened accents, somewhat broken:

"Will you give me your arm, my son? Help me to my chamber."

The arm was given in silence. When the two had entered the old man's chamber, he said, brokenly:

"You will take care of yourself, my son. Be a man! And God be with you and bless you."

And he put his arms around the son's neck and kissed his cheek tenderly. There was no answering embrace, kiss, or show of affection.

The old man burst out in one of his passionate ejaculations.

"Great God, young man, is there no blood in your body, no spirit in your soul, no feeling in your heart? What means this apathy?—this cold-blooded, insensate lifelessness? Ay, deadness of everything that should be precious to manhood? Speak, sir, and tell me what it means?"

"What would you have me say?" answered the youth, gloomily.

"Say? Say anything! Curse your father, if you will, only show some signs that you live—that you feel—"

"I feel, but do not live! Is it not enough that I obey you? You have not suffered me to feel or live as I would, and in coercing my will with your own, you take my life! I am your creature, not my own."

"Ha!—and why the devil, sir, have you submitted to me? Why did you not resist before? Why do you submit now? Why not bid me defiance? Better a thousand times that you should rebel against a tyrant father, than forfeit the rights of your own soul and manhood!"

"You never taught me this lesson before. You have cursed your son when you suspected him of such defiance."

"It is not too late! Curse me, sir. Curse me now, for your own sake, if you would regain your liberty."

"It is too late, sir. You have doomed me."

"Walter!—my God!—how much he looks like his mother now!"

Walter was gone. The father sank down upon the side of his bed, and covered his face with his hands. What a history was embodied in that last sentence which broke so unconsciously from his lips! What a story did it tell of the despotic husband, terrible in his self-esteem, ruling his household with the rod of iron; savage, if resisted in his despotism; and in the sustenance and growth of his self-esteem, utterly blind, deaf, and in every way insensible to the sweet sympathies, the loving feelings, the warm tenderness, which, at every step, he trode down beneath his feet.

Yet, old Dunbar fancied himself a Christian. He had daily prayers in his family. He himself delivered them; read from the Bible, and rose up always with a delightful sense of satisfaction. His loud tones, his imperious manner, even while he prayed, with eyes open, but cast upward, seemed all the while to say to the spectator, "God should be very grateful to me now, for all that I am doing in his behalf on earth."

Alas! alas! this miserable Humanity!

The groans of the father, which followed the flight of the son, and which grew from that obtrusive memory of the pitiless past, failed to effect any change in the mood or manner of the son. He himself, full of his own agonizing sense of humiliation, had no uttered anguish. The house, but for the groans from that upper chamber, was all in silence, and these groans might be due quite as much to the gout as to the human susceptibilities.

Yet, no! The son *had* struck a blow at the very heart of the father which he felt through all the iron which incased it.

# CHAPTER XXVI.

## A L'OUTRANCE.

Lovers have modes of telegraphing each other without waiting on the wires. Somehow, Martin Joscelyn could always discover when the field was clear for him at the Sand Hills—when old Dunbar retired early—when Major Alison was about—and briefly, when there was no danger of any intrusion upon his *tête-à-tête* with the fair Annie. It is just possible that Alison suspected these secret meetings, if the father did not. But Alison was not the person to declare his suspicions. He was not the less vigilant, though silent. We shall see.

When Walter, gloomy to desperation, descended the stairs to the parlor, he found Martin quietly sitting beside his sister. The good aunt had graciously retired also, but not till after Martin arrived. The young men shook hands; Martin as eagerly as ever; but he recoiled suddenly from the passive surrender to his own, of the hand of his ancient comrade and friend. There was no grasp—no cordial gripe, full of assuring friendship; and when the eyes of the two met, the vacant, blank, unmeaning glance of Walter utterly astounded Martin.

"Why, Walter, what's the matter? Are you sick? Has anything happened?"

The other answered evasively.

"You know that I leave for the hill country to-morrow."

"Yes, Annie has been telling me. How long will you be gone?"

"I know not. It is on business of my father."

Martin watched the face of the speaker, uncertain what to gather from its expression, or rather want of expression. But he resolved to go on talking to, or at him, in order to bring him out. Annie Dunbar, whose countenance betrayed thought and anxiety, seemed not unwilling to second this object, and freely joined in the conversation.

But in vain. Walter remained taciturn, responding only to direct inquiries, of which he also seemed impatient. He strode the room with his head drooping forward, his hands folded behind his back, stopping occasionally in his walk, and sinking listlessly, at times, into a chair, from which, as suddenly, he would rise again, only to resume his walk.

Martin, meanwhile, continued seated beside his betrothed, and finding all his efforts in vain to elicit from Walter the secret of his seeming malady, he gave up the effort, and in low tones addressed himself only to his fair companion. This forbearance, in respect to himself, seemed to afford Walter evident relief. He grew more composed, seated himself, and appeared lost in thought as he was in silence.

The parties were thus grouped, when they were surprised by an unexpected and unwelcome intruder. The door was opened quietly, no footsteps had been heard without, and Major Alison made his appearance in the centre of the parlor, before either of the group had become aware of his presence or approach.

The effect was magical. Martin started up from the sofa, but not before Alison had fully discovered the proximity of his head to the brown tresses of the damsel. It is just possible, too, that he may have seen that the left arm of Martin was hidden behind her person, on the back of the sofa.

Our friend Martin, though a brave fellow, was decidedly beflustered. He rose hurriedly, as we have said, and without seeming to notice the intruder, walked hastily across the room to the spot where Walter was sitting. The latter appeared wholly unmoved, and, as it would seem, almost unconscious of the entry of the visitor, till fully recalled to consciousness by the approach of Martin.

"So! so!" muttered Alison, *sotto voce*, while a bitter smile spread itself over his lips.

He advanced with a somewhat lordly salutation to the lady, a bow to the gentlemen, and an inquiry after old Dunbar, addressed to his son. The lady answered him.

"My father has retired for the night, Major Alison. He is somewhat unwell."

"Is it not possible for me to see him?"

"Hardly, sir; he is really quite unwell, and much suffering from a sudden attack of the gout."

"A gentlemanly disorder, at all events," was the remark of Alison, as he coolly took the seat on the sofa which had just been vacated by Martin.

"D—n the fellow's impudence!" was the almost audible exclamation of Martin. "What the devil could have brought him back so soon and so suddenly?"

As if anticipating some such reflection, Alison said to Annie:

"I had not hoped for the pleasure of so soon seeing you again; but a sudden exigency—really, I could wish to see your father, if possible, to-night."

"I should be quite unwilling to disturb him, Major Alison, and you would find him, in his present state of suffering, to be quite unfit for any business."

He beat with his foot impatiently upon the floor, his eyes curiously scanning the face of Martin, as the latter stood leaning against the mantel. The poor fellow looked bewildered. A cold, malicious smile passed over the features of Alison, as he surveyed him, while one almost of contempt succeeded to it on his face, as he looked at Walter.

"Ahem!—Mr. Dunbar—" It was thus, though somewhat hesitatingly, that Alison challenged the attention of Walter.

The latter started as from a dream, and replied abruptly:

"Well, sir—what?"

The voice was harsh, the tones stern, the whole manner of the speaker denoted dissatisfaction and dislike. Alison was taken aback for a moment. Walter's voice sounded like a defiance.

"You seem unwell, sir," said the other, half deprecatingly. "I—"

"I do not accuse you, sir," was the seemingly inconsequent reply.

"Oh! no, sir; of course not—my purpose was simply to request that, as I have to depart again to-night, you will communicate to your father the message—"

"Sir, I shall not see my father again until I return from a mission upon which I depart by to-morrow's dawn. Nay, I know not that I shall ever see him again! I can undertake no mission to him. You must see to it yourself."

There was something in the burst of passion contained in this reply that produced a profound sensation in the whole party. The eyes of

Annie Dunbar settled upon her brother with a mournfully pleading expression. Martin stared wistfully anxious and more bewildered than ever. Even Alison was silent during a long pause, which he at length broke abruptly.

"Then I *must* see him to-night."

"That you can *not,* sir," said Annie Dunbar, with much firmness of tone and manner. "My father suffers too much under those attacks, and every disturbance increases his suffering and irritation. You will please reserve your communication for the morning."

"Impossible! I must ride to-night."

Saying this, he paused, and seemed to meditate. Suddenly his countenance changing completely, and now wreathed in smiles, he bowed towards the young lady, and in a manner much more familiar than courtly, said, while he pointed to the harpsichord:

"Will you give me some music, Annie, before I go?"

The flush covered the cheeks of Annie Dunbar. She gazed steadily at the offender, and in silence; but the voice of Walter Dunbar rang sharply over the apartment:

"*Miss* Annie, sir, if you please."

"Oh! *Lady* Annie, sir, if *you* please."

The lady rose, her bosom heaving with indignation. Martin Joscelyn strode towards Alison with flashing eyes, and fists clenched; but Walter darted forward, flung Martin aside, and, confronting Alison, who sate carelessly smiling on the sofa, exclaimed in suppressed but emphatic tones:

"This insolence, sir, deserves the horsewhip, and shall have it."

Terribly effective was the sarcastic rejoinder:

"Let the infliction take place in my school-room, with a score of my boys about me, and I shall feel myself honored by it."

Walter staggered back as if under a blow. His humiliating secret was then already blown abroad! Shame stared him in the face on every hand. But he recovered himself in another instant, and advancing towards Alison, he said hoarsely, but distinctly:

"You shall hear from me, sir."

"No, Walter," interposed Martin. "He shall hear from me."

"You!" said Alison, scornfully.

"Yes!" And, with the reply, Martin Joscelyn approached him, and with something of the look of his powerful, though crippled brother, stooping, he hissed in his very ears:

"Yes, dog as you are, you shall hear from me, and by ——, you shall *feel* me, too, from the crown of your head to the sole of your feet."

Alison now rose. He no longer held his calm of aspect. But, before he could speak, Annie Dunbar passed between the parties.

"No, Walter; no, Martin. This man shall hear from *me!* You have, sir," said she, turning to him, "abused my father's hospitality. He shall know it. You have wantonly inflicted insult upon a woman. Take with you, wherever you go, the consciousness of your baseness, and the absence of character among all honorable men."

She turned from him, and deliberately walking up to Martin, she laid her hands upon his shoulder, and to his own and the surprise of all parties present, she kissed him upon his cheek.

The act was conclusive! Alison's face paled again. What were his emotions we cannot say. He had lost a point in his game. In his malice of heart he had, for a moment, lost his head. He had not thought that things had gone so far between Miss Dunbar and Martin Joscelyn; and seeking, perhaps, to create a false impression in the mind of the latter, he had forced the lady to the assertion of her womanhood, in the revelation of her heart. He little knew the fiery spirit, or the clear sense, or the exquisite sensibility, leading to power, in that seemingly slight and trifling girl.

But the scene had reached its crisis—its climax.

The impudence of Alison was not wholly to be rebuked. He rose, and bowing right and left as he went, he said:

"A very courtly company of lords and ladies! I wish you a very good evening."

Martin Joscelyn touched him on the shoulder as he left the room.

"And to you, sir, such good morrow as you shall deserve. We shall become better acquainted, sir, before you get your full deserts."

"All in good time, sir." And, humming a song, Alison disappeared from the entrance. It had been easy for him, hitherto, to come and go, and he made his way directly to the leafy covert where his steed was fastened. Here, after muttering some bitter curses, he mounted his horse, and, in a few moments, disappeared from the precinct—whither, we need not now inquire.

## CHAPTER XXVII.

### TOUCHED TO FINE ISSUES.

"Martin! Walter! I exhort—I command you not to seek this war! There must be no fighting on my account."

So spoke Annie Dunbar, with her hands laid on an arm of each of the young men. Her fine face was flushed. Her voice was tremulous, but commanding. Her form was raised to its fullest height. The tears were in her eyes, but she looked very beautiful.

Martin was silent; but Walter spoke.

"*You,* at least, Martin, must take no step in this business. The task is mine. It is my sister that he has insulted."

"She is my affianced, Walter."

"That is nothing," answered Walter, impatiently. "She must not be committed in the public eye, which would be the case were you to interpose in this matter. And how should I suffer you to interfere, when it is under my own eyes, in my own presence, in my father's house, that the insult was given? It is for me, and me only, to resent and punish the insulter. I will do it, and you must not step between us."

"You forget, Walter, that you are to depart to-morrow."

"I will not go. I will stay till I ferrit out this scoundrel."

"You must go, brother! My father will never forgive you!"

"Ha! ha! ha!" was the wild, bitter laughter of the young man. "He forgive! When did he ever forgive? What chance have I now of his forgiveness? I have no hope from him. I do not dream of it."

"You will obey him, my brother!" said the young girl, grasping both his hands with hers. "For my sake, you will obey him. And—remember his condition. Remember the trusts which he confided to your hands. He tells you—he has told me—that they are of vital importance to his interests—that he can trust the commission to you only, and that it needs all possible dispatch. Do not trifle with this sacred demand upon your duty."

The young man shook off her grasp, and paced the floor in silence. Martin Joscelyn joined his entreaties to hers. He followed Walter, caught his arm, took him into a corner of the room, and whispered in his ears.

"Leave him to me! You have no time to waste upon him now. We must wait. To hunt him up at present would be like looking for a needle in a haystack."

"*I* know where to find him!" cried the other, hoarsely.

"But you must *not* find him, brother—you must not seek him," cried the sister, again approaching the two. "Do not, I entreat you, for my sake, take any step in this business—either you or Martin. I know—I see—what you meditate. I know what the passions of men are, and the false notions of what you call honor; but, mark me, Martin Joscelyn, if you come to me with the blood of this man on your hands, shed in personal combat, you shall never have hand of mine—never!—never!"

"But, Annie," said the lover, beginning to expostulate.

"Never!—never!"

"My dear Annie!"

"I have said it, Martin. Never, never will I give my hand in marriage to one who seeks, or has sought, in single combat, the blood of any fellow creature. It is bad enough if such deed be done in war —but in the duel! Oh! Martin Joscelyn! solemnly, sadly, I tell you now, that all must be at an end between us, unless you forego the unlucky purpose which you have declared, and which I see is working in the minds of both of you."

"But shall a man not defend himself?"

"Oh! Martin, do not trifle with me by such evasions. Surely he must defend himself, as a man, if assailed. I do not speak of such a case, nor is it such a case that you meditate. I say, if you seek this man in any way to fight him, as an individual, for his offence to-night, we part forever. Now, do you understand me?"

Martin would still have expostulated, but she waved him to silence, while she turned to her brother. But he gave her no heed.

"Oh! brother, will you not hear me?"

"What more can you say that you have not already said?" he replied. "Now, hear me, Annie. I have resolved."

"Ah!"

"I will do somewhat to satisfy you. I will go on the mission of our father to-morrow. I will not suffer the pursuit of this scoundrel to defeat that object. But this is all I will promise you. Be content with this, Annie. It is all that you get from me now, though you should plead all night. And now, go to bed."

"You will then go to-morrow?"

"Yes."

"I will be up in the morning before you start, and give you breakfast."

"Let it be early. I must be off at the very break of day. I shall probably have to ride fifty miles to-morrow."

She kissed him, and gave her hand to Martin. He, too, would have kissed her, but she shook her head.

"No, Martin!—not again until you promise me."

He dropped his head.

"Ah!—is it so, Martin? And so hate triumphs over love!"

Martin groaned, and, as she gave him a sad look at retiring, he suddenly turned, caught her in his arms, and kissed her—then said:

"It shall be as you say. I will not seek this man; but——"

"But what, Martin?"

"He must not cross my path!"

She was gone.

When her last footsteps were heard ascending on the stairs, Walter closed and locked the door.

"Martin," said he, "I will not seek this scoundrel, Alison; I feel that I must yield myself for the present to the requisitions of my father, but I will leave a message for him. I will not ask you to deliver it, for two reasons. I would not, in the first place, involve you in any situation which might lose you the regards of my sister. The other reason I shall keep to myself. Sit while I write."

He seated himself at a desk and hastily penned two brief notes, one addressed to Major Alison, the other to John Cummings, Esq. The note to Alison was covered in that to Cummings.

These done, he gave them to Martin.

"Deliver this to-morrow as soon as possible to Jack Cummings. I will say nothing of its contents. You, accordingly, know nothing of them. You have promised Annie, so I understand it, to do nothing yourself in this business. There is hardly a possibility that Alison will force any meeting upon you, nor is it likely that any opportunity will occur for a rencontre between you. You will keep your word to Annie, I know, and I need not ask you for any promise to me. We must part now, Martin. But, before we do so, I must refer vaguely to another affair about which I can tell you nothing. You will hear of it soon enough from other parties. You will then understand why my mood is such to-night. It may be that the action of which I have been guilty, and of which you will surely hear, will outrage all your sensibilities, possibly lose me all your sympathies."

"Oh! never, Walter."

"Do not be too fast. You will be shocked. Your wonder will be great, that I should have so forgotten your claims upon me in the passions which were provoked by another. I am shocked and revolted myself, and wonder at my own insanity when I think of it; but my humiliation is beyond description. It is my proper punishment, and it crushes me to the earth. All I can say is, Martin, that I am full of remorse at my offence, and despise myself at my folly. Will you give me your hand, at parting, my friend? You can tell me hereafter whether you can forgive me!"

"Give you my hand, Walter?" cried Martin, throwing his arms round the neck of the other. "You have hand and heart, old fellow, as you have ever had, since the days when we were playfellows. What mysteries are these that you are talking of?"

"They will be no mysteries to you by to-morrow night! You will then understand the whole. You will see how great has been my folly—you will, perhaps, conceive the cause of it—you will know too well what is my offence to you, and I can only hope that you will forgive it, in the conviction that, in its commission, I was under a sort of insanity. Let us part now. You know not how great is the effort I make to say so much, and to say it calmly. I seem to myself like the victim of some cruel fate that shapes me, as the winds shape the light clouds of an April sky, to what ridiculous forms they please. One embrace, Martin—and now leave me! I can talk no more—say no more—nothing to explain a matter which you will soon hear from other lips than mine. Enough that my present humiliation is fully proportioned to my offence!"

Walter had really made a great effort at composure when he made this speech. It was much broken in the utterance. He frequently paused, and turned away. But he nerved himself to a renewal of his task, and finally, as we have seen, delivered himself of it. He could do no more. Martin's anxiety, greater than his curiosity, would have made assurances—would still have lingered over the subject, but Walter would not hear him—would not respond. He could only say:

"Leave me now, Martin; if still my friend, leave me now. I can bear no more! Farewell, and, whether we meet again or not, do you forgive me!"

"Forgive you! Oh! Walter—oh! my friend—there is nothing to forgive. You are forgiven by Martin Joscelyn whatever your offence!"

"Ah! *Joscelyn?*"

The full name spoken touched the sensitive cord, and the young man shuddered, as he waived Martin off.

"Ah! when you shall hear."

Martin only answered by embracing him; then, with slow steps, he left the house.

"It was a bitter medicine!" said Walter, when he had gone—"it was a bitter medicine! And the taste will long remain in the mouth!"

He threw himself upon the sofa, in gloomy meditations, and if he slept at all, it was in that situation. It was dawn when he parted with his aunt and sister.

## CHAPTER XXVIII.

### GRACE AND STEPHEN.

Walter gone upon his doubtful mission, Martin Joscelyn proceeded upon his finding Cummings, and delivering the mission of his friend; but of this matter nothing more need be said at present.

It was not very long after this had been done, when, as Walter had told him, Martin soon heard those tidings, which filled him with equal pain and surprise. He could now comprehend the mystery of Walter's deportment, and find a clue to the occult matter of his language. The story of the encounter between Walter and Stephen Joscelyn, and the prompt action of the school-boys, was very soon spread abroad over Beach Island, Augusta, and the surrounding precincts. But the jeer and the jibe did not reach the ears of the fugitive, who rejoiced that he was already far from the scenes of his humiliation. We are yet to see what other scenes fate had in store for him, of a more grateful character.

Martin rode over to Beach Island to see and sympathize with his brother. But Stephen would hardly listen to any remark upon the subject.

"Say no more of it, Martin. I pity the poor fellow. He is *your* friend. That is enough for me. He knew not what he did. He has some good qualities, but there is a fatal weakness in his moral, or mind, which will always defeat the good he has in him. He pauses when he should proceed, and darts ahead at the very moment when he ought to pause and reflect. He is infirm of purpose. And the annoying consciousness of this infirmity, when felt acutely, is very apt to impel the party to a rashness, if only to satisfy himself that he is not *wholly* infirm—that he has the will, the courage, the decision, about which his own consciousness is yet full of perpetual misgivings."

"He is gone with despatches from his father to certain parties in the Highlands."

"Ha! what parties?"

"I do not know. I did not ask."

"Stop a bit, Martin." Then addressing his pupils, Stephen cried out:

"Boys, you are dismissed for the day. Let me see you soon to-morrow."

They were gone, tumbling out headlong, and soon their whoops and halloos tore the air without.

"And now," said Stephen to his brother, "were it possible, I should put out with my troop, try and overhaul Master Walter Dunbar, and see to the contents of the despatches he carries."

"Good God, Steve! what is this?"

"War, Martin! Have you heard the tidings? Have you seen Col. Hammond, lately?"

"No! He is absent from Snow Hill."

"With his troop? Why are you not with him? But you will be called out. Advices have just reached me which will require me, you, and all of us, to take the field pretty soon. Major Williamson, with three hundred of our men, Colonel Thompson, with his Rangers and three hundred foot soldiers, and Colonel Richardson, with another force of three hundred foot, are already on the march to meet the King's men, as they call themselves, and Drayton's proclamation is out denouncing them as enemies of the country."

"How do you hear all this, and we not a syllable in Augusta?"

"It is a secret with me why I should hear—why you should not have heard also, through Colonel Hammond, I do not see; for my advices assure me that he will shortly take the field also, and I know that he has received the intelligence. Captain Andrew Pickens is now moving down to join him with his company, and Hammond's company will unite with Drayton. We are all to concentrate upon Kirkland, and take him front, flank and rear, and if he will only wait for us, we'll do it."

"I must get back to Augusta, and put myself in readiness."

"You will find orders waiting you, I doubt not, as soon as you get back."

"And you, Steve? Do you still persist in forming this company of cavalry?"

"Forming! It is already formed, and you shall soon see in saddle fifty as fine troopers as ever straddled a wild horse. It is quite probable that I shall be in the saddle at the head of them, in less than three days. I expect my messenger with dispatches, this very night—dispatches from Drayton himself."

There might have been some little pride of manner and swell of voice, on Stephen's part, when he told his brother of his distinguished associations; but he did not tell him *all*.

When Martin was gone, Stephen took out his private letters, and brooded over them for awhile. He read aloud at intervals, and soliloquized as he read.

"No," said he, "it will not do to mention this as yet." Then he read from the dispatch:

"It is rumored that there is a squabble among the tory leaders. Some of them are for fighting it out; but others betray the white feather. Among these—such is the report—Kirkland himself is scared; and the rumor, last night, was to the effect that he had stolen off from their camp, and was nowhere to be found. He is probably seeking to make his way below. If these rumors shall be confirmed, I shall issue a new proclamation, framed to suit the event, and calculated to still further cause dissention in their ranks."

Stephen soliloquized.

"Kirkland stolen away! This letter is a week old. Three nights ago a stranger reached the abode of Mrs. Kirkland. Bridges reports that a horseman rode thither at a late hour last night. He saw him enter, but could distinguish nothing about him in the darkness. Who should this stranger be? Who so likely as Kirkland, seeking temporary refuge with his sister-in-law? And it is only a two days' ride from hence to Salt Water."

And so he brooded for awhile. He then rose, took out a bunch of quills, and proceeded to convert them into pens of fine nib, which he manufactured very nicely with a directing hand. These, when made, he put up carefully in a paper box, with several quires of paper, a box of wafers, and a bottle of ink. He was then employed about his school-room, throughout the morning, and long after the boys had gone from the premises.

That night, when the darkness had fairly set in, he rode from the house of Dick Marvin, taking the package which he had thus made up under his arm, and taking Marvin along with him. As they rode together, in the direction of Mrs. Kirkland's dwelling, Stephen said to him:

"Dick, take this little slip of paper; keep it secret, but so convenient to your fingers that you may be able to find and use it at the first opportunity. You say you have to see Mrs. Kirkland about that lot of bacon and flour."

"Yes, Captain Stephen, but what am I to do with the paper?"

"You shall soon know."

"But don't you mean to go in?"

"No; I'm coming to that matter. I shall hardly enter that house again."

"What, Captain, and when they think so much of you too, and after all you've done for them?"

"I do not think, Dick, that *all* of them do think so much of me, or value so very highly all that I have done for them."

"Then they're a dod-durn'd ungrateful set, and don't deserve any favors."

"Hush, Dick," said Stephen, gently. "You know not what you say. I have reason to think that some of them are grateful, and have always been kind to me, but not all."

"Then it kin only be that Queen of Sheba, or that Queen of Huzzies, rather, with her fine feathers and tossing head of curls. Ah! I thought from the first that she was a fool, and now I know it."

"Hush, Dick Marvin; again I tell you, you know not what you say. And—we have no need to talk of this. Hear me. I shall not enter the house, nor shall you speak of me as having come with you. I shall stop behind the garden, while you ride forward to the house. Do you ride into the yard, and up to the piazza, and make as much noise in riding up as you possibly can. See then to your business with Mrs. Kirkland, but contrive some plan for slipping that note into the hands of Miss Grace, without letting any other person see you; and if she leaves the room, do you remain there till she come back. I expect her, when she reads the note, to come out and meet me."

"Ah! Steve, you're on the sly. Well, I always thought Miss Grace a thousand times the best of the two, and what's more, I always conceited that she had her eyes on you, Steve."

"Pshaw, Dick, don't be a blockhead."

"Blockhead or not, Stephen, I've got a good pair of eyes in the block."

"But very little brains behind them, Dick. You're a good fellow, Dick, but your studies of young women have not yet taught you understanding, so far as they are concerned. Do you do as I tell you, and keep your tongue busy while you stay in the house; but say nothing of me, if you can help it."

The note contained but a single sentence:

"Grace, I shall await you at the bottom of the garden, and must see you on a matter of great importance.

"S. J."

The mission confided to Dick Marvin was not beyond his power to manage, and it was not long that Stephen had to wait beneath the apple tree, before he caught the glimpse of a female figure approaching. The stars were out, shining brightly, but not so brightly as to suffer the warm coloring of Grace's cheek to be perceptible to her companion, as she put her hand silently in his.

"You are well, Grace—all are well, I hope."

She answered him in the same low tones, in the affirmative. The question satisfied, Stephen proceeded directly to the business which had brought him. He was a man of purpose.

"Grace," said he, "I have reason to believe that your house will be searched by the 'Council of Safety' within the next forty-eight hours."

"Oh! Stephen! Searched—The Council—"

"It is suspected that you harbor there a person who, as I have reason to believe, will be denounced within that time, as a traitor to his country. It is not improbable that I myself will be designated as the leader of the squad which may be sent to take him. I give you now my conjectures only, and do not ask to know any of the secrets of the house. It will be for your mother to say in what degree this communication will affect her, and to take her precautions accordingly. If there be any suspected person with you, it will be easy to send him off before the search is made. It is on your and your mother's account that I give you my advice and opinion, before it shall become my official duty to act in such a manner as might annoy you, and possibly bring you into danger. My patriotism, Grace, has not been able to hold its ground against my affection for your family."

"Oh, Stephen, I so thank you! There is a person—"

"Tell me nothing, Grace; and let me entreat you to say nothing to your mother, or to any one, of your source of information."

"You are so good, Stephen," was the murmured answer. Then becoming bolder she said:

"We have so missed you, Stephen."

"Ah! Grace! Can it, indeed, be so? What is there in me, that my presence or absence should occasion thought or regret in any of your sex?"

"And why not, Stephen? Are you not—"

Here she paused, seized with a sudden trembling, which caused her to grasp a branch of the apple tree for support. "Had she said too much?" "Had she gone too far?" These were the questions which her conscious and sensitive heart asked of her unwitting tongue.

"You are faint. You are ill, Grace," and he put his arm about her waist to support her, and she then trembled more violently than ever. She felt that she could die gratefully under the acute sense of pleasure, in that seeming expression of pain.

"Lean on me, Grace. You are chilled. You are faint. I was wrong to bring you out here. But you know I could not enter the house, and it is to your prudence alone that I could trust in this delicate matter. Lean on me."

And she rested in his arms, and on his bosom. Her eyes closed. Her lips murmured. She seemed, for a few moments, to have lapsed away in her faintness, in her dream, to him, in his ignorance, into a seeming death.

"Grace! Grace! my God! she will die?"

But, in the next instant, she broke away from his bosom, and stood erect. He still would have grasped and sustained her; but, with a sudden growth of energy, she waived him off, and said, in very low but decided tones:

"No, Stephen. It is over. I am better now. It was a strange, sudden faintness, and—and—"

The sentence was concluded with an involuntary sigh, while her eyes closed again, as if to sleep, and recall the happy dreams which had been lost in her awaking.

Stephen was still solicitous for her, and would have supported her back to the dwelling, but she would not.

"I am better—I am quite well, now, Stephen. I don't know how it was that I became faint so suddenly."

When assured that she was recovered, when, in brief, she had resumed that calm, gentle, placidly resigned woman by which he had always known her, he said, lifting up the package which had been lying at the foot of the tree:

"You asked me, Grace, months ago, to make you some fine pens, and I take shame to myself for having neglected them so long. I have brought them now, with a little supply of paper, wafers, and ink. There is enough here for all the family, and it may be long before I can again supply you."

"Oh! thank you, Stephen. Are you going already?"

"I must. Thank you, Grace, for so kindly coming to meet me. I should not have taxed you to do so, but that there was no other mode of giving you this information without endangering what is possibly a secret of much interest to your mother. Good-bye, Grace."

"Good—good-bye, Stephen."

The voice again faltered. The long, taper-fingers trembled, as his hand closed over them; and her face, could he have seen it, would have shown itself as pallid as at first it had been flushed with the hues of the carnation. How little did he conceive of that drama of the sensibilities through which her poor yearning heart had gone, in that small fragment of time which they had spent together.

Slowly she went from sight, slowly, sadly; but with a sweet sensation of a new kind, which kept trembling in all her arterial pulses.

And he! Poor Stephen!

He did not watch *her* departing progress, nor note with what reluctant steps she passed from his sight. His eyes, with intense stare, were fastened upon the windows of that southwest chamber, where flickered the faint light of one little lamp, shadowed, at moments, by the flitting of a female form, between its faint glimmer and his straining gaze.

In a quarter of an hour more, he was joined by Dick Marvin, and the two rode home together, Stephen Joscelyn yielding to him the exclusive field of speech, for which the eloquence of Dick Marvin was duly grateful, as he recounted the long dialogue which he had enjoyed with the old lady, what he said and she said, what they mutually answered, and especially all that the good woman had been pleased to say of a loving nature in respect to Stephen himself, of whose neglect she complained sadly, while admitting that she had reason to complain.

Stephen sighed only in reply.

"As for the fool girl, Angelica," continued Dick Marvin, "she hardly gin me the time of day; but soon as she seed who it was, she flung out of the room, singing a sort of air, as if to say, 'what the devil's this fellow to me?' "

"You saw nobody besides the family, Dick?"

The answer was in the negative. Yet Stephen gathered from Dick, without provoking the suspicions of the latter, that they were a long time in letting him in; and that, when they did so, "they looked as much frightened as if I had been a whole regiment of dragoons. But women are all of them so cussed scary."

## CHAPTER XXIX.

### FETES AND FATES.

Three days after these events, there was great stir on Beach Island. Everybody was on the *qui vive.* Stephen Joscelyn had summoned his troopers to the field. The "old field school" was broken up. There was a great gathering on that occasion. Parents and children assembled alike, to receive the farewell of the well-beloved teacher. They came from various distances, and brought their supplies of food and viands along with them. The reunion was resolved into an extempore *pic-nic* beneath the trees. Stephen Joscelyn divided a large number of his books among the pupils and their parents. He distributed paper, pens and ink—distributed himself, as it were, among a people whom he might never see again. Such, at least, appeared to be the thought among many, and all hearts were saddened by it. There were eyes of good mothers full of tears. There were eyes of old men watching, with a fond gravity, the enthusiastic play of every muscle of the brave young teacher's face, as he discoursed in turn to parents and pupils. Never had a little community more confidence in its local leader. He was about to conduct into the field of danger fathers, sons and brothers. By this time, all parties knew that the discontents in the highland country had culminated in the absolute issues of war. Armies were being massed, and were marching upon each other. Settlements were divided, and contiguous districts and precincts were arranged under hostile banners. Very earnest were the moods of men; very grave their thoughts; very serious their apprehensions. When men invoke the god of battles, they know not what fate will take the field, interposing between right and justice, in behalf of mortal power, passion and usurpation! They forget that the true God sways not to His ends of justice through the arm of violence; and how monstrous to appeal to Jehovah to engage in any issue where Moloch has been already chosen as the presiding Deity! As well expect the intervention of a god in a conflict of mad bulls, scouring the plains in their fury, and relying solely on the length of their horns and the thickness of their skulls!

Stephen Joscelyn disbanded his scholars with an affectionate address, full of loving counsel. He followed up this address by one to the people, to the parents and connections of the boys, and, when all had left the school-house, and wandered off to the shade trees where the several contributions of food had been spread, he closed the doors of his wigwam, and retired for a while within its recesses. When he came forth again, it was with his raccoon cap on head, his spurs at heel, in his long, blue hunting shirt, and with long, bright sabre clanging at his side. His steed stood at the door, and, even as he went forth, up rode his Lieutenant, Dick Marvin, at the head of fifty-four gallant troopers, all in like costume with their captain.

A few seconds of awkward foot-marching took Stephen Joscelyn from the door of the school-house to his steed, and, once in saddle, the cripple had become the cavalier. Here it was that Stephen felt his manhood, while all who beheld him acknowledged it. There was a grand shout; and, leading his troop, Stephen coursed over the field, and exercised his troopers in an hour's drill, to the satisfaction of all the delighted spectators.

And while the parade went on, there came the wagons to carry off to the house of Marvin the furniture of the school-house, which was soon to lose the cheery echoes of those scores of happy children, which had, for so long a time, made it a wildly musical precinct.

Stephen alone, that solitary man, came back to it that evening, and sate till long after night, brooding over all its solitude as too truly teaching of his own. It was that night that, obeying orders, transmitted by Colonel Hammond, he dispatched a small squad, under Marvin, for the search of Mrs. Kirkland's house. Her kinsman, Colonel Moses Kirkland, was under the ban of treason. The search was in vain. Kirkland had not been there, and the unknown party who had been mistaken for him, was, as we happen to know, no other than our old acquaintance, Major Alison. He had eluded the search. It was at the school-house that Stephen awaited the return of the report of his Lieutenant.

Alison's hurried visit to old Dunbar, at the Sand Hills, and his equally hurried departure again, on the night when he insulted Annie

Dunbar, and aroused equally the ire of her brother and lover, were the result of his own discovery of the danger in which he stood while in that neighborhood. That sudden departure from the precinct of Augusta, as well as of Beach Island, necessarily prevented him from receiving the hostile message of Walter Dunbar.

For the present, we do not see the course which he has taken, but doubtless he will turn up again at the moment when he is least expected, and, perhaps, when his appearance will be least desirable to any of the parties.

Meanwhile, Stephen Joscelyn as suddenly disappeared from the scene as did the other parties. The squadron of Colonel Hammond, his chief, had already shaped its course upward, and was gone from sight, and Stephen was commanded to follow with all expedition. The hostile parties were understood to be converging to one common centre, and they were supposed to be very nearly equal in point of numbers, and, we may add, in efficiency and material. It is doubtful whether, at this early period, there was any remarkable development of military ability on either side. Drayton, nominally the leader of the forces of the movement party, was professionally a civilian, and the militia Colonels and Captains under him, though many of them had seen service against the red men of the mountains, had scarcely arrived at much, if any, distinction in such a service.

On the other side, the case was not materially different. The *personnel* was very much the same. They had stout men among them, bold, sturdy, uncompromising, and somewhat reckless leaders, such as Browne, the Cunninghams, and others of some local eminence; but, in point of ability, in military respects, most of them were yet to be tried.

Meanwhile, Walter Dunbar pursued his solitary way through a comparatively savage country. Vast tracts lay in the original forests. The settlements were few and far between. Colonies had been formed in remote precincts—Scotch, Irish, French, Dutch, which scarcely knew each other. Wild wastes of wood and water separated them. The roads were few—communication was little desirable, where these colonies, representatives of so many distinct foreign nationalities, were still tenacious of their native tongues—the Dutchman, Scotchman and Frenchman, each speaking the language of his people. The Irish settlements alone exhibited that flexibility, still so characteristic of that race, which gradually breaks down the social barriers, and accommodates itself to a more various convention.

Walter saw but few persons on his route, and still fewer habitations. Here and there a cabin, possibly one, two or three, rarely more, in a whole day's ride; and these were generally poor, low, squalid habitations, indicating the very humblest beginnings of frontier civilization. The inmates showing themselves at these cabins were generally women; few men were to be seen, and these were generally of the aged and infirm. The vigorous young men of the country seemed generally to have disappeared. The women encountered the stranger with anxious looks, showed some reluctance to entertain him, and were evidently relieved when he was about to depart. The fare was very humble, being commonly nothing better than hoecake and bacon. For this no charge was made usually, though it was evident that something was expected. Such an extreme condition of poverty, of itself, sufficiently appeals to the liberality of the guest.

Occasionally, as he rode, Walter encountered some wayfarer like himself. But these all showed themselves singularly uncommunicative. They passed hurriedly, at a trot mostly, sometimes at a canter, eyeing the stranger askance, nodding, perhaps, and darting by without a word. Most of them were armed, carrying the long rifle of that day across the saddle, as if ready for immediate use.

Walter was slow to conceive the condition of the country. He could not persuade himself that this was war; the evidence, at all events, of that approaching conflict, which was to spread throughout the country, and cover the face of the land with blood. Surprised at the strangeness in this conduct of the men, as well as the women, he yet did not rise to the full appreciation of those popular moods which needed nothing but leadership, a popular cry, some sudden outburst of passion in the multitude, here and there, to set all the sleeping volcanoes in a flame.

Though surprised, and somewhat wondering at what he saw, he was not disposed to resent the rude indifference of those whom he met, and from whom he failed to extract a civil or satisfactory answer. His own moods were of a sort too vexing to make him desirous of much companionship, or social intercourse of any kind. He rode on, brooding over his own melancholy experiences, preferring that he should indulge his humiliating reflections without the consciousness of a stranger's eye watching his emotions. We need not say how bitter were all these reflections—how deep was his sense of humiliation, and how little there was in his experience of the last six months upon which memory could look back with any degree of satisfaction.

It was in the midst of these gloomy meditations that he was suddenly aroused from them, by a troublesome notion that he had somehow lost his way. This was no difficult matter in an unknown country, so little traveled, with roads almost undistinguishable, and which frequently disappeared in a mere blind path. He had been conscious, some hours before, that several diverging paths had opened before him; but, as he was incapable himself of deciding on either, he had left the decision to his horse, who knew just as little of the country as himself.

The path he now followed led him to a spring and branch of clear, cool water, buried deeply in a dark, thick forest of oak and hickory, and as it was noon, he threw himself from his horse, left the animal to graze about among the long, thick grasses which grew along the margin of the water course, and, taking from his saddle-bags his wallet of smoked venison and biscuit, he proceeded to make his simple noonday repast. This he did in silence, in a continued muse of melancholy thought, which perpetually carried him back to the long chapters, immediately preceding, in his life, which were all so teeming full of humiliation. This last mishap, that of losing his way, however seemingly insignificant in comparison with all that had gone before, of defeat and misfortune, yet sufficed to bring up the whole tissue of events in full array before his imagination, and, in the bitterness of his mood, he gave vent to his anguish in outspoken soliloquy.

"It is a fate!" he said; "it is a fate! I am surely under a doom; else why should this record be one of unvarying defeat, disappointment, humiliation and overthrow? Do what I will, work out the problem as I may, think with whatever caution, deliberation, under whatever guidance of law, authority, the wisdom of the past, the experience of the present—all the same! In my case, the authority fails, the precedent is worthless—the argument is gainsayed by the experience—the experience, otherwise universal, is dashed in my case, by the one exception! The very stars fight against me, and where, with the same cause, the same argument, the same convictions, and the same course of conduct, other men would triumph, I alone fail—I alone am cast down, baffled, defeated, and humbled beneath the heel of circumstance! There is a fate that pursues, a perverse demon that hangs about the steps of some men, thrusts itself between them and fortune, and turns their own weapons forever against their own throats! And such a fate is mine."

"Nothing more probable—nothing more true," answered a voice from the copse just behind him. Walter started to his feet at the words, and turned in the direction of the speaker, who continued speaking as he came:

"Yes, indeed, my excellent friend," he said, coolly, as if the parties had been intimate for a hundred years. "There are some diabolical fates that follow every man's footsteps—sometimes trot ahead of him, and lie in ambush for his coming. But take my word for it, every man makes his own fate, and it depends simply upon his own individual manhood whether the said fate shall become friend or foe, master or servant."

## CHAPTER XXX.

### HIGHWAY ADVENTURES.

Walter Dunbar started to his feet. The stranger was only a few feet from him as he spoke. He had emerged from a thicket covert, which spread in the rear all along one side of the little rivulet, where Walter had partaken his repast; and had probably been resting there at the time of his arrival. He had heard with ease every syllable which, in the full belief that he was alone, Walter had spoken aloud, but, as he fancied, only to his own senses.

A fiery blush overspread the cheek and face of the young man, as he found that he had been overheard: but he was too much taken by surprise to speak. He could only gaze vacantly upon the new comer, who was a young man scarcely older than himself. He was garbed in the long hunting shirt of the mountain country, with cape and fringes, which seemed once to have been of better material than was commonly in use. But his garment was frayed and torn, and there were stains of the soil upon it which argued a life recently of some experience. He wore leggins and moccasins of Indian fashion. A knife at his belt, and a long rifle which he bore carelessly in his grasp, constituted his only weapons. His coon-skin cap, somewhat dilapidated, scarcely covered his head, and could not conceal the thick shock of brown hair which broke from under it in curling masses. The face was fair, frank and florid, full and massive, and was lighted up by eyes of a bright blue, and a marvellous expression of vitality. All the features were well pronounced, and the breadth of the jaws terminating in a well developed and finely rounded chin, spoke for energy and prompt decision of character.

There was a vague notion in Walter's mind that he had somewhere before met with the stranger; but the more he surveyed him, the less assured he grew in respect to this previous knowledge, and he soon dismissed it from his thoughts.

"Talking of the fates, my friend," continued the stranger, who now drew nigh, dropping, as he did so the butt of his rifle to the ground, "talking of the fates reminds me of food. We must feed even the fates; and one of them has been pursuing me till I am hungered in his behalf. There is no other way of getting rid of him, or subduing his ravages but by feeding him. Now, you have eaten. Have you anything left in your satchel? Give me to eat, if you have it. I have had a long chase to-day—that is, I have been *under* a long chase, and pretty well winded, and will need a good half hour to recover before I set forth again; and I shall probably have to run till night. What have you got?"

And the stranger threw himself down on the sward even as he spoke, with the careless grace of the hunter, and the confiding ease of one who has no doubts of his companion.

Walter Dunbar was not insensible to this proof of confidence, but he combatted it with a sudden question, the result of a suspicious temperament. The stranger seemed to him a little too much at his ease. Silent still, for he knew not well what to say, and had not yet recovered from his surprise, he yet proceeded, promptly enough, to comply with his guest's application for food. His saddle-bags, which he had just locked up, were reopened, and he soon unfolded to the eager eyes of the famishing young man a goodly prospect of hoecake, wheat biscuit, and a tolerably solid mass of smoked venison.

In an instant the *couteau de chasse* of the stranger was whipt out from his belt, and he proceeded to slash away at the meat with the avidity of one who had enjoyed no such opportunity for the last thirty-six hours, and even as he eat he spoke:

"Yes, my friend, there are fates, scores of them, for every man, and they behave just as he knows how to manage them. Hunger is an obtrusive fate. Well, I meet you, and obtain your help to pacify him. He will obey me, for the rest of the day, as dutifully as if I had paid him a week's wages. Well, in dealing with this, or any other fate, what is my process? A very simple one. I find you, for example, with food in your wallet, and I have none. I do not mince the matter with you—do not hang off, with petty affectations; but come to you frankly, assuming you to be human, and say to you: 'Give me to eat?' Deal with your fate as frankly as you do with your fellow, as I have done with you, and as boldly, and he will set the table for you, and provide the meals, and put up the fragments carefully in your wallet for to-morrow."

And all this time Walter knew not what to say. The other continued:

"Now," said he, "I have a sort of dog-fate pursuing me at this very moment. I have been a fugitive for more than thirty hours, and I am still pursued. I have scarcely more than half an hour to spare for rest, and then I must take to my heels again. Your wallet will help me wonderfully in the chase."

"What pursues you?" queried Walter, almost speaking for the first time.

"My Alban villa! You remember the rich man who was pursued by his Alban villa in the time of Sylla? *(See Plutarch.)* Well, I have a pretty farm and cottage. It is just now impersonated as my fate! If I can be hunted down, as a rebel, it becomes the property of a beautiful rogue of a loyalist! you see. Well, this Alban villa of mine is my fate, represented by a human rascal. He has got a small troop of like rascals at his heels. They beset me yesterday. They are still at my heels, and, when I have swallowed this last bit of hoecake, and this last slice of your venison, I must tramp again."

"Do not spare them," said Walter.

"Don't intend to! My hunger-fate is an unsparing one, and, with this venison of yours and beautifully browned hoecake, he declares himself perfectly content, so far as the food is concerned, but he suggests shrewdly that the same wallet of yours, which contained the venison, is just as likely to contain the wine! Eh? It is certainly a capacious one, and could you, by any magic, by the interposition of any benevolent fate, find me a flask of rosy Jamaica in that same wallet, I should be quite able to show you that the fates are never hostile to man when they are properly commanded."

Walter laughed out, and at once proceeded to open out from his saddle-bags a corpulent Dutch flask, containing a full pint or more of the very liquor indicated by the stranger, to whom he handed it without speaking.

"See what it is to have a sagacious and well-determined fate in the service. By word of mouth!"—carrying the flask to his lips—"and may your liquor never be less because of a thirsty fate in attendance. I have been something of a fate to you, and am not yet done with you. Do not yet put up that venison. I will but hack off a bit of it for supper, and put a few of your biscuits in my pouch."

He suited the action to the word, and in the twinkle of his *couteau de chasse*, divided the fragment of venison, very equally, between himself and the proprietor, conveying his moiety to the pouch in his hunting shirt, to which he also transferred some half dozen biscuits. "You see, my friend, how I provide for certain of the fates—danger, trouble, doubt, anxiety—all of them are of the same breed with hunger, to be disarmed, subdued and made subservient, if we once know how to manage our servants. There is not a dog-fate in our homestead, not a trouble, fret, bore, difficulty, danger, which is not, in some way, designed for our servant! Only learn how to whip in the brutes, and the rest is easy."

Walter said something, sufficiently commonplace, about the wisdom of such a philosophy, could one command it always.

"And why not?" said the other. "This is the very business of life —the only process, indeed, by which life developes manhood. What else has life to do? We are engaged in fighting the fates all the while; but"—and he stooped, with ear to the earth, and listened without breathing. As he rose—"Do you hear?" said he.

"Nothing!" said the other.

"My fate hath a keener ear," replied the stranger. "A horn was blown, and I know the blows. He would impersonate my villa! Now, my friend, I tell you confidentially that he is rushing on his fate, and the pursued shall become the pursuer."

Here he caught his rifle. "I know it, just as if I beheld it before me. This dog-fate has pursued me a few miles too far. He will discover this before nightfall—but too late. I must leave you. Thanks to your wallet, I am strong enough for another heat. I shall bury myself in yonder opposite wood, where my fate, grown quite good-humored on your venison, tells me that I shall find succor. We must part; but before I leave you, Walter Dunbar"—

"What? you know me? Who are you, then?"

"No matter; I am Nemo for the nonce! But I will give you such a token before we part, that you shall know me. Take my counsel before parting. Hurry forward! Do not linger in the neighborhood! Stop not to look behind you, and be prompt in making your fate subservient. Before you have ridden many miles, you will have need of all your wits! Your danger is from the two stools which your fate will offer you, and which are always stools of repentance to him who does not know how to choose promptly between them! Of one thing take heed always—never let your enemy get the first clip at you! The man who can strike the first blow is very apt to make his fate what he pleases! Go forward promptly, and strangle every doubt, by instant action, without consultation with that damning thought which so prevaricates with the human understanding as to take from it all aim and purpose! This is the fate you have to fear, Walter Dunbar. Beware of it! Farewell!"

"But, who are you? The sign—the sign!"

"Have you, then, no memories of boyhood, and Thompson's old field school? Do you find no meaning in the counsel—*"Never let your enemy get the first clip at you!"*"

The stranger was gone, waiting for no answer. With one bound he left the covert—with another, he crossed the road, and was buried in the thick woods on the opposite side.

He left young Dunbar in a stupor of doubt and vague conjecture, working in a vain effort to recall old school memories—to discover who it was who knew him so well, and of whom he could recall so little! But he remembered the injunctions of the stranger to hurry on his way. He looked about him for his horse. The beast had wandered off several hundred yards, in search of grass, and some little time was consumed in finding him. The saddle-bags were put on at length, and the young man mounted. He had scarcely done so when he heard distinctly the sound of a distant horn. It might have been a mile off. He fancied also that he heard, still nearer, the deep bay of a beagle.

The story of the stranger, and of the hot pursuit of his foes, appealed to his imagination, and he sate motionless upon his steed, his curiosity making him momently forgetful of the warning of his late companion, to hurry upon his way. Very soon after, he heard the dog distinctly, and, unconsciously, he moved forward to the open road. Here he stood, keeping in his steed by involuntary rein, and looking backward along the stretch of open ground over which he had passed an hour or two before. On a sudden, a hound trotted out upon the highway, if such it might be called, ran back into the woods quickly, and soon after was heard approaching under cover towards the rivulet which Walter and the stranger had so lately left.

Supposing him to be on the track of the stranger, it occurred to Walter that this route pursued, would probably bring the dog upon himself. He put spurs to his horse accordingly, and cantered away some two hundred yards forward. But a sort of fascination held him bound to see what was to be the result of this chase. He dismounted again, fastened the horse to a swinging limb, and, on foot, passed out to the highway, taking a position on a little hill, which enabled him to scan the road for a quarter of a mile back or more. Very soon his curiosity was rewarded. The hound, nose to earth, passed again out of the covert, and over the very spot which he had recently left. He took directly for the opposite woods. In ten minutes after a party of four men, on horseback, crossed the road also, and were soon covered by the thickets on the opposite side. At intervals, the hound could be heard, giving tongue, as on a hot trail. Then there followed a sudden howl, as if from the same animal; but it was no longer the bay of the beast, exulting in successful chase, but an expression of suffering and pain. Only fifteen minutes more had elapsed after this when the sharp spang of a rifle shot echoed throughout the woods.

All this seemed to argue strife and danger. The fates were at work in some way. Walter remembered the warning of the stranger, but he could not tear himself away from the spot. A fearful fascination bound his feet, and he stood, fixed, rooted to the ground, his lips parted in lively emotion, while his eye-balls were strained, in earnest and intense stare, over the long stretch of open ground over which he had traveled, and which his vision could command.

How long he thus watched, he knew not. It seemed but a few moments. It was an hour; and at length his curiosity was rewarded, and the fascination which had so spelled him was changed into a sort of horror, as he beheld *three* men, on foot, suddenly reappear from the forest. *Four* had *ridden* in on horseback; *three* only had re-appeared on foot. These two facts rose prominently to his thought, and, when he further saw that two of the men bore an inanimate body between them—when he saw the limpness of the lower limbs, as they hung down on the one side, while what he assumed to be the *head* of the corse hung equally limp, nerveless and muscleless on the other, he felt that the fate of the stranger had realized the prediction with which he had left him—that the "dog-fate," which had hunted him for his "Alban villa" would pursue him a little too eagerly and far, and that the time had come when his "hunger-fate," refreshed by his venison and Jamaica, would indulge in its decreed revenges!

The party emerging from the thicket seemed something at a loss. One of them re-entered the thicket, while the other two laid the body upon the sward beside the road. From their demeanor, Walter took for granted that the victim, whoever he might be, was quite dead.

Then it was that, suddenly, he was recalled to the propriety of pursuing his way with all favorable promptness. He remembered all the injunctions of his late companion, not to loiter, but to keep his wits about him, and, suddenly putting spurs to his steed, he went forward at a hand-gallop, which quickly put a mile or two between himself and the suspicious party which he left behind him. He could only conjecture that his late companion had fulfilled his own prediction, and that the aim of his rifle had proved fatal to his pursuer. Had he known that the brave stranger had first throttled the bloodhound, throwing himself directly in his way, as he found him so much ahead of his human pursuers, and had driven into his body the blade of the same knife which had so lately sliced his venison—his curious interest, in his new acquaintance, would have undergone proportionately a great increase. The hound slain, the stranger crouched beside his body till he beheld his human enemy, and his shot was then as fatal as it was prompt. When the other pursuers reached the body of the beagle, the fugitive was already far on his way, and pursuit was no longer prudent in the case of one who carried so long a rifle, and held the fates in such beautiful subjection.

## CHAPTER XXXI.

### NIGHT ADVENTURE IN THE HOVEL.

Leaving the dead to bury their dead, leaving the fates to take care of themselves, as, perhaps, it is always wise to do, unless you can conquer them, Walter Dunbar rode on, seeking to dismiss from his mind, as much as possible, what he had seen, and to address himself wholly, as well as he could, to the main objects of his travel. He still fancied that he had dispatches of importance to deliver, and these he was resolved to deliver at the peril of his life—so far was he resolute.

But it was not so easy to dismiss from his mind the stranger, his adventures, and the catastrophe which had seemingly followed them. Still less was he disposed or able to free himself from much vexing and troublesome thoughts which grew naturally out of this interview with the stranger. Who was the person who knew him so well, and whom he did not know? Vain were all his efforts to recall him to his memory; and yet the voice, the action, the free and easy manner, the bold and confident tones of the other, seemed to him strangely familiar, but blended with all his conjectures and reflections, one thing grew ever uppermost in his mind, the creature of his morbidly awakened self-esteem, and the feeling which it occasioned found its utterance in outspoken soliloquy.

"Everybody thinks himself privileged to give me counsel. Here is a man whom I may have met before, who seems not a day older than myself, who yet undertakes to tell me how I shall go—how carry myself—how use my wits—how avoid two stools—and how to coerce fate! What is there in my action, or my aspect, to justify people in supposing that I need any such counsel? Yet, Martin Joscelyn will counsel me, and my own sister looks gravely upon me, deals in wise saws and modern instances, and seems to think that I need them. If I could distrust my own manhood, I should feel that something were wanting—something, I know not what, to make me as other men.

And yet, have they no justification? This self-esteem but mocks me! What have been these defects, these disappointments, these cruel humiliations, which I have had to endure, even where my intellect was proudest, and my will as confident as if all were easy to my hand? Why should this stranger be able to see humiliation written in my face? Why his lesson about the fates? Am I, alone, incapable of seeing the way before me? Am I, alone, incapable of meeting any encounter with circumstance, or, if you prefer it, fate? Alas! there would seem to be still one fate which I cannot baffle or escape. But who comes now?—prudence for a season."

His soliloquy, in which he simply chewed the cud of bitter thought, was broken by the heavy tread of a horse's feet immediately behind him. He turned to behold a stranger. Some natural but cold salutation passed between them. Walter was shy. The new comer might be of the very band whom he had seen pursuing his recent guest. What Walter had seen had been sufficient to arouse his apprehensions, and to make him more suspicious than usual. His new companion seemed disposed at first to be communicative enough, but he met with little but repulse. Walter put spurs to his horse. The stranger kept at his side. Walter then drew in his rein, and walked his horse. The stranger was equally accommodating.

Was it worth while to quarrel? Such was the question which Walter asked of himself. He concluded otherwise, and rode on, and so riding, the two together, almost at the same moment, and just before dark, rode up to a low habitation, and asked, almost in the same breath, for quarters for the night. The stranger seemed to anticipate all the movements of his companion.

Walter had now an opportunity of observing him more clearly than he had done while they rode together. He was of medium size, dark of complexion, with a downcast expression in his eyes, one of which had a squint which was more significant than persuasive. His costume was simple, like that of the plain farmers of the country, and he seemed to be weaponless. The two eyed each other for a moment only, then turned to meet the woman who appeared at the door of the hovel.

She was a stalwart, tall, raw-boned creature of a very ordinary type, but with features which seemed to denote decision at least, if none of the gentler virtues.

"And what may you men be wanting?" was her homely question. Walter waited for the stranger to speak. He answered readily enough, and to the point, for himself.

"Some place to sleep for the night, and some supper for myself and for my horse, if I can get it."

She looked to Walter as if for his answer also, before replying to the first speaker. He made the same application, in somewhat more courtly terms, and with some difference of manner.

"Well, now, young men, look you both. I'm a most lonesome and poor woman, living here just now by myself. You see what a house it is, and you may guess for yourselves that there ain't much of anything in it. I can give you a bit of hoecake, and a slice of rusty bacon, for your supper, and there's good water from the spring. There's some fodder in the old stable, and that may sarve your horses. As for the sleeping, there's a room with one bed in it, and if you can sleep together—" Walter cast a glance at the stranger, then said:

"This gentleman is a stranger to me—"

"How's that?" asked the old woman, quickly, and somewhat suspiciously—"how's that, when you come together?"

"It has happened so, but I never saw this person till the last half hour."

"Nor I him," said the other, "but I overtook him, and we rode on together, a leetle agin his wishes, I'm a-thinking."

This was said with a sort of grin, which might have been designed for a smile.

"Well," said the woman, eyeing the last speaker keenly, "that's onlucky; for you'll have to sleep together anyhow, onless one of you is willing to make his bed on a bench in the eating room."

Walter promptly replied that the bench would answer his purposes.

"Well," said she, "it's well you're so easily satisfied. And now," she continued, "I warn you that you'll have to keep watch for yourselves on one another, seeing that you're onbeknown to one another. You may be both very good people, but then again you may be great rogues. I don't answer for either on you, and I can't be answerable for anything you do. But I warn you, considering the bad nature of men in general, and the troubles that's going on now all through the country, that you have business enough for all your eyes to keep them on the stretch all night. There's hardly anything here that's worth your robbing from me. You knows best if there's anything very vallyble between you that you can rob from one another. That's all my say. Look ayont now, over that turnip patch, and you'll see the old stable. You'll find the fodder in the loft—so you may see after the beasts as soon as you please, and I'll do what I kin for your supper by the time you come in again."

She pointed to the stables, and the two young men proceeded at once, after watering their steeds, to bestow them away for the night. The stranger made some few remarks as they rode, but to these Walter made no reply, certainly none which was calculated to encourage his companion to more familiarity. He appropriated one of the stables, and there were several, to his horse, filled the rack with fodder, and, as the beast proceeded to eat without delay, he left him and proceeded to the house alone. The stranger lingered behind for a few moments, and followed slowly.

If Walter Dunbar thought of any one thing more than another, in leaving his steed for the night, it was the rickety condition of the building. It seemed to him that a good puff of wind would upset the whole establishment, but there was no choice, no alternative. He would have ridden farther, in search of better accommodation, for his hostess did not come up exactly to his standard, but he was somehow more fatigued than usual. He had ridden forty miles that day, and he knew nothing of the country. He knew not how much farther he would have to ride, in that sparsely settled region, before he should find better accommodations than the one before him. He loitered a while in front of the dwelling, looking around him, before he re-entered it. The stranger, meanwhile, returned from the stables, and approached him. Somehow, Walter had taken an aversion to this man, and he turned away at his approach, and passed into the dwelling.

A few seconds will suffice to show how the poor lived in that day, and in this unsettled region. The house was old and narrow, built of logs, and consisted of three compartments. The centre was the hall or eating-room. On each hand a door led into a chamber; one of these chambers was held by the landlady herself, the other was yielded to the stranger, and a long bench in the central room afforded Walter the only means of sleep.

By the time that the two young men had re-entered the dwelling, the hostess was busily engaged over the fire, browning her hoecakes and frying her bacon. To the butter-dish she added a few fresh eggs, and the odor which these sent up seemed to gratify very equally the nostrils of our young men. They drew towards the table, which was already spread with a few delf plates, and as many tin cups, and two oak-bottomed chairs enabled them to confront each other at opposite sides. Very soon the old woman spread her dishes, hissing-hot from the fire, and bade her guests fall to, while she waited upon them. The tin cups, it was found, were made to hold a supply of very thin and watery coffee. It was evident, however, that with all her rough simplicity of manner, the old woman was doing her best to make their supper palatable. They found it so, were hungry and eat heartily. When this performance was fairly ended, she said to them, while removing the supper things—

"Now, look ye, men, I've given you both warning! You've got to look to one another. You may be good men enough, but you may be both rogues for what I know. You've seen to your horses, young men; you've got the fodder, and I hope that will do them for the night. I've got too little corn for myself to be giving any out to these dumb beasts, though I reckon, if they could talk, they'd be axing after it. I've told you where you kin sleep for to-night; one of you's got that room, and the only bed, and the other says he'll take the bench. All that's just as you please. And now, if you've got any means, or the will to pay me anything, you kin do so. If you havn't got anything, don't pay anything, and I rather reckon I won't be any the worse for it, till my son comes home again."

"Where's your son now?" asked the stranger.

"What's that to you?" she answered, with a sharp, fiery look and accent. "That's his business, and none of yours or mine. So just mind your own business, and remember what you must have l'arned at school, if you ever had any schooling, ax no questions and I'll tell you no lies!"

The stranger laughed—a sort of dry chuckle—drew from his pocket a couple of English shillings, and laid them beside his plate. Walter had already laid before the woman a couple of English crowns.

"Ah! ah!" quoth the stranger, with a grin, "the Crown forever!"

To this Walter made no reply.

The woman quietly gathered up the silver, and dropped it into her pocket.

"And now," said she, "men, I'm gwine to bed; you kin set up as long as you please; there's firelight enough for a blaze all night, and when you want more, there's wood; lay it on—airily to bed, you know, and airily to rise! Ef you're honest travelers, you'll sleep easy; but you've just got to keep watch on one another!"

And, without a word, she opened the door of her chamber. Here, however, she paused, though but for a single moment. Walter Dunbar followed her with his eyes, while the stranger strolled towards the door opening upon the highway. In that single moment of pause, and while the woman lingered at her chamber door, ere she disappeared from sight, Walter was surprised to see a significant pressure of her uplifted finger upon her lips. This was evidently addressed to himself. Was it a sign of warning? Had it any meaning? Why warn him more than the other? She had warned them both, it is true, emphatically enough to watch each other. Why, especially, make sign to him of caution? The jealous self-esteem rose uppermost in his thoughts, and a flash of indignation passed over his cheeks as he murmured—

"Even this old woman would counsel me in some fashion, if she only knew how! What is this fate which marks me out to everybody as in need of advice and warning?"

It was long after midnight. Walter Dunbar slept at last, and everything was hushed, and everything was dark in the hall where he lay, stretched along the narrow bench, with his saddle-bags beneath his head. He had not undressed. His purse, well filled with British coin, was in his vest bosom. His father's despatches were in his saddle-bags beneath his head. He had felt both securely beneath his grasp ere he delivered himself to sleep. He was awakened suddenly by a shock, and in the same moment he heard a sharp voice, almost ringing in his ears, which he recognized as that of the hostess—

"Ah! wretch! would you murder the young man, and he sleeping?"

He started to his feet. A torch was blazing in the hands of the old woman, where she stood in her doorway. It gave sufficient light to the apartment, and Walter came to his perfect consciousness only on perceiving the outer door unclose, while a figure, which he conjectured to be that of the stranger, his late companion, was making his way through it. He sprang after him, but the door was hastily shut in his face, and when he had succeeded in making his way into the open air, he found himself in such utter darkness, that pursuit and search were seemingly in vain.

He returned to find his saddle-bags cut open, and lying upon the floor. The shock which had awakened him was occasioned by their sudden withdrawal from beneath his head, and that the robber was arrested in his attempt, was due to the sudden glare of the torch-light upon his proceedings, and the sharp, hurried interrogation of the woman.

Walter was greatly relieved, upon examination, to find that his packet of letters, his father's despatches, though actually withdrawn from the saddle-bags, had fallen from the grasp of the robber, and lay beside them upon the floor. The prompt interruption of the woman alone had saved him from loss of property and possibly of life. No attempt had been made upon his purse.

"He is gone!" said she to Walter; "you could not see him."

"It was too dark to see a step before me."

"Ah! what a thing it is to get sleep when you want it, for young people can sleep; but it's not so with the old ones. I was jubous about you two men, and when I heard a noise in the bed-room, where that man slept, I was more jubous. He overthrowd my barrel of peaches, and made such a noise that if you hadn't been dead with sleep, it must have awakened you. Then I watched, and then I waited and listened. It was a long time before the man moved again. He was afeard. But when I heard the door creek, I know'd he was moving; so I got up and just lighted the pine, and when I opened the door, there he was, with his knife opened and standing over you, just ready to kill; then I screamed out, and then he run. But, Lord love you! young man, here I'm a-keeping you talking when there's no knowing what mischief he's a-doing now. You couldn't find him in the dark. You—but, Lord love you! why didn't you push for the stable? Your horse, man, your horse!"

Walter had forgotten his steed. He immediately bolted forward, and had already opened the door, when the woman said—

"Here! I'll go along with you, and carry the fire!"

They reached the stable together, but too late. Both horses were gone.

# CHAPTER XXXII.

## CONFERENCE AND CONFIDENCE.

"Oh, Lord! oh, Lord! have mercy on this wicked generation. What are we coming to? I ought to have know'd what would happen, and I tried to make you know, young man, just as much as I darst to. Lord! Lord! Why, where upon the airth, young man, was you *brung* up, not to know better what to do? I warned you both of the villainies of people everywhere; and to think that you should travel with a stranger you don't know, and put up your horse along with his'n, and no lock to the stable; and you knowing just nothing about the character of the man. Oh, Lord! oh, Lord!"

"Why, what should I have done, my good woman?"

"Done? Well, I'll tell you, since you don't seem to know for yourself. You should hev watched your time, and hid your horse in the bushes, and in the bottom of some of the hills, perticklarly when you didn't know who 'twas you traveled with. Better if you had taken to the bushes yourself. I told you both mighty plain, and I *gin you* a sign with my finger, and *that,* to a man who had his five senses about him, or any one of 'em, ought to hev been enough to make you think of all that consarned yourself, and of what mought be the dangers of the road. Oh! I reckon you've had a most foolish mother, that jest let you play about always, with a great nigger or two to follow you about, and pick you up whenever you tumbled down. Lord! Lord! There air such mothers in the world, and I've known some of them!"

This was the last feather on the camel's back. It capped the climax of mortifying commentary upon himself, which had furnished the chief matter to Walter in his humiliating soliloquies. He uttered a bitter laugh as he turned away from the now eloquent old woman, and stalked off into the darkness, as if to escape the glare of the firelight, which, at every sentence, she was flashing in his face.

She followed him in her zeal to administer counsel and rebuke.

"And now, young man, what is it you're agwine to do? I kain't guess at your business, or where you're agwine; but I'm sorry for you, and ef you could say something that I could do for you, I'd like it."

"I know not what to do," was the gloomy response. "My horse was necessary to my progress, and I have before me a ride of a day, and possibly two days more."

"Well, don't be caist down. You must take hairt and keep up as well as you kin. It's the right determinatin, after all, that brings a man out right and straight. Now, ef my son was only here."

"Ah!—well, what could he do?—what would he do?"

"Well, I'll tell you what he'd *try* to do."

"Let me hear that."

"He'd try to take the track of this fellow that stole your horse, and he'd *nose* him, I reckon, for a thousand miles till he tuk him by the throat."

"And that is what I should do—what, indeed, I must try to do."

"Ah! you hevn't had sich a schooling for it as Clym Carter; but it's not onpossible that, if I gives you a leettle help and advising, you may get upon Clym's track, and though I warn't willing to tell the other man about my son and his business, I've rether a trust in you, and don't think 'twould do him any hurt to tell you."

"On my honor——" Walter began.

"Oh! never mind your honor—it's in your face, my young man, that I sees the honesty. You're a gentleman born—that I know'd from the time you first rode up. There's no disguising a gentleman born from the eyes of a woman what's got a son of her own; and, what's more, let me tell you, there's no putting off upon her the false kine, (coin). You may put what fine clothes you please upon a lacky, but let him try his best, he kain't keep you long from seeing the tail of the fox, or the nose of the coon! Now, ef you had been a person quick to see, and find, take a trail, and run down a fox, 'twould be no harm to you to be a gentleman. But, being, as you air, only a gentleman, I knows that you kin be trusted with a secret business."

Walter repeated his assurances of good faith, to which she did not listen.

"Well, now, you seems to be upon some business of your own that I don't ax *you* about, and don't want to know. And you're in a country where you don't seem to know the pints of the compass; and you're in rather a bad fix, now that your horse is stolen; and you're a gentleman; so when I put all these things together, you see, I'll jest let you a leetle into the sort of doings that's a-working in this part of the country, among this gineration. You heard what that thief of a man said when you laid the two *crown* pieces upon the table as pay for your supper. Well, I seed that you didn't know his meaning. He cried out with a halloo for the *crown*, and by *that* I knowd that he was a *Scoffilite*." *

"Now you see," drawing nearer to Walter, and speaking in a whisper, "my son, Clym Carter, is one of the Regulators, and he's out now with a party in sarch of this very gang of horse-stealing Scoffilites. Ef you could only know where to find him now."

"Has he a spare horse?"

"I kain't say that he has; but, if any man kin get back your'n for you, Clym's the man to do it, ef you could only find him."

"And where's he now? I should be willing to pay well."

"Oh! jest shet up about the pay. Clym's on the track for the good of the country. He's for making a clean sweep of the wretches. They burnt us all out not quite a year ago, and he's now death on all the tribe."

"Is there no way to find him?"

"Well, that's the pint. He's here to-day, but fifty miles off to-morrow, clean away up among the mountain settlements, and into North Carolina. But the fire's gone out, and we may as well be getting back to the house, where we kin finish all we've got to say."

Here she shook her expiring brand, but failed to rekindle it, and, in the darkness, Walter followed her as closely as he could around the turnip patch, till they gained together the log-house. Closing the

---

* The Scopholites, or Scovilites, so called after a certain leader, were a band of outlaws, refugees from other parts, mostly foreigners, gamesters, plunderers, horse-thieves especially, and altogether a mere banditti, in the wild and unsettled regions of the Carolinas. Their organization finally became so powerful, in the early times of the Colony, and their depredations so atrocious, as to provoke another organization, called the "Regulators," who, by a sort of wild justice, which was summary enough, succeeded at last in putting the outlaws down. At the opening of the Revolution, out of the *débris* of these parties, in the same region, grew those of Whig and Tory, the Regulators generally becoming *rebels* to the common authority, while the Scovilites as generally became its adherents. They were the "*loyalists*" of that day, whose lineal descendants may be found in this.

door behind her with the massive bar which was employed to cross it, she threw some fresh brands on the fire, and the apartment was once more lighted with a cheerful blaze.

"Now," said she, resuming the conversation, "you, young man, hev got to tramp, and take the tramp afoot, may-be, for the rest of your journey. You kain't be toting that heavy saddle-bag on your shoulder, and kin leave it with me till you get a horse, whether it's your own or another man's. Ef you could git to find my son, Clym, he'd help you along, for I's give you *my own mark* to him, and *a sign* that would put you on the right tarms with him, jest as soon as he seed it. But the trouble's here—I don't suppose you know that jest now, hardly ten miles from here, Ginrel Fletchall's got an army of maleshy soldiers, and there's fifties of these Scoffilites among 'em. They calls themselves "Loyalists," and "Saracents of the Crown," and "King's Men," and "King George's Men," but they're Scoffil's men, a good chaince of 'em, and devil's men, too. But they've got king's officers among 'em, and there's bloody work, I reckon, jest to begin, and there's no saying who's safe, ef you once happen to fall in among 'em, promiscus-like. I reckon this horse-thief man is pushing, fast as he kin, straight for their camp. He tried to see what you was when he hurrah'd for the Crown."

The face of Walter brightened as he heard that the forces of Fletchall, to whom one of his letters was addressed, were within ten miles. A tramp of that small distance would, (as he fancied,) end his embarrassments. The woman did not note the hopeful change in his countenance. She continued:

"But Ginrel Fletchall hasn't got the thing all his own way, you see, and Ginrel Drayton, with the patriots, is a pushing right up at him, fast as he kin, from below, and there's no telling how soon they'll all be fighting. They've fout some small skrimmages already. Now, my son, Clym Carter, is on a scouting move for Ginrel Drayton and Ginrel Richardson, and he's on the look out, you see, to cut off recruits, fast as they push in; and if you'll jest take the track I give you, and keep it for ten miles, there's a chance, and a good one too, that you'll meet Clym Carter, and to make him know you, I'll jest give you my own sign and a token, which is as good as gould between us."

She brought forth from her chamber a small bit of leather, on which was rudely inscribed, with ink, the figure of a horse-shoe, within which, traced in rude but distinct letters, were the initials "C. C.," with a cross, or asterisk, between them.

"Jest you show that to Clym Carter, ef you meets him, and tell him all what you know, of what's happened to you here. You won't tell him any lie, for I sees that you're a gentleman; but even ef you was to do so, he'd see through you in a twink, and a'ter that, he wouldn't hear to a word that you could say. Clym's not a born gentleman, mind you, I don't say that, but he's what a gentleman ought to be, he's as honest as broad daylight! I'm his mother, and ought to know, young man, though, I reckon, you're a thinking in your secret heart that I ought not to say it; but I only say it bekaise I thinks it will be better for you to know what he jest is, as a man of sperrit!"

She proceeded to indicate the route which Walter should pursue, in which he would be most likely to find her son, and so direct was her description, so clear, so free from unnecessary words or any circumlocution, that he felt no difficulty in fixing all the details in his memory at once. This done, the good woman said:

"And now, young man, I'll give you a bite of breakfast, and then the sooner you sets off the better. You've got no time to waste in scratching the head after a thinking that is slow to come. You've got all the thinking now in your head that's needful, and the next needful thing is to work it out after the fashion of the thinking."

We must take for granted that, as a gentleman, Walter was duly considerate in making his acknowledgments. He handed his saddle-bags to the old woman.

"Good Lord! what a slash the villain made in 'em! It was a sharp hunting-knife, young man, that made that cut."

She proceeded, without more words, to tumble out the clothes, which constituted the chief contents of the saddle-bags.

"The Lord save us!" she exclaimed, as she counted the several articles—"The Lord save us! no less than seven fine shirts, of the best Irish linen, and drawers to match, and gloves, and hank-chers, and—oh! bless me, young man! the only nation wonder is, how you git on in the world at all, with all this luggage. Why, my Clym will go off for a month, and ef he carries with him one shirt only, it's bekaise I stick it in his coat-pocket. Why, with all this clothing, he'd never do anything useful or sensible in the world. He'd be for dressing himself up with clean shirt and stockings at every running water he'd come to!"

Walter could only smile faintly. His self-esteem was becoming singularly circumspect and timid.

"I'll take care of everything for you, so long as I'm a living woman."

She, with this assurance, was about to take the things into her chamber, when he stopped her, and pulling his purse from his bosom, said:

"Mrs. Carter, perhaps I had better leave with you some of my money also?"

" 'Twould be more sensible."

"Here is some gold."

She counted the guineas as he passed them into her hand.

"Lord save us from temptation! Eighteen gould guineas, as I'm an honest woman! Why, Lord! young man, the wonder is, with sich a head as you carry, that you got so far without losing gould and life together. That horse-thief guessed you had this gould, I reckon; he know'd it, jest from the way that you left your horse, knowing how you hed fought shy of him. Don't you see?"

Walter did not see; but he did not attempt to show that the good lady was illogical. He simply said, in a kindly and gentle manner:

"I confide to you, Mrs. Carter, as you have confided to me, you will find me a gentleman, though, perhaps, by no means as wise as I should be. Keep this money for me till my return, and if I should never return, keep it for yourself. The silver which I have will be quite enough for my purposes."

Hoecake and fried bacon for breakfast, at the dawn of day, and then Walter Dunbar departed from the rude dwelling which had sheltered him, and the rude but honest woman who had counseled him, on foot, light of burden, if not of heart, and following, as he did with ease, the route prescribed for him by his hostess, which was one leading directly to the camp of Fletchall, but sheltered by hill and thicket all the way, though moving all the way within bugle sound of the main trace through the country.

## CHAPTER XXXIII.

### SUMMARY PROCESSES OF REGULATION.

Some time before daylight that morning, a group of five men separated after some consultation, along the main road some five miles from the dwelling where Walter had found shelter, and, taking opposite sides, but still in close proximity to the road lying *perdu* behind trees or amidst covering brushes, one of the party alone, not seeking a cover while the darkness prevailed, strode to and fro, patrolling up and down the road, but never so far as to be beyond hearing of the party. All of these persons were afoot. It was hardly an hour after this arrangement, when the tramp of horses might be heard coming up the road.

Our sentinel fell back, and the whole party was in an instant on the *qui vive*. The result almost immediately followed in the arrest of a person who rode one horse and led another. His bridle rein was seized without a word, the horse backed upon his haunches, and the rider commanded, in brief, but imperative language to alight and "show his papers."

The new comer was slow to consent to this proposition, on the contrary, he made desperate efforts by spurring his steed to send him forward, but another grasp quite as vigorous as that which held his steed, was laid upon his own shoulder, and he was drawn from the animal to the ground, while striking blindly right and left, in the effort to defend himself.

This violent effort, more spasmodic than sensible or well directed, was made with a sharp hunting-knife of large blade, any one of the strokes of which, well delivered and with resolute will and aim, might have sufficed to hew off a man's arm at the wrist, and as the fellow sought to defend himself rather by *chopping* than stabbing, this was the danger to his assailant.

But keep his seat, hold and guide and spur his horse forward—all of which he strove to do while smiting at his foe—required a combination of muscle and faculty, wit as well as will, which the rider was not able to command. A few moments found him prostrate on the earth, a powerful man kneeling on his breast, the knife wrested from his grasp, and a rope passing around both his arms, binding him effectively in a manner to show that the capturing party was expert and well trained by practice in such operations.

The prisoner was then lifted to his feet and bade to show the virtues in his legs. He walked into the cover of the thicket, while one of his captors walked beside him. Another was, in a moment more, mounted upon one of the captured horses and leading the other. He, too, disappeared within the forest.

Very soon they were passing into the gorges of the hills which now thickly strewed the face of the country, and effectually concealed all parties passing through them from persons traveling the road. The rest of the group of scouts resumed their post of watch, but it does not lie within our purpose to remain with them.

This scene took place with as little noise as possible. Few words were spoken on either side. The stranger was taken by surprise, and though struggling, spoke but once or twice, and then in simple exclamations, the consequence of his situation. He addressed nothing to the assailing party challenging their explanation. It seemed as if both parties had enjoyed a degree of experience of this sort, which needed no words for comprehension. It is just possible, also, that the captive had a lurking consciousness which rendered him wary and circumspect, especially in the use of his voice. The old offender at the assizes knows how wiser it is to use the tongue of his counsel rather than his own. Enough now to say that when day dawned, the prisoner found himself quietly disposed with four other prisoners in like condition of *duresse*, in the hollow of a group of hills which completely fenced in the spot from all casual observation. All the prisoners were securely tethered with ropes, their persons first being examined and all weapons taken from them. They lay, or rather crouched about among trees and boulders of rock, while a sentinel, well armed, kept watch over all their movements.

Walter Dunbar proceeded on his way somewhat slowly, the better to be sure that he followed the directions of Mrs. Carter. His progress was not gratefully beguiled by any reflections of his own. We can easily conjecture of what character they were, and how naturally they grew into self-questionings, the answers to which, however, softly whispered in his own soul, were not calculated to lift it out of that sea of humiliations into which the uniform experience of the last few months had sunk his spirit beyond his own power to recover. Darkly brooding over his vexing thoughts, he had probably gone some five miles upon his way, when, rising from a hollow, and turning short around a huge boulder in the road, he encountered a rifle muzzle at his breast, while a stern voice cried to him—

"Stop, and give the word!"

"I have no word to give," was the sullen reply. The mood of Walter at that moment, shaped by the thoughts of the last hour, made him comparatively indifferent whether the man shot or not.

"That's bad for you," said the other, lowering his rifle as he saw that Walter was weaponless and exhibited no hostile movement. "Look up, my man, and let's see the color of your eyes?"

Walter looked up with an expression of quiet indifference.

"Where from, stranger?"

"Home!"

"Where's home?"

"Augusta."

"Ah! well they've been cracking crowns in this quarter! What do you think of a *cracked* crown, any how?"

Walter paused. There might be a snare in the words, which were equivocal. When he did reply, it was coolly and calmly, and perhaps in the proper spirit.

"My friend, I am unwilling to be questioned, except when I know who it is that questions me. I am unarmed, as you see, and you have your rifle, which I suppose is loaded."

"I reckon it is that, and with a half ounce bullet!"

"You have then no need to fear from me. Now, I am in search of a person to whom, however, you can conduct me."

"And who's the person?"

"One Clym Carter."

"And why the dicconer didn't you say *that* at the beginning? To be sure I can bring you to him; but who sends you? That you must *say* to me, or show to me in some way. Have you got no token?"

Walter showed the bit of leather with Mrs. Carter's sign manuel.

"That's quite enough; and I'll take you to the Captain's quarters just so soon as I'm relieved here. You see I'm on duty, and we're getting mighty strict. It'll be a good two hours before the 'relief' comes, and you'll have to kick your heels with me, behind the rocks, for that time at least; and, even then, when we get into camp, there's no sartainty that you'll see the Captain before nightfall. He's got his hands pretty full, not too many men, and several pints of road to cover."

Walter threw himself down upon the sward, and against a convenient boulder. The sentinel was good-humored and talkative, but had little to communicate, except in broad generalities. He was in a company of rangers. His company was an integral of Mayson's Regiment. Mayson's Regiment was a portion of Richardson's Brigade, and this brigade was a part of Drayton's army, raised for the defence of liberty, &c. In like manner, a summary report was made of the troops raised by the loyalists, and under the leadership of some half-dozen of the chief men among the mountaineers, of whom we have heard already.

"We'll have a fight out of them mighty soon, I reckon, since both parties are gathering to a head, and the fighting won't be very far off from here. We're bound to lick 'em, though they do brag mightily upon the British officers they've got. But the Scoffilites are not going to make good fight, and, just as soon as the bullets begin to fly, hot and heavy, they'll break down all the bushes in the country, but they'll find a way out of the skrimmage. We've licked 'em too often before to expect to see them stand fire now."

But, though the dialogue was lively enough between the two, it does not concern us to pursue it farther. In two hours, rather than one, the relief came, and our sentinel was at liberty to conduct Walter in the direction of the "rebel" camp. It was not long before something of the din of an encampment reached the ear. There was a hum, a buzz, a faint murmur, and the impatient whining of several horses. But the guide soon changed the direction which he took, and led up a more sinuous path, winding around the steep sides of a hill somewhat higher than the general elevation of the ridge. Suddenly turning down a gorge, they went, as it were, right into the heart of the mountain, and passed into the shelter of a sylvan tent of poles, covered with green bushes.

Up started a couple of rangers, as they entered this tent, and challenged them. The guide of Walter made his report, and the Lieutenant who received it, very cordially invited our wayfarer to the modest hospitalities of his command. Clym Carter, the Captain, would not probably return till noonday.

Walter bore with the delay with what patience he could, having no reason, in the meanwhile, to complain of the civilities of the Lieutenant and of such parties as appeared occasionally. He had shown the token of Mrs. Carter, and it commanded instant respect.

At noon, a bugle sounded among the hills, and very soon Walter was told that Captain Carter had returned and would soon see him in his tent.

Meanwhile, one of the rangers proceeded to spread a rude table of planks on benches, covered finally with green leaves, upon which he spread the simple but sufficient dinner for the party. There were no plates; only a few tin cups and a bucket for water. The meals were abundant and barbecued. The entire quarter of a mutton, huge collops of beef, in strips, and hoecakes, finely browned before the fire, constituted the fare, which was all spread upon the green bushes, in readiness, some time before the Captain made his appearance, the Lieutenant excusing him by suggesting that some examination of prisoners was taking place; but it was not long after that before he came. By this time, Walter Dunbar had instinctively become impressed with the conviction that he was to see in Clym Carter no ordinary man. The mother had impressed him. She was a coarse woman, it is true, but how full of character! and she had never spoken of her son as the Captain of a formidable band of regulators, as a vulgar vanity might have done. Then, the deference with which the sentinel and the Lieutenant had severally spoken of him; all these things had impressed him, and when the stalwart form of Clym Carter entered, stooping, into the tent, rising within it to his full height, erect, with great breadth of shoulders, admirable symmetry of form, with lofty and commanding forehead and massive face, whose jaws seemed to indicate a leonine capacity of gripe. These impressions of Walter were confirmed and strengthened, when, over all, he beheld the large, bright, blue eyes, lighting up a smooth face, carefully shaven of all signs of beard, and beheld the grace of his carriage, which, in his open and flowing hunting-shirt, reminded him of the heroic aspects of the great chiefs of the red men, the Metacoms and Powhatans, and Attakullas, famous in the history of that day. He could fully comprehend the secret feeling of the mother when she dwelt so earnestly on the subject of "the gentleman," to "the MANNER *born*."

There was a certain feeling of awe in the heart of Walter when he beheld this noble presence, and he rose respectfully at his approach, and simply presented the rude token which had been confided to him by his mother. The welcome of the Captain was as simple as it was gracious. When Walter would have made his report to him, he said:

"Not now, sir, if you please. That will keep warm, but not so our beef and mutton. I must make you at home here, sir, by first showing you that I make myself at home. Fall to, Lieutenant, upon that mutton!"

The practice of Lieutenant Sandys as a carver, had been considerable. Very soon he had served all parties, and there was none present who did not testify to the virtues of the viands by the rapidity with which they were consumed. The only beverage was water from a cool mountain runnel, which gurgled away pleasantly at the foot of the hill. The repast finished, the *débris* was quickly removed, and then the Captain signified his willingness to hear the report of Walter, the Lieutenant being requested by the Captain to continue present.

Walter began by telling who he was, but forbore to say anything about his mission, and, indeed, confined his narrative wholly to the period when the stranger, who first robbed him of his horse, first joined him on the road. All that followed was given in full detail, avoiding all prolixity. The Captain listened with an attentive gravity, which was sometimes enlivened with a smile. Once or twice he looked, with a nod of the head, at the Lieutenant, who bowed in seeming acquiescence; and, at the close, when Walter had ceased to speak, he said:

"I am happy to think, Mr. Dunbar, that we have been fortunate enough to recover your horse. We have also caught the thief."

"Indeed! Is it possible? So soon!"

"A party of our scouts captured the fellow within an hour or two, as I reckon, after his felony was committed. He was in possession of a led horse, which, from your description, must be yours. The scoundrel is an old offender, who has now fully run the length of his tether. Unluckily for him, there are more crimes chargeable to his account, which should have sent him to his last account some years ago. There can be no doubt," looking to the Lieutenant, "that it is Red Pyatt!"

The Lieutenant nodded affirmatively.

"The wonder is, Mr. Dunbar, that having gold in your bosom, he had not murdered you."

"His knife was drawn!"

"Ah! you had not mentioned that. He is, however, as great a coward as scoundrel, and the voice of my mother, and your awakening at the right moment, no doubt, saved your life. Your danger was chiefly while you slept. But you will be able to identify him. Lieutenant Sandys, you will please attend Mr. Dunbar; be convenient, so that when I give you the signal, he may come forth and confound the scoundrel. We shall close the books with him now and forever."

So saying, he went forth, and after awhile Lieutenant Sandys followed him, accompanied by our wayfarer. A circuitous walk of a quarter of an hour brought them within view of the encampment, which lay generally within the hollow of the hills. As they wound along the heights, they could see the Rangers in sundry groups; had glimpses of smokes curling up through the thickets, and beheld where, in a long, narrow gorge, the horses of the troop were picketed. The utmost silence prevailed over the whole scene. When at length they had descended to the valley, the Lieutenant led the way to a thicket, where, throwing himself down, he motioned to Walter to do likewise. It was not long before voices were heard, as if from a group in front of them, concealed by the thickets and a line of massive boulders. But nothing was distinguishable. Suddenly, there was a shrill whistle, and the Lieutenant rising, motioned his companion to follow. He led the way for some fifty yards, passing through the thicket and flanking the line of boulders, and Walter suddenly found himself almost in the midst of the whole body of the troop. Some stood, while others sate; the Captain occupying a small boulder, while just in front of him stood five persons, all prisoners, each roped strongly, and guarded by as many riflemen.

Among these prisoners, Walter in an instant recognized the features of the robber. It seemed that these parties had all been severally under examination. One or two of their faces exhibited defiance; others doubt, while that of the robber, whose person has been more particularly brought to our notice, was the very picture of terror and despair.

As soon as Walter made his appearance, the Captain said to him:

"Mr. Dunbar, do you recognize either of the five prisoners you see before you?"

"I do, sir."

"Single him out."

Walter did so, saying, "this man overtook me on the road last evening, and kept along with me till we reached the house of Mrs. Carter, where we both sought lodgings for the night. About midnight, I was awakened by having my saddlebags pulled from under my head, and by the cry of Mrs. Carter at the same moment. By the light of a torch in the hands of Mrs. Carter, I distinctly beheld this man, with a large hunting-knife in his hand. He had cut my saddle-bags open, and most probably would have murdered me but for the cry and presence of Mrs. Carter."

"Would you know this knife, were you to see it?"

"I could say if the shape and size were apparently the same."

"How does this weapon answer the description?"

Here the knife was shown.

"It has the same general appearance, and is about the size of the knife which he carried."

"What followed your awakening?"

"He fled through the front door; I pursued him; but, in the great darkness of the night, could see nothing. I returned to the house, and after a conference with Mrs. Carter, she suddenly remembered what I had quite forgotten, my horse. She lighted me to the stables immediately, but we were then too late. Both horses were gone."

"Do you know your horse so as to be able to identify him?"

"Among a thousand."

"Be pleased to accompany Sergeant Mullens."

Walter did so, and returned in ten minutes leading the animal.

"That will do, Mr. Dunbar."

Walter bowed, fell back, and took a seat upon a boulder, while the Sergeant led the horse away.

"Where's Corporal Harris?"

"Here, sir."

"You brought in the horse this morning, which Mr. Dunbar says was stolen from him last night?"

"I did, sir."

"Is the horse the same?"

"The very same, sir."

"How did he come into your possession?"

"My scout caught this prisoner, Red Pyatt, before daylight this morning. He was riding one horse and leading another; and this other led horse is the one which Mr. Dunbar claims."

"Do you know these facts of your own knowledge?"

"I pulled him with my own hands off one horse, while Jim Oakes jerked away from him the halter which had the other."

"Where's Oakes?"

He was brought forward and confirmed the testimony.

"That is enough. Lieutenant, you will see that Mr. Dunbar has his horse restored to him; find him a saddle and bridle, if you have them to spare, and when he is ready to depart, give him conduct beyond our line of pickets."

Turning to Walter, he then said:

"You will be quite free to depart, Mr. Dunbar, as soon as you think proper, and perhaps it will be prudent that you should do so before we move. Before midnight, we shall ourselves be gone."

At this moment Walter looked towards the prisoner, and caught a look from him so pitiful, that he could not forbear saying to the Captain, in low tones:

"May I ask, Captain, if this proceeding will affect the life of this man?"

It was with a grave aspect and cold accent that he replied:

"It certainly will!"

"Horse-stealing?"

"Is with us not merely a felony, but a peculiar crime, from the great value of the horse in this country, the facility with which he is stolen, and the great frequency of the offence. This fellow has long since proved himself a master in the business."

"And yet, Captain, if this penalty be consequent on the wrong done to me—"

"Feel no concern, Mr. Dunbar, on this score. Had the case concerned your affair only, his punishment would have been light, if a first offence only; but horse-stealing is the very least of his crimes. He has been duly convicted by his peers and neighbors, before your presence was invited, of burglary, arson, and murder. He is one of the most notorious of all the outlaws that for years have infested our country. He is already judged."

"And doomed?"

"And doomed!"

Walter could not trust himself with another glance at the miserable criminal, and turned away. Captain Carter, meanwhile, made a single motion of his hand, and the Rangers grounded their rifles simultaneously, the butts coming heavily to the ground. At the sound, the felon started, looked wildly about him, and suddenly cried out to Walter:

"Oh! Mr. Dunbar, ef that's your name, pray to the Captain for me! 'Twas only your horse, you know, and I might have killed you, you know, when you was sleeping."

"Come!" said the Captain quietly, laying his hand on Walter's shoulder, and leading him away from the scene. As he went, the miserable wretch cried out:

"He won't speak for me a single word. Oh, Lord! Oh, Lord!"

Captain Carter never turned, or suffered Walter to turn, but led him off upon the track by which he had descended from the hill where stood his quarters. When they were midway up the hill, a horrid shriek burst from the valley, and looking back with a shudder, Walter beheld a man struggling with several others, in frantic efforts to escape from their clutches, while shriek after shriek made the hills ring with echoes that told of the agonizing terrors of a weak and desperate heart, without hope, and in the grasp of a mortal fate. Soon a horn was blown, and when next Walter ventured to look back upon the valley, the troopers could be seen in groups returning slowly to the camp, while pendent from the swinging limb of an old oak, there dangled a human form which still struggled feebly in the air, in the last dread agonies of death.

# CHAPTER XXXIV.

### THE FATES STILL AT WORK.

A faint sickness seized upon the heart of Walter Dunbar, as he turned from the miserable spectacle, and followed his companion up the ascent, and into the sylvan tent of the latter. Here, still sick with what he had seen, he took his seat upon the rushes, and the Captain somewhat abruptly said to him:

"And now, Mr. Dunbar, that you have been so fortunate as to recover your horse, I would counsel you to proceed at once upon your journey. You *cannot* remain with *us*. Our duty and the prospect before us forbid that you should do so. If I understand it rightly, *you* are *not one of us*, and it is not so clear that you are not one of those who are opposed to us. But I do not wish to learn your secrets, and I take for granted that, whatever steps you may take, and into whatsoever company you may happen to fall, you will respect ours, and say not one syllable of what you have seen."

Walter very promptly gave the assurance desired.

"I have," continued the Captain, "so far as I know, fulfilled all the promises that my mother was pleased to make for me. You may be sure that she will fulfill all her own. Your gold is in safe hands whenever you shall be pleased to call for it. Let me beg that you will do so as soon as you can. It will be a danger to her, as it is a temptation to others. I must now leave you. Lieutenant Sandys will accompany you on your way beyond our outposts. God be with you, sir, in mercy."

And, hardly waiting for the warm thanks of Walter, the Captain passed out of the tent. Scarcely had he done so when Lieutenant Sandys entered, followed by one whose appearance aroused a variety of emotions in the bosom of Walter. This was no other than the dashing stranger who had made his appearance beside him at the *branch*, shared his bread and meat so frankly, and subsequently disappeared in a manner so mysterious as to awaken in the bosom of Walter the most lively concern in respect to his fate.

He darted towards him eagerly with extended hand, and a warm expression of recognition. But, to his equal surprise and mortification, the other neither gave his hand, nor exhibited any such eagerness as his own. He accordingly drew himself up with *hauteur*, bowed his head, and looked calmly upon the new comer.

"We must be upon no terms, Mr. Dunbar," said the latter, "as long as we do not know where you are. You have not chosen *your* fate, and the fates are never single. There are always two in conflict, foil and counterfoil, and they never suffer any mortal to *play* between them. What I say to you now is dictated by a kindly feeling. I have such knowledge of you and your situation, that I must presume to counsel. Until you can decide with which fate to grapple, in hearty, hardy, enduring and resolute conflict, go back upon your course. *Go not forward.* If you do, you rush upon an adverse fate, and the consequences may be ruin. Let me speak more plainly. Within three hours from this point you will meet with the forces of the crown, under the lead of Fletchall, Browne and others. Within the next twenty-four hours they will probably be in conflict with the forces of the patriots, under General Richardson. How will these things affect you?"

"I have despatches to some of these very persons—to Col. Fletchall, Robert Cunningham, Pearis, Kirkland and others."

"Kirkland is fled, Fletchall and Browne are at loggerheads, and it is doubtful if the loyal militia do not disband before fighting. But, are you sure of the nature of your despatches? You think them of value. Open them, and see."

"Never, sir! The letters are from my father. They are sacred."

"And their purport?"

"I know not, but I am assured of their importance."

"And they are valueless! Their sole object is to send you away from the supposed influence of Martin Joscelyn upon you, to the control of those leaders who, like your father, are devoted to the crown. I assert this without fear of contradiction. Open, read them, and you will see for yourself."

"That, sir, I cannot do, as a man of honor."

"You are not dealing with men of honor, Walter Dunbar."

"My father, sir."

"Your father is an honorable man, but obstinate, wrong-headed, and under the influence of some of the vilest scoundrels under the sun. He has lately harbored in his dwelling one of the most venomous serpents that ever lay in coil upon human hearth."

"Who?—Alison?"

"I see you know; you suspect, if you do not know. It is fair in war, in such times as these, that you see that you do not carry your fate in your own wallet. Read your letters, and they will tell you that you are used simply as a puppet; your veneration for your father being made use of to neutralize all your own properties of manhood."

"You speak without circumlocution, sir."

"The only way, in a season like the present, and when we would serve or save a friend. Read your letters, and you will rather burn than deliver them. Proceed with them, blinded as you are, and you rush upon your fate!"

"Be it so! But I must go forward. Delusive as these letters may be, I have pledged myself to deliver them; and I will do so, though the fate shall take me by the throat a moment after!"

"Well!—well! You are warned. I would save you from yourself."

"Who are you, sir, who know me and mine so well?"

"You are slow, Walter Dunbar, in a voyage of discovery. I fancied that I had given you a sufficient key-note already, which would carry you back some ten years or more. I can only repeat it, and leave you to con its meaning, and take counsel from its warning, 'Never let foe or fate get the first *clip* at you!' "

"Ah! I know you now—Ned Melton, my friend!——"

But the party spoken to had gone, and Lieutenant Sandys, entering and interposing at the moment, warned Walter that his horse, properly equipped, was ready for him in the valley, while he, Sandys, was prepared to accompany him to the outposts. Walter recognized this communication as in the nature of an *order*, and, with an involuntary sigh, looking curiously around him as he went, he followed his guide and escort to the valley, and was finally conducted to the outposts of the troopers.

When alone, riding forward slowly, he said to himself:

"So Ned Melton turns up at last! How could I have forgotten him? Yet how changed! And where can he have hidden himself all this while? Verily, I *should* have remembered the significant warning, 'Never let the enemy get the first *clip* at you!' He said *that* when John Cummings gave me my first threshing at school, bunging up my eyes at the very first clip, and before I was quite certain that we should fight at all!"

We need not pursue these musings, which brought up a whole volume of school-boy recollections, making Walter forgetful of his steed and road, until suddenly and roughly awakened from his dreaming mood, by finding himself arrested by a squad of militia men. By these he was hurried off to the camp of the loyalists which was just at hand.

Here, on the slope of a gentle eminence, he found himself in the presence of a formidable array. The leaders of the loyalists were mostly present. Fletchall, Browne, Pearis, McLaurin, Cunningham and others, all on horseback, and in an irregular circle, appeared to be engaged in some serious conference. Colonel Browne was the most conspicuous figure in this group. But he had undergone an extreme and curious change from the person he displayed when we last met him. He was no longer the tarred and feathered, matted, squalid and utterly disfigured savage, which he then appeared. All traces of his cruel punishment, inflicted by the patriots, had been removed from his person, and, instead of the ragged and filthy fugitive, he was now habited in the rich uniform of a British Colonel, as fine as feathers and scarlet, gold lace and *chapeau bras* could make him. His uniform, sent him from Charleston by Lord Wm. Campbell, was well designed to impose upon the senses of the ignorant backwoodsmen; and he had his vanities. He was not insensible, seemingly, of the fine show he made, in wonderful contrast with the simple gray hunting-shirts of all around him. His air and manner betrayed to all eyes the consciousness of power. His tones were loud and arrogant, and he faced the sullen countenances of Fletchall and others, of the rangers, with a look of haughty superiority, which, it was evident, had already given great offence to all parties, especially outraging the claims of others, who, from their local influence, believed, and with reason, that they should outrank him.

And so, indeed, Colonel Fletchall did. But Browne possessed a *will* such as Fletchall did not bring to the support of his authority; and he looked on, and listened, with the gorge rising momently as he heard the other, in language which assumed the whole command for himself, while tone, look and manner declared equally his scorn and contempt for most of his associates.

To the great surprise of Walter, who had been kept on the outer edge of the circle, still a prisoner, he beheld, in front of Browne, no less a person than Stephen Joscelyn, a single glance at whom sufficed to awaken in his bosom a throng of bitter memories.

Stephen, accompanied by another Captain, of Hammond's command, was present in the character of a Commissioner to treat for a pacification. He was sent to demand the surrender and disbandment of the "Loyalists," under penalty of being held to answer to the State authorities, as public enemies and traitors. He had already fulfilled his mission, and made the demand in terms equally proper and impressive. He had just finished speaking as Walter appeared upon the scene.

It was then that Fletchall approached Browne, and said to him in low tones:

"We should assemble in council to consider these terms."

"In council!" replied Browne, scornfully, "and why in council? Am I not here, in the King's commission? Do I not know what are the counsels of his majesty's representatives? We need no *council*, sir, nor *counsel*. My counsel lies in my sword."

Then, as Fletchall sullenly fell back, he turned to Stephen Joscelyn, and replied:

"Go back to your masters, sir, and tell them I accept no terms from rebels to their king. Let your Drayton, and your Richardson, and your Williamson, your Mayson and your Hammond, bring on their rapscallions as soon as they please. Their crippled diplomat is but a fitting representative of their crippled policy and party, which we shall cripple much more thoroughly if they only pluck up courage to maintain impudent language by bold actions."

"You might have spared your *personal* insults to a *cripple*," was the calm reply of Stephen, though his face was deeply flushed, and his voice slightly trembled from the effort which he made to subdue his passion. "Cripple as I am," he continued, "if you will only face me when we do meet in the shock of battle, as bravely as you now show yourself in words, you will find nothing of the cripple in my *arm!*"

Walter's cheeks flushed as he heard these words, and recalled his own humiliation at the school-house.

Browne replied, scornfully:

"What! *you! You* confront me! Ha! ha! Get hence, fellow, to your fellows; and beware how you cross my path!"

"Remember what I say," retorted Stephen. "That I *will* cross your path, you may be assured, and, as God is living above us, I hope to make you remember the *arm* of the cripple to the latest moment of your life."

"Be gone! be gone!" was the only answer, as Browne wheeled his horse about, and confronted Fletchall and the sullen group about him.

At that moment, Walter, as a prisoner, now dismounted, was brought forward by his captors. His sudden appearance, under the circumstances, was quite a surprise to Stephen, who gave him but a single look, and then rode off with his companion, escorted by a small squad of his Beach Island troopers. They were all sturdy fellows, and their bugler, a mere schoolboy, sounded a lively note of defiance, as they wound upon their way along the hills.

"Who is this?" demanded Browne, as Walter stood before him. Walter answered for himself.

"And what do you here?"

"I have letters for certain persons from my father."

"Give them to me."

"There are none for you."

"The letters, man—no fooling here."

"The letters are for Col. Fletchall, Col. Cunningham, Mr. Cameron, Mr. Kearns, Mr. McLaurin, and others. There are none for you, sir."

"Search him," was the order.

"It will not need. I see some of the parties present to whom they are addressed. Here they are."

The package was snatched from his grasp by one of the soldiers, and handed to Browne, who immediately tore wide the envelope, and was about to tear open one of the letters.

"What are you about, sir?" demanded Walter, in tones of indignation. "That letter is not for you. There is *no* letter for you in the package."

And as Browne proceeded, without regarding him, to open the letter, Walter sprang forward and grasped the packet from his uplifted hand. In the next moment he was stricken to the ground by a heavy stroke from the butt of his horseman's pistol, which, quick as lightning, Browne had drawn from his holster.

"Take that, fool!" was his ejaculation, as he struck. The youth fell incontinently, while the blood streamed from his forehead. There was a murmur among the officers, Fletchall and others now running forward and lifting the body from the earth.

There was a call for Dr. Smyzer, as they took the now insensible man to the dwelling in the rear. Walter Dunbar had again encountered with his fate, and had not been permitted to follow the counsel of his friend, in getting "the first clip" at his enemy.

## CHAPTER XXXV.

### BEFORE THE BATTLE.

A stormy conference succeeded that night among the Highland chieftains. Though something of an imbecile, Fletchall had his self-esteem, and this had been goaded to extremity by the reckless scorn and indifference of Browne, whose will, violent as powerful, conscious of purpose, goaded by passion, and capable of performance, kept no terms with imbecility. We have seen that he was a man of intense passions. These were not quieted by the possession of power, and the very slight resistance, more negative than positive, which he had met from some of his associates, had made him doggedly regardless of their sensibilities. He answered their expostulations with an almost contemptuous heedlessness, that frequently disdained all answer; and to the murmurs—for, as yet, their discontent had taken no louder utterance—he replied only in the reassertion of his will.

Fletchall's self-esteem, at the open outrage to which he had been subjected, in the perusal by Browne of a letter addressed to himself, spoke out, at this conference, in terms more than usually emphatic. Pearis and others, similarly treated, were also prepared to second him in his assertion of right and position. They made points of two matters—the refusal of a consultation on the proposal of Drayton to treat, and the opening of their letters, when they themselves were present, as if the letters had been common property.

"We should have called a council of war," said Fletchall.

"A council of war," retorted Browne, "is only a cover for cowardice! In nine cases out of ten, the General who calls for a council of war, simply desires an excuse for not fighting. We have got to fight. That should be understood. There's no use for any counsel, treating of peace, when this necessity is before us. We shall never be anything, or do anything, until we make these nabobs of the seaboard feel the weight of our arms. I have put my hand to the plow, and I'm not for turning and looking back."

"But we have a right to speak in this matter, Colonel Browne."

"You have a right, have you? I don't see! What will you do? Sir, let me tell you that when the ship's about to founder, the right lies with the brave man who is ready to take the helm! The storm is upon us, and the day of counsel and councils is quite gone by. I have taken the helm simply because I do not see, whatever may be your rights, that there is any bold seaman among you, who is prepared to do so, and there you have my answer! Here's the King's commission, and you have yours, you say, and yours dates some months, perhaps, before mine. What of that? The commission don't make the man! Well, I'm here, and I am prepared with the manhood as well as the commission. Show me your better titles. If, with fifteen hundred men in hand, you will go forward against the thousand that Richardson leads against you, and they have no more; if you will lead to-morrow and make fight, why you shall command; but if you temporize and treat, and call for councils of war, which are generally pacific enough for a Quaker meeting, I tell you, I will take the helm, and guide the vessel. Here you have it! I see enough to know that we are all swamped unless somebody is prepared to lead, and unless that lead means fight! Once for all, gentlemen, I mean to fight, and in order that you should do so, I mean to lead. You have my answer on this head, and my resolution! As for this boy of Dunbar's, and your letters, let me say that the boy is a blockhead, of no use to us or to anybody else! I've seen him tried. He's a milk-sop, who stops to weigh scruples with the storm upon his very shoulders. If you could take the pluck of the old man, his father, and drive it into his brain—well, along with what he's got there,—we might do something with him. The letters were nothing of value; but, even if they were, a commander takes leave to read all letters, if he pleases, which fall into his hands. This is the law of war, and while I am in command, no letters shall pass me, to any person in this or any camp of mine, which I shall not examine if I please. It may be that our security shall depend upon it. We are not so sure, gentlemen"—shaking his head significantly—"that every man here is sound of heart, within the beat of our enemy's drum! Here, you have had an instance which you ought to remember. Where's Moses

Kirkland? With his fifteen hundred men, he might be, this day, in possession of Augusta; yet, at the very moment when he should strike his blow, he abandons his troops in a panic, and clears out to the seaboard!—takes to his heels, like the braggart that he is, and turns tail at the first sound of the trumpet. And are we, and shall I, risk the King's cause, which is our own cause, upon doubtful things like him? No, gentlemen, I am in command here now; my hand is on the helm, and I don't mean to deliver it into other hands until I see the good ship of State in safety—"

"Or see it wrecked!" said Fletchall.

"Or see it wrecked!" was the cool reply. "Wrecked it will be, if left to such hands as have been managing before! We incur no greater danger in fighting than in running the vessel upon the rocks. I will be answerable for what I do, and I beg you to understand that, come what will, we fight the rebels to-morrow. The King's standard must not be spread abroad in vain, or as a mockery. Be you but men, and do your duty like men, and we shall whip these rapscallions before noon to-morrow! Ours is the sword of the Lord and of Gideon! and I stake my life upon it!" And he finished his speech by quaffing deeply from a stoup of Jamaica; turned upon his heel, and disappeared from the dissatisfied assembly, without further question or reply. He was accompanied only by Colonel Cunningham, who sought, but vainly, to make him understand that conciliation was an act not to be undervalued in the present condition of affairs; but he pleaded in vain.

"It is useless, Cunningham, to hope for anything from this people till you have made them fight! That done, that beginning once made, and they fully committed to the cause, they will feel the rope about their necks, and use the sword freely to escape the gallows! They must fight, they shall fight to-morrow, if Richardson brings his fellows up to the scratch; and if not, we shall hunt them down, till every fox has taken to his hole!"

With the next day's dawning, Cunningham roused up Browne, whose potations of the night had made him particularly drowsy.

"Well, what's it now?"

"It is as I feared," answered Cunningham; "they are gone!—Fletchall, Pearis, and the rest—carrying with them both the regiments, at least a thousand men! The scouts are coming in with the report that Richardson is marching down upon us, hardly two miles off, and we have but four hundred foot soldiers left, and less than two hundred horse."

"The miserable dastards! But thick grass is easier cut than thin. We shall fight, nevertheless. He who shows best front, and holds on the longest, is sure to win!"

He had risen, looking wild and haggard, and, for a moment, seemed to hesitate; then he plunged his head into a bucket of cold water, gave it several immersions, and rose from it, shaking it as a water-dog after swimming. He hurriedly dressed himself in his grand uniform, strapped on sword and sash, and his horse, by Cunningham's orders, was already in harness at the door. Catching up his holsters, he was soon in saddle, and proceeding as coolly and promptly to put the troops in order of battle, as if nothing had happened to disturb his equanimity or lessen his confidence in his strength and fortunes.

Cunningham, who acted as his chief Lieutenant, and had command of his cavalry, had already set the men in order according to previous arrangements, and the two rode forth together to the front. There was a savage buoyancy about Browne, glaring in his eyes, and showing itself in voice and action, as if his spirit rose in due degree with the diminished chances in his hands.

"Now shall you see, this day," said he, "what may be done by men, however few, whose hearts have the proper pluck, and whom a proper pluck conducts to action. Numbers do not constitute an army. It is in the will of the Captain who commands, and the readiness of those he leads to surrender themselves blindly to the direction of that Captain's will. I shall set my teeth firmly, and those who see will set theirs, unconsciously, and go forward as I show them. These raw militiamen of Richardson will hardly stand a good charge of your cavalry. We shall need to rely upon them. We must use our foot soldiers as skirmishers. All the passes have been occupied?"

"All but the rear. Fletchall has drawn off every man from that quarter."

"We shall hardly be assailed in that direction."

"I don't know that! There was a report last evening of a company of rebel rangers coming up from below."

"Well, we must look sharp about us."

"The further report now is, that Richardson's force will be fully two thousand men, and one-third of them horse."

"Nonsense! Hardly one thousand, as I know. Drayton had but one hundred and twenty-five all told, when first he pushed Fletchall from his quarters below."

"Besides four swivels and eighty horse from the Savannah river."

"The swivels scared Fletchall."

"But they have had large increase swelling their strength, and I apprehend that our former estimates will scarcely do justice to their present numbers, which have had large accessions from the sea-board. Richardson has been joined by Thompson, with his rangers from Orangeburg and the Santee country. This we *know* from a person brought in last night. The intelligence is certain."

"Well, well, your present estimate?"

"Would make them quite two thousand men."

"Impossible! impossible! But whether two thousand or twenty thousand, matters nothing. *We must fight.* Show them a bold front, and these sea-coast nabobs will be apt to show their heels. They will hardly stand a second fire."

Cunningham shook his head, doubtingly.

"At all events, Cunningham, we know what's to be done. The duty is before us—let us about it like men, and you need not fear what will happen."

A busy two hours passed, but the revolutionary troops did not yet appear. Meanwhile, Browne and Cunningham reviewed all the ground, chose the most elevated ridges for their defence, sent out scouts and *videttes,* placed sentinels, and, out of the small force left them, detached small squads for covering the nearest passes, some of which had been left entirely uncovered by the withdrawal of Fletchall's and Pearis's regiments. This done, and all precautions taken, Browne seemed to abandon himself to a leisurely and composed calculation of his resources, and the chances of his situation. He quaffed his Jamaica, meanwhile, without a scruple; and in his deportment exhibited that savage *riancy* of the Hun, rioting, as it were, in the suggestive fancies of the rapturous strife before him. He was a savage, a brute, in many respects, ferocious and cruel; but cool even in his most fiery moods of passion, and capable of an audacity that seemed very like the efforts of despair, even at the moment while his eye took in all the aspects of the field, and his mind revolved quietly all the advantages or the dangers of its every position. He said to Cunningham, with a fiendish smile playing upon his face, as he passed the sides of his sabre over a grindstone:

"Always see, Cunningham, that your sabre has the teeth to bite. Men who carry dull sabres into the fight, do not calculate to use them. The Turks knew better, and were the most brilliant cavalry in the world. Now, if you could but slice off a man's head, sheer at a blow, and send it spinning across the field, it would do more to strike a panic into his followers, than any solid charge which you could make, stirrup to stirrup, with your masses. Sharpen your sabre, Cunningham—give it teeth to bite shrewdly."

Then, after a moment—

"Did you note that crippled fellow yesterday—that Commissioner from Drayton—and see how he defied me? That fellow will fight, cripple as he is. He has it in him. His eye met mine with as cold and brave a stare as I ever beheld in eye of man. I shall meet him. He will certainly keep his word, and meet me if he can. I am whetting my sabre especially for him, and if we do but come to close quarters—"

He finished the sentence by a whisk of the blade above his head.

"That we shall come to close quarters, I nothing doubt. It will be pretty much a hand to hand fight, if any. That's what I want. I rely upon your troopers, Cunningham; for, look you, if your reports be true, our game will be to choose the best pathway for cutting our way through them. Our foot will open the play as skirmishers. The hills afford here a sufficient cover for riflemen, and to command all the approaches."

"In front and on the right; but I somehow fear from left to rear. This delay—it is now ten o'clock—and they do not yet come on. They wait, I apprehend, in their main assault, until their detachments shall sufficiently work round us, and we have no troops to cover all the points of the compass."

"Apprehend nothing. We are as ready and as well prepared as we can be. You know my plans. By the way, what became of that younker, Dunbar?"

"He was left in Fletchall's hands, who has doubtless carried him off. They carried the surgeon off with him. You hit him a hard blow."

"Yes; my hand is rather a heavy one when I am angry. Why the devil did the blockhead oppose me?"

"I am rather sorry for it. The father is a true friend of ours—a loyal subject, and brave."

"Yes; had the son the pluck of his father, and his principles, he would do us good service. But he is good for nothing. He was a pet boy, and was never weaned. He is still a milksop. Hark! Who comes?"

"From the front—the pickets are driven in."

The two men were on horseback immediately. Random shots were heard approaching, and trooper after trooper appeared, dashing into camp at full gallop.

## CHAPTER XXXVI.

### THE BATTLE.

"Well, Purvis, what report?"

"Three thousand, sir, at least."

"Three thousand what?"

"Troops, sir!"

"Pshaw! man; you're dreaming."

"It's with eyes open, then, sir. I saw them from the hill. They're marching in three separate bodies, and not less than a thousand in each. They've got artillery."

"Artillery, ah! And what's artillery? There are some lumbering things, called cannon, on cart-wheels; and, by putting powder into cannon, and applying a match, there's a noise—a bellowing across the hills, that troubles nothing but the ears. Don't take in a fright through your ears, Purvis! I wonder what the devil mischief their cannon can do among these hills. You may laugh at the cannon, Purvis!"

"I think they're trying to surround us, sir."

"Very likely. That means coming upon us front, flank and rear! eh? But don't let even that trouble you, Purvis. Get back to your company now, and remember that I am to see you out of these pleasant surroundings. Don't listen to the cannon, Purvis. It hits none but the fool who listens. Away now, and think of nothing but to follow as I lead!"

And so Browne dismissed Sergeant Purvis to his squad; and so he dismissed a dozen others to their several stations, himself moving to all points in turn, and letting himself be heard, as well as seen, and always with a scornful sort of levity in his speech, that seemed to mock at every suggestion of danger.

The apprehensions of Cunningham, confirmed in a measure by the report of Sergeant Purvis, were soon realized. Detachments of the revolutionists had worked their way equally to flank and rear of Browne's position, while the main body came on in front.

From the defiles the firing, at first scattering, became fast and furious. Soon the small bodies of Browne's men, occupying the passes, were driven in, fighting as they gave ground, with resolute courage, and only overborne by numbers. Anon, a random fire was opened in the rear, which found corresponding echoes from the flanks, and Browne discovered fully that he was in a net. His foot soldiers gradually came dropping in from the heights, bearing occasionally a comrade upon their shoulders. Their places were supplied by new bodies from the slender reserve which Browne had kept in the back ground; but it was very soon evident that this resource would be quickly exhausted. The troops of the patriots were everywhere rising to the heights, and pressing back the small bodies whom they encountered. Already a considerable column had crossed one of the several ridges in front, and they, seeming to hesitate, were supposed to do so, simply to mass themselves more effectually before making their charge down into the area, which had been occupied as the camp of Browne. The latter observed all the signs around him, and his eye continued calmly to take in the aspects and events with which he had to contend. He was never more cool, resolute or inflexible of purpose than at the present moment. Cunningham rode up to him at this juncture.

"Should I not charge them at once, before they are massed for the advance?"

"Not yet!—not yet! We must spare your troopers as much as possible for the final effort. Meanwhile, see that our rifles keep up a brisk fire upon the body on yonder ridge, thinning out the epaulettes as fast as possible. We must do all the mischief we can before making our final dash."

A trooper now rode up.

"Captain Bergman is killed, sir, and his men are falling back. Lieutenant Cox begs that you'll send him some help. The rebels are rising over the 'Red Hill' now."

"What numbers?"

"I reckon about three hundred, mostly foot soldiers, but I saw, just as I rode off, a troop of cavalry coming out of the 'scrubby oak thicket,' and making towards the 'Rocky Hollow.' "

"Ha! Cunningham! You must see to that quickly. It is by that path that they can most easily gain our rear, and cut us off from all retreat. Take a sufficient squadron of your troopers, and meet them before they reach the 'Hollow.' How many troopers did you see, Phillips?"

"There might have been fifty or sixty, sir."

"Good! Leave me fifty or sixty of your fellows, Cunningham, and take the rest. Take what you please."

Cunningham dashed off for the threatened quarter, leading some seventy-five of his cavalry.

Meanwhile, the forces of Richardson appeared, crowning the hills on several sides, and, from their elevations, using their rifles with considerable effect. Browne's skirmishers, among the hills, and under cover of rocks and trees, still kept up their fire; but, as both parties fought in Indian fashion, either squat upon the ground, or from behind some shelter, whether of trees or rocks, the casualties were not great on either side. Browne knew that the grand issue would only take place after the assailants should be massed for a charge, seeking, by mere pressure of numbers, to force their way into the encampment.

Suddenly, a wild yell was sent up from the whole line of Richardson's army, in front and along the flanks. Simultaneously, a merry blast of bugles blazed out from the rear, and, looking around him, Browne saw the squadrons of Cunningham in full retreat, down from the "Stony Hollow," with a strong corps of the assailing cavalry following close at their heels. He had been overpowered, but fought with a Parthean skill and spirit even as he fled, turning ever and anon upon his enemy, and showing a fearless front.

Browne's trumpets sounded for the rally. He now drew his sabre, and put himself at the head of his remaining cavalry.

It was time to do so, for the assailants were now pressing down from the heights, on three sides, driving his skirmishers before them. These, it was soon seen, were no longer to be rallied. Driven in several quarters, scattered in several directions, each sought his several shelter, and possibly, from heights and hollows tolerably secure, they looked down upon the conflict in which they were no longer willing or able to share. The rest of the battle remained to the cavalry.

The squadron of Hammond was in full pursuit of Cunningham, when Browne, at the head of the force left with him, rushed desperately to the rescue. He darted between the pursuers and the pursued, the latter massing themselves as fast as possible in his rear, while he opposed a sturdy and well set column to the attack.

In an instant, the two opposing forces were in collision, and a pell-mell conflict ensued. Suddenly, and when the conflict was at its wildest, Browne found himself confronted by Stephen Joscelyn.

"Ah! ha! my brave fellow, you are there!" shouted the former, as with sabre whirled in air, he rode down upon him.

"I am in your path, and will cross it!" answered Stephen.

The stroke of Browne's sabre was delivered with all the weight of his arm. It was handsomely parried, and the two steeds came together; when, instead of smiting with his steel, Stephen, throwing back the blade of his weapon, smote Browne with the iron hilt of the sabre heavily in the mouth, and hurled him from his horse. Rising in his stirrup, on his sound leg, he was about *to give him point* as he lay upon the ground, when a bullet from Cunningham's pistol passed through the brain of his horse, and the beast staggered forward and fell; not, however, before Stephen had succeeded in extricating his feet from the stirrups and sliding safely to the earth.

In an other moment, Cunningham had succeeded in remounting Browne, and as the other, raging like a wild beast, was about to turn again upon his opponent, Cunningham seized the bridle of his horse, and turned his head, forcing him away from the *mêlée*.

"We have not a moment to lose," said he, "if we would cut our way through the enemy. Our course is by the 'Stony Hollow.' The game is up for the day! Away! away!"

So saying, he bade his bugles sound, massed his men in a brief space, and gave the command to charge! He broke through the scattered troopers of Hammond, already broken by the recent pursuit and attack, and, after some severe fighting, he succeeded in escaping from the net. Browne, though very reluctantly, submitted to his guidance, looking behind him and sending back his curses as he rode.

Stephen Joscelyn, provided with another horse, leading his Beach Island Troop, was quickly in pursuit; but the day's work had been already too much for horse and man, and our patriot partisans had the mortification of a chase for five miles, made utterly in vain.

---

Here ends our present chronicle. We have done what we proposed at first—to give the *opening* scene in the grand drama of the seven years' war of the Revolution in the South. The *dramatis personæ*, such as yet remain undisposed of, are yet to survive for long conflicts, frequently renewed. Of their fate, their fortunes, we may speak in future pages. That they were various and dubious, alternately saddened with defeat and exulting in triumph, the reader can readily conceive; but we trust to gratify all curiosity in respect to these several parties, when our readers shall again meet with us, under the auspices of the publisher.

THE END.

From the S. Lewis engraving, Plate VIII of the Atlas accompanying John Marshall's *The Life of George Washington* (1807).

# EXPLANATORY NOTES

by

Stephen Meats

These notes are intended to identify persons, places, events, quotations and obscure or archaic words and terms in the text of *Joscelyn*. Special emphasis has been placed upon the Revolutionary War history in this novel, including, when possible, the identification of Simms' sources and his departures from them.

1. epigraph: Shakespeare, *Henry VIII,* III, ii.

3.1 "It was a pleasant day": Simms visited Augusta to gather local information for *Joscelyn* between 23 July and 1 August 1858. A single page of notes mostly on the geography of the area and a hand-drawn map of Augusta and the surrounding vicinity are the only documents surviving from that visit. General Hammond was James Henry Hammond, a former Congressman, Governor of South Carolina and United States Senator. John Bones was a friend of Hammond's at Augusta.

4.4-5 "Hernando De Soto": De Soto visited the Augusta area in May 1540. He died 21 May 1542 and was buried in the Mississippi River.

4.32-33 "seizure and imprisonment": An account of this seizure of the Cacica of Cutifachiqui, as she was called, appears on pp. 62-68 of *Narratives of the Career of Hernando De Soto* (New York, 1866); see the following note.

4.34-37 "Let the reader": The book Simms refers to here is *Narratives of the Career of Hernando De Soto in the Conquest of Florida as Told by a Knight of Elvas,* trans. Buckingham Smith, New York: [The Bradford Club], 1866. The Bradford Club also published *The Army Correspondence of Colonel John Laurens in the Years 1777-78* (1867) for which Simms wrote a memoir of Laurens.

5.1 "Uchees": An Indian tribe along the Savannah River; also spelled Euchee and Yuchi.

5.10-11 "to have tried men's souls": Thomas Paine, *The Crisis: Introduction* (1776).

5.16-18 "Hammonds, Cummings," etc.: In this list of ten names Simms seems to be mixing real and fictional persons; the actual names that could be identified are as follows: The Hammonds were apparently Captain Samuel Hammond, a noted soldier in the Revolution, and Colonel Le Roy Hammond, Samuel Hammond's uncle, who owned a home, Snow Hill, north of Augusta on the Carolina side of the Savannah River. Colonel Hammond also served with distinction in the Revolution. Samuel Hammond's appearance in *Joscelyn* is a mistake since he did not arrive in South Carolina until his family moved from Virginia in early 1779. The name Cunningham undoubtedly refers to Robert and Patrick, brothers who were prominent loyalists in the back country civil war which provides the historical framework for *Joscelyn*. Alexander may refer to William Alexander, a landowner near Augusta, who was Justice of the Peace in 1759; he does not appear in the novel. Hamilton is apparently Captain Hamilton, perhaps Robert, whose troopers tarred and feathered Thomas Browne; see note 8.28 and pp. 73-83 of the novel. Cooper may have been Richard Cooper, a landowner near Augusta, who signed a resolution supporting American independence in 1775; Cooper was a common name, however, and appears frequently in the standard lists of Georgia Revolutionary War soldiers. Thomas Browne (also spelled Brown) was perhaps the most notorious loyalist in the South during the Revolution; for a more complete discussion of Browne, see note 8.28. Colonel James Grierson was a staunch loyalist who occupied Augusta with Browne in 1780 after the fall of Charleston. He was murdered by whigs after Augusta was recaptured in 1781.

5.19 "ninety years ago": *Joscelyn* takes place in the summer and fall of 1775; this reference, then, is to the time of the writing of the novel in 1866.

6.1 "The city": On the page of notes from his Augusta visit, Simms noted that "Augusta ought to be estimated at 600 in the Revolution." A letter quoted in Berry Fleming, comp., *Autobiography of a Colony* (1957), p. 90, gives these figures for the year 1765: "138 men and 402 Women and Children, 501 Negro slaves and about 90 Checkesaw Indians."

7.9-10 "'when George the Third was king'": Byron, *Don Juan*, Canto I, stanza 212.

7.27 "'Deckard' rifle": Jacob Dechard was the maker of this famous rifle.

8.24 "Cameron": Alexander Cameron, a Scotsman, was Deputy Superintendent of Indian Affairs in the Southern Department until the death of John Stuart in 1779 when he became Superintendent of the Western Division.

8.28 "Tom Browne": Thomas Browne is the historical character most important to the novel. Simms first made use of his story in *Mellichampe* (1836) in which he attributed portions of Browne's history to the character Barsfield. In the preface to this earlier novel, Simms wrote that Browne was "one of the most malignant and vindictive among the southern loyalists, and one who is said to have become so solely from the illegal and unjustifiable means which were employed by the patriots" to convert him to the revolutionary cause (*Mellichampe* [New York, 1853], p. 2). A contemporary account of these "unjustifiable means" in the *Georgia Gazette* of 1 August 1775 reports that the "Sons of Liberty" (also called Liberty Boys) from Augusta visited New Richmond, S.C., to charge Thomas Browne and William Thompson, "two young gentlemen lately from England," with having made statements against American independence. Thompson escaped when he heard of their approach, but Browne refused to run and was captured. The Liberty Boys then "politely escorted him to Augusta, where they presented him with a genteel and fashionable suit of tar and feathers, and afterwards had him exhibited in a cart. . . ." The next day the *Gazette* reports that Browne retracted his objectionable statements. Hugh McCall, an early Georgia historian, adds the detail that Browne and Thompson made their remarks "accompanied by toasts at a dinner," after which they fled and were pursued by the Liberty Boys (*The History of Georgia* [1816], II, 46). According to a more recent biographical study, Browne was not a Scotsman, as Simms implies in *Joscelyn*, but was instead the son of Jonas Brown of Whitby, England. He came to Georgia in late 1774 to establish a plantation, and apparently would have succeeded if he had not been interrupted by the civil conflicts of 1775. According to Browne's own later testimony, which disagrees somewhat with the *Georgia Gazette* account, a party of one hundred men came to his plantation demanding that he renounce his loyalty to the British government. When he firmly refused, most of the men left, but a few remained, and later, by burning his feet with torches, forced him to sign an oath of loyalty to the revolutionary cause. (Simms' fictionalized version of this event agrees most closely with the *Georgia Gazette* account.) When allowed to escape, Browne hurried to South Carolina to join with loyalist forces there. After the events of 1775, he was active in attempting to implement an unsuccessful plan to use the Indians against whig forces along the frontier, and later he was commander of the Florida Rangers. In May 1780, he commanded the loyalist forces that occupied Augusta. From that position of power he began his revenge upon the whigs in the Augusta area for the pain and humiliation they had caused him five years earlier. His most notorious atrocity was the hanging of several wounded prisoners in his own presence so that he could watch them die, and the release of others to the Indians to be tortured to death. After the war Browne was exiled and settled on the island of St. Vincent in the Bahamas, where he died in 1825.

11.20 "Scottish type": Cameron was Scots (his nickname was "Scotchie") but Browne was English; see the previous note. Simms apparently based his belief in Browne's Scots nationality on John Drayton, *Memoirs of the American Revolution* (1821), I, 366, where Browne is called "a Scotchman." Simms' statement at 11.22-23 that Browne was an Indian trader is not supported by history.

15.1 "Lord William Campbell": Campbell, a Scotsman, was the last Royal Governor of South Carolina. His active role in the office lasted only from early June until 15 September 1775 when he fled from Charleston, after finding the Provincial Congress hostile and intractable, and took refuge on the British warship *Tamar*, which was anchored in the area of Charleston Harbor known as Rebellion Roads. His flight suspended royal authority in South Carolina until the British capture of Charleston in May 1780.

15.32 "Drayton": William Henry Drayton was among the foremost proponents of American independence in the South during the Revolutionary period. His actual visit to Colonel Le Roy Hammond's home, Snow Hill, occurred on 29 August instead of near the first of the month as it is described here. He was on an official journey through the area between the Broad and Savannah rivers attempting to persuade the inhabitants of that region to sign the articles of association (see note 125.15) in support of American independence. He left Charleston on 2 August accompanied by the Reverend William Tennent and several other men, notably Oliver Hart. Drayton's and Tennent's reports of the journey are printed in Drayton, I, 324 ff.

19.13 "stirring up the red men": On the basis of certain passages in the correspondence of Alexander Cameron and John Stuart (see the following note) which came to the attention of the governing body in Charleston in May 1775, and on the basis of several letters which were seized at the Charleston Post Office in early July, these two men were suspected of attempting to incite the Indians to attack the Carolina-Georgia frontier. When the alleged plot was discovered by William Henry Drayton and Timothy Dwight, Stuart fled from Charleston to Savannah and finally to Florida while Cameron withdrew into Cherokee territory. Historians in this century have shown that in the early stages of the war, at least, both men resisted British pressure to bring about Indian support of a British invasion, though Cameron actually led the Indians in some of the battles of 1776; for further information, see note 62.8-9.

19.28 "Colonel Stuart": John Stuart, a Scotsman, became Superintendent of Indian Affairs in the Southern Department in 1763. He served in that capacity until his death at Pensacola, Florida, in 1779.

23.19 "Fletchall's Regiment": Colonel Thomas Fletchall, a Scotsman, was the most influential loyalist in the Ninety Six District of South Carolina just prior to the Revolutionary War; in the summer of 1775 he could muster a militia force of 1500 men. When the fighting actually started in the fall of that year, Fletchall proved to be a somewhat timid and ineffectual leader. He signed a peace treaty in September, the terms of which were dictated totally by William Henry Drayton and were favorable only to the whig side—a virtual betrayal of his army. Later he deserted the army to hide from the pursuit of a strong whig force under Richard Richardson, but was captured early in December and sent to Charleston as a prisoner.

23.21-22 "Saluda, Broad, Tiger, Little Rivers; Dutch Fork": The first four are rivers in the northwest section of South Carolina. Dutch Fork is the name of the region between the Broad and Saluda rivers, and is so named because of the large number of Germans settling there before the Revolution.

23.24 "Kirkland, Pearis": Moses Kirkland, a Scotsman, was first a captain of cavalry-rangers on the whig side but switched to the loyalists in July 1775, after betraying the whig garrison at Ninety Six and its commander, Major James Mayson, into the hands of Major Joseph Robinson and his loyalist troop. The garrison contained a quantity of the King's arms which Kirkland had helped to capture from Fort Charlotte on the Savannah River in late June. In late August it was rumored that Kirkland had raised a body of troops and was threatening an attack on Augusta. On 30 August, after learning of Kirkland's plan, W. H. Drayton declared him an outlaw, called out whig troops to protect the back country, and offered a reward for Kirkland's capture. Kirkland fled to Charleston in disguise and then went on to Florida where he worked for John Stuart. He was later captured near Philadelphia while carrying dispatches to General Gage. Richard Pearis, also a Scotsman, was an Indian trader and agent before the war; he was involved in various land acquisitions of questionable legality in the Indian territory of South Carolina. In the 1775 conflict he switched from the whig to the loyalist side in October after the Council of Safety failed to appoint him as Indian Agent of South Carolina. While a member of Patrick Cunningham's small band of loyalists, he was captured by Richardson's forces early in December, and was sent to Charleston as a prisoner.

23.27 "Committees of Safety": The first Council of Safety in the South was created by the Provincial Congress of South Carolina in June 1775. Local committees were also established in the various parishes.

23.30-31 "Ashley and Cooper Rivers": The peninsula on which Charleston is located is situated between the mouths of these two South Carolina rivers.

23.31-32 "Dorchester, Monk's Corner": Small villages a few miles inland from Charleston. Dorchester, at the head of navigation on the Ashley River, and Monk's (Monck's) Corner, at the same point on the Cooper River, were gateways to the interior of the state, and so were of great strategic importance during the war. After the Revolution Dorchester rapidly died out, and by Simms' time was little more than a ruin.

24.19 "Beach Island": Also spelled Beech Island, this was then the name of the region south of Augusta on the Carolina side of the Savannah River. Simms included this location on his hand-drawn map of the Augusta area.

25.18 "Lochaber": Cameron's 2600 acre plantation was northwest of Augusta near Long Canes Creek in South Carolina, and was granted in 1765, about the time Cameron became John Stuart's deputy.

43.25 "Indian wars": The Cherokee Indian Wars in South Carolina and Georgia occurred in 1759-1761.

43.32 "chewing the cud": Shakespeare, *As You Like It*, IV, iii.

44.32-33 "Amaryllis . . . Naera's hair": Milton, *Lycidas*, 67-69.

44.35-38 "This is no world": Shakespeare, 1 *Henry IV*, II, iii (slightly misquoted).

50.9 "Galphin and Redclyffe settlements": Near the lower end of Beach Island was a place called Galphin's Mill. Redclyffe was later James Henry Hammond's plantation. Simms noted both locations on his hand-drawn map of the Augusta area.

50.12 "Sand Bar Ferry": Ferry across the Savannah River south of Augusta. Simms noted the location on the page of notes taken in July 1858, and on his hand-drawn map of the Augusta area.

51.24 "Main street": A street map of Augusta in 1780 shows no street by this name. Simms was probably referring to Augusta's principal street which was apparently Broad Street.

53.22-23 "Scotch was the more conspicuous element": In describing the loyalties of the various factions in his *History of South Carolina* (1860), Simms indicates that the Scottish, English and German immigrants who had settled in the frontier regions were more likely to become loyalists, while native born persons, Irish immigrants and persons from the low country were usually whigs. After the Battle of Culloden in 1746 the British Government, especially during the administration of Lord Bute, seemed intent on compensating the defeated Highland Scots supporters of Charles Stuart by offering them attractive opportunities for position and land in the southern colonies of America. Indeed, by the time of the conflict of 1775, a substantial number of the prominent landholders in the back country were Scotsmen, as were most of the Indian agents and other government officials at all levels: the royal governors of East Florida, West Florida and South Carolina were all Scotsmen. Professor George C. Rogers, Jr., suggests in a recent article (*Richmond County History*, 6 [Summer 1974], 33-51) that much of the factional animosity in South Carolina at this time was perhaps caused by a strong anti-Scots feeling among the natives, and that Simms saw the back country divisions in this light. Statements by Simms in several of his works other than *Joscelyn* seem to support Professor Rogers' supposition. In a five-part review of Ward's edition of Curwen's *Journal and Letters* (1845) in the *Southern Literary Messenger* Simms states in a note that "John Stuart, Thomas Brown, [Evan] McLaurin, Moses Kirkland, the Cunninghams, Alexander Cameron, Andrew McLean, and others, were all Scotchmen, and were the active men at this period, in behalf of the British, among the people of the back country" (12 [June 1846], 328). Earlier in the same article he remarks "that three out of four Scotchmen, scarcely enter the country, when they are raised to office—made judges, magistrates, and surveyors, by Royal Patent" (12 [June 1846], 325). The result, wrote Simms, is that the Scots, who owed their positions and lands to the generosity of the Crown, were not likely to revolt against British rule, and also that the native population resented an administration "which thus studiously subjected the native to denial and inferiority . . ." (12 [June 1846], 325). In an unpublished lecture, "The Battle of Fort Moultrie" (1853), Simms says that "Loyalty, at least since '45, is the Scotchman's instinct. The Highlanders, deported to the South, because of their support of the Stuarts, became, in America, the steady champions of the Guelph. . . . The question, with the Highlanders, then, was no longer between rival sovereigns,—but between King and No King,—and their loyalty did not require a moment to decide" (17).

59.27 "Hamlet": Shakespeare, *Hamlet*, I, iv-v.

62.8-9 "original letters": There is some doubt whether such letters as Drayton displays here actually existed. In May 1775, certain suspicious passages in the Stuart-Cameron correspondence were brought to the attention of the patriot government in Charleston, but there is no indication that the letters in which these passages appeared were seized or intercepted; the passages are printed in Drayton, I, 267-290. On 2 July 1775 a number of letters (printed in Drayton, I, 338-350) were seized in the Charleston Post Office because they were believed to contain information about a conspiracy to incite the Indians to attack the frontier. Simms states (*History of South Carolina* [1860], 175, 176) that Stuart's correspondence was intercepted, but Drayton gives no such indication. The belief of the conspiracy was apparently based on a long-standing suspicion of such activities by Stuart, and was seemingly confirmed by reports from the Indians and by the passages from his correspondence with Cameron mentioned above. Stuart obviously did not consider these passages to be incriminatory since he voluntarily showed them to agents of the Charleston Council of Safety. None of Stuart's correspondence was in the 2 July seizure, although the Council of Safety learned that letters to Lord William Campbell, Royal Governor of South Carolina, and to Stuart had been forwarded before the seizure was made (Drayton, I, 310). The Council probably assumed, as Simms seems to have done, that the letters to Stuart contained instructions similar to those in the intercepted letter to Governor Martin of North Carolina; see Drayton, I, 344-346. See also note 19.13.

71.17-18 "the chimes of midnight": Shakespeare, 2 *Henry IV*, III, ii.

73.22-23 "Broad street": A street map of Augusta in 1780 shows Broad Street as one of the principal streets running parallel to the Savannah River. The marketplace is shown on the map in Broad Street between Centre and Elbert streets.

79.33 "New Windsor": Then a village on the Carolina side of the Savannah River about five miles southeast of Augusta.

87.12-13 "Man delights not me": Shakespeare, *Hamlet*, II, ii.

105.16 "'Walter, my son, do you know me?'": According to Mary C. Simms Oliphant, Simms' granddaughter, Walter's delirium scene is based on an actual occurrence in the Simms family just after the Civil War: ". . . that delirium scene . . . actually happened to my father [William Gilmore Simms, Jr.]. The good doctor sent for Simms to come, that his son was in a coma, that the only chance of life was to rouse him. Simms arrived, dug his nails into my father's wrist and commanded: 'My Son, you speak to me.' My father opened his eyes, uttered the one word 'Father' and turned over and fell into a deep, life-saving sleep . . ." (personal letter from Mary C. Simms Oliphant to Stephen Meats, 3 September 1975).

112.16 "Some natural tears she shed": Milton, *Paradise Lost*, XII, 645.

114.6 "McLaurin": Evan McLaurin was a Scots trader in South Carolina who kept a store located in the "Dutch Fork, at a place he called Spring-Hill; fifteen miles from Saluda River, on the road from thence to

Kennedy's Ford on the Enoree River" three miles to the west of Broad River (Drayton, I, 363). He was an active loyalist leader in the conflict of late 1775.

114.11 "Congaree": A large river in central South Carolina formed by the confluence of the Saluda and the Broad.

116.5 "Regulators and Scovilites": Simms provides an explanatory note on this topic on p. 273 of the novel. The Regulators were a group of mostly respectable landholders in the South Carolina back country who banded together in the years 1767-1769 in a sort of vigilante body for self-protection, first against outlaws such as horse thieves and murderers, and second against a segment of the back country population known as the "lower people," who, though not exactly criminals, were vagrants, ruffians, petty thieves, loafers and other social undesirables. In 1768, to combat the increasingly unbearable outrages of the outlaws, Governor Montagu commissioned two companies of rangers made up of Regulators; these effectively purged the back country of the criminals by late that year. But the landholders' conflicts with the "lower people" were not so quickly and satisfactorily dealt with. In the absence of adequate supervision by the royal authorities, the Regulators had assumed the responsibility of providing government for these people even to the point of enforcing morals and personal industriousness by whipping and other painful means. Several of the victims of these excesses sued the Regulators in the Charleston court, and some of the Regulators were actually convicted. The Regulators then brought the wrath of the royal government down on themselves by defying official attempts to take the convicted persons into custody. As a result, early in 1769 a Moderator movement arose among the "lower people" to combat the illegal excesses of the Regulators. This group was led by Joseph Coffell (often spelled Scovil or Scoffel), a man of very questionable character, who was appointed the group's leader by Governor Montagu. A dangerous confrontation between the Regulators and the Coffellites (or Scovilites) occurred in March 1769, and would almost certainly have culminated in a battle except for an unexpected and somewhat dramatic turn of events. Almost at the last moment, Richard Richardson, William Thompson and Daniel McGirt arrived at the scene and by their personal intervention averted a civil war. Richardson and Thompson at this time were the two men of greatest stature in the back country. Both had been sympathetic with the Regulators' desire for law and order but had remained aloof from the actual conflict. As a result, they still commanded enough respect from men on both sides to enable them to persuade the opposing forces to put down their arms. After this confrontation the excesses abated and the judicial reform act of 1769 established a system of courts and law enforcement which satisfied the needs of the back country population. Simms' statement in this passage and in the note on p. 273 that the South Carolina Regulators generally became whigs while the Scovilites became tories in the Revolution is supported by evidence in Richard Maxwell Brown's *The South Carolina Regulators* (1963), pp. 123-124, and by the fact that in the list of the loyalists taken prisoner at the Battle of Great Cane Brake, several are identified as "Scophilites" while none are identified as Regulators.

116.16 "The curse of the colony": The following paragraph is adapted from Simms' *History of South Carolina* (1860), p. 151.

117.1 "Companies of infantry": The Provincial Congress of South Carolina organized three regiments of troops in June 1775. The circumstances related in these two paragraphs are historically accurate and seem to be derived mostly from Simms' *History of South Carolina* (1860), pp. 177-178.

121.26-27 "Ford's Station": The actual confrontation between Drayton and Browne occurred at this location on 23 August 1775. Colonel Thomas Fletchall, the militia commander in the Ninety Six district, had been ordered to muster his regiment of 1500 men to meet with Drayton and Tennent, but he had instead told them that attendance was not mandatory, that the men needed to attend only if they wanted to hear the Commissioners. As a result only about 250 attended (Simms says 300 on p. 125.8-9). The loyalist leaders Simms identifies as present were actually there: Fletchall, Robert and Patrick Cunningham, Moses Kirkland, Thomas Browne and most likely Joseph Robinson, although Drayton's *Memoirs* (Simms' apparent source for much of the actual history in *Joscelyn*) does not mention him directly. In the novel Simms has Browne arrive unexpectedly at the muster still disfigured by tar and feathers, while actual history reports that he had been in the area for some time prior to this meeting, and had already argued with Drayton on at least two previous occasions, at King's Creek on 15 August and at Fletchall's plantation, Fairforest, on 17 August; see Drayton, *Memoirs*, I, 365-367, 368, 370-371. Browne and one of the Cunninghams did interrupt Drayton rather dramatically at the first of these meetings, but there is no indication that Browne still had on his tar and feathers; in fact, one source notes that he attempted "to conceal his disgrace" by cutting his hair short and wearing "a handkerchief around his head" (Lorenzo Sabine, *Biographical Sketches of Loyalists* [1864], I, 261). In this scene Simms seems to have combined the most dramatic elements of the two meetings of 15 and 23 August. In general, however, the circumstances of the 23 August confrontation, such as the open hostility of Browne and Kirkland and their attempts to seduce the Commissioners into violence, are historically accurate.

124.15 "Robinsons": Major Joseph Robinson was a loyalist leader throughout the conflict of 1775 in the back country. It was into his hands that Moses Kirkland betrayed the garrison at Ninety Six in July 1775. Robinson was also the leader of the loyalist forces in the brief skirmish with whig soldiers under Andrew Williamson near Ninety Six in November 1775. It was in this encounter that the first blood was shed in battle in the Revolution in South Carolina.

124.20 "McLean": An extract from a letter by Alexander Cameron printed in Drayton, *Memoirs*, I, 366, is addressed to Andrew McLean. An Andrew McLean was a prominent merchant in the Augusta area, but no association with Stuart or Cameron has been discovered. In an 1846 article, Simms lists Andrew McLean among the Scots leaders of loyalist forces in the back country; see "The Civil Warfare in the Carolinas and Georgia During the Revolution," *Southern Literary Messenger*, 12 (June 1846), 328.

125.15 "articles of association": These articles were formulated by the Provincial Congress in June 1775. They called for the signatures of all supporters of American independence; anyone who did not sign was to be considered an enemy.

129.8-9 "*ordered* this performance, in Charleston": Drayton's *Memoirs*, I, 273-274, 300-302, gives information about the first tar and feathering ordered by the Secret Committee of the Council of Safety. The order was signed by W. H. Drayton in a disguised hand.

135.14 "arrival of the British army": South Carolina was attacked by the British for the first time in June 1776, when Sir Peter Parker's fleet was defeated at Sullivan's Island by a small garrison of whig soldiers commanded by Colonel William Moultrie.

136.28-29 "the Ridge": An area about halfway between Augusta and the present site of Columbia; Drayton's *Memoirs*, I, 379, reports that W. H. Drayton spoke among the people at Augusta, Snow Hill and the Ridge. The Long Cane Settlement, where the Rev. William Tennent visited on this expedition, was on Long Canes Creek north of Augusta near Fort Charlotte in South Carolina.

141.8 "black dog": Shakespeare, *Titus Andronicus*, V, i.

145.11 "maiden meditations were all fancy free": Shakespeare, *A Midsummer-Night's Dream*, II, i.

176.21 "He is infirm of purpose": Shakespeare, *Macbeth*, II, ii.

177.34 "This is no fiction": No information on this incident has been found.

179.4 "Sheridan": See Thomas Moore, *Memoirs of the Life of the Right Honorable Richard Brinsley Sheridan*, 5th edition (1826), I, 348.

186.5 "Galphen": George Galphin was a powerful Indian trader before the war. Early in October 1775, he was appointed Indian Agent of South Carolina by the Council of Safety, and later during the Revolution he used his influence on the whig side as Assistant Superintendent of Indian Affairs.

193.9 "Secret Committee": The central Council of Safety resided in Charleston; in support of it each parish also had its own Council. The Secret Committee, which was headed by W. H. Drayton, was created by the Council of Safety; it was a secret police organization which planned and executed subversive activities. No confirmation of the existence of Secret Committees on the parish level has been found.

201.14 "Barmecide": From a story in *The Arabian Nights*, this phrase is used to describe an imaginary or illusory meal.

208.29 "dome": This term probably refers to a bee-hive.

223.36-37 "life of maiden solitude": Similar to Hamlet's speech, III, i: "Get thee to a nunnery."

227.15-16 "right hand perfect in its cunning": Paraphrase of Psalm 137.

243.20 "Major Williamson": Andrew Williamson, the leading whig in the Ninety Six district, was called the "Arnold of South Carolina" after the war. He fought the loyalists in 1775 and the Indians in 1776, but was regarded as a traitor for failing to come to the aid of Charleston in May 1780. He then took protection and moved to Charleston, where the British apparently expected to employ him in various minor capacities, although no evidence exists that he actually aided them in any material way. While in Charleston, he may also have supplied information on British activities to the American commander, General Nathanael Greene. In July 1781, Williamson was captured by whigs led by Colonel Isaac Hayne but was rescued by British troops. He was allowed to remain in South Carolina after the war.

243.21 "Colonel Thompson": William Thompson (also spelled Thomson) was the leading whig in the Orangeburg area, and had been a colonel of militia before the war. In June 1775, he was appointed lieutenant colonel of rangers by the Provincial Congress, and later led his detachment of troops in the attack against Cunningham in the Battle of Great Cane Brake which Simms used as the basis for the battle that ends *Joscelyn*; see note 301. Thompson is perhaps most well-known for his defense of the east end of Sullivan's Island against forces under Sir Henry Clinton during the attempted British invasion of June 1776.

243.22 "Colonel Richardson": Richard Richardson, the leading whig in the Camden area, was a colonel of militia who commanded the troops sent to pursue Patrick Cunningham's loyalist forces into Indian territory prior to the battle at Great Cane Brake. William Thompson's troops were a detachment from Richardson's force. The proclamation Simms mentions here was the one against Moses Kirkland; see note 23.24. The paragraph here comes almost directly out of Simms' *History of South Carolina* (1860), pp. 184-185, which in turn seems to be derived from Drayton, *Memoirs*, I, 380-382.

243.30 "Captain Andrew Pickens": Pickens was from the Long Cane Settlement. He fought with Williamson against the loyalists in the November attack on Ninety Six and served under Williamson on the frontier for the next two years. He was promoted to general after the Battle of Cowpens.

258.12 "My Alban villa": *Plutarch's Lives*, the translation called Dryden's, corrected and revised by A. H. Clough, 5 vols. (1859; rptd. 1909), III, 184.

263.26-27 "wise saws and modern instances": Shakespeare, *As You Like It*, II, vii.

285.15 "Jim Oakes": A soldier of this name served in the 2nd Regiment under Francis Marion later in the war, but no reference has been found to his participation in the 1775 conflict.

297.17 "chief Lieutenant": The actual leader of the loyalist force in this encounter was Patrick Cunningham. Browne's presence is not supported by history, although Simms had some justification for placing him at the battle since his whereabouts were unknown between early November, when he was seen in Dorchester on his way to the back country, and 26 December, when he was seen passing through Augusta apparently on his way to Florida.

301 "THE BATTLE": The Battle of Great Cane Brake occurred on 22 December 1775 between loyalists led by Patrick Cunningham and whigs led by Colonel William Thompson, a detachment from Richardson's forces. Great Cane Brake was on the north bank of the Reedy River near the present site of Greenville, S.C. Simms gives the following description of this encounter in his *History of South Carolina*:

> Richardson marched against the loyalists. His force soon reached three thousand men. Their approach overawed the insurgents, who gradually began to disband. Several of their chief men were made prisoners—Fletchall, Pearis and others. . . . The junction of

> Richardson with Williamson and others, including a few Georgians, made the army four thousand strong. A detachment, under Colonel Thompson, proceeded against Patrick Cunningham, and had nearly surrounded his camp, when they were discovered. The insurgents were overcome at a blow. Cunningham made his escape on a fleet horse (p.193).

As this description indicates, the actual battle was smaller in scale than the one described in *Joscelyn*; Drayton's *Memoirs*, II, 132, reports five or six loyalists killed and only one man wounded on the whig side. A list of the loyalists taken prisoner during the campaign, which was called the "Snow Campaign" because of a deep snow that fell a few days after the battle, can be found in R. W. Gibbes, *Documentary History of the American Revolution . . . 1764-1776* (1855), pp. 249-253.

305.5-6 "Of their fate . . . we may speak in future pages": In a letter to Evert A. Duyckinck dated 11 December 1868, Simms expressed his intention of writing the "few chapters" necessary to conclude the narrative, but so far as is known, he never returned to the story of the characters in *Joscelyn*.